Advance Praise for *Drift* by Sharon Carter Rogers

"Sharon Carter Rogers is an adept storyteller. In Rogers's novel *Drift,* she has woven suspense and the supernatural with a writing style that keeps the reader glued to the page. Rogers's multifaceted ability as a writer is on full display in *Drift.* Touching hearts in one passage while horrifying us in the next, the pacing of *Drift* is superb. I highly recommend this reading journey to all."

—Garrett Wang, actor (*Star Trek Voyager*)

"*Drift* is my kind of book! An edge-of-your-seat novel with a touch of the paranormal. I look forward to more books by Sharon Carter Rogers. This one's a keeper."

—Linda Hall, award-winning novelist of *Black Ice* and *Shadows at the Window*

"From its first chilling chapter to its last gripping page, I found myself irresistibly tethered to *Drift.* Filled with hair-raising chills and sublimely plotted detail, *Drift* does anything but 'drift,' sending you on a fast-track adventure into the heart of darkness and the spirit of redemption. THE. PAGES. WOULDN'T. FLIP. FAST. ENOUGH! (On a side note: could someone please figure out the identity of Sharon Carter Rogers? It's killing me!)"

—Matt Bronleewe, founding member of music supergroup Jars of Clay, and critically acclaimed novelist of *Illuminated, House of Wolves,* and *The Deadly Hours*)

"*Drift* is brooding, ghostly, romantic, and utterly sexy—something to read on cold nights under warm blankets!"

—Ethan Van Sciver, fan-favorite DC Comics artist (*Green Lantern* and *Superman/Batman*)

Praise for

Unpretty by Sharon Carter Rogers

"*Unpretty* is the kind of thriller that comes along all too rarely for my tastes: a daring, original plot with rich, fascinatingly odd-ball characters . . . Leaves you bound and helpless against the need to turn the page. Great stuff!"

—Gail Simone, DC Comics writer (*Wonder Woman; Action Comics; Birds of Prey*)

"A fast-paced thriller filled with plenty of action—and more action."

—Harriet Klausner, Amazon.com's #1 reviewer

"Gritty and creepy, with a compelling cast of characters. Rogers keeps readers guessing."

—*CBA Retailers + Resources*

"If you like murder and mayhem, if you like books a little off center, and if you like books that are just a bit creepy, this is the book for you."

—*Baker Book House Store Fiction Blog*

"*Unpretty* weaves a plot of art and death."

—*The Big Thrill*

"*Unpretty* throws the reader directly into the action and does not stop delivering spine-tingling twists and turns until the very last page."

—The Nearsighted Bookworm

"If I would have a Book of the Year Award to give, Sharon Carter Rogers would have won it this year with *Unpretty*."

—*Reviews Plus+*

"A great book, and it kept me well entertained!"

—*Mystery, Suspense, and God, Oh My!*

"*Unpretty* is a gripping, fascinating tale fed by a multitude of plot twists that keep you guessing."

—Nancy Moser, Christy Award–winning author of *Time Lottery* and *Just Jane*

"Once you start reading, you might as well plan to stay up until the early morning hours . . . Whoever she is, Sharon is a phenomenal writer!"

—Tyoramoody.com

"An interesting plot line . . . A very suspenseful read!"

—Tree Swing Reading

"Only a gifted author such as Sharon Carter Rogers could write a novel of such gritty suspense, leaving a trail of bread crumb clues that hold you until the very end. And what an ending it is!"

—Deena's Books

"*Unpretty* is marked with unforgettable scenes."

—Eric Wilson, critically acclaimed author of *A Shred of Truth* and *Facing the Giants*

Praise for Sharon Carter Rogers's debut novel,

Sinner

"Heart-pounding adventure."

—*CCM* magazine

"A thriller fantastic."

—*Aspiring Retail* magazine

"A gritty mystery that's unpredictable and delightful."

—*InFuze* magazine

"Engaging. Haunting. Innovative . . . Reminiscent of Dean Koontz on a dark night."

—Alton Gansky, bestselling suspense novelist

"A great suspense thriller starring two incredible antagonists."

—Harriet Klausner, Amazon.com's #1 reviewer

"The story draws you in and the action keeps you reading long after you should have turned out the lights."

—BuddyHollywood.com

"Truly a wonderful story . . . captures the mystery and intrigue of *myth*."

—The Bookshelf Reviews

"A fantastic job . . . leaves you turning pages faster and faster with each line!"

—1340mag.com

"Rogers deftly weaves an intriguing tapestry, leaving unexplained miracles to enhance the story's sense of wonder. *Sinner* is unique, hopefully the first of many novels."

—*Press & Sun Bulletin*

"A supernatural tale that is hard to put down . . . *Sinner* is a riveting book!"

—*The Phantom Tollbooth*

"A tale that is thought-provoking, lingering, tightly woven, heinous, and redemptive."

—*Reviews Plus+*

"A fine concoction that pleads for cinematic realization."

—Grady Harp, Amazon.com Top 10 reviewer

"By far, one of the best Christian thrillers."

—Christian Book Previews

"Sharon Carter Rogers [is] in the big leagues of gritty, spiritual suspense."

—Deena's Books

"An intriguing book . . . From the opening scenes . . . [*Sinner*] speeds along."

—Eric Wilson, critically acclaimed suspense novelist

"Like sitting in the front row of a theater and watching a hair-raising thriller!"

—Clay Jacobsen, critically acclaimed suspense novelist

"*Sinner* is the kind of book I love. The kind that I never want to end but cannot stop reading in order to make the adventure last longer . . . Rogers weaves the threads of the story together seamlessly, in a way that will keep you turning pages to discover what happens next."

—"My Years of Reading Seriously" at CJReading.blogspot.com

"*Who is Sharon Carter Rogers?*"

—The Suspense Zone

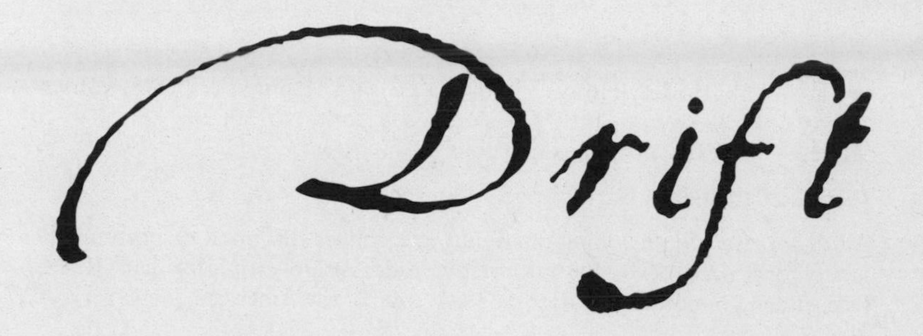

a novel of suspense

Sharon Carter Rogers

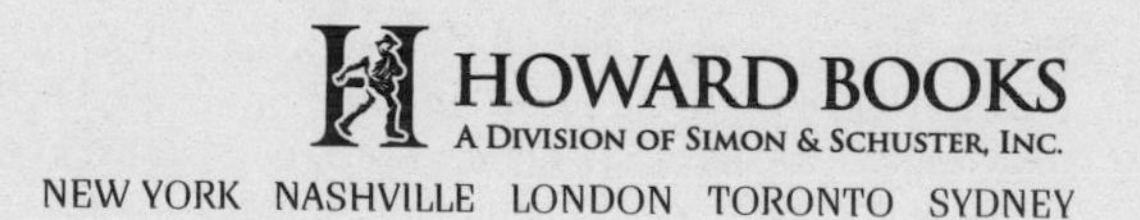

Published by Howard Books, a division of Simon & Schuster, Inc.
1230 Avenue of the Americas, New York, NY 10020
www.howardpublishing.com

Drift is published in association with Nappaland Literary Agency, Colorado, www.NappalandLiterary.com

Library of Congress Cataloging-in-Publication Data
Rogers, Sharon Carter.
Drift : a novel of suspense / Sharon Carter Rogers.
p. cm.
1. Adoptees—Fiction. 2. Organized crime—Fiction. 3. Identity (Psychology)—Fiction. I. Title.
PS3618.O468D75 2010
813'.6—dc22 2010000269

ISBN 978-1-4165-6653-3
ISBN 978-1-4391-7086-1 (ebook)

10 9 8 7 6 5 4 3 2 1

Manufactured in the United States of America

Edited by David Lambert and Lissa Halls Johnson
Cover design by Nate Salciccioli, Faceout Studio
Interior design by Jaime Putorti

For Jacob Kurtzberg and Joseph H. Simon

—SCR

Souls flow through history like a river in time.

And in that river, I have recently come to believe,

some may be lost in the drifts . . .

—SOLACE THE LESSER
PHILOSOPHER AND HISTORIAN, 431 B.C.

Drift

One

FRIDAY, FEBRUARY 18

I am cold.

I think I should be grateful that this is a dry February. There is no snow or sleet covering my frame or stinging my face and neck. But the numbness in my fingers and toes, and the biting that seems to come from inside my earlobes, rob me of the comfort of that thought.

The dirt beside me is tumbled and stirred, but already I can sense the hardness forming within the mass that extends six feet below me. Simon lies beneath that mound of earth, his body colder than the frigid air that now surrounds me.

The cemetery is empty, though I see cars pulling into the parking area to the north. There is another casket that has been set up for a ceremony about fifty feet away, but right now that means nothing to me.

I tethered to Simon six years ago or so, when he was a teenager. He still seemed too young to die, too young to leave me locked to his presence in this unforgiving cold.

I feel the cold in my pure physicality. In my skin, in my pores, down into my bones. I want to moan and cry, not for Simon, but for myself. But I cried my tears out long, long ago.

I am not angel, nor am I demon. I am not a ghost as some would like to believe. I am a Drifter, something God created in his spare time and then forgot on the fringes of reality.

A few mourners enter this graveyard. They pass me by without notice. No surprise.

I've only met two others like me, but I've heard stories. I know there must be many Drifters out there. I wonder what they are doing, if they are warm and fat, or freezing and hollow like me.

—

The first one I met was a girl. She looked about twenty-four or twenty-five, but one can never be sure about our kind. I was standing on a street corner in the summertime, outside a drugstore and soda shop, wondering if I had enough room to go inside and steal a cold drink. She was with another woman, a redhead likely in her mid-thirties. I didn't even know she was a Drifter. Just thought they were two friends.

The redhead walked out sipping on cream soda in a glass bottle. She glanced up the street and then back down again. That was when she saw me.

She stopped and stared, looking directly in my eyes. I felt the churning, the knotting in my stomach and the mild dizziness that begins the tether. My breathing relaxed involuntarily and I noticed a light grin play at the corners of her mouth.

"I see you," she whispered. "I see you!" Louder that time.

Then the other Drifter stepped between us, shoving the redhead backward and breaking our gaze. "No!" she said fiercely. She spat at me, "This one is my tether. Mine, you understand?"

Since I'd never seen another Drifter, for a moment I didn't. And before I could say a word, the girl pulled a blade from her back pocket and stuck it, hard, into my belly and then pulled it back out again.

I felt my eyes roll up in my head as the pain spun inside me in several different directions. I couldn't speak, couldn't do anything but groan and collapse onto the warm pavement, writhing and swimming in an ever-expanding pool of my own blood.

The girl leaned in close to my face. "This one is mine. You understand now? Mine." I couldn't respond because I couldn't breathe. But, yes, now I understood.

The redhead was blinking with mild uncertainty, peering across the street, looking as if she'd suddenly lost something she had only moments before been pleased to find. The other Drifter moved close to her, putting hands on her shoulders and commanding the redhead's attention.

"You okay?" she said to the redhead, locking eyes with her in a forceful gaze.

"Yes, I think so," the redhead responded. "Who was that, Jill? Who was that man?"

"Nobody," Jill said quickly, willing the other to believe it. "Nobody."

"But he seemed real. And he had your mark in his eyes."

"No," Jill said again.

"Yes! Yes!" I groaned at their feet. "Look at me! I'm right here . . ."

"No," Jill repeated. "You didn't see anyone. There's only me. There is always only me. You know that."

"Yes, of course." The redhead appeared to be forgetting already, though she couldn't seem to shake a certain sadness.

Jill released her grip from the redhead's shoulders and shot a glare back toward me. I felt the oxygen racing out of my body along with my blood, and watched as darkness began to swim in the edges of my vision. There was a severing in my soul, and my heart seemed to sputter and spark.

"Please," I begged. "Why?"

"Because I choose it to be so," the other Drifter hissed at me, "and you are an unhappy consequence of that choice." Then she said nothing more.

When I regained consciousness, they both were gone and my insides felt mangled and raw. It seemed as though my heart were stopped, but my bleeding never ceased. I lay on that pavement for three hours, always bleeding, never dying, always waiting. That's where Alondra finally found me.

Alondra . . .

—

I feel the wind like freezing breath race around my collar, whipping away the warming thought of Alondra and bringing me back to the coldness of this cemetery. God, why couldn't I at least have had time to grab a coat? Or gloves?

More mourners move toward the other casket. Apparently whoever is to be buried over there was well loved. Or at least well respected, judging by the men in dark suits and the bejeweled ladies solemnly gathering beside the hole in the ground. I am unseen by any of them, and I wish desperately to rip one of those long, faux-fur coats from the back of any of the women who pass me by. But they are too far away from me now.

Simon's death has weakened the tether, but not broken it. I can only wait, and hope that I will freeze to death. But, of course, I know this won't happen. Not to me. I will simply freeze, and never greet the death that usually accompanies it.

My eyes hurt from the cold. I close them and finally give in to the ground below me. It is cold like me, but it holds me without complaint. I sit next to the freshly filled grave and curl into as much of a ball as I possibly can.

—

The second Drifter was different, but the same. He walked alone, as though he were tethered only to himself. He bore the mark in his eyes, but he also had a solidity about him that wasn't quite right. As if he once had been something besides a Drifter; as if he'd once been a man. I met him in a library while I was waiting for . . . for . . . funny. I can't remember that one's name. He was an old one . . . What was it? Well, it doesn't matter.

In the library, I was sitting on a bench, waiting. The Drifter walked in, walked past me, and then stopped. He turned back toward me and spoke.

"I have seen you," he said. "And yet you are not seen."

"Have you come for me?" I asked.

The stranger shook his head slowly. "No. Not for your kind."

Then I saw the mark in his eyes. "You bear the mark," I said. "Who are you?"

His face grew grim and hard. "No one," he said. "Just a sinner like everyone else."

I felt something stir inside. This one could help me. I knew it.

"Please," I said, "I have questions."

"There are no answers," he said. Then he stepped away and disappeared behind a corner. I longed to follow him, but I was prevented. As usual.

—

"At least that one didn't stab you in the heart!" That's what Alondra always said whenever I mentioned the sinning Drifter.

Alondra . . .

—

I am cold.

Here on the ground I feel feral, like the animal that knows only pain and wants only revenge.

I am not angel, nor am I demon. I am no ghost. I am simply me. A soul lost in the shallows. Where are you, Alondra, now when I need you?

Where are you?

Two

She almost didn't see him at first.

He was hunched over, arms hugging his knees, sitting in a curled-up ball next to what appeared to be a freshly filled grave. She almost didn't see him, but something within her told her that she could never have missed him either.

He must be freezing, she thought. *Another grieving idiot, I suppose. Not my problem. Not today at least. Another day I might care, even do something to help. Maybe, if only to make the nuns from my old grade school happy. But not today. Definitely not today.*

In spite of herself, she couldn't stop from wondering why he wasn't wearing gloves, or even a heavy coat. She turned away from him and immediately, noticeably, forgot the features of his face.

That won't do.

She prided herself on her skills of observation; if she didn't, she probably wouldn't have stayed alive—and she definitely wouldn't have known to get out of Charlie Murphy's house before it was too late.

Charles Franklin Murphy. The general consensus was that he was her father. Her adopted father. Her stepfather. In reality he stole her away from his girlfriend's ex-husband when she was only thirteen months old. That girlfriend—her dear departed ma—died less than a year later, and old Charlie decided it was easier to change the baby's name and raise her himself than to risk having the police discover he had kidnapped the child. Of course, "raising a daughter" for Charlie Murphy mostly meant passing her off to whichever of his flunkies was nearby at the time, which was usually fine by her. You can get away with a lot when your guardian is an imposing "enforcer" known for his ability to inflict pain in barely perceived places. They weren't interested in the minor mischievous behavior of a child.

Yeah, you can get away with a lot. But not stealing from your wicked stepfather. And certainly not being the one responsible for the end of his miserable life. At least not for long.

Maurits was moving them closer to the grave. As she followed, she tried to hang back a step from Maurits in the cemetery so she could shoplift another glance at the boy by the grave, but Maurits was watching her more closely than usual. She saw the frown begin to crease his face as he looked down at her; she quickly picked up her pace. In this kind of mood, her dad's old bodyguard might actually break her fingers just by grabbing a hand to pull her along. She couldn't let that happen. Not before she could get away.

She let out an unexpected sigh, and saw Maurits's features soften just a bit. Surprisingly, he reached out and gave her a quick squeeze on the shoulder.

"Don't worry, Baby Doll," he said through icy lips. "We'll get the imbecile who set this up. We'll get 'im before the cops do. And we'll make him suffer. You got Maurits's promise on that score. Okay, Baby Doll?"

She nodded mutely, trying to swallow her terror. He was gallant and protective—in a murderous, Hitler-as-a-father kind of way. And she realized he knew something wasn't right. The death was not what it seemed.

She'd known Maurits Girard since, well, since before she could remember. When she cried in the night, she had a distinct memory of his musky smell wrapping her up in strong arms, rocking her and humming until the night terrors would fade. She never remembered his face from those moments, though, but she knew it must have been him. A man's true smell never changes.

It was funny how callused hands with as much blood on them as Maurits's could also be the gentle ones that comforted a small child. She couldn't help but think of what those hands could do to her—would do to her—if they knew of her role in Charlie Murphy's unexpected death.

Maurits looked at her, and she could tell that he thought she must have been cold from the chill in the air. Without a word, he stopped walking, removed his topcoat, and wrapped it around her shoulders, then walked on a step ahead of her. *His mistake,* she thought, *because I can feel the spare pistola stashed in the inside pocket next to my left forearm.*

Pistola. Funny word.

Maurits had heard it in an old spaghetti-western film once, and took to calling his special guns by that name ever since. She knew the gun that hid next to her in the topcoat. It was a small, .22-caliber, short minirevolver. A backup weapon, the kind that a guy like Maurits could actually conceal in the palm of his hand if necessary.

I can use this gun, she thought. *Five shots, used wisely, would all be deadly.*

Maurits was one of the few who knew her name from before the "adoption." He knew that she knew he held that knowledge, but he'd never let it slip. Not once. Not ever. Maurits simply wouldn't betray her father like that, not even for her.

A new thought wandered unbidden through her mind. *I wonder if I could kill Maurits? If I could pull this pistola out of his pocket, place a bullet behind his ear, and then run like madness out of this cemetery, out of this city, out of this world? Just disappear.*

They'd probably track down her real father and kill him for revenge. She could live with that. She'd been an orphan since that loser was careless enough to let her get kidnapped anyway.

But could she kill Maurits?

She wasn't sure.

But she thought so.

Despite what they tell you, she figured, it's actually easier to kill someone you know—even someone you like and trust—than it is to kill a complete stranger. At least that's what Maurits always said. With a friend, you know all the faults, all the reasons why that person deserves to die. But with a stranger, there are too many unknown variables. Too many reasons why he should live—like maybe he's got kids who depend on him, or maybe he's an artistic genius and if he lives he might create the next Sistine Chapel, or maybe he's just some SOB who deserves a second chance simply because you got a second chance once or twice in your life.

A new thought slipped into her head. *I wonder if I could kill that poor sap freezing by that grave behind us? Put him out of his misery?*

She turned to get another look at the boy. He was still there, freezing like a moron too stupid to do anything different. She felt a sudden hatred and pity for that boy. Then she blinked, and was shocked to see him appear to shimmer in the cold, as if he might disappear if she wasn't careful. She blinked again and he was solid once more, as if he'd never changed.

Her head was turned away from Charlie Murphy's resting

place, so she missed the fact that Maurits had put out his arm as a signal for her to stop. It didn't matter, because even after twenty years Maurits was still strong enough to stop her in her tracks without really trying. She stumbled into his arm, nearly fell down, then righted herself beside him. She glanced up at him and could see he'd barely noticed their collision.

Charlie's grave was just ahead of them. Already a small collection of people had begun gathering around the coffin, waiting for the interment of the body. Maurits was frowning again, this time with true maliciousness. She quickly saw why. Police Detective Honoria Lopez was dawdling by the grave with a disdainful smirk dressing her face.

Maurits often said he didn't like hurting a lady, so it was a good thing that Honoria Lopez was no lady. The woman had absolutely no fear, not of Maurits, and definitely not of Charlie Murphy. But she could never make charges stick against either one of them. And everybody knew that one day either Charlie or Honoria was going to end up six feet down—it was just a matter of time.

Looks like you won this round, Detective Lopez. Good for you.

"Wait here." Maurits didn't bother to look back at her as he strode purposefully off to chase away the unwelcome mourner. After all, for Maurits, the grave site of Charlie Murphy was like holy ground.

She exhaled and watched the misty breath fly away from her mouth and dissipate into the freezing cold of mid-morning. Her eyes wandered back to that stupid boy. He was rocking back and forth now, eyes closed like he was trying to remember a warmer place and time.

She was surprised to discover that she'd already forgotten the color of his hair.

From here it looked black. Straight. Falling down over his eyes and just past his ears. She watched the rocking of his frame and realized that while he was trim, he was also muscular, almost like a middleweight boxer. Small, but thick. His skin was pale, but not white. More like an olive color, or a light shade of something you might find on a visit to the Middle East. He wore dark jeans, a T-shirt, and a button-up shirt over that. No hat. No gloves. No sunglasses.

She was memorizing him now, determined to remember this boy if only as an exercise in mental discipline. She imagined a piece of charcoal in her hand, and mentally traced his features on a blank page in her mind.

Then something in the back of her head told her that maybe now was the right time to make a break for it, to get out while Maurits was occupied with other things.

But she couldn't take her eyes off that boy.

She saw his rocking stop, his body stiffen. He raised his head a bit, as if he'd heard a sound he didn't recognize. Or maybe one that he did recognize, and one that required his attention. Seeing his full profile now, she discovered that he was not really a boy at all, despite her original impression. The face was clean and straight, but also weathered, with hints of worry wrinkles that originally seemed out of place, and then seemed perfectly normal. Something about him made her wonder. At first she thought he must be only fifteen or sixteen years old. But looking at his features and his manner now made her think he must have been mid-thirties or early forties. And then she was immediately sure that was wrong too.

He wasn't hard to look at. Some girls at her college would have probably thought he was attractive. She couldn't decide. But she also couldn't stop looking at him.

She saw a spurt of warm breath fire unexpectedly from his

mouth. His head turned slowly toward her, and his eyes locked onto hers.

Do you see me? He mouthed the words, and somehow she understood them.

She nodded slowly.

With a deliberate sadness, he released his arms from his legs, uncurled his body, and rose to his full height. He seemed smaller on the ground. Now she realized this boy—this man?—was actually closer to Maurits's height than hers. She was five six, and Maurits about six three. This stranger, she guessed, must hit six feet even; maybe six one.

He stared directly at her.

"What are you looking at?"

Maurits's voice rang unexpectedly in her ear, but she didn't jump at the sound, despite her surprise. Instead she nodded in the direction of the freezing boy, never breaking her gaze from him.

"What?" Maurits said. "That tree?"

"That boy over there," she said. "The one by that fresh grave."

The boy began walking toward her now, slowly, as though he were worn out from a lifetime of walking. She couldn't take her eyes off his.

Maurits grunted. "No time for games, Baby Doll. Not today. I already had to deal with Detective Lopez and I'm just not in the mood. Understand?"

The boy came close to her. He never took his eyes off hers. They were dark eyes, not quite black, but definitely one of the darker shades of brown. He gave her an appraising look, and then exhaled again.

"Do you see me?"

His voice was surprisingly calm and rich. Like a Gibson

acoustic guitar that's aged well over a few decades. Almost comforting. And a little bit frightening at the same time.

"Yes," she said.

"Good," Maurits said. Then she heard him muttering to himself. "Your two minutes are just about up, Detective. Best be on your way now. Don't make Maurits do this to you today. Not here."

"Name?" The boy said it like they were meeting over coffee.

"Baby Doll."

He grimaced. "Not your adopted name. Your real name."

She felt a chill inside her, a familiar absence.

"I don't know."

"Stop talking to yourself, Baby," Maurits said. "People'll think you're crazy. Bad for business."

She tilted her head toward Maurits. The boy followed her question with his eyes, then looked back and shook his head. So, Maurits didn't see him. For some reason, this made sense to her.

She raised her eyebrows, silently asking another question. She watched his eyes sweep over her face as if he were reading the page of a book.

"I've long forgotten it," the boy said after a moment. "Just call me whatever seems comfortable to you."

She was tempted to be annoyed, but her curiosity overruled the temptation. The power of naming is not something to take lightly.

"Okay, the cop is leaving," Maurits said. "Let's go. It's time to pay our last respects to your father."

Wicked stepfather, she thought as she turned away from the boy to follow her bodyguard/jailer. She saw Detective Lopez ambling toward what appeared to be an unmarked sedan in the parking lot to the north. Of course, they all knew Honoria Lopez's Crown Victoria, so it might as well have been emblazoned with the police department logo and flashing lights like the marked cruiser parked next to hers.

Detective Lopez glanced back in her direction. At first she seemed disinterested, probably still gloating about the fact that Charlie Murphy had preceded her into the afterlife. Then she did a double take, and Baby Doll felt a flicker of worry in her gut. Honoria slowed down, stopped, then fully turned around. Baby Doll was uncomfortably aware that the plainclothes detective was staring directly at her.

Baby Doll said nothing and instead focused on the back of Maurits's thick neck, following him obediently to the grave site. She wondered what kind of gun Maurits had holstered as his primary, next to his chest, and if he had realized yet that his secret, spare gun was now in her possession. She felt the little pistola thump, thump, thump against her heart, matching the rhythm of her footsteps on the hardened ground.

The boy fell in step behind her.

Apparently wherever Baby Doll was going, he was going too.

Three

The tether is always strongest at the beginning. Later—a few days, a few weeks, maybe even a year—it will loosen like a used rubber band, allowing me more freedom to roam. But at the start, the tightness of the newly formed bond is strict, as if it were a leash wrapped around the neck of a dog. For now, I must stay reasonably close to this girl. Within twenty or thirty feet at most.

It is old habit; I begin measuring distances to see how far I could go before feeling the painful tug of the tether beneath my rib cage. Perhaps as far as the fifteenth grave site to the south. Perhaps as far north as that parking lot where the cars have gathered. I wonder if I should hang back now, pay last respects to Simon. But—and I marvel that I don't feel ashamed by this thought—he is already fading from memory for me. They all do eventually. Well, most of them. Six years is not very long, after all.

The health of the tether has begun flowing through me, and I feel my extremities beginning to warm. Soon I will feel almost normal again, even in this biting February air. And then I will sleep, cementing the tether and healing the damage to my frost-bitten toes.

It strikes me suddenly that this girl is wearing two coats—a man's overcoat and what appears to be a woman's hip-length leather jacket underneath. The overcoat slaps awkwardly against her body on the left side. Something there is heavier than the pocket that holds it.

Two coats, yet she doesn't offer one to me. Something to remember about her.

The flush of first tether brings with it images as well. I see her, briefly, as a child. A different man holds her close, then he is gone, replaced by others. I can't hear her name, but I perceive that she has more than one. I can't see more of her past, but I see that she is hiding it behind her eyes. I'll learn more when the dreams come.

She follows the large man, silently, sullenly. She doesn't grieve like he does. His is a deep sorrow. His is the dangerous kind. She, though, grieves only that she must be here. Her face is a mask that others do not seem to penetrate. But no face can fully hide itself from me, not after all these years. The person she is going to bury meant very little to her. Much like . . . what was his name? Yes, Simon. Of course. Much like Simon.

It was foolish of me to get caught sleeping when they removed Simon's body from the morgue. Even more foolish to let myself get separated from Simon's coat and gloves. Fortunately I woke before the full agony of Severance, but the dying tether still makes its presence known, even in its fading. I wonder sometimes what would happen if, after death, a new tether didn't form. If, for once at least, there was a time when I needed no tether but myself. But that's a question for which there is no answer.

And so they delivered Simon to the graveyard, and I was dragged along behind, feeling the tether both fade and constrict, hostage to a dead man.

Rest well, Simon.

Despite our differences, you deserve at least that. You were still so young. Who knows what you might have grown into?

The girl is breathing heavily now, but not because of the walk. It's a nervous kind of panting, with quick intakes through the nostrils and short blasts of moist air flushing back out through her teeth. I step closer to get a better look at her face. Her lips are flat and stretched in a thin line. Her eyebrows are knitted together, forming small wrinkles across her forehead. Her eyelids are raised a millimeter higher than they should be.

She is afraid.

But of what?

"Stop staring at me." She's turned to look at me straight-on, anger now wrapping itself over her fear. "I don't like it, so just cut it out."

She inhales deeply, exhales, and her face loosens into what she must suppose is a mask. I can see her willing the muscles in her body to relax as well. But the topcoat still gathers awkwardly with each new step that she takes. It doesn't take a genius to intuit what's in there.

I nod and fall a step behind. And then I see the woman who is seeing the girl.

I see that the large man has noticed the woman as well. "I can't believe she's coming back," the big man mutters to himself.

It appears this is going to get interesting.

Suddenly I am stopped short because the large man has stopped the girl in front of me. We are almost to the grave. But no one steps away from the burial site to greet us, or to mourn with the girl, to wrap an arm around her shoulders and tell her that it's okay to cry.

"Wait here, Baby Doll," the big man says. The sorrow in his voice is blanketed by anger. He motions and two other large men

separate themselves from the small crowd now surrounding the grave site. All three of them stride purposefully toward the woman. To her credit, she moves forward to meet them. A wave of her hand and two uniformed police officers detach themselves from a cruiser in the parking lot and begin following her footsteps toward a showdown with the three men.

"Get me out of here."

The girl is suddenly inches from my face. Her skin up close has the look of raw sugar that's been powdered, hardened, and then freshly scrubbed. The shape of her features indicates a mishmash of heritages. Irish eyes, Asian cheeks, nose and jawline from European stock. She would pass for white, but the light shading of her skin color and her thick mane of dusky hair suggest that American Indian also figures somewhere in her background. She smells faintly of lilac soap. Or maybe it's shampoo. She wears a wrap around her neck and ears that obscures the back of her head. She is so close to me that the mist of her breath feels warm and wet on my neck.

"Listen, Boy," she says, "you've got to get me out of here."

"Is that my name then?"

Her eyes flick back and forth, searching mine, looking for something to pin a hope upon. She nods quickly. "Yes. Your name is Boy. Now, please, Boy, get me out of here. Right now."

She pauses and catches her breath, and I recognize the moment when a human first sees the mark. "Your eyes, in your eyes, there's . . ." She trails off.

"Yes," I say.

"What is it? What does it mean?"

"It's the mark of a Drifter."

"You mean like a vagrant or something? That doesn't seem right. It must mean something more than—"

She is interrupted by shouting. The woman and the large man are now in full confrontation mode. Words are sprayed like machine-gun fire between them, words that are pregnant with threats, insults, and more than a few profanities.

The girl, Baby Doll, grabs my shoulders and leans in. "Boy, I need to get out of here, before Maurits comes back. Before Detective Lopez starts to ask me questions. Now, can you get me out of here or not?"

It is more a command than a question. I don't like taking orders, but I also have reasons to be cooperative, at least for now.

I nod.

"Good," she says, shooting a glance at the feuding people across the lawn. "Let's go."

"I can get you out," I say patiently. "But I didn't say that I will."

She looks at me like she is going to spit. Instead she swings a hard backhand against my jaw. She's stronger than she looks. I feel the contact of her middle knuckle on my cheekbone, and lightning from her blow splinters through my face. I am so surprised by this, I almost want to laugh.

"You go to hell," she seethes.

"I can't," I mumble in return. But she doesn't hear me. She has already turned away, apparently unafraid of any retaliation I might be contemplating behind her back. If she hadn't hit me so hard, I might have admired this display of bravado toward me. Still, she did hit me. Something else to remember about her.

Her right hand slips inside the topcoat; I see it tremble slightly and I know it's not from the cold. Perhaps it's time for me to get involved after all.

"Give me the gun," I say.

"What?" She whirls back toward me.

"Give me the gun."

She looks at me, deciding whether or not to lie about the existence of the pistol in her pocket.

"No," she says finally.

"Give me the gun and I'll get you out of here."

She looks worriedly toward the arguing group. A few more men have broken away from the grave site and are making their way toward the area of confrontation. The woman has started waving a pair of handcuffs.

"Not Maurits," she whispers, and her voice is suddenly pale. "Don't kill Maurits. Not today."

I see unexpected compassion flash quickly through her eyes. Interesting.

"And not Detective Lopez—that lady Maurits is yelling at. Don't kill her either."

"Give me the gun."

"Promise me. Not Maurits or Detective Lopez."

I hold out my hand. I make no promises.

She regards me with a mixture of contempt and hope. A moment later I feel the cool steel of a minirevolver in my palm.

"When this is over," I say, "you will owe me a favor. You understand?"

She stares at me, and the compassion I saw previously is replaced with new loathing. I take that to mean yes.

"At the right moment, run straight for that car."

I point to a blue Ford Crown Victoria parked next to the police cruiser, which is blocking the exit for the cars of the other guests. I expect her to ask how she will know when the "right moment" will be, to demand a signal or a cue. But she doesn't. Smart. Something else to remember about her.

I measure the distances with my eyes, and wonder if I've got enough room in the tether to get to where I need to go. No matter. I can at least get to Detective Lopez, and that's far enough for a start.

And after this is over, Baby Doll will do me that favor. I will see to that.

I turn toward the north and begin walking.

Four

Boy.

It was a stupid name. She knew it was. But Baby Doll was angry, and he deserved it. And after she said it, after it was out there, it just *was* his name, as though it had always been his name. As though it were his when they were first introduced. Besides, it wasn't any worse than Baby Doll. And besides again, he deserved it.

She didn't trust this Boy. Not really. But she needed him, and sometimes needing someone means you have to trust him and hope for the best. She had to admit, though, that mark in his eyes kind of freaked her out. Sure, she believed in God, probably more than most people. Eight years of Catholic school helped with that, and she even kept a Bible hidden in her room as a kind of comfort. But these weren't enough to make her believe. It was her home life that had convinced her. When you grow up in the kind of world Baby Doll did, you see pretty quickly how terrible people are. When you can't believe in humanity, what's left to believe in but God?

The mark in Boy's eyes was so faint she didn't even see it at first, but once she knew it was there, she couldn't help seeing it. Couldn't avoid seeing it. Because even though she believed in God, she couldn't say she'd ever really believed in angels. Or demons. And she couldn't say for sure which one this Boy might be.

Oh, God, she thought suddenly. *Why did I give him the gun?*

Was she praying?

Baby Doll felt a twisting in her stomach, a reminder of the guilt she had swallowed three days prior.

The Boy was walking toward Maurits and Detective Lopez, the gun held loosely in his hand. She could see this was not the first time he'd held a pistola. She watched him walk directly into the small, furious crowd, and wanted to close her eyes. He slipped in front of Maurits and then out of view.

Why can't I blink my eyes?

An unusual calm settled over the cemetery. It was almost as if Maurits and Detective Lopez were temporarily spent from yelling at each other and were taking a time-out to catch their breath and reload for the next round. Lopez still held the handcuffs as a threat; Maurits and the five or six men behind him stood like a wall in front of her. The two uniformed officers looked grim, and one rested his hand on his holstered gun, preparing to spring into action in the event that violence broke out.

But where was Boy?

Almost against her will, Baby Doll felt herself being pulled toward the little group of enemies. One step, then another, she began to slowly move in that direction. She could feel the brittle grass crunching beneath her feet, and below that, the uneven layers of earth made it feel like she was walking across bumps on a giant's head.

A movement in the distance caught her eye. The passenger door on Detective Lopez's Crown Victoria had popped open—not wide, but enough to be able to swing the door open without lifting the handle. Then she saw the driver's door was slightly open as well.

Baby Doll now found herself only about five feet away from the silent, hostile gathering. Detective Lopez saw her first. A slim smirk flashed onto the detective's lips.

"Baby Doll Murphy," she called out over Maurits's shoulder. "May I have just a moment of your time?"

Maurits's head swiveled to see his charge standing behind him as well. "Baby Doll," he growled over his shoulder, "go back to your daddy's grave and—"

A gunshot rang through the air, echoing through the cemetery as sound waves bounced from tombstone to tombstone. Maurits instinctively reached inside his suit coat. Then he also seemed to remember he wasn't wearing his overcoat. His eyes flew wide as he searched Baby Doll's hands to see if she was holding his gun. The men around him melted backward and down, trying to identify where the shots were coming from. The two uniformed officers drew guns and dropped to one knee, and everyone started shouting again.

"Drop your weapons and lie down on the ground!" one uniform commanded as he waved his gun toward Maurits's crew.

"Do it now!" screamed the other uniform, apparently trying to assume his most assertive manner, yet unaware that his voice cracked in fear on the word "now."

Only Detective Lopez and Maurits refused to bow or run. Maurits, after discerning that Baby Doll didn't have a gun, had begun scanning the cemetery with a practiced eye, picking out echo points and tracing them backward to the origin of the sound. Detective Lopez ignored the gunshot completely, and instead took two steps toward the girl.

"Ms. Murphy," she said loudly, but calmly, "I need to speak with you for a moment, please."

It was only after the second gunshot that Baby Doll realized the time had come for her to run. She threw off Maurits's topcoat and broke into a trot toward the parking lot. Detective Lopez must have thought she was running to her for protection because she gave a reassuring, albeit stale, smile and reached an arm toward the girl. Baby Doll blew past her before she quite knew what was going on, and had fifteen to twenty steps on her before Honoria Lopez even started to come after her.

"Baby Doll!" Maurits's voice carried both concern and anger.

Three more gunshots cracked the air in rapid succession. By now it was obvious they were coming from the parking lot—and that Baby Doll was running directly toward them.

Her foot hit the pavement and immediately skidded on a previously unseen, glossy, iced-over patch of the parking lot. She fell hard on her right hip. But she was up again in a breath, and when she reached the Crown Victoria two seconds later, Boy was already in the driver's seat with the engine running. He didn't wait for her to close the passenger door before backing out of the parking space. Then he gunned the engine forward, and as her door swung shut Baby Doll caught sight of the police cruiser. It appeared the two back tires were flat, and it was still blocking the other cars.

She didn't ask where they were going; she didn't care at that moment. All that mattered was that no one would follow them.

Baby Doll chanced a look back at the cemetery grounds. Maurits stood tall, following the path of the car with his gaze. A few feet away from him the two uniformed officers appeared to have gained the upper hand on Maurits's crew, standing over them with guns drawn while the associates of her father knelt in the grass with hands clasped behind their heads. Detective Lopez stood near the trunk of the police cruiser, apparently cursing and angry. Lopez kicked the bumper of the car, and Baby Doll couldn't help wondering if she'd picked up that move from an old *Starsky and Hutch* episode or something.

And then it dawned on her.

She was free.

At least for the moment.

Baby Doll looked over at the Boy in the driver's seat, expecting him to grin or laugh or do something to indicate relief that they'd gotten away. He just glanced at her and kept driving. After a moment, he reached in a pocket and pulled out the mini-revolver.

"You're out of bullets," he said calmly.

"Right," she said as she took the gun from his hand. There was quiet that followed, punctuated only by the sound of tires speeding across the lumps in the road. It almost seemed as if Boy had forgotten she was there. To break the silence, Baby Doll said the first thing that came into her head. "How did you get the keys to Detective Lopez's car?"

"Pickpocket," he said. "Years of practice."

She heard a buzzing and realized the police band radio had sprung to low-volume life. She turned the knob up and heard chatter across the airwaves. Then her name was being spoken on the police band. ". . . Baby Doll Murphy . . ." Reflexively, she quickly shut off the police radio. She didn't want to know what they were saying about her.

And then it hit her: she wasn't free at all. She was a rat in a maze, trying to figure out where to turn next to avoid people who would most definitely be coming after her. In a city like Lehigh, West Virginia, you might be able to stay hidden from the police by going to someone like Maurits and to her stepfather's Organization. Or you might be able to get out of the reach of the Organization by going to the police. But how would a twenty-year-old college kid like Baby Doll be able to stay out of the clutches of both Maurits *and* the police? Especially when they found out what she'd taken?

The sound of ringing shattered the silence.

Of course—how could she be so stupid? Her cell phone went everywhere she did—and that meant as long as she held on to that cell, they could find her anywhere, anytime. She didn't hesitate. She grabbed her purse, and before the call even went to voice mail, her $400 mobile was crashing into pieces on the pavement. In fact, she threw it so hard out the passenger window that it actually bounced off the asphalt and spread its remains all over the sidewalk and underneath a bus-stop bench.

She stared inside her purse, at all the things that pointed to her—driver's license, credit cards, even her monogrammed makeup case—and knew it was time to say good-bye. First she pulled all the cash out of the wallet. Fifty-seven dollars. Not a lot, but she wasn't worried about that at the moment. Next she started flinging plastic out the window. Visa cards (two). JCPenney and Nordstrom cards. Driver's license. College ID card. Library card. Only at this last one did she hesitate, but not for long. Out the window it went too. When her wallet was empty, she chucked it outside as well. Then she dumped the rest of the contents of her purse through the window, and finally dropped the handbag out as well. Some lucky girl was going to find a slightly scuffed, $750 Louis Vuitton black with multicolor designs Alma handbag by the side of the road today. Good for her.

On the seat next to her she saw Maurits's now-empty minirevolver. *If I can't allow myself a library card, then I certainly don't need to keep this.* A moment later, the gun skidded and bounced on the roadway as well. She felt suddenly invisible, lost to the world, and realized it was not a new feeling. A shiver ran through her, and she realized that all this littering outside the window was whipping ice-cold air into the car. She rolled up the window and then reached over to turn up the heat on the console. She felt her ears begin to sting as numbness in them subsided and feeling returned.

Baby Doll looked over at Boy and caught his eye. She could tell he was reading her face like the morning news. She tried to read his, but nothing she'd learned in Psychology 201 could penetrate his freakish eyes. They drove along in silence for a while, and then he finally spoke.

"You hungry yet?"

And just like that, she realized she was starving.

Five

It was crazy. An absurd notion. But Alondra's grandfather had been an Episcopal priest before his retirement, and she had decided he was finally senile enough to go along with the charade. "Besides," she'd said happily, "I'm fifty-six years old now and have never been married. People think I'm crazy anyway. Why not take advantage of it?"

Glitter danced in her emerald eyes, and I wondered how anyone could ever say no to her . . .

—

"How did you get the keys to Detective Lopez's car?"

The present rushes into my senses at the sound of Baby Doll's voice, reminding me that Alondra is gone, has been gone for some time now. It is so easy to forget where I am, what I am doing. I am lost in the drifts, and sometimes even that seems like home.

"Pickpocket," I say. "Years of practice."

She quickly becomes preoccupied with her belongings, as though it's just now that she's realized that when you run, people follow.

I need to sleep; to heal from the cold. But first we must do what's necessary, what even she doesn't notice about herself. I wait for the moment when her racing mind will pause and take a breath. Her face is open to me right now, and that makes choosing the right moment easier. Finally it comes.

"You hungry yet?"

She looks surprised, then nods.

"Starving."

Five minutes later we are standing at the counter of an Arby's, and she is nervously chewing her fingernails while we wait our turn.

"I don't know if we should have come in," she says. "What if . . ."

I nod. "We have to leave the car somewhere soon, because everyone is looking for you in it. That's why I parked it across the street. In here, we blend with the crowd. And we can sit at a table inside a fully windowed structure, so windowed in fact, it provides views out of three sides of the building. We'll know minutes ahead if anyone is coming after us. That should be enough time for us to make our way out one of the four exits in this room."

She slowly affirms my assessment, and then steps away from me to the counter and orders two Beef 'n' Cheddar sandwiches, with a large curly fries but only one Dr Pepper. Enough food for both of us, but she's clearly uncertain about how to explain ordering two drinks.

"That's a lot of food for a pretty little girl like you," the man behind the counter flirts. She fakes a smile, puts a hand on her stomach, and says, "Yeah, well, I'm eating for two." It strikes me that she lies spontaneously with practiced ease. I wonder how she will react when she discovers that I am not easily lied to.

"Oh, congratulations," the counterman says insincerely. Suddenly, his flirtatious intentions are apparently needed elsewhere.

She carries the food to a table and we begin to eat. "So, what do we do now?" she asks. I shrug. She nods thoughtfully. I can see her trying to decide if she is more hungry than worried, or more worried than hungry. Hunger apparently wins out because she attacks her sandwich with the ferocity of a wolverine.

When she begins to slow down, I speak. "You owe me a favor."

"I don't owe you anything yet," she snorts. "All you've done so far is give me a ride to a fast-food joint. I bought your lunch, so we're even as far as I'm concerned."

She wears a light gray, cable-knit sweater over the top of black dress pants. Appropriate attire for a funeral, I suppose. For the first time, I notice that the sweater fits her oddly.

Now she's looking at me, trying to read my thoughts.

"Who are you?" she says softly. "Why can't anybody else see you?"

A small group of people comes laughing into the restaurant. They appear to be led by a young man with a wide smile and a flamboyant air. Two girls hang on his arms, and all three look like they've just found hidden treasure.

"It's difficult to explain," I say. "People are aware of me—enough to walk past or around me. Enough to not question that there are two sandwiches in front of you. But not enough to see me. I'm here, but unnoticeable." I know this isn't enough explanation for her, but I'm weary, and this is one of those things that takes time to comprehend.

A teenager comes smiling by. He seems too old for high school, but not old enough, or maybe not mature enough, to be out in the workaday world by himself yet. A junior college junkie, I assume. He has shaggy blond hair and a surfer's grin. Mischievous blue eyes that reveal to me he is skipping freshman English today. And that maybe he skipped biology yesterday as well.

"Hey," he says to Baby Doll, "you should get in on this. That guy up there says he's buying whatever anybody wants as long as they order within the next five minutes."

"Thanks, but no thanks."

The kid shrugs and starts to leave, but then Baby Doll grabs his arm.

"Hey," she says when he turns back. "What's your name?"

"Will." He smiles. He can't tell if she is flirting or just talking, but he is willing to wait around long enough to find out.

"Want to earn a quick fifty bucks, Will?" Baby Doll says sweetly.

The teen looks suspicious. "Maybe," he says.

She puts her hand on the table, palm up, fingers gently moving, signaling me without looking in my direction. "See that Crown Victoria across the street? It belongs to my auntie Honoria. She works down at 104th and L.K. Fine Street."

"Isn't that where the police station is?"

"Yeah, so you know the area?"

"Well, sure."

"Great. Well, I borrowed the car from her this morning, but was supposed to return it by noon. Only my boyfriend just called and wants me to go with him to the movies. He's supposed to meet me here in a few minutes."

"What's that got to do with me?"

I place the car keys in her left hand while she pulls $50 out of a pocket with her right hand.

"Here," she says, handing him the keys and the cash. "If you'll return it for me, you can keep the money."

He looks dubious. "How do you know I won't just steal your aunt's car and take it for a joyride?"

Baby Doll favors the kid with a sly grin and shrugs. "Hey, it's not my car."

She then turns her attention to the stack of curly fries in front of her. The teen looks up at the counter where the young man and his two girlfriends are indeed buying lunch for the gathering crowd.

"Ah, it's too crowded up there anyway," he says, smiling back at Baby Doll and pocketing the money. "I'll tell your auntie you said hi."

"Thanks, you're a lifesaver."

The teen exits the front door and we watch him cross the street. A moment later he drives away in a direction that is definitely not headed toward the police station. Baby Doll smirks.

"Never underestimate the power of human weakness," she says softly. I nod. She is smart, and she apparently knows how to pick a mark out of a crowd. More to remember about her.

"Okay, that should lead the police on a little bit of a wild-goose chase," she says to me. "Which brings us back to you."

I wait. She shoves what's left of her food aside.

"Last night I had a dream about you," she says.

This is interesting.

"Well, not about you specifically. But about you anyway. I was on a stage at the front of a great theater. I was surrounded by people who wanted to hurt me."

"Maurits?" I ask.

"Maybe. I don't know. No one had a clear face in the dream. But I knew they wanted to hurt me, and that I had to get away. As they were closing in, I heard the squeaking of a pulley. I looked up and a boy was being lowered onto the stage from above, like an angel."

"Deus ex Machina."

She nods, admiration sneaking into her face. "So you know a little literature. Good for you. Yes, Deus ex Machina—God out of a machine—coming down on a crane, ready to set things aright in whatever Greek tragedy is playing on the stage that day. Or, in your case, an angel representing God maybe?"

"I'm not an angel."

"Demon?"

I shake my head.

"So why are you here, Boy? I can't figure out where you fit into what I know or believe. If you're not my Deus ex Machina, what are you doing here?"

"I don't choose the tether," I say slowly. "I have no control over it. It controls me."

She leans back in her chair, arms crossed. "I have no idea what you just said."

I lean in closer, locking my eyes onto hers. "I am a soul lost in the shallows of history. A Drifter. That's all I know. The mark in my eyes confirms it. If you can see the mark, if you can see me, then you are my tether, at least for the time being. That means I am bound to you until the tether is broken."

"Bound to me," she says thoughtfully. "Like a slave or servant or something?"

"No. Just bound to you. Not subservient to you."

Her eyes narrow, as if she doesn't quite believe me. I am surprised to see a flicker of compassion behind the hardness in her eyes. She is thinking of the power of lostness. Does she feel sorry for me?

"What's your name?"

"Boy," I say. It feels like that's what it's always been. I honestly can't remember what others have called me.

"No, what's your real name. Your birth name?" I can see frustration on the edges of her eyes.

"I don't know."

"Where are you from?"

I shrug.

"Where did you grow up?"

I don't bother responding at all.

She sighs, a long annoyed exhalation that seems to indicate she's trying not to lose her temper.

"Okay, how about this," she says. "Tell me about your childhood. Any random memory from when you were a kid. How about we start there?"

"I've lived a hundred childhoods. And I've died a hundred deaths. I've been old, young, and everything in between. As far as I can tell my life has no purpose or meaning. I'm a Drifter, forgotten by God. I have no past; I have no future. I have only my tether, and right now that tether is you."

"So you say," she says. There is a moment of silence between us, and then we both see a police cruiser drive casually past on the street outside. Her eyes match mine, and I know what is next.

We leave our unfinished edibles and paper wrappings on the table and push our way out a side door of this now-crowded little eatery.

"Just a minute," she says, running back inside. I see her enter the ladies' restroom, and feel the hint of tugging inside my rib cage. I measure the distance with my eyes—about thirty-five feet. Maybe tomorrow it will be thirty-five yards, or fifty. Maybe even one hundred yards. Hard to tell at this point. A few weeks, I think, and the tether will loosen. For now, though, I know what must be done. I reenter the restaurant and wait for her outside the door of the ladies' room. In a moment she is out again, looking a bit tousled, as though she had to remove both her coat and her sweater to go to the bathroom.

"Okay," she says, "let's go."

Six

She was vaguely aware that it was unnatural for her to just run away with some random guy she'd picked up at a funeral, but something about Boy was beginning to jibe with her mental state. Sure he was frustrating, obscure, and possibly dangerous—judging from the way he'd handled that minirevolver. Still, being with him was also beginning to feel normal to her, as if they'd been friends for a long time but had only just met.

And it was weird that no one else could see him but her. That alone was enough reason to keep him around. In a desperate moment an invisible friend might come in handy, if only for the fact that he wore pockets.

She stuffed two hundred-dollar bills in the pocket of her black dress pants, straightened her sweater, and swung the leather coat on top of it all, then walked out the bathroom door. Boy was waiting for her there. "Tethered" to her apparently. *Deo dignus vindice nodus.* She thought of the Latin saying when she looked at him. *A knot worthy of God to untie.*

Out loud she said, "Okay, let's go."

A normal person would ask where we're going, she thought. *But this Boy just follows along like a lost puppy.* She led them south down Harvey Avenue for a bit, then wondered herself, *Where are we going?*

"The Crown Victoria will have been spotted by now," Boy said. "How far away do you think that would be?"

Baby Doll checked her watch. It was 12:19 P.M. now. Charlie Murphy's funeral had been at 10 A.M., and the interment ceremony had been scheduled for 11:30. Now, just forty-nine minutes after that, she was on the street, a fugitive, with an apparently imaginary companion haunting her every step. "At least fifteen miles east, maybe more, depending on how fast our joyrider drives."

"I need to sleep. To heal."

She looked at the Boy and saw pain in his eyes. Weren't supernatural beings, or at least invisible ones, supposed to be immune to simple human needs like sleep? She hesitated. "Do you want to try wearing my coat?"

"I don't need a coat, not anymore. But I need to sleep. To heal."

"I don't understand exactly what you mean."

He didn't say anything then, just waited. Baby Doll was beginning to hate his silences. They seemed to indicate both infinite patience and nagging restlessness at the same time. She continued walking down Harvey Avenue, trying to figure out what to do next. Boy followed closely behind in silence.

Okay, she thought, *it was a half-baked plan. Go to the funeral. Find an opportunity. Then run. It seemed pretty simple when I hatched it last night, but now that plan A has worked, what am I supposed to do for plan B?*

In the distance a row of cheap motels gave her answer.

"Fine," she said aloud. "We'll get a room up there. Hide out until tonight, and then figure out our options."

She had to pay cash up front at the reception desk of the Super 12 Motel, but the attendant didn't seem to mind that she used a fake name and completely left an address off the registration form, so that was good enough for Baby Doll. Inside the motel room were two double beds, drab curtains, a TV set that looked like it might have come from a Goodwill store, and three clean towels hanging in the bathroom. But it was quiet, and it was isolated. A good place to catch a breath and think.

Boy sat on the bed closest to the bathroom and looked at her for a moment.

"Go ahead," Baby Doll said. "Get some rest. I'll be here when you wake up. I'm just going to do some thinking while you sleep. Maybe I'll even take a nap myself."

He nodded, and then stretched out on top of the bedclothes and closed his eyes. Baby Doll noticed that he didn't even remove his shoes or take off his shirt.

Guy must have been exhausted, she thought. Then, *Tell you the truth, I'm exhausted too.*

She thought about taking up space on the empty bed, but then decided she wouldn't allow herself to sleep until she'd figured out what her next move was going to be. She didn't even grant herself permission to sit on the wooden chair next to the scratched-up table under the lamp in the corner of the room. Instead, she pressed her back against the wall by the bathroom door and slowly slid down until she was seated on the floor, staring at the curtained window and wondering why light always seemed so bright through the slits that inevitably showed between the curtains in a cheap motel room.

Finally she allowed her mind to wander back over the events of the past few weeks. It had been the Sunday before last when she'd first gotten the idea.

—

She'd been sleeping in her room on the second floor of Charlie Murphy's mansion in North Downtown. It was the same room she'd occupied since she was four years old when Charlie took over from the Captain and moved into this house as part of the claim of his rightful place in the Organization. Although Baby Doll's room had been painted and redecorated a few times over the years, it still held the air of a little girl's bedroom; pink, safe, small, and just cluttered enough to remind a visitor that someone lived here.

Baby Doll had stayed up until midnight or so studying for a Latin exam. Others took Spanish or French or even German to fulfill their foreign language requirements, but not Baby Doll. The things she wanted to know were hidden in languages like Latin and Greek, so she'd convinced the university to let her take Latin as her language requirement for graduation. It's possible that Maurits had had something to do with that exception being made, but also just as likely that the administrators at the university wanted to encourage learning in all its forms and so made accommodations for Baby Doll without regard to her family connections. She liked to assume the latter, though she never could really rule out the former.

After studying, she'd stacked her books on the desk and gone quickly to sleep. It was around 1:30 A.M. when the screaming started.

Baby Doll had drawn her pillow over her head and tried to put the noise out of her mind. She thought of waterfalls and daffodils and even Saturday-morning cartoons. But the yelling continued, longer and more violent this time. She heard a crash and understood the splintering of wood against a wall. She heard footsteps racing down the hall outside her door and Maurits's voice barking commands. There was a moment of silence, then another crash, the opening of a door, and a stream of profanities that raged from the mouth of a truly angry man.

Baby Doll got up, put on her robe, and cracked open the door of her bedroom, then opened it a bit wider. Two of Charlie's "associates" raced by her door in the direction of the yelling. She glanced down the long marble hallway to the other end of the floor where Charlie Murphy's massive bedroom was. The heavy oak door was open, and standing on the threshold was Charlie. He wore his boxers and nothing else. His face was pink with rage, and the area around his eyes blue-black from either alcohol or lack of sleep or just plain sickness. But the thing that made his associates halt halfway down the hall was the classic Scottish broadsword he held in both hands, swinging it back and forth with malicious fervor.

"*Facta non verba,* you miserable, worthless piles of refuse! *Facta non verba* or I'll kill you all!"

Baby Doll's first thought had been a selfish one. *Hey, I taught him that.* Facta non verba—*"deeds, not words." I didn't even know he was listening.* Her next thought was for the safety of those getting closer to her manic stepfather. Charlie Murphy was not a gentle man. If he wanted to hurt someone, it was best to stay out of his way.

Just then Maurits had come up the stairs, holding a small plastic bottle in his big hand. He walked calmly, without fear, toward his boss. When he came to Baby Doll's door, he paused.

"Go back to sleep, Baby," he said quietly, twisting a bottle of Lamictal back and forth in his hand as he spoke. "Your dad just forgot to take his medicine for a couple days. He'll be fine in the morning. You go on back to bed now, and let Maurits take care of your dad."

Baby Doll nodded, stepped back, and started to close her door. She left it open a crack, though, to hear what would happen next. She heard Maurits walk up to Charlie without hesitation.

"What, you gonna kill ol' Maurits now, boss? After all we

been through? Well, if that's what you think is best, then I'm with you on it, just like always. Go ahead, boss, take your swing. I won't fight it. Just make it quick for ol' Maurits, will you, boss? At least I deserve that much respect, right?"

And then the sobbing. Charlie was sobbing. And the sword clattered to the floor, cracking one of the marble tiles where the heavy gold-plated hilt struck the ground.

"Shh, it's all right, boss." It was Maurits again. "Nobody here but family. Nobody but us. Here, I got your medicine, and—" Baby Doll heard Maurits's fingers snap. "Leo over there, he's going to get you a nice stiff shot of gin to help it go down right."

Baby Doll heard Leo's footsteps pounding down the hallway. Charlie's sobbing continued, but more quietly now. A moment later she heard the door to Charlie's bedroom click shut, and the house was silent again.

She closed her door the rest of the way and went back to lie in bed. While she lay there, two phrases flitted through her head.

Bonitas non est pessimis esse meliorem. It is not goodness to be better than the worst.

Facta non verba. Deeds, not words.

—

Baby Doll sat with her back against the motel room wall, staring at the dilapidated curtains pulled across the window directly in front of her. The Drifter slept without moving on the bed. The sun still strained to break through the filth of the window, waning in intensity.

She replayed the episode from that Sunday night once more in her head, until she could almost recite the events by rote.

Yep, she thought to herself grimly. *That was when I finally decided to kill him. And when I knew how to do it at last.*

The gift of sight is fraught with frailty.

Eyes cannot see what the soul touches,

nor can the lens of vision capture the true nature of a thing.

All we see is just a reflection in muddied water,

and we must hope that it is enough.

—SOLACE THE LESSER
PHILOSOPHER AND HISTORIAN, 429 B.C.

Seven

SATURDAY, FEBRUARY 19

When Baby Doll opened her eyes her first thought was that she had gone blind. The darkness was so thick, and she was so disoriented, that it took her a full minute or two to realize that her face was pressed up against the greasy thickness of old carpet, that she had, in fact, drooled into a puddle that now dampened her left cheek and even seeped into her ear. She sat up with a start and discovered herself in a shadowed motel room, hips sore from sleeping on a hard floor, and her back to a wall. She blinked a few times, willing her eyes to adjust to the darkness until she could make out shapes. Two beds. Curtains. A window. She cursed under her breath. The sunlight no longer fought to break through the draperies, no more were there bright lines and edges around the frame of the window. She blinked again and then felt her heart jump. There was a shape, a man, sitting on the edge of the bed staring right at her. Memories flooded back into her head, and she groaned, both because of the soreness of her muscles and back, and because she was annoyed with herself for being caught off guard by a bogeyman in the dark.

"What do you want, Boy?"

"You owe me a favor."

"Yeah, well, right now I owe my bladder a favor." She got up and stumbled into the bathroom. A moment later she returned to find the Boy still sitting on the bed in the dark. She sighed again.

"All right, what's the great big favor that you so desperately want?" She searched the room for the clock and saw 1:14 glowing red on the nightstand. Had she really slept that long?

"I need to go back to Simon's apartment. I left something there, and I need to get it."

"Fine. Go. We can meet up later if you want. Just tell me where." She crossed the room in the darkness and let herself stretch out on the empty bed.

"I can't go unless you do. You're the tether, and it's always strongest at the beginning."

"So what are you saying, you can't go anywhere without me? That's a little bit needy, isn't it, Boy?" She closed her eyes in the darkness. It felt good to lie on a mattress, even if it was in a seedy motel. *I could actually go back to sleep right now,* she thought to herself in surprise. *Am I really that exhausted?*

"Baby Doll." Was that the first time he'd used her name? "We have to go anyway. We can't stay here much longer, or someone will figure out where we are."

"You're right. Just give me a few minutes to wake up."

"And then we'll go to Simon's?"

She didn't answer.

"Baby Doll."

She rolled to her side, facing away from him. She felt a little guilty about ignoring the Boy at first, until she remembered his frequent, frustrating silences toward her earlier. *See how you like it when somebody doesn't respond to you,* she thought in dreamy satisfaction.

She heard Boy lie back down on his bed, heard his breathing, soft and steady like a lullaby. *I should get up,* she thought. *Now's a good time to find a more permanent hiding place.* Boy continued breathing. In the sound she thought she heard wind chimes, and then flutes. *I like those flutes,* she thought. *I wonder where they're coming from?*

She walked down the second-floor hallway of Charlie's house and peeked into her pink bedroom. No. No flutes in there. She turned and peeked over the railing down to the first floor. Nothing there either. She heard the flutes whisper behind her, so she turned and found herself facing Charlie's bedroom door. When had he painted it red? The handle was broken, so she tapped on the door quietly. To her surprise, it gave way under her touch. She pushed it a little harder and the door swung wide open. The inside was bigger than she remembered, but the sound of flutes was definitely coming from this direction. *Has Charlie moved his bed to another room?* she wondered. In the corner she saw Charlie's bedroom desk, a large rosewood piece that was always covered with papers and books. The chair behind the desk was occupied; Baby Doll felt a tremor of fear, knowing she shouldn't be in this room without an invitation. "It's all right, Baby," the voice behind the desk said. "Come on in. We need to talk anyway."

The flutes beckoned from behind the voice. She took a step closer, then another. She heard wind chimes now. Another step, but the desk never seemed to draw any nearer, as if it slid one step away for every step she took toward it. The voice behind grumbled, and suddenly she was at the desk, and it was larger and wider than she could have imagined, so big that her chin barely reached over the top of it. And behind the desk was not just a chair, but a throne made of iron and glass, and full of jagged points that rose like spires around its edges. The man on the throne leaned forward into the light. *Maurits!*

"Hello, Baby Doll," Maurits said. "I believe this is yours." In his outstretched palm he held a .22-caliber short minirevolver. It was stained with blood on both the handle and the snout. "You know what to do with it, yes?"

Baby Doll peered over the top of the desk with the wide eyes of a child, wishing her feet had not been fastened to the floor.

"No? Well, that's all right, Baby, 'cause I know what to do." He aimed the revolver between her eyes and pulled back on the hammer.

Maurits, wait . . . She no longer saw his face, or his throne, and even the desk had disappeared. All she could see was the muzzle of that deadly little gun. She tried to close her eyes, but they wouldn't shut. She watched as Maurits's forefinger began to close, almost in slow motion, pulling the trigger to release her death.

Her eyes flew open. Was that a gunshot she'd just heard? She blinked hard, staring at the dingy curtains once again. But something was wrong; something was different.

She heard Boy rise from the bed next to her.

In the crack of the curtain she saw a pale, gray-yellow light slipping through. *Oh, no . . .*

"They're here." Boy said it as though announcing the weather outside.

Baby Doll felt her heart racing. She almost wished she could have a heart attack. At least then she wouldn't have to face this moment. She heard another thundering knock on the door, a pounding that sounded like three staccato gunshots in her ears. She swung her head around and looked at the faded red numbers on the clock. It was 5:29. Four more hours. She'd slept four more hours! What was wrong with her?

"I told you it was time to go. We should have left during the night."

I toldjaso? That was the best this annoying Boy could come up with?

"Just shut up, Boy," she snapped. She could feel the pressure building inside, threatening to overwhelm her. She almost wanted to drop to the floor and start crying for her mommy like a little lost child, but it had been a long time since that had been a option for her. "Just shut—"

"Baby Doll, open the door." It was Detective Lopez's voice. "Come on, Baby Doll. No one's going to hurt you. We just want to talk to you. We think you might be in danger from your father's associates. We want to help."

Baby Doll jumped from the bed and ran to the bathroom. No luck. No window. She searched the motel room for a hiding place, for an exit, for anything. And all the while the Boy just stood there, watching.

"Open the door, Baby Doll. We can help you. I can help you."

"You get your car back, Detective?"

The muffled snickers let Baby Doll know that there were at least three other people outside that door with Honoria Lopez. Two men, apparently, and another woman.

"Well, sort of," the detective said. Her voice was not smiling. "We found it—well, what was left of it—at the racetrack. It appears I won't be driving the Crown Victoria any time soon."

"How did you find me, Detective?"

"Credit card trail."

Baby Doll raised her eyebrows. *How could that be?*

"After you bought everybody lunch at that Arby's down the road, your card activity popped up on the grid."

Bought everybody lunch? What . . . ? Then she remembered. *"Hey, you should get in on this," that stupid teenager had said. "That guy up there says he's buying whatever anybody wants as long as they order within the next five minutes."* She shook her head in disgust. *That guy and his two girlfriends must've found one of my Visa cards on the street and then gone on a shopping spree, starting at Arby's. Figures.*

"After that, it was just a matter of establishing a perimeter and showing your picture around until somebody recognized you. Was nice of you to buy everybody lunch, though. You celebrating something?"

"Am I under arrest?"

There was a pause. Then, "No, of course not, Baby Doll. Open the door, and let's talk."

"What about your car?"

"Oh, that? We've arrested a teenage boy for grand theft, auto. Seems that he and a few of his friends stole it to go joyriding. They'll get a slap on the wrist, do some community service, and be done. No harm, no foul." There was a significant pause. "That's it, Baby Doll. *Teen boy stole my car.* You understand what I'm saying?"

She shot a glance at Boy, but his face said nothing. "Yeah, I understand, Detective."

"So what do you say, Baby Doll? Got a few minutes to talk with a poor old lady who got her car stolen by some joyriding kids?"

Baby Doll drew in a deep breath, then walked carefully across the room and opened the door. She was surprised to see that two of the backup police officers had guns drawn, and a third had handcuffs at the ready. Her eyes flew wide and she started to slam the door shut, but Honoria Lopez was too fast, blocking the opening with both her forearm and her foot. In the same motion she waved a hand toward the cops behind her. "Doggone it, Sam, put that gun away. And we definitely won't be needing those handcuffs." She looked meaningfully in Baby Doll's direction. "Will we, Baby Doll?"

The girl shook her head slowly, and then stepped out of the motel room. Boy followed closely behind.

"Of course we won't," Detective Lopez said soothingly.

"I'm not under arrest?" Baby Doll asked again.

"No," Detective Lopez answered, but Baby Doll thought she heard one of the backup officers whisper, "Not yet," under his breath as they stepped away from the motel room entrance.

"So why are you chasing me then?"

"I'm not chasing you, Baby Doll. I'm trying to protect you. There are some interested parties who seem upset by the untimely death of your stepfather—"

"Adoptive father."

"Yes, of course. My mistake. Adoptive father. Anyway, we were worried about your safety, especially when you unexpectedly, um, disappeared yesterday."

"I'm fine. Can I go now?"

"Now, Baby Doll, I can't let you just wander the streets knowing that you might be in danger. And besides, it turns out I have a few questions myself about your step—I mean, *adopted* father's recent passing."

"Why would I know anything? I'm just a third-year philosophy student. That's what I do. You can check it out with the university."

"Of course that's what you do. I believe you, Baby Doll. No need for me to check out *your* stories, now is there? And don't worry. When the motel clerk told us that you hadn't paid for your room yet, we went ahead and took care of that for you."

"He's a liar. I paid cash for this room last night."

"Of course you did. But we made sure to clear your debt this morning anyway. After all, that's what friends are for, aren't they?" Honoria Lopez smiled like a fox just preparing to enter a chicken coop.

"Now," Detective Lopez said warmly, "how about we take a ride in my new car?"

Eight

Only in the dreaming do I feel really alive.

But this time it was a healing sleep, not a dreaming sleep, though after I wake I have the feeling that I have not quite remembered something.

I flex my toes and no longer feel the deadening void and painful blistering that had inhabited the front of my feet earlier in the day. I hear the sound of Baby Doll, lightly snoring to my right, but I do not open my eyes just yet. The room feels cool, but I can't yet gauge how much time has passed.

And I feel it's important to remember something from my sleep.

I wait, but nothing comes. I open my eyes and see shadows in the room. A glance out the window reveals that I have slept through the best part of the day, and now it appears to be close to midnight. My senses tingle with the freshness of sleep and a strong tether.

For some reason, Baby Doll is sleeping on the floor next to the bathroom.

We've been here for twelve hours now. Long enough. If we are really on the run, we can't stay in one place too long until we've found a safe house or created a new place for ourselves. And besides, now is a good time to go back to . . . to . . . Again,

I can't remember his name. But I know where he lives—lived—and I know where I've hidden my box in his apartment. We must get that box before it's too late.

I move to the edge of the bed so I can get a better look at Baby Doll. She seems truly gone to the world. Of course, given what she's been through in the last twenty-four hours, it makes sense that she would need time to recover, to sleep and heal herself.

Simon. That's his name. Was his name. Simon. I must remember it. I rarely remember the names, although I try. There are so many and they come and go in my mind. I concentrate harder and remember some of the others. Like Elia. Like Galway. Like Caroline.

Like Alondra.

I force myself to think of Simon, pushing back the memories of Alondra until I am sure that his name is imprinted in my mind. Simon. Simon's apartment. In the space above the ceiling tile, behind the door, just inside Simon's guest bathroom.

—

I hid it like that for seven years before Alondra found it. She was only twenty-seven years old then. Still wearing a young woman's clothes and the fresh face of optimism that reflected itself in the children she taught five days a week at the grammar schoolhouse. Even then, she wouldn't have seen it if the snow hadn't melted into the attic and then flooded the ceiling above her room.

"What's this?" she'd asked me when she discovered it among the water-damaged ruins in the attic. "It looks old. Maybe it holds a secret treasure or something! Who do you suppose might have left it here?"

It was not a large box—certainly not big enough to hold

much in the way of treasure, but she immediately plopped down on the floor and began examining it.

"It's barely much bigger than a little girl's first recipe box," she said gleefully. She turned it over and over. It fit nicely in her hands. "It seems to have escaped the worst of the snowmelt—that's good luck, isn't it? The wood must be some kind of mahogany—look at the deep red color. Oh, it's just beautiful, isn't it? I think it must be a hundred years old at least!"

"Alondra," I said.

"Shh," she said quickly. "Let me have my fun first. You can look at it next." She turned it over again. "It's so light, but I can feel weight shifting inside every time I turn it over." She held it up to her ear and shook it gently. "Yes, there's definitely something hidden inside there."

She placed it on the floor in front of her and gave it an appraising look. "Hmm. Eight corners, all covered with filigreed brass of some sort. Look at the detailed craftwork on this. Those corner pieces must have been done by hand. Two metal buckles on the front, and two more on the back. But the buckles seem to be just decorative. They don't open or connect to anything at all."

She reached out and flipped it carefully to its side.

"Strange," she said. "There is no slit or crack anywhere on this box. Nothing to indicate where, or even if, it opens."

"Alondra," I said again.

"Shh! You know the rules when we have a game like this. Me first, then you. I promise you'll get your turn."

She picked up the box and held it close to her face, actually sniffing the lid. "Musty. But also a bit perfumed. Perhaps there's potpourri inside."

"Alondra." I said it a little more forcefully this time; I was afraid she might be tempted to lick the dirty old box, just

to see if it tasted like gold. She gave me a pout and held it out to me.

"Fine," she said, "you can see it now. But let me look at it again when you're done. There must be some way to open it that I can't quite figure out yet. I know something is in there. I wonder if old Mr. Jellico left it up there when he passed on and my father bought this house. I'll have to ask Daddy if he knows of any stories that go with this home."

"Alondra," I said, taking it from her hands. "It's my box."

She looked at me with sheer delight, as though I'd just told her that Christmas was coming three times this year. "Well, what are you waiting for? Open it, you silly. I'm dying to see what's inside."

How do you say no to someone like Alondra? Even with something as valuable and private as this? You don't, really. You can't. But that was something special about Alondra; she knew when you wanted to, and when you didn't. She never forced a yes out of a no.

"No, wait a minute," she said softly. She rose to her feet and looked into my eyes. I felt her fingers sweep softly against my cheek. "No, I don't want to know. Not yet anyway. Someday, maybe. When you are ready. But not today."

She brushed her lips against mine, not long, but long enough. Then she smiled. "But it is such a pretty box," she murmured. "We should at least keep it on the dresser where it won't collect cobwebs or get lost in a flood of melted snow."

I nodded, and handed her the box. She placed it on the dresser next to a photograph of herself in an orchard. As far as I know, she never touched it again.

I always meant to open it for her one day, to let her see the treasures inside. For some reason, I thought I had plenty of time.

—

Baby Doll groans, and even in the darkness of the motel room I see her face form itself into a grimace. I look at the clock. It's just after 1 A.M. *now. We really need to leave this place. To get my box from Simon's apartment and then find another place to hide it away. In the darkness I see the girl's eyes flutter, and then open. She seems confused at first, unsure of her surroundings. So I wait. After a moment she sees me, and she groans again.*

"What do you want, Boy?" she says.

"You owe me a favor."

"Yeah, well, right now I owe my bladder a favor." And she steps away, into the bathroom. When she returns, she is in a foul mood. But this is important. Still, she doesn't listen. Instead she lies back down on the bed opposite me.

"Baby Doll," I say to her. She doesn't answer. She rolls away from me, turning her back to me. Telling me with her posture that she wants me to go away. She doesn't care.

Another thing to remember about this one.

And she promised me a favor, one that she has failed to keep. As I think on this I begin to remember what it was that was shown to me in my sleep.

I lie down on the bed beside hers. We will wait, then.

In the darkness, the minutes turn to hours. And in the darkness, the pictures from my sleep begin rearranging themselves into a meaningful order. There are still gaps, but it is coming back to me now. And I see why my mind kept insisting that it was important to remember.

Baby Doll groans from time to time. Once she mumbles the words "Maurits, wait . . ." And then, just as the first streaks of sunlight begin to peek through the cracks in the curtains, the knock comes on the door. Baby Doll comes to wakefulness sud-

denly, almost unsure of what she has heard. I rise from my bed and get ready to go.

"They're here," I say. I assume she knows whom I mean.

She doesn't say anything, but her eyes are scanning the room, looking for a way out.

"I told you it was time to go. We should have left during the night."

"Just shut up, Boy," she says. And so I do.

A few moments later, we are riding in a police cruiser, heading to a place where neither one of us wants to be. And while I am staring out the backseat window, the memory from my sleep comes fully, finally, into focus.

Before this day is over, Baby Doll is going to try to kill me.

Nine

Baby Doll resisted the urge to walk over to the two-way mirror and stick a finger up her nose. She had only been in an interrogation room once before, and that was on an eighth-grade class field trip to the Police Services Center. At the time she had promised herself that she'd never have a reason to be back in one of these rooms. So she'd worked hard through high school and talked Charlie Murphy into paying for her to go to college at the state university in Lehigh. Now, two and a half years in, she had expected to graduate early in the fall. Of course, Charlie's death had interfered with that plan.

She took a seat on the back side of the little table that was the only furniture in the room. Boy stood behind her. He hadn't spoken the whole trip here. He'd sat in the backseat beside her, but spent the whole ride staring out the window, hands clasped in his lap. Detective Lopez, unaware of his presence, had tried to be chatty at first, asking about school and TV and such, but she was obviously not good at small talk, and eventually had probably decided it was better to give up than to risk ruining any rapport she might have with the suspect.

When they arrived at the Police Services Center, Detective Lopez had ushered her through the security scanners with everyone else, but then moved her past the normal check-in for suspects and had taken her directly to this interrogation room instead.

"Aren't you going to fingerprint me? Or strip-search me or something?" Baby Doll had asked.

"Of course not, Baby Doll." Detective Lopez had chuckled. "That stuff is for criminals. You're not a criminal, are you?"

Baby Doll shook her head no.

"Then why would you need to be searched and fingerprinted? You're a guest of the department."

"A 'person of interest'?"

Detective Lopez's face relaxed into an almost natural smile. "Yes, that's a good way to put it. A person of interest. Because, Baby Doll, I am very interested to hear what you might have to say about Charlie Murphy's death."

"I don't have anything to say."

"Well," she said brightly, "let's just talk about it anyway, shall we?"

Then she'd deposited Baby Doll in this room and left her with two armed security guards, both female, standing at the door. In spite of Honoria Lopez's reassurances, "guest" was not the word Baby Doll would have used to describe her current situation.

"May I take your coat, Ms. Murphy?" one of the guards asked politely, but it was evident that offer was not a request. Baby Doll grimaced and peeled off the leather jacket and handed it to the woman. She noticed the guard's name badge read "M. Chester." Officer Chester nodded, again politely, and then immediately took the coat out of the room.

"She won't find anything in there," Baby Doll said to the other security guard, one with a name badge that read "J. Hummel." "There's nothing in there to find."

"Yes, ma'am," Officer Hummel replied, equally as polite as

the first guard had been. She nodded, and Baby Doll understood that conversation was over as well.

She stared at herself in the two-way mirror, and wondered how long the charade would go on. She wondered how much she could say to Honoria Lopez without saying too much. And she wondered why this Boy standing behind her didn't do something. If this were the movies, he would have suddenly sprung into action, effectively—but humanely—disabling the security guards and then transporting her out of the Police Services Center in either a blaze of adrenaline-pumping martial arts and gunfire, or in an equally adrenaline-pumping stealth escape through the air ducts or something. But instead, he just stood there, taking it all in as though he were memorizing a play.

"Some Deus ex Machina you turned out to be," Baby Doll mumbled.

"Excuse me?" The security guard leaned toward her. Politely, of course.

"Nothing."

A few minutes later Officer Chester returned to the interrogation room and took up her former position beside the door. Baby Doll's expensive leather coat was nowhere to be seen. Then they all waited.

It was a full forty minutes before Honoria Lopez returned. She was full of energy, as though she'd swallowed four or five cups of strong coffee before coming into the interrogation room. She carried a folder and wore a gun in a shoulder holster. When she entered the room, one of the security guards leaned over and whispered something short into Honoria Lopez's ear.

"Comfortable, Baby Doll?" Lopez said cheerily.

"No. Can I go now?"

Detective Lopez only smiled. "Officer Hummel," she said to the second security guard, "would you please get our guest a soda or something. Dr Pepper okay, Baby Doll?" Baby Doll didn't answer, so Detective Lopez gave a quick nod to the security guard, and she immediately left the room.

"So," Detective Lopez said. "It's been a busy week for you. College exams. Family business. Stepfather kills himself. Or so it seems."

"Adoptive—"

"No need to play games with me anymore, Baby Doll. We both know what your father was and was not to you."

"What do you want from me?"

"I just want to talk for a bit. To learn more about you, about how you're doing."

"I'm fine. Can I go now?"

Detective Lopez ignored the question. "We've been keeping an eye on you, Baby Doll. We're worried about you." She opened the file folder. "Let's see. Eight years in Catholic school before transferring to the public system for high school. And it says here that now you're already a junior at the university, even though you're only twenty years old. A go-getter, aren't you? Good for you! Charlie Murphy must have been proud. Also says here that you're majoring in philosophy, with a minor in Latin of all things. Well, no one ever said you weren't a smart little cookie, did they? Looks like you make good grades—very good grades—although there was that blip with college algebra, wasn't there? Ah well, one can't be a genius at everything, can she?"

The door opened and Officer Hummel returned to the room carrying a Dr Pepper can. She set it, politely, on the table in front of Baby Doll. "Thanks very much, Jan," Detective Lopez said absently.

"Oh, now this doesn't make much sense though." She thumped a page in the folder with a little more drama than necessary. "According to this report, you know a lot of people at your school, but aren't really friends with any of them. Never joined a study group. Never invited anyone over to your house for a Friday-night get-together. Never visited friends in the dorm or attended a sorority party. Now that's just sad, isn't it?"

Baby Doll said nothing. Instead, she started reciting Homer's *Iliad* in her brain, trying to take her mind off the pressure she felt building inside her.

"Aw, not even a date for homecoming." Detective Lopez tilted her head and gave a look of mock sympathy. She closed the folder and slapped it firmly onto the table.

"Well, you know what we need to do, girlfriend? We need to help you make a few new friends. And since you're not going anywhere for the next few hours, I think I can hook you up in that regard."

"What? What do you mean?" Baby Doll felt her heart begin to race.

"Officer Hummel, would you please escort Ms. Murphy to the women's holding cell on the fourth floor?"

"Wait, why? I thought you wanted to talk. I thought you wanted to hear my stories." She tried not to sound panicky, but the high-pitched tone in her voice gave her away.

"I do, sweetie, I really do. But, you know, I think you might feel a little more talkative after you've been able to relax and make new friends in the women's holding cell."

"No, I'm relaxed. I'm fine. You wanted to talk, let's talk."

"I see. Well, how about this. What can you tell me about 'deus ex machina'?"

Baby Doll instinctively shot a look at Officer Hummel. The security guard gave a curt smile and nod.

"'Deus ex machina' is a Latin phrase that references a contrivance in Greek tragedies. It means 'God out of a machine' and it describes the moment in a play when a Greek god or an angel is let down through the rafters—on a crane or a pulley or something—just in time to save the day."

"Mm-hm. Very interesting. Tell me more."

"That's it. That's all it means."

"Really? You don't think it might have something to do with, I don't know, maybe a method of succession in Charlie Murphy's Organization? That maybe it means Maurits Girard is taking over your stepfather's place?"

"What? No, of course not. It's just a literary term from ancient Greece. That's all."

"I see. Well, maybe you'll think of more to share after making new friends. Officer Hummel?"

The second security guard stepped forward and put a hand on Baby Doll's arm.

"Wait, you can't be serious. That's really all there is to know about 'deus ex machina.' It's a literary term. I'm telling the truth."

"Mm-hm. I believe you, Baby Doll. You know that."

"Then why are you sending me to jail?"

"Not jail, sweetie. Just a holding cell. A little room where a few girls gather to get their heads together before they do something really stupid. And hey, there's even a TV set in there. Maybe you'll get to watch *Jeopardy* or *Wheel of Fortune.*"

"Am I under arrest now?"

"Of course not, honey. We just want to keep you safe here, and while we're at it, there's no harm in helping you make new friends, now is there?"

"You can't do this! If I'm not under arrest, then I can refuse to go. You can't make me go."

"Oh, I'm not making you go, Baby Doll. You're going to spend a few hours in holding voluntarily. Didn't you know that?"

"You're crazy. Why would anybody *voluntarily* go to jail?"

"Safety, of course. It's a dangerous world out there. In fact, you remember that kid who stole my car and took it joyriding? Well, now he's saying some girl gave him the keys and paid him to steal it. On the surface, the girl he describes sounds a lot like you. You and I both know that kind of talk is just foolishness. Still, it is probable cause, so it would make sense, since you are here already, to go ahead and place you under arrest while we check out his story. That would mean I would keep you here for a full forty-eight hours while I decide whether or not to charge you with a crime. In that situation, Baby Doll, I would have to go ahead and run your fingerprints, do the strip search, the whole nine yards. Standard procedure and all that." She shrugged sympathetically. "Or you could volunteer to spend a few short hours in holding, just to relax and gather your wits about you while we make sure it's safe for you on the outside."

Baby Doll was speechless.

"So relax, Baby Doll. Go make some new friends. I'll see you again in a few hours, and we can talk more about deus ex machina, about Charlie Murphy, and most importantly, about Maurits Girard. Officer?"

Baby Doll felt Officer Hummel's grip tighten on her arm, felt herself practically lifted out of the chair and moved toward the door. She looked wildly back at Boy standing behind the table. "Do something!" she hissed.

"Oh, I am, Baby Doll," Detective Lopez replied while paging through the folder on the table. "You can bet your life on that score."

Boy said nothing. But he followed the procession out the door. Baby Doll wanted to say something smart, something cavalier and brave as she left the interrogation room. She turned to Officer Hummel with the best of intentions, but the only words that came out were, "You're not nearly as polite as you pretend to be."

Officer Hummel just smiled.

Ten

I wonder what she is hiding.

She handled the stress of preliminary interrogation reasonably well for a woman as young as she is. She was definitely caught off guard by Detective Lopez's sweat-it-out tactic, but even then managed to keep her wits about her. It was only at the threat of strip search that Baby Doll finally flinched.

It hadn't occurred to me that she might be hiding something on her person. Until now. Whatever it is, she covers it up well.

After twenty-four hours in the same clothes, she looks reasonably unscathed. Her dress slacks have a few wrinkles now and hang with the looseness of fabric that needs a good washing, but still hold sharp lines and the texture of affluence. Her cable-knit sweater appears a little stretched out under the shoulders, but also has managed to avoid stains or grime one would associate with normal wear. She didn't wear much makeup to start with, so apart from a little extra shading around the eyes, and a little tiredness at the edges, her face looks normal. Hair could use a stiff brush, but even that was mostly tamed earlier in the morning with only a few quick glides of her fingers from front to back.

I can tell that she is hiding something. I have my suspicions where, but I can't be sure. And I have no idea what it might be.

For some reason, this makes me like her just a little bit, even though I know I can't trust her.

The holding cell is a large, windowless, rectangular room, about sixteen feet by twenty feet, with benches placed strategically around the concrete flooring and bolted to the ground. Two sides of the cell are white-painted brick walls, the other two sides an array of woven steel rods that intersect at one large, gated entrance. A TV set is mounted on a wall just outside the entrance and is blaring a generic morning talk show. Inside, the room is only sparsely populated. Two women stretch out on benches, sleeping off the effects of alcohol, or just trying to block out the awful chatter on the television. Three women are sitting near a corner where one would normally expect a window to be. One woman stands alone, lazily pacing in a circle. All of them look intensely bored. Video cameras are positioned outside the cell at various angles, apparently giving surveillance officers outside the room clear views of anything inside.

"Officer Hummel," the pacing woman calls out when she sees us arrive. "How much longer you gonna keep me in here? Ain't my man posted bail yet?"

"A little while longer yet, Maryanne," Officer Hummel replies. "I think I saw your husband downstairs, though. I'll go check on it as soon as I'm through here."

She opens the gate and indicates for Baby Doll to enter the cage. I hesitate. I could remain outside the cell and still be close enough to my tether. Baby Doll takes a breath and strides forward with confidence into the cell. Without really thinking, I follow her lead and, a moment later, hear the lock engage behind us.

"Whatcha brought for us this morning, Officer?" one of the three women in the corner says comfortably. "She's kind of a fancy one, huh?" Hummel doesn't respond, but instead turns and leaves.

Baby Doll quietly surveys the room, looking for an inconspicuous place to pass the time. She finally settles on a spot near the middle of an empty bench along the left-side steel wall. She looks uncomfortably at her hands, as if she doesn't know what to do with them, or what to do at all. The only thing to do here, it seems, is to wait. I sit next to her, unnoticed, and she leans her head back against the steel and closes her eyes. Sleep is one way to pass the time. To my surprise, she reaches out slowly and grasps my hand. Only then do I notice that she is trembling.

"You look like hell, sweetie."

One of the women has separated herself from the trio in the corner and is making her way toward us. Baby Doll's eyes snap open, taking in this new person. I can see her measuring her thoughts, trying to come up with a response that is neither friendly, nor antagonistic.

"Been a long few days," she says at last, then she looks away, trying to give the hint that this conversation is over.

"Aren't they all?"

The woman is the sturdy sort, one you might expect to see doing chores on a family farm or shooting pool in a local tavern. She wears jeans, a rock concert T shirt, and a blue flannel man's overshirt, sleeves cut off, that hangs open and loose on her frame. Her hair is short, brown, with a lazy curl barely nuzzling up against the collar of her shirt. She sits down comfortably on the other side of Baby Doll, as if invited.

"My name's Linda," she says casually, but without a tone of friendship. "What's your name, sugar?"

Baby Doll doesn't respond at first, then she says, "Nice to meet you, Linda, but I'm really just looking to pass the time and get out of here."

Linda laughs. "Now aren't you just the sweetest thing." Suddenly Linda brings the back of her forearm up against Baby

Doll's neck, pinning her against the steel wall and making Baby Doll gurgle and sputter. "Maybe you didn't hear me, honey. When Linda asks you a question, you answer? Understand?"

Baby Doll tries to nod, while also clawing at Linda's meaty arm. After a second, Linda releases her grip and relaxes again on the bench. Baby Doll leans forward and starts coughing, face red with anger and surprise. Linda's two friends in the corner are laughing.

"So," Linda says again. "My name's Linda. What's your name, sugar?"

Baby Doll gulps and glares. "Get lost."

Linda laughs. "Nice to meet you, Getlost." She raises her voice and calls out to her two friends in the corner. "Hey, guess what? Her name is Getlost! That's what your parents should have named you, Cynthia!"

Baby Doll starts to stand up and walk away, but Linda grabs the back of her sweater and pulls her down, hard, onto the bench. I slide a bit away from her, watching.

"You're not going anywhere, Getlost. Not until Linda says you can go."

"You don't know who I am, or what I can have done to you," Baby Doll says fiercely. "So why don't you just go on back to your friends and leave me alone."

She starts to get up and walk away again, and once more Linda pulls her back down onto the bench.

"Pretty tough for a little thing, aren't you, Getlost? But you sure do dress nice; I'll give you that. I just love this cable-knit sweater you're wearing. Where'd you get it?"

Baby Doll leans back against the wall, folds her arms across her chest and says nothing.

"Oh, so that's the way it is, is it?" Linda laughs again. She seems to truly be enjoying this moment. Unexpectedly, she

swings her substantial arm back toward Baby Doll's neck again, but this time the girl is too quick. She ducks under, and then springs off the bench, and turns back to face her attacker as Linda's hand smacks the wall. Linda stands slowly, rubbing her hand. "Doggone it, Getlost, you done made me break a fingernail. Now what are you gonna do to make things right with me again?"

Baby Doll says nothing, but her whole body is tensed for a fight. Linda easily outweighs Baby Doll by sixty pounds, maybe more, yet the college girl refuses to back away. I admire her courage, in spite of myself.

From the corner of my eye, I see Linda's two friends get up and begin to quietly walk toward us. I wonder if I should give a warning, but then I don't. I am remembering a few things about Baby Doll, like her unwillingness to keep a promise, like her own fierce backhand to my face in the middle of a cemetery. Instead, I slide even farther away.

At almost the last moment, she, too, catches the movement of Linda's cronies. Just as she turns to face them, Linda pounces, grabbing a thick handful of Baby Doll's hair and yanking it down, hard, toward the floor. In spite of herself, Baby Doll is caught off balance and drops to one knee, which is all the advantage a woman like Linda needs. Without releasing the hair, she swings an ample fist toward Baby Doll's upturned face. I see the young girl's eyes flutter and roll up, briefly, behind her eyelids. Now the other two women get involved. One—Cynthia, I think—slides behind Baby Doll and pins her arms against her back. The other begins randomly kicking at the mess her friends are holding. A few more blows from Linda, and Baby Doll is limp, bleeding from the mouth and nose, and groaning involuntarily.

Linda and Cynthia release the girl, and let her slump to the floor. A string of saliva drips over the edge of Linda's lip for a moment, but she doesn't seem to notice.

"What size sweater do you wear, Cynthia honey?" Linda says eventually.

"I don't know. Size six maybe."

"You like that sweater there?"

"Sure do, Linda. Can I have it?"

"It's my gift to you, sugar. Help yourself."

In spite of the situation, Baby Doll tries to fight off the theft. So they kick her a few more times until she can barely breathe, let alone resist. When they remove the sweater, they find a surprise.

"Well, look at that," Linda says admiringly. Wrapped several times around Baby Doll's rib cage, just beneath the cups of her bra, is a large, thick, tan gauze bandage. But the bandage isn't what attracts Linda's attention; it's what is partially falling out of the lower edge of the gauze under Baby Doll's right arm.

"Do you see something green peeking at me there, Cynthia?"

"Why, yes, I do, Linda. I surely do."

They rip off the first layer of gauze with hunger in their eyes, and are delighted when several thick packets of hundred-dollar bills, spread evenly around Baby Doll's rib cage, fall to the floor. Under the third layer they find another surprise. A large, gold ring. A man's ring, about the size of a professional sports team's championship ring—and just as gaudy. The edges are encrusted with diamonds with a larger diamond adorning the top; the center is a thick slab of onyx; and engraved onto the onyx are an ax and a scepter, crossed like swords and also encrusted with diamonds.

"You do have some secrets, don'tcha, Getlost," Linda murmurs in admiration.

The three attackers take the bounty and return to their corner of the holding cell. A moment later, Cynthia starts counting the hundred-dollar bills; she squeals with delight when she reaches the end. "Ninety-eight of them," she says excitedly to her cronies. "Nine thousand eight hundred dollars in cash—plus an expensive cable-knit sweater."

But Linda is preoccupied with the ring. She turns it over in her hands, and finally places it on her index finger, where it stays.

After a while, Baby Doll crawls back toward the bench, where she raises herself up against it and then curls into a ball.

"Why didn't you do anything?" she hisses finally, never really looking at me. "Why did you let them do that to me?"

"I'm no angel," I say. And I am still remembering.

She curses at me. I realize I have now given her something to remember about me.

Linda stands suddenly and separates herself from her group. She walks over to Baby Doll and kneels down beside her, almost motherly in manner.

"How you doing, Getlost?" she says.

Baby Doll says nothing.

"Funny, isn't it? They got cameras all over this place, but not a single cop came in to help you. Know what that means?"

Baby Doll says nothing.

"It means somebody out there don't like you, sugar. Somebody out there wanted me to hurt you, and they sent the guard monitoring the video out on an unscheduled coffee break or something. You know, what you don't see can't be charged against you, that kind of thing. Otherwise, they'd have been in here in a heartbeat to save your pretty little self." She shrugs. "Still, it worked out pretty good for me, though, didn't it?"

Linda stands, pausing long enough to admire the ring on her finger. Then she hesitates. She takes off her flannel overshirt and drops it at Baby Doll's feet. "Guess I at least owe you that much," she says.

Baby Doll says nothing.

Linda returns happily to her friends in the corner. After several minutes, Baby Doll finally leans over and clutches the flannel shirt. A few minutes after that, she lifts herself heavily onto the bench and pulls the shirt around her bare shoulders. She is breathing better now, and her nose has stopped bleeding. She's young. She'll recover faster than some.

"You have to get me that ring back," she says quietly, still not looking at me so she appears to be muttering to herself.

I don't respond.

"The money they took is nothing. But you have to get me that ring."

"Why?" I truly am a bit curious at how this is playing out.

"You just have to, that's why."

There is a moment of silence between us.

"You owe me a favor, Baby Doll."

She spits blood in my direction, and I see true anger in her eyes. But she says nothing.

Eleven

Baby Doll let her mind wander while she tried to regain some semblance of normalcy. *It's funny what you think of just after you get your butt kicked,* she thought finally. For Baby Doll, it had begun with sheer anger toward the Boy, for his placid inactivity while the other women were attacking her. Then it transitioned to a replay of the fight.

I think I could have taken Linda by herself, she thought. *She's big, yeah, but she's also clumsy. I could have worn her down. A few quick shots to the throat like Maurits taught me. She wouldn't have lasted long.*

Then, *Never should have taken my eyes off Linda, though. Once she had my hair, it was over.*

Then, inexplicably, *I wonder if I should cut my hair. I might look cute in a nice little bob, maybe just above my shoulders.*

And finally, *So now the ring is gone. No matter what happens, I have to get that ring back. Either that, or die trying.*

About half an hour after the beating, Baby Doll felt bruised and sore, but otherwise whole again. Dried blood inside her nostrils was an annoyance, but one she could deal with. She didn't feel like running a marathon or anything, but at least she was ready to walk again.

She took a moment to observe the trio of women who had attacked her—and the three who had stood by and done nothing while it happened. One woman had simply slept through it. The other two ignored her, moving away from the fray and minding their own business. It was as if they thought that by not getting involved, it meant that they were not responsible for anything that had happened to her.

Baby Doll watched Linda admiring the ring, memorizing her face, her voice, even her bulky frame. That would be important when she got out of here.

She felt certain Boy could simply go over and steal back the ring—didn't he say he was a pickpocket or something? He could probably even get a sizable chunk of the money back as well. But he simply was not cooperative.

"Why are you even here," she grumbled in his direction. "What do you do, anyway?"

"I'm a Drifter," he said simply.

"Wow, thanks for that enlightenment."

About forty-five minutes after the beating, a uniformed guard appeared at the door of the holding cell. "McDavid?" he said. "You can go now." He opened the gate.

"Thanks very much, Officer," Linda said, jumping up and heading toward her freedom. Cynthia and the other, nameless woman followed.

"Just Ms. McDavid right now," the guard said, using his body to cut off the other two women before closing the gate in front of them.

An unpleasant idea planted itself in Baby Doll's brain.

"But, wait a minute," the nameless one said. "We all were brought in together. Why aren't we getting out together? Why does she get to go free and we don't?"

The guard shrugged. "I'm sure it'll all be taken care of shortly." And he was right. Within the next fifteen minutes, a different guard came and released Linda's two friends. One by one, over the next hour, the other three women were also released, and two new women were brought in as well. Baby Doll said nothing to any of the new prisoners; she just sat on her bench, occasionally closed her eyes and tried to sleep, and occasionally watched whatever was on the TV set above her. She actually managed to see two back-to-back reruns of *Jeopardy,* and one particularly confusing segment of a soap opera.

It was after 3 P.M. before Detective Lopez and a uniformed guard finally came through the door to the holding cell.

"Well, hello there, Baby Doll. I hear you made a few new friends today."

"I'm done 'volunteering,' Detective," she said wearily. "Either arrest me, or let me out of here. Right now."

"Of course, Baby Doll. All you had to do was ask."

Lopez motioned to the uniform, and he stepped forward to unlock the gate. Baby Doll walked toward the opening, and Boy dutifully followed her. Just at the gate, she took one step out, then said, "Wait, I forgot something," and started to go back inside. Boy stepped back away from the entrance to let her in, but again she halted. "No, I got it. Never mind," she said. Then she slipped quickly through the opening and, before even the guard could react, she reached behind her and clanged the gate shut. The uniform moved in quickly and locked the cell, and then they all turned to leave.

The look on Boy's face was almost enough to make Baby Doll regret what she had done. He stared at her from inside the cell, through the woven steel bars, and for the first time she actually saw both surprise and fear in his eyes. His mouth fell slightly open, as if he wanted to say something but his throat and tongue wouldn't cooperate. His eyes grew wide, and he stepped forward and pressed his hands against the steel rods of the holding cell. Invisible or not, he was trapped.

Baby Doll paused long enough to catch his gaze. She felt a wrenching disgust for herself, for what she was about to do. She almost changed her mind, but then she thought back to his passive presence while she endured the worst beating of her life; while he let Linda McDavid take the only thing she'd been working so hard to keep safe, to keep hidden. She pictured that ring on the big woman's finger and felt a new kind of fury toward Boy that overruled any sympathy she might have otherwise felt for him.

"Good-bye," she said firmly.

She was better off without him. As far as she was concerned, he could just "tether," or whatever he called it, to someone else in that jail cell. Maybe they'd be glad to have an annoying, invisible friend. She turned to follow Detective Lopez and the uniformed officer out of the holding area. She had taken only a few steps when she heard his voice.

"Baby Doll, don't go," he said. Was he pleading? "Baby Doll—"

She kept walking.

"Baby Doll." He was almost shouting now. "Baby Doll! You owe me a favor! You owe me a favor, Baby Doll!"

And then his voice was just a muffled sound. A moment later she was in an elevator, headed back to an interrogation room on the first floor, and Boy's voice was nonexistent, except in her head, where she still heard the panic in his timbre. *You owe me a favor . . .*

—

"I think you owe me a favor," Detective Lopez said once they'd all settled back into the interrogation room.

Baby Doll looked at the bruises and cuts on her face in the two-way mirror. "How do you figure that, Detective?"

"Look at yourself, Baby Doll. If this is what happens to you after only a few hours in a minimum-security holding cell, imagine what might happen if you had to spend three to six years in a federal prison for, I don't know, say car theft or something?"

"What's your point?"

"I did you a favor, sweetie. I showed you what your life could be like, and now I'm here to help you avoid that kind of future altogether. You see how it works? I did you a favor, and now I want you to do me a favor in return. Got it?"

Baby Doll sighed. "What do you want to know?"

Twelve

It begins in my abdomen, almost as soon as the outer door closes to separate Baby Doll and me. It's barely felt at first, just a warning tremor of sorts. Something to alert me that the tether is in danger. But I know what is to come and all I can do is wait for it. I don't move for a while, feeling the first pangs of rupture begin, waiting for the full agony to come. I foolishly think that the waiting is just as bad as the actual Severance will be. An hour or so later, I realize the absurdity of that thought. Now it starts in earnest, and it is as if an invisible hand has reached inside me, squeezing its grip on my spleen and then yanking, trying to pull my inner organs out of me and being halted by the skin that shells my body.

"Baby Doll. You owe me a favor, Baby Doll."

She is long gone now, but I can't stop repeating those words.

I am still pressed against the woven metal that makes this room a cage, feeling my insides twist and rearrange. I can no longer tell how much time has passed; to me it seems as if time simply stops instead. For some reason, I try not to scream. There is no practical motivation for this suppression of the natural urge; no one can hear me, no matter what comes out of my mouth. Maybe it's pride, or stubborn anger. I will not scream, not this time.

But I do allow myself to groan.

Unexpectedly, ever so briefly, the tether restores itself and I feel almost normal. A bit out of breath, yes, but the interior agony has gratefully disappeared. Then, as quickly as it left, the hardship returns. My mind works it out ruefully. Somewhere in the building, perhaps on a floor above or a floor below, Baby Doll passed by. Close enough to reestablish her connection to me, and then swept away into a distance that severs me again.

Even Simon, for all his faults, never did this to me. Not ever.

I feel a hatred for Baby Doll that borders on the insane. I want to kill her until I realize that this desire really is only because I secretly wonder if that would be enough to kill me as a result. But I know the answer already. Death weakens the tether, yes. But it doesn't break it. Nothing breaks an existing tether except a new tether.

I feel the Severance resolve itself into splinters that shoot from my abdomen outward toward my extremities. I have the first myocardial infarction, and feel almost paralyzed on my left side.

I search the room around me. There are three women left in the cell.

"Hello," I shout. "Help me."

No one responds.

I struggle to move, dragging myself toward a wilting blond woman with darting eyes and a swollen cheekbone. I grab her wrist in my good hand, shaking and shaking it. I am desperate for a new tether, for the pain to subside.

"See me," I say. I try to pull her arm so that her head will be close to my mouth. "I exist. I'm here. Do you see me?"

She allows her wrist to be manhandled, yet doesn't seem to notice. Her glazed eyes finally fix on the TV set above us. I am as lost to her as she is to me, nothing more than a shadow she doesn't see.

The pounding begins in my head. I think this must be what an aneurysm feels like. Mercifully, blackness swirls at the edges of my vision. Unconsciousness is only a temporary respite, but it is a respite nonetheless.

"Baby Doll. You owe me a favor."

I hear a cracking sound and realize it is my skull slapping the hard concrete floor. I don't know how long I have been on this floor, but the pain shooting down my right leg, and the spasms in my spine and neck, make it clear to me that I won't be getting up any time soon.

I finally give in to the screaming. It bursts from me like vomit, rinsing my mouth with a putrid smell that stings as much as it stains. I feel my muscles constrict and twist, and then I finally pass out from the pain.

—

When I awake, the world is gray and colorless. The body still battles within me, but now it is an exhausted conflict. Now it hurts too much to scream, to fight, to squirm. Now it almost feels better to simply give up and embrace the pain. I am color-blind and dizzy. I taste blood. My skin feels tight against my bones, as though it is shrinking, decaying around me. I am dying, but never dead.

The light flickers around me, then flashes brightly and leaves me fully blind. And in that blindness I see my solace.

—

Alondra.

Ah, but she is weeping now. Dressed in costume, but no longer playing the part.

"He is here. I know he is here," she says to those who try to comfort her.

The Marilyn Monroe partygoer says nothing and just wraps a tender arm around her shoulders. The middle-aged woman in the cheerleader costume looks uncomfortable. She whispers disapprovingly to the old man in the priestly collar.

"How could you, Grampa?" she says. "You, of all people, should have known better."

In the great room of the house, the party continues with laughter and music and dancing. Spiced punch, pumpkins, trays of cookies, and party snacks happily being eaten. Decorative witches, ghosties, and goblins swing from the ceiling. A large bowl of candies sits by the door for the inevitable stream of children who keep coming through.

I stand in the doorway between the great room and the kitchen, caught between the joy and the sorrow, feeling nothing of either.

An hour ago Alondra was the happiest I had ever seen her. She wore a bridal gown rented from one of the local costume shops, complete with tiara and weathered veil. But no lace covering could diminish the brightness in her eyes, the sparkle of her smile.

"This is absurd," I had whispered.

"Of course it is," she'd murmured back at me. "But it's worth it all just to see you looking so dapper and stylish in Daddy's old tuxedo."

"Alondra, this seems a little absurd," the elderly man in the priest's collar had said to her. The confusion in his eyes seemed a normalcy; the bent, beleaguered posture a hazard of his many decades.

"Of course it is, Grampa," she'd said lovingly toward the old man. "That's what makes it fun. This is a party after all."

The old one blinked rheumy eyes and must have seen a pleasant memory. He smiled, shuffled a bit, and pulled a small

New Testament from an inner pocket. "What will your sisters say?"

"Who cares?" Alondra laughed. "They're out dancing with their husbands in the other room, leaving you and me to console ourselves here in the kitchen."

"It just seems disrespectful . . ." the old priest began, hesitating.

Alondra became very serious then. "Oh no, Grampa. This is not that. Not ever." Her eyes pleaded. "Please, Grampa. Humor me this time. Pretend he is here, that he stands right next to me, wearing a classic black tuxedo. Looking young, and strong, and very much in love. Play the game with me tonight, Gramps. For old times' sake."

He chuckled. "For old times' sake?"

Alondra nodded.

"I suppose I did marry you a dozen times to plush animals and imaginary princes when you were a little girl. Even married the dog to the cat once, if I remember correctly."

"Yes, Grampa," she whispered. "Yes."

And so the old one did his part.

"Do you, Alondra, take this man . . . what's his name again?" He paused, waiting. "Does your invisible friend, does he take you, dear little granddaughter?"

"Yes," I whispered in her ear. "Yes a thousand times over." I reached into my pocket and pulled out a surprise that I'd been saving. I slipped a diamond solitaire ring onto her hand, realizing too late that it was about one size too big for her finger. Alondra smiled through teary eyes anyway, admiring first the ring and then my face.

"You may now kiss the bride, er, the groom. Or whatever it's supposed to be, Alondra dear."

She hugged the old man delightfully to thank him for his part in the ceremony, then pointed him out the door with directions to the buffet table. Next she was back at my side.

"You look the same as you did when I first met you," she said as she reached for my hand.

"So do you," I said.

"Liar!" She laughed. "Is that any way to start a marriage? By lying to your poor, old, ugly wife?"

"You will never be ugly to me. Never."

Her lips felt like wine upon mine. "I think," she said, "that now is a good time for a toast. Be a dear and go get us something to drink, will you, my husband?"

I bowed slightly. "As you wish, my wife."

"Wait," she said quickly. She handed back to me the diamond ring I had placed on her finger. "Keep this in your pocket for me. It won't do to have my sisters see it today. We'll get it resized tomorrow, and then I'll just tell everyone I bought myself an early Christmas present." She kissed me again. "Now go get us some punch or I'll start to think you're a lazy husband!"

In the great room the celebration felt like a wonderful fall reception. I leaned over the punch bowl, smelling that someone had already added a little alcohol to the mix. It was absurd, I know, to think a Drifter could even pretend to marry a Tether. But with Alondra, even the absurd seemed normal, felt almost like coming home. And we had been bound together for thirty-six years already—the longest tether I'd ever had. I would happily stay by her side for thirty, or fifty, or a hundred years more. I would be there when her eyes failed, when her health gave way. I would sit beside her and tell her stories when she could only wait to discover what lay beyond death. And I would—

I would—

"What are you?"

I felt trembling inside me.

"What are you, I said."

He was just a boy, not more than eight or nine years old. He wore what appeared to be a hastily constructed cowboy outfit, which mostly consisted of a hat, boots, and a plastic six-gun tucked into the pocket of his jeans.

"I . . . said . . . what . . . are . . . you?"

My mouth went dry. Over his shoulder I could see the doorway to the kitchen, brightly lit and inviting me to return.

"Do you see me?" I asked in disbelief.

"Of course I do, silly. What are you supposed to be dressed up as? Howard Hughes?"

I felt a mild dizziness and the involuntary relaxation of my breathing.

"No," I said slowly. "Not Howard Hughes."

"So what are you then?"

I saw the light flicker in the kitchen. Alondra's face appeared at the doorway. I waved in her direction, but she didn't see it. Her eyes scanned the room, first with light annoyance, then with gentle concern.

Inside me, the world crumbled like a sand castle beneath a wave.

"Nothing," I said finally. "No one."

She started calling out my name then. She said it softly at first, but I could hear the syllables float by like music. Then panic tinged her tune. She cried out for me louder and louder, until her sisters broke away from their dancing and came to her side. I tried to walk to her, but the new tether was too tight to let me even cross the room.

The sisters ushered her back into the kitchen, and the senile old Grampa followed close behind. I worked my way as far toward her as I could, until I found myself in the doorway, the sounds of celebration on one side of me, the hollowness of tears on the other.

The little cowboy retreated to a corner of the great room where he sat sullenly, flicking the trigger of his six-gun and giving the impression that he simply couldn't wait for this dumb, grown-up party to be over.

"He's here. I know he is here," Alondra was saying.

Suddenly the little cowboy stood up and ran over to me. "I hate you," he spat, punctuating his pronouncement with an attempt to kick me in the shin. Then he ran back to his corner of the great room, still holding his little gun, glowering at me and everyone else in the room.

In the kitchen I saw Alondra weeping. The old priest was shaking his head, confused and unsure of anything except that he'd made his beloved granddaughter cry. The Marilyn Monroe sister was crying a little bit too, and I wondered if she knew the truth, and if she did, if she also believed it.

The boy across the room aimed his six-gun at me and mouthed the words again. "I hate you."

"That's okay," I mouthed back to him. "I hate myself too."

—

I feel a piercing in my hands and feet, sharpness between my ribs, a crushing weight pressing upon my lungs. I am crucified on the floor of this cursed holding cell, unnoticed, abandoned. Dying and not dead.

I can no longer find respite in my memories of Alondra, not even here, not even now. It hurts too much to do that. So I inhale deeply and immerse myself in the Severance, in the pain of my newest consolation. And for reasons I can't quite explain, I think of Baby Doll.

I hope that she is okay.

Thirteen

It was close to 10 P.M. when Detective Lopez finally announced that the questioning was over.

"So that's it, then?" Baby Doll asked. Her voice felt like gravel. "You've got everything you wanted to know?"

Detective Lopez grimaced. "No, sweetie. Not by a long shot. But I think now I've gotten everything you have to tell me. At least for the moment."

Good, Baby Doll thought. *Now to play the helpless-kid role.*

She tried to give the impression that she was holding back tears. "So what happens now, Detective?"

Honoria shrugged. "I guess that's up to you, Baby Doll."

"Should I go back home? Maurits won't be happy to know that I talked to you."

"Do whatever you want," the detective said as she gathered up her things. "Honestly, you told us little we didn't already know."

Baby Doll smiled within herself. That was what she'd been trying to do for the past several hours. The Organization had a rulebook to follow with the police; Maurits had gone over it with her a dozen times. "You can't avoid getting picked up from time to time," Maurits had said. "But you can avoid being a liability to your daddy."

So she had tried to follow the rulebook during the interrogation. Get a hint about what the police already knew about Charlie's operation, and then spill that detail as if it were a hard-fought secret that Lopez had finally wrung out of her. In the process, she had been able to steer the conversation away from her own involvement in Charlie Murphy's death and get Detective Lopez wrapped up in minutiae surrounding organizational structure and timelines that, thankfully, were easy to flub and easy to pretend to get confused by.

"So you think it's safe for me to go home?"

Detective Lopez sighed theatrically. "I think I've spent more time on you than was necessary. I think it comes down to this; you're a spoiled little college brat who had the bad luck of being in the same room when Charlie Murphy offed himself, and that really, nobody gives a flying fig what happens to you at this point. Least of all me. Understand?"

Baby Doll made her lip quiver just long enough, and then burst into tears. "But now what do I do? Charlie Murphy was my f-father after all."

Detective Lopez shot a glance at Officer Hummel. It had been a long day for everyone.

"All right, sweetie. No need to get emotional. You're going to be fine."

Baby Doll sniffed away her tears. "You think so?"

"Of course. Look, here's my card." She produced a small rectangle of paperboard from her pocket. "You call me tomorrow. I'll make arrangements for you to sit with a grief therapist to help you, um, get through this tough time. Okay?"

"Thank you, Detective."

Baby Doll was feeling pretty good about her charade, about her performance in front of this cunning old detective. And then, almost as if it had been threatening to do so for ages, the face of the Drifter appeared, swallowing all of Baby Doll's thoughts. She felt a sickness inside, wondering what he'd been through over these last several hours. She thought, at first, *Why do I even care*? Then, *What kind of person would I be if I didn't care? Who am I turning into?*

"Officer Hummel," Lopez said, "would you please get Ms. Murphy's coat from the storage room. I understand it's going to get below zero outside tonight."

The security guard nodded politely and exited the room.

"Detective Lopez," Baby Doll said thoughtfully. "I think, um, I think I left my sweater in the holding cell."

Lopez snorted. "If you did, honey, it's long gone by now."

"Right, well, but could I go up there to check for it anyway?"

"Look, it's late . . ."

"But Detective, Charlie gave me that sweater himself. It was a birthday present, and—"

"Fine. Yes. Okay. Sure. As soon as Officer Hummel gets back, you can go look for your sweater."

They waited in silence for a few more minutes until the security guard returned with Baby Doll's leather coat. She was pleased to discover that nothing was missing and that the coat looked none the worse for wear.

"Officer Hummel, Ms. Murphy here believes she may have left her sweater in the women's holding cell on the fourth floor." The security guard snorted. "Would you be so kind as to escort her up to the holding cell to see if it may still be there?"

"Of course," Hummel said.

"And after that, she is free to go."

"Yes, Detective."

Baby Doll smiled wanly at Detective Lopez as she left, fully aware the good detective no longer cared whether she lived or died at the hands of Maurits or some other of Charlie Murphy's associates. As far as Lopez was concerned, Baby Doll was no longer anything more than an irrelevancy in a long, complicated investigation. And as far as Baby Doll was concerned, that was exactly what she wanted to be. If she no longer had to fear the police, then that gave her much more flexibility in what had to be done.

Baby Doll followed Officer Hummel up to the now-familiar fourth floor. When they entered the exterior area just outside the holding gate, she put her hand to her nose.

"Whew," Hummel said. "Smells like something died in here."

They walked to the gated entrance of the holding cell, and Baby Doll felt sick to her stomach.

"Do you see your sweater in there?" Hummel asked, crinkling her nose at the smell.

A woman called out from a bench inside the cell. "Officer, you've got to do something. A rat died in the vent or something. It stinks to high heaven in here—and that's cruel and unusual punishment. My lawyer's gonna sue the whole department."

"Maybe your lawyer is what's in the vent, Janice," Hummel said amicably. "But don't worry. I'll get the custodial staff up here right away, and we'll get it taken care of." She turned back to Baby Doll. "Well, Ms. Murphy?"

Baby Doll wanted to cry. Lying in the middle of the cell floor, the Drifter was curled into a ravaged ball. Dried blood stained his mouth and ears. Blood only she could see was crusted on the bench and floor where he'd thrashed in pain. His bones stuck out at awkward angles, suggesting that one, or more, might have grown so brittle that it had broken while he convulsed on the cement ground. His hair was torn and patchy, as if some had fallen out and some had been ripped out. His body was emaciated; skin clung to his face as though it had been wrapped too tightly around his skull. His eyes were open but unseeing, and sunken into his head like holes in a pocket billiards table. He had apparently soiled himself more than once. Baby Doll looked at this ghastly being and felt what she never expected to feel.

Compassion.

"Officer Hummel," she said quietly. "I don't feel safe outside tonight."

"No need to worry, Ms. Murphy. Detective Lopez knows what she's doing. She wouldn't let you leave if she thought you were in any real danger."

"Just the same," she said, never taking her eyes off the Drifter in the cell, "I think I'd like to, um, volunteer, to stay here tonight. For my own safety."

She heard a groan from the middle of the cell floor. Boy's head suddenly snapped back, his unseeing eyes blinking in her direction.

"Now, Ms. Murphy—"

Baby Doll turned and looked directly into Hummel's face, but said nothing. The security guard paused, and then said, "Let me make a call first."

A few moments later, Officer Hummel reported that Detective Lopez had given permission for Baby Doll to spend one night in the holding cell, with the understanding that they would be sending her home at eight in the morning. "Detective Lopez says we simply can't be your babysitting service, and if you want to stay here longer you're going to have to break the law like everyone else. Got it?"

Baby Doll ignored the attempt at humor and waited for the gate to open. The Drifter had seemed to sense her presence, and by now had sat up on the floor and pushed himself backward until he was leaning against a bench along the back wall. His breathing was ragged and harsh, but he was breathing. She waited until Officer Hummel had locked the gate behind her, and the others had returned their attention to the television. Then she walked over to where Boy was. After a moment's thought, she sat cross-legged on the floor next to him. They said nothing at first. Finally, after about fifteen minutes, the Boy spoke to her through blistered lips.

"Why did you come back?"

Baby Doll didn't answer. Instead, she reached around his withered shoulders and gently placed his head in her lap, smearing her pants and Linda McDavid's overshirt with blood in the process. She was surprised to find herself stroking his ravaged head.

"You owe me a favor." His breath reeked of mildew and halitosis.

"Shh," she said softly. "Go to sleep. And heal. I'll be here when you wake up. I promise."

"Are you looking for forgiveness? Is that it?"

A pause. Then, "Shh."

A tremor worked its way through Boy's back and up to his head, causing him to jerk and painfully smack Baby Doll in the ribs. She grunted in discomfort, but never stopped caressing.

Across the cell a woman sniffed the air. "Finally," she said aloud to nobody. "They must have found that rat in the ventilation system. Seems like that horrid smell isn't quite as bad as before, doesn't it?"

Baby Doll looked down at the Drifter, now twitching as he slept in her arms. *Funny,* she thought. *Eight hours ago I wanted to kill this Boy. Now I feel like I might die without him.*

Boy opened his eyes suddenly, staring fitfully into Baby Doll's face. She returned his gaze without wavering.

"Do you see me?" he whispered at last. Something lost inside him called out to her.

"Yes," she said. "Now go to sleep."

Boy closed his eyes again. A moment later Baby Doll felt his body relax and his breathing even out to almost normal.

What are you? she thought. *Are you a Deus ex Machina? Are you my angel? My demon? Or like me, just another misplaced thing waiting to be found?*

Baby Doll leaned against the bench behind her and sighed. Although it had been a long time, she felt like praying. She needed that comfort. Guidance. And she had a lot of thinking to do before morning.

There are hidden things among men and among angels. But the only real secrets are the ones hidden in the mind of God. His alone are the mysteries known exclusively to One. And so we wonder, should we fear God's secrets? Or embrace them, knowing that what we don't know could easily end us all?

—SOLACE THE LESSER
PHILOSOPHER AND HISTORIAN, 428 B.C.

Fourteen

SUNDAY, FEBRUARY 20

This Maurits person is an imposing figure.

He stands in silence for a moment, staring at Baby Doll while she sleeps on the bench beside me. She was sleeping in a crumpled pile on the floor when I awoke, her hand twitching upon my chest, my head still resting in her lap. It had been a healing sleep for me; no dreams, no memories or visions. Just sleep. And now I am awake, feeling the health of the tether flowing inside the marrow of my bones.

I am tired, yes. But not cold. Not alone.

It was around 5:30 A.M. when I finally felt strong enough to lift her and place her gently onto the bench. She hadn't really noticed, except for a pained expression that creased her face briefly when she finally stretched out her legs. But even then she hadn't woken up. The ability to sleep undisturbed is a gift that not many humans enjoy. It makes me wonder if she is even aware that she owns that gift.

Baby Doll's return still surprises me. I had expected to endure the Severance for who-knows-how-long until finally a new tether appeared there in the cell. After all, no tether is permanent. Some are just longer than others. The shortest was only a few minutes;

some have been only a few hours or weeks; most last a few years at best. One lasted much longer . . . but I don't want to let myself go there again. Not now.

Still, there is always a new Tether, sooner or later. If I can make it through the torture of Severance, there is always the hope of a new Tether on its way, somewhere, somehow, sometime. But to endure a full Severance and then reunite with a previous Tether? This is something new. And for someone like me, "new" is a rare and mystifying thing.

I cannot read her face while she is sleeping. I do not trust her motives; I'm unsure of exactly what she wants from me now. But I can't deny her actions. She did come back. And she stayed, waiting beside me until the sleep could work its healing. Something new to remember about her.

I look at her on this bench and feel an emptiness emanating from inside her. It feels dull and ragged, like hunger unsatisfied. She has lost something that means more to her than she can even admit to herself. Something more than just her name or that gaudy ring that Linda McDavid stole from her. I can relate to this. Hidden things always feel lost.

It is almost seven-thirty when Maurits and his, well, I suppose they would call Maurits's companion a bodyguard, come into the outer area of the holding cell. There are two security guards in police uniforms accompanying Maurits and the bodyguard to this location. Both of the uniformed officers appear nervous, painfully aware that they are in the presence of a powerful man who is also an enemy. They stand ramrod straight, and maintain a stiffness and pseudoprofessionalism that communicate a hint of personal fear. They don't want to be overly friendly toward this man, but they don't want to make him angry either.

The bodyguard looks most out of place here. For one thing, he is a full six inches shorter and about forty pounds lighter than the man he is supposed to be protecting. True, he is at least twenty years younger than Maurits, but it's obvious that in a fight the bigger man would make short work of this bodyguard. The curl in the young man's lip and the spiderweb veins in his neck suggest that he's wishing for a cigarette right now. That also means that if he were called into action, his lungs would be a weakness—something a smart attacker would notice and use against him. But, for the moment at least, I am not worried. I suspect that he has more weaknesses to be exploited than just an addiction to tobacco.

The bodyguard is clearly uncomfortable inside this building, as though he has spent some time in prison and doesn't relish the idea of going back, even if it is to visit a simple, temporary holding cell like this one.

Maurits is a stark contrast to the body language of the bodyguard and even to the uniformed officers. The eyes are what make the difference here. Yes, the first thing you notice is his size—about six feet three inches and well over two hundred pounds. He carries the build of a former athlete, thick but firm. Flat stomach. Broad shoulders. Walking on the balls of his feet, always leaning slightly forward as if ready to assert his ownership of any situation. The next thing you notice are the tufts of white hair that color his temples and stray streaks of gray that are salted throughout a still-thick head of hair. A vainer man would dye his hair to an almost-natural black color. Instead, Maurits seems proud of his age, proud to have lasted this long. It's as if he likes the fact that a man in his mid- to late forties could still transform a much younger man into pudding with a few well-placed blows from his fists.

But, again, it is the eyes that make the biggest difference. There are plenty of fit, middle-aged, former athletes in the world. Yet only one man like Maurits. His face is one that hides its se-

crets well, even from me. His eyes, though, are too proud to hide anything. They sweep the room in an instant, immediately taking in everything, assessing assets and obstacles, playing chess with the people and pieces of the situation, planning not his next move but his next six moves. I see him collecting knowledge he doesn't need—the show droning on the television set, the difference in height between his bodyguard and the first uniformed guard, the number of steps from the gated entrance to where Baby Doll still sleeps. His eyes file this information away, just in case it will be something he needs tomorrow, three weeks from now, even five years in the future. This man's eyes set him apart from everyone else in this room; they tell me that everything he does has a reason, has a purpose. Which makes me want to study the bodyguard once more.

Why would a man with Maurits's mind choose a bodyguard who is obviously his physical and intellectual inferior?

I watch his eyes, and the secret betrays itself. The bodyguard is not a bodyguard after all, but an escort of sorts. Someone sent to keep an eye on the big man; someone the big man has grudgingly allowed, and someone he has made sure could be quickly neutralized if that possibility ever became a necessity.

The bodyguard/escort coughs uncomfortably, and I see Maurits grin ever so slightly.

Baby Doll's guardian stands in silence, letting minutes pass while he makes everyone around him wait. The bodyguard/escort starts to say something, but Maurits stops him with a glare. The security guards shuffle their feet. One steps forward to unlock the gate to the holding cell, but Maurits stops him with a large hand placed to the shoulder.

"Let her sleep for a few minutes more," he says quietly. A more confident person would have recognized that the big man had no authority to give that command. A more experienced

guard would have ignored Maurits, opened the gate, and done his job as he was trained to do. But this guard works on a Sunday morning; only those stuck with a night shift rank lower than he does. He has been trained to respond to authority with unquestioned obedience, and in this room right now, Maurits is definitely the authority figure.

I move to the front of the holding cell and get as close to Maurits as the woven-steel rods will allow me to get. His face is a mask, but his eyes are still calculating. He has to make a decision soon, and he doesn't yet know which is the right one. Baby Doll, his *Baby Doll, is either a friend or an enemy. Twenty years of watching her grow up in Charlie Murphy's house is telling him she is still an innocent little girl, a small ray of light yet unsullied by the dirt of the Organization. At the same time, events of the last two days are telling him that she could be a traitor, a Judas inside Charlie Murphy's own home; inside his home now.*

He will make a decision soon. But at this moment, his decision is to not decide.

"Baby Doll." The words pop out of his mouth like a general giving an order. The bodyguard/escort stands up straighter in spite of himself. I turn to look behind me and see that Baby Doll's reaction to his voice is almost immediate. She sits up on the bench before her eyes have fully opened.

Maurits motions to the security guard and he puts a key into the lock on the gate.

"Let's go, Baby Doll. It's time to go home."

She is still foggy with sleep, but her natural reaction is to nod and obey. She stands and moves toward his voice, eyes blinking awake until it all comes rushing back. There is a half second of hesitation, one that no one notices except me. And maybe Maurits. Then Baby Doll nods her head again and walks with certainty toward the gate.

"Yes, Maurits. I'm coming."

The door swings open. I fall in step behind Baby Doll. I will be glad to finally get out of this sterile little cage. At the opening, she stops and looks up into Maurits's eyes. They are unreadable now, but Baby Doll nods again anyway. Then, without looking behind her, she reaches out, leaving her hand hanging in the air.

Maurits frowns slightly. "Let's go, Baby."

"I'm coming, Maurits." But she doesn't move. Instead she shakes her hand in the air behind her, and I finally realize what she's doing. I reach out and take her hand in mine. She squeezes it once, and then pulls me through the opening with her. She doesn't let go until we are all inside Maurits's black Lexus sedan outside the Police Services Center, driving away through a frigid, gray morning.

The bodyguard/escort sits up front with the driver. Maurits sits in the backseat with Baby Doll and me. I sit in the middle. Maurits is unaware of my presence beside him. He takes the morning paper the driver hands him and flicks it open to the front page.

"Take us home, Stanley," he says to the driver before glancing over at Baby Doll. "Nice shirt," he says without smiling.

"Yeah," she responds ruefully, looking down at the beat-up overshirt Linda McDavid bestowed upon her yesterday. "Traded my sweater for it."

Maurits nods and turns his attention to the newspaper.

Baby Doll closes her eyes and whispers. I think she might be praying, but I can't tell for sure.

Fifteen

Sunday morning. The world was so much different today than it was just one week ago for Baby Doll. This time last week, Charlie Murphy was watching one of those TV preachers who kept saying that God wanted him to be pretty and rich like she was. Monday was Valentine's Day; a holiday that went unobserved in the Murphy household. Tuesday Charlie Murphy shot himself in the head in his bedroom.

Baby Doll sat in the backseat of Maurits's car and tried to make room for Boy without being too conspicuous.

"Nice shirt," Maurits said without smiling.

Baby Doll looked down and remembered afresh what the last twenty-four hours had cost her. "Yeah," she said. "Traded my sweater for it."

She was relieved to see Maurits bury himself in the Sunday paper for the rest of the car ride home. For the moment, at least, she appeared safe. But it was hard to tell with someone like Maurits. And she didn't recognize the new bodyguard sitting up front with Stanley either. That couldn't be good; a new face without an introduction rarely was. She closed her eyes and unexpectedly found herself thinking about God. Even in Charlie Murphy's house, she had, from time to time, felt as if God were close by. And then there were times like right now, when he seemed to have misplaced Baby Doll and left her exposed to things she didn't like to imagine. She wondered briefly if God knew all her secrets, and if he did, how long it would be until God let Maurits or Honoria Lopez—or both of them—know what she was trying so desperately to hide.

—

Maurits had been out of the house when Charlie Murphy finally ended his miserable life. Baby Doll still hadn't decided if that was simply lucky coincidence or the providence of God. Regardless, her plan had been set into motion, and the results were making themselves seen.

She'd come home from classes last Tuesday to find the household staff scurrying worriedly around the mansion—and everyone avoiding the second floor where Charlie had taken his refuge. Even Charlie's bodyguards were loitering around the kitchen instead of staying up near the boss as Maurits had ordered. Charlie had apparently chased them away with his broadsword and a fireplace poker.

They barely acknowledged Baby Doll when she walked in through the kitchen entrance at the back of the house, and she noticed that one of them bore a nasty, poker-sized bruise across his left cheek. It only dawned on her later, at Charlie's funeral, that she never saw those bodyguards again after that. Tradition on this side of town was that bodyguards stayed alive only as long as their charges did. Baby Doll shuddered to think about how Maurits had terminated their employment, and only at the funeral had she admitted that she bore some measure of guilt for their deaths as well.

Baby Doll had gone quietly to her room on the second floor. She set down her books and coat and then peeked out into the marble hallway. It was empty, save for the muffled sounds coming from the king's bedroom down the hall. She felt adrenaline surging into her bloodstream until even her chest and shoulders trembled with the primal instincts for fight or flight. She took a step toward Charlie's room and waited. Nothing happened, so she took another step, then another, until she stood in front of the closed door, listening.

In her mind's eye she pictured the contents of that room. Bookshelves lining the back walls. His large table/desk to the right, probably filled with papers, his laptop computer, and a few stacks of cash that had no doubt been recently collected and turned in for his approval. On the wall behind him would be his Scottish broadsword and a shield decorated with a red falcon holding blue arrows in its talons. Charlie said it was his family's coat of arms, but Baby Doll had researched that on the Internet once and had never found anything like it in the records of Scottish noble houses. She suspected that he had simply made it up and had passed it off as the truth for so long that he eventually came to believe his own lie.

On the other side of the room would be his couches and a few chairs, the place where he held his councils with Maurits and maybe one or two other trusted advisors. And Charlie's oversized bed stood in the middle of it all.

A skylight overhead was the only real window in the room. Sure, there were other broad picture windows that could bathe the entire room in sunlight, but after the death of the Captain, one of the first things Charlie had done when he took over this room was to cover those windows with dark wooden shutters that could only be opened from the inside. As far as Baby Doll could remember, they had never been opened since she'd moved in here.

Through the closed door, she could hear Charlie Murphy muttering and pacing the room. Occasionally he would shout a profanity, and once she heard a crashing sound that seemed to indicate he had thrown something heavy across the room. She looked behind her, and still the rest of the household stayed away. They knew only Maurits would be brave enough to face Charlie when he was in one of these moods.

Baby Doll felt her fingers tingling. She wondered if he might be drinking, as he usually did when these fits hit, or if old Charlie might soon pass out from the effects of alcohol, and she could sneak into his room and remove evidence of the dirty deed she'd set in motion.

It was at that moment the bedroom door swung open and she found herself face-to-face with her stepfather.

"Where's Maurits?" he said through ragged breath. Yes, he had been drinking. In his left hand he held a half-empty bottle of Scotch.

In his right hand was a .45-caliber, Glock model 36 automatic handgun.

Baby Doll felt herself trembling, but now she couldn't tell if it was because of adrenaline or fear. "I don't know. I just got home and he wasn't here."

Charlie stared at her dully for a moment, and then waved the gun. "Come here," he said, turning to walk back in his room.

"I don't know, Charlie," she started. "Maurits will be here soon and—"

The sound of a Scotch bottle crashing on the floor interrupted her.

"I said, come here." His speech was slightly slurred on the word "said," but Baby Doll got the message. She entered the room cautiously and watched as Charlie dragged himself to his desk and sat in his chair. "Sit down," he said.

Baby Doll eyed the door, wondering whether to leave it open or not. It seemed a split-second decision, but inside Baby Doll knew she must have been thinking about it subconsciously for days. She reached behind her and closed the door to Charlie's room. Only after it was shut did she then go over and sit in the chair situated in front of his desk.

"You think you're a smart girl, don't you, Baby Doll." It was a statement, not a question. Baby Doll didn't answer.

"We all know you're smart. Everybody knows it. What you don't know, though, is that I am smarter than you are. I always have been."

"I know you are, Charlie, I—"

"Don't lie to me!"

Baby Doll fell silent.

"Don't lie to my face, you ungrateful daughter of a prostitute! I saved your life, I did. I raised you like one of my own family."

Baby Doll wanted to say something then, but the sight of the Glock 36 kept her from speaking what was on her mind.

He leaned across the desk, placing the body of the gun on the table between them, and putting his weight upon the hand that held it.

"I know what you did, Baby. I know. Did you think I wouldn't figure it out? You don't get to be Justice of the Organization by being stupid. And you don't stay Justice for more than sixteen years by being stupid. You know what you get by being stupid, Baby Doll?"

She shook her head.

"You. You're what being stupid gets you."

He sat back heavily in his chair and waited.

"I—I don't know what you're talking about, Charlie."

There was silence between them. Then Charlie Murphy smiled.

—

Maurits folded his newspaper as Stanley pulled through the gate into the long driveway that led up to the Murphy mansion. Stanley parked the car at the back entrance, where a member of the kitchen staff held the door open. Maurits gave Baby Doll a quick once-over.

"Get yourself cleaned up, Baby Doll. Throw out those clothes; I never want to see them again, got it?"

Baby Doll nodded mutely.

"You need a doctor for your face?"

Baby Doll shook her head.

"All right. Well, wash up and put some makeup over it. It won't do for people to see that Charlie Murphy's daughter got touched with harm. Understand?"

She nodded again. Maurits opened the car door, and then apparently felt a moment of compassion. "Go ahead and get some breakfast," he said. "Then meet me in Charlie's old room in two hours." He looked at his watch and frowned. "No, meet me at noon," he said. "I have business to take care of first."

He didn't wait for Baby Doll to respond, but exited the car and walked through the kitchen door without looking back. The new bodyguard followed close behind. Baby Doll sat in the backseat, feeling weakness in her wrists and ankles, feeling like crying but not allowing herself to give in to that pleasure. She glanced up and noticed Stanley grinning at her in the rearview mirror.

"You look like garbage, Baby," he said warmly.

"Yeah, I know, Stanley, you sweet-talker, you. Bet you say that to all the girls."

He laughed appreciatively, and Baby Doll realized how much she liked laughter—and how long it had been since she'd been able to laugh.

"You want me to take you round to the side entrance so you don't have to face the kitchen crew before you get cleaned up?"

Baby Doll sighed in relief. "Yeah. Thanks, Stanley."

"No problem, Baby."

The driver pulled away from the kitchen and turned the wheel so that they drove past the large garage and around the curve to the side of the house. Baby Doll suddenly realized that it was odd for Stanley to still be here. He'd been Charlie's driver for years. Now that Maurits was in charge, it was protocol to replace the old boss's driver with a new one, just to make sure loyalties weren't mixed.

If Stanley's still here, she thought suddenly, *that means Maurits still hasn't been confirmed as the new Justice.* A flicker of new hope welled up inside her.

"Hey, Stanley," she said casually as they rolled toward the side entrance. "You've been around here a while, right?"

"You know it, Baby Doll." He grinned at her in the mirror. "Stanley Lieber's been driving your pop around for nearly seven years now."

She returned his smile. "Listen, I, um, *loaned* something to a new friend I met back at the Police Services Center."

Stanley shot a dismissive look toward the ragged overshirt that Baby Doll now wore. "Don't look like you got much for it in return—if you don't mind my saying, Baby."

"Yeah. Right." Baby Doll flicked a finger against the overshirt and shrugged her shoulders. "Well, anyway, I'd kind of like to look up my new friend, but I forgot to get her address before we parted ways. Her name was Linda McDavid, and she's a real piece of artwork, if you know what I mean."

Stanley chuckled appropriately.

"Think you could check around and find out where she lives for me?"

Stanley stopped the car at the side entrance. He turned around and looked uncomfortably at the girl. "Yeah, you know,

Baby, a week ago that woulda been no problem. But things are . . . *different* now. I probably shouldn't do any favors, not even for you, unless Maurits tells me to do it." He looked apologetic. "You know what I'm saying, Baby Doll? You understand, right?"

Baby Doll felt herself flush. She hadn't counted on the fact that Stanley would be worried about his own standing in the new regime. That he, too, had probably noticed the disappearance of two former bodyguards. "Yeah, sure, Stanley. I understand. No worries, okay?"

"Okay, thanks, Baby Doll," he said with genuine relief. "Now you go get cleaned up. Your uncle Maurits will be waiting for you soon."

She stopped short. "Uncle?" she said. That was a new one.

Stanley shrugged and grinned. "I don't know. It just seemed right, considering the circumstances."

"No, sure. Yeah. Uncle Maurits. I'll try it out, you know?" She pasted a smile on her bruised face and opened the door. "Thanks, Stanley."

"No problem, Baby Doll."

She held the door open long enough for Boy to slip out of the car and stand beside her, then waved as Stanley drove the car away.

"I think Stanley is about the same size as me," Boy said after the car turned the corner of the house.

Baby Doll turned and shot a confused look at the Drifter. "What?"

He motioned to the soiled wreck of clothing that he wore. "I think that driver is about the same size as me," he said again.

Baby Doll sighed. "Right. I get it. We'll stop by his room on the way up to mine."

"And then?"

"We'll get cleaned up and eat. Then, obviously, I have to see what Maurits wants."

Boy nodded.

"And then," Baby Doll said as she turned to walk in the side door, "I believe I owe you a favor."

Sixteen

The driver is not exactly the same size as me, but close enough. From his closet I filch a pair of brown corduroy pants and a belt, a clean pair of boxer shorts, and a white cotton dress shirt. I consider a pullover sweater with muted blue stripes, but in the end I decide against it. No one will be able to see it once I'm wearing it, and it's warm enough indoors. I keep my own shoes, but go ahead and steal a new pair of socks to fit inside them. When I have the clothing in hand, Baby Doll leads me up to the second floor. My first impression of her room is that it's decorated a little young for someone her age, with pinks and pastels and even a few plush animals decorating the shelves. But she doesn't seem to notice, or to be embarrassed by having her childhood represented in an adult's room.

"The bathroom is there," she says, pointing to the small anteroom adjoining hers. "I'll have to be in there a while, so you can shower first. Toss your dirty clothes out to me before you get in, and I'll make sure they get disposed of with mine."

Moments later, it feels good to stand in the warm, streaming water and wash away the memories of Simon's funeral, of the Severance, of everything except the comfort of steam, soap, and shampoo. When I am done and dressed, I find Baby Doll sitting at a little desk, staring out a window. She is now wearing a pale yellow pajama set covered by a red silk robe. Outside the sky is grayish-pink, and intermittent snowflakes are beginning to fall.

"We're not safe here," Baby Doll says when she sees me. "Well, I'm not safe. Not for long." She pauses and looks at me with what appears to be genuine concern. "If something happens to me," she asks, "what happens to you?"

Before I can answer, there is a knock at the door. "Miss Baby? It's Leticia."

Baby Doll doesn't take her eyes off me, but she calls out toward the door, "What is it, Leticia?"

"Mr. Girard sent me with your breakfast."

Baby Doll opens the door to reveal a maid carrying a tray of food. Eggs with cheese, bacon, toast, and juice in a large wine goblet. A cloth napkin and flatware fill out the tray. The smell alone would make anyone hungry.

"Thank you, Leticia. You can set it there." She points to an empty space on the desk. After Leticia has gone, Baby Doll turns toward the bathroom. "Save me the bacon, and some of the juice," she says. "You can have the rest." A moment later I hear the shower start to run.

The breakfast is simple, but good. I eat exactly half of everything and leave the rest for her, including the full goblet of orange juice. Then I cover the tray and wait.

The snowfall is coming down in earnest now, spattering across the windowpane with actual style, as if some cosmic Jackson Pollack were flinging moisture as paint across the sky. Something inside me wants to open the window behind Baby Doll's desk and jump through the snow to the ground below, and then begin running—any direction will do—until I find myself free of this tether, free of any tether. Free to wander and make my own way in this world.

—

"Why don't you go?" Alondra had asked me once during another February snowstorm. "Why don't we go, I mean."

She was forty-two then. Europe was in shambles as madmen ravaged it in search for power and, some said, peace. For fifteen years she had saved, planning a trip to tour the Continent, her starry-eyed dream of youth. But after last December 7, it was clear she wouldn't be going there for some time.

"I don't mean today, of course. And maybe not even until spring or summer or after this horrid war is finished. But honestly, why can't we be free together? At least for a little while?"

"You're talking nonsense, Alondra," I had said.

"And you're being obstinate," she'd said, pouting.

"Okay, tell me what you mean."

"Look, for twenty-two years you and I have been together. And for twenty-two years you have followed me wherever I've gone. From Charleston to Philadelphia. From Philadelphia to Boston."

I grimaced involuntarily.

"Yes, I know that Boston was a mistake, but still you came, and we didn't stay there for long. And from Boston to Chicago, and from Chicago to here."

"Yes. And?"

"Well, look. Now that I am teaching at the university, I have much more freedom. I have full summers off, and I can even take a sabbatical if I want to. So why not run away? Why not follow that urge to roam wherever you want to go?"

She was the first to ever even suggest such a thing. I didn't know what to say. She reached toward me and stroked my hand. "You can lead for once. How about if you be the Tether, and I will be the Drifter who follows you. I have money saved, you know that. We can go anywhere. To Africa. To India. To Brazil or Denmark."

She begins rummaging through a drawer and pulls out a stack of postcards she has saved over the years. The postcards reveal images of places all over the world—the Eiffel Tower in Paris, Big Ben in London, the Uffizi Gallery in Florence. Her "dream collection," she calls it, because she likes to look at these cards when dreaming about exotic trips to foreign lands.

"Where would you go if the world were your train station?" She looks at me with delight dancing in her eyes.

The answer had been easy for me. "I would go wherever you are."

Her pout was both flirtatious and genuine. "You're missing the point. I'm offering you freedom, of a sort. Yes, I would still have to be with you, but you for once could decide where to go and what to do. It will be my gift to you, a memento of gratefulness for the last twenty-two years."

"I am no angel."

"Nor demon, I know. You are no ghost. You are just who you are, a Drifter. My Drifter. So why don't we drift a while together?"

I held her in my arms a while, thinking. Where would I go if the world were my train station? What would I find if I started over again with Alondra by my side? No one had ever offered this option to me, not in many lifetimes of years.

"I've already seen this world, Alondra," I said at last. "Every corner of it. It is all the same to me. The world that matters right now is only you. I've already found where I want to be."

I meant the words; they were true to me at that moment. But I could see that I had disappointed her. She was like a child giving something precious to another; I was like a grown-up, missing the magic of the crayon scrawls on paper.

She patted me on the cheek. "You will probably regret this someday," she'd said wisely. "And now, I'm going to bed."

I had stared out the window, watching the snow fall all night long, thinking of Alondra's words and her offer to me. "How about if you be the Tether. I will be the Drifter who follows you . . ."

It was a lovely dream.

But my world doesn't work like that, Alondra. In this world I am always the Drifter. I am always alone.

—

"Boy?"

Baby Doll sits on the bed behind me. She is dressed in blue jeans and a dark green sweater. Her hair is clean and dry, flowing stylishly across her shoulders. She wears a long string of pearls, wrapped twice around her neck, with earrings that match. Black boots, black belt, gold watch. Makeup covers most of the remaining damage to her face. She looks every bit the college coed, ready to go out for pizza or a study session with friends.

"Boy?" she says again. "I'm sorry to interrupt, but it's time. We have to go see Maurits now. It won't do to be late."

I nod. Have I been here that long, lost in my thoughts? Even the snow outside has stopped falling, leaving barely a glaze of white on the ground outside.

"I waited as long as I could," she says by way of apology. "I could see that you didn't want to be disturbed."

"No, it's fine," I say. "I'm fine."

She nods slowly. "I'm sorry, Boy. For whatever it was that made you so sad. For whatever it was that takes your mind back to that sadness."

I feel a heat rising from my neck to my face. Am I that transparent to her already?

"How long have you been waiting?" I ask.

"More than an hour," she says. "But it's okay. We had the time, and it was almost peaceful just to sit with you in silence here."

I nod and stand. She starts toward the door, then stops and turns back to me.

"Do you want to tell me about it? About whatever it is that makes you look so lonely like that?"

Inside I think that yes, I very much do want to tell Baby Doll about it. I very much do want someone to know about Alondra, about the woman who meant more to me than eternity. But I know that no one can really be trusted. Least of all myself.

"It's nothing," I say quickly. "Right now we've got other things to worry about."

She bites the corner of her lip, and I see a glimpse of the fear I first noticed on her face at her stepfather's funeral.

"Boy," she says slowly. "If anything happens to me in there . . . while we're in there with Maurits . . ."

"I know," I say to her. "It will be up to me to get back that ring."

Seventeen

Maurits's new bodyguard stood at the entrance to Charlie's old bedroom. He looked barely five years older than Baby Doll. When she stepped into the hallway, it was clear that he liked what he saw. *Have to remember that,* Baby Doll thought. *Might come in useful in the future.*

She took a deep breath and walked down the marble hallway toward the oak door to Charlie's old bedroom. She stopped at the entrance and took in the new man. "I don't think I know you," she said politely.

He gave a mock bow and a smile. "Name is Ellsworth," he said easily. "Whitney Ellsworth."

Time for a test, Baby Doll thought. "Whitney?" she said, wrinkling her nose a bit. "Isn't that a girl's name?" A true bodyguard would simply ignore the insult and announce her to Maurits. A man with hormones, though, would get defensive at the idea of being dismissed by a pretty, snobby young girl.

She saw his face turn slightly red and a familiar anger flash in his eyes. "No, of course not," he said too quickly. "Whitney is a man's name. Has been for centuries before women started using it in the recent past. Baby Doll"—he said her name with dry sarcasm—"now that's a woman's name."

Baby Doll smiled inside. Immature. Prideful. And flirtatious to boot. This one was definitely not a bodyguard. Maurits would never put up with that kind of security in his household. That meant that Whitney Ellsworth was an outsider, someone playing a role instead of a part.

"My mistake," Baby Doll said sweetly. "Maybe later you can tell me more about yourself."

Another mock bow. "It would be my pleasure, Miss Baby Doll."

Another flub on his part. No bodyguard in this house would ever risk his position by flirting with Baby Doll or any other woman in the house. Maurits would have none of it, not even when Charlie was alive.

She leaned in close and whispered, "So who are you really, Mr. Ellsworth? And what are you doing here?"

He looked both surprised and pleased that she'd spotted his ruse. "Someone you'll be glad to know, if you know what I mean," he whispered back.

She nodded and smiled, and wondered how long it would be before he disappeared like Charlie's final bodyguards.

"I see," she said. There was a moment of silence. Then she nodded toward the door behind Mr. Ellsworth. "Well, maybe you'd better tell *my uncle* that I'm here." Stanley was right; calling him "Uncle Maurits" might have its advantages after all.

Whitney Ellsworth nodded and then turned and disappeared into the bedroom. While he was gone, Baby Doll spoke quickly to Boy.

"Wait out here with him. See if you can pickpocket anything that will give us a clue about who he works for and why he's here."

Boy nodded. Baby Doll had another thought.

"And see if you can steal his gun. He's the kind who would be too proud to let on that he'd lost it—and who would be dangerous if he kept it."

Boy nodded again. "If you need me in there—"

She stopped him short. "If I need you in there, then it's already too late for both of us. Just wait for me. And take care of this dumb Whitney Ellsworth for me. Okay?"

Boy said nothing, but he took a step back and placed himself in a spot where he would be directly behind the bodyguard's left shoulder when he returned. Baby Doll took another deep breath and waited. A moment later the door opened and Whitney Ellsworth grinned ingratiatingly at her. "Mr. Girard will see you now."

Baby Doll stepped inside.

"Come on in, Baby Doll," Maurits said from behind Charlie's desk. "Let's have a look at you now."

The first thing Baby Doll noticed was that Charlie's bed was gone; the space it left was smaller than she'd expected it to be. The lights were dimmed in the room, except behind Charlie's rosewood desk. In the shadows she saw Charlie's dressers had been emptied and the drawers stacked on the floor. Piles of papers, clothes, and boxes were also spread across the room. Someone had been looking for something hidden in here.

"It's all right, Baby," the voice behind the desk said. "Come on in. We need to talk anyway."

The second thing Baby Doll noticed was that four of the shuttered windows had been opened. The light from outside was pale like dusk, despite the fact that it was mid-morning and threatening to retreat into snow flurries again. But there was light nonetheless, and it was coming in through dusty windows that had not been opened for more than a decade.

She walked toward Charlie's old desk and was surprised to see it was clean, organized, and uncluttered. The only things on the surface of the desk were Charlie's laptop and a telephone. There were no bloodstains, which also surprised her. Either this desk had been thoroughly washed, or someone had simply restained the surface with wood polish and covered over the blood. She took a deep breath and decided the latter.

Maurits sat behind the desk tapping something onto the keyboard of the laptop in front of him.

"Sit down, Baby Doll. I'll be finished with this in just a second."

She took a chair on the opposite side of the desk from Maurits. Only after sitting did she realize it was the same chair she'd sat in the last time she'd been in this room. Inside, she felt her skin crawl. She looked up behind Maurits's head and noticed that the Scottish broadsword and Charlie's "coat of arms" were no longer on the wall. When she looked back down, Maurits was eyeing her from behind the computer screen. He kept her gaze while he finished typing something on the laptop. Then he closed the lid and pushed the computer aside.

"Hello, Baby Doll," Maurits said quietly.

"Hello, Maurits," she responded.

He nodded in approval. Then he opened a drawer behind the desk and reached inside. "I believe this is yours." In his outstretched palm he held her driver's license. "And this." One of her Visa cards—the one not used to buy lunch for the greedy at Arby's. He reached into the drawer again. "And these." Her second Visa. Her JCPenney card. Nordstrom. College ID.

"Thanks," she said, avoiding Maurits's penetrating gaze.

He dug back in the drawer one more time and threw a few more items on the desk. Louis Vuitton black with multicolor design Alma handbag. Scuffed, scraped, and basically ruined for public use. A monogrammed makeup case. An empty wallet. Maurits waited as she gathered her belongings from the desk.

"Something missing?" the big man asked casually.

Baby Doll looked sheepish. "Well, I was kind of hoping for my library card."

Maurits shook his head. "We'll keep looking."

Baby Doll nodded.

"Oh, but there was one more thing," he said. "I believe this is yours now." He held out a gun so small it barely filled his monstrous palm.

Baby Doll's eyes widened. "Maurits, I don't . . . I mean . . ."

Maurits never took his eyes off hers, just held out the gun, waiting. Finally she reached over and took it from his hand.

"It's out of bullets," he said. "You know where to get more?"

"Yes," she replied. She held the gun in her hand and felt it tremble. "Yes. Of course." She stuffed it inside the Louis Vuitton, and then swept all of the other items Maurits had given her into the purse as well.

Maurits leaned back in his chair and seemed to relax for the first time. "Your daddy's death got you feeling a little mixed up inside, Baby?"

Baby Doll didn't know what to say, so she said nothing. Maurits continued.

"This is a difficult time for everybody. Things are changing. Some for good, some not so good. But you don't need to worry about anything, okay, Baby Doll? Old Maurits is still here, and as long as he is, nobody's going to do anything to disturb what Charlie Murphy built from the ground up. Not Honoria Lopez"—he said the name with disgust—"not some coward from the inside, nobody." He paused and looked hard toward Baby Doll. "Not even you. You understand that, Baby Doll?"

The girl felt a tightness in her throat that prevented her from speaking, so she gave a quick nod instead.

"You need to tell me anything?"

She shook her head. It felt awkward and juvenile.

"You follow the rulebook when Detective Lopez pulled you in?"

She nodded. "To the letter."

Maurits said nothing, just looked at her, trying hard to read her face. She did her best to return his gaze and not look like a lying, thieving betrayer. "Good," he said finally. "So how's school going, Baby?"

Baby Doll was caught off guard.

"You going to be able to make up the classes you missed, with all the drama of last week?"

"Oh, yeah," she said finally. "No problem with that, Maurits." Then she had a thought. "I'll probably have to spend some extra time at the library to make up a few assignments in art history and Latin studies. But other than that, it shouldn't be a problem."

Maurits nodded, and Baby Doll noticed that his eyes flicked toward the laptop to his right. *He is ready for this talk to be over,* she thought. *He is suspicious, but he doesn't know for sure. He is ready to chalk up my crazy behavior to grief over Charlie's suicide.*

"That's good, Baby. You get back into that school routine, now, okay? You just focus on making good grades, making the memory of your dad proud."

"Right."

"Now Maurits has got business to attend to. You need anything, you ask Stanley to help you. Got it?" Maurits reached over and pulled the laptop to him, signaling that it was time for Baby Doll to go. She stood up almost involuntarily.

"Right." She paused. "Um, Maurits?"

He looked toward her expectantly.

"Listen, for my art history class, I need to track down this classic piece of artwork. It's a McDavid original. They said it was on display here in town somewhere, but with all the excitement that has been going on, I didn't get a chance to find out where it is. You think Stanley could find it for me?"

"Of course."

"Well, he said that I should talk to you about it first."

Maurits grunted and picked up the receiver of the telephone on his desk. "Put Stanley on," he said. After a moment he continued, "I want you to find something for Baby Doll." He looked up at the girl. She mouthed "McDavid piece of artwork" to him. "Some piece of artwork, a McDavid or something. Baby Doll can give you details. Yeah. Find out where it is and let her know so she can go check it out." He hung up the phone and turned back to Baby Doll.

"Okay, Baby," he said. "Now I have to get to work. You stay out of trouble."

"Right. Thank you, Maurits." She started to go.

"Oh, Baby Doll, one more thing." She turned and was surprised to see that Maurits was already standing beside her. "Something went missing right after your daddy, well, right after. Something important." His eyes were searching, looking for clues. "You see anybody come in here that shouldn't have been? Somebody from the household staff or something?"

"No, Maurits," she said, realizing too late that she'd probably answered too quickly. "What was taken?"

"Nothing for you to worry about," the big man said, also too quickly.

Suddenly he reached down and tilted her chin to the side, studying her face with new scrutiny. An angry frown appeared. "And don't you worry about that either," he said with a nod toward the swollen part of her jaw. "I'll make sure that's taken care of as well. No one touches you and gets away with it. No one."

"Thanks," she mumbled, not thinking much about what Maurits might do or who he might find to punish for her pain.

"This happen before or after your time with the good Detective Lopez?"

Baby Doll felt a dull panic start to grow inside her. If Maurits's associates tracked down Linda McDavid in order to exact revenge for the beating she'd given to Baby Doll, then it was likely they'd find her before Stanley did—and before Baby Doll could get to her and recover the ring she'd stolen. And if they found Linda McDavid and *explained* to her that it was unwise to touch Charlie Murphy's daughter harmfully, they would undoubtedly find the ring on her finger. And if they found the ring on Linda McDavid, it would only be a matter of time before Maurits came back to Baby Doll with a new *explanation* about why it was unwise to steal a ring from a secret compartment in her dead stepfather's desk.

"Yeah, it happened before Detective Lopez," Baby Doll said. She hoped that lie would buy her enough time to get to the ring before Maurits's men did.

Maurits nodded. "Stay out of trouble, Baby Doll," he said again. And then he turned back to his desk.

Baby Doll turned to leave, and then felt herself jump involuntarily at the loud bang and floor tremors that thundered through the room. She turned to find Maurits swearing over a heavy wooden shutter, now split in half and plastered across the floor.

"Blasted relics," he spat. "Old rusted hinges, I bet. Have to get these all replaced." Maurits looked up at Baby Doll. "Nothing to worry about, Baby. Just some old furnishings that your father should have replaced a long time ago."

The big man suddenly frowned. "That reminds me," he said as he began rummaging through a drawer in his desk. A moment later he flicked a wrist and a small missile came flying toward

Baby Doll's face. She reacted instinctively and caught the cell phone before it did any damage. "Keep this one turned on, and with you, at all times," Maurits said, looking her in the eye to communicate the seriousness of his command. "No more 'accidents' like what happened with your last cell phone. Got it?"

Baby Doll nodded mutely. Maurits watched her pointedly until she turned on the phone.

"I had 'em transfer over your address book and phone numbers from our backup database. Should be good as new."

"Thanks."

Maurits nodded. Then he gestured toward the door. "Tell that execrable Ellsworth he should have been in here the second he heard that shutter drop, and that if something like that happens again, he won't get a second chance."

Baby Doll took that as a dismissal. She exited the room and was surprised to find Boy standing with a gun in his hand, and Whitney Ellsworth unconscious on the marble floor.

I watch her enter the room where Maurits waits, and notice her hands trembling. I wonder which she fears more: that the big man might one day kill her, or that she might one day have to kill him.

Whitney Ellsworth takes up his position in front of the bedroom door, but it's clear his heart is not in it. His eyes wander back toward the bedroom frequently. He even leans his ear close to the door a few times, apparently hoping to hear what's going on between Baby Doll and Maurits on the other side. It's a false hope, as this oaken door is thick and solid. Eventually he gives up and stares out and up, willing the time to pass.

From my position behind his left shoulder I trace the outline of his clothing. There is a smooth lump that slightly raises the fabric of his suit coat along the left side of his rib cage. A bulge at the small of his back, at belt height. And a knot above his right ankle that wrinkles the cuff that sits below it.

Since I am standing behind him, my first target is the weapon stashed at the back of his belt. It's a delicate dance I must do. The untethered are not consciously aware of me, but the subconscious mind is not so easily fooled.

"I don't understand what you mean," Alondra had said to me once, back during the earliest days when she was young and fresh and still filled with the curiosity of a child. "Either they can see you, or they can't, right?"

"Yes," I had said, "and no."

"You're infuriating sometimes, you know that?"

How does one explain mysteries that he himself doesn't yet understand, even after all these years?

"Okay, so let's start at the top," she had continued. It was a problem to solve, and for Alondra few things were more attractive than an intellectual puzzle.

"Alondra," I said, "some things have no explanation. Some things just are."

She, of course, ignored me.

"Okay, to me, you are real. Flesh, blood, breathing. Something that can be seen, touched, smelled, heard, and even tasted, I suppose. But that's only because of the tether. Am I right so far?"

I nodded.

"To everyone else, you don't exist. Right?"

This time I shake my head. "No, I never stop existing. I'm just unseen. Well, unnoticed."

"So what happens if you are walking in a crowd and someone comes barreling toward you?"

"It's difficult to explain."

"Everything about you is difficult to explain."

I sighed. "The person coming toward me won't see me. But he will—how do I say it?—accommodate me."

"What's that supposed to mean?"

"As best I can tell, the untethered can't experience me through their five senses, but there is a sixth sense of sorts that knows I am there. And that sixth sense swishes at my presence the way a

horse's tail flicks at flies. It's not something they think, it's just something they do."

Alondra had thrown up her hands in frustration at that point, growling like a little girl kept from a cookie jar. "Show me," she'd said finally.

So together we walked down to the kitchen of the boarding house where she was staying. The landlady was in the kitchen preparing stew for dinner.

"Hello, Alondra dear," she'd said. "Is there something you need?"

I motioned for her to stall for time. "Um, no, Mrs. Snelling. Not really. Just thought I'd see if you needed any help in the kitchen today."

"That's sweet of you, dear," the landlady had said. "Here, you can peel these potatoes for me while I cube the meat for the stew."

At that moment I took the paring knife off the counter and held it up in the air.

"Now what did I do with that potato knife?" Mrs. Snelling had said. "I had it just a moment ago." She looked around until her eyes locked onto a spot in the sink. "Ah, there it is," she said brightly, and as she reached toward the sink her hand swept across the handle of the knife, effortlessly taking it from me and placing it herself in the sink bay where she then picked it up with a smile. "Here you go, dear. And I thank you for the help."

Alondra's eyes grew wide with wonder. I held out my hand and she delivered the knife to me again. This time I flipped it around into a weapon, and before Alondra could stop me I rammed it directly at Mrs. Snelling's throat. Alondra stifled a scream; the landlady, on the other hand, casually flicked her body sideways and her head to the left, leaving me to careen harmlessly past her and crash into the shelf.

"Did you hear something, dear?" Mrs. Snelling said pleasantly. "I thought for a second that someone might be at the door."

Alondra's face was flushed and damp. "I'm not sure, ma'am," she said shakily. "Maybe I'll go check."

"Thank you, dear. But I'm still counting on you for the potatoes!" she chirped.

In the hallway Alondra was breathless and in a mild state of shock. "What," she said, "just happened in there? You almost killed her!"

"No, Alondra. I couldn't. Her sixth sense wouldn't let me. She's not aware of me, but something inside her makes sure that she will always accommodate me. Even with the knife, she subconsciously sees it where it makes sense for it to be, even though it's clearly in my hand. Do you understand now?"

"No."

"Well, that's okay, because I don't fully understand it either."

Alondra took a moment to catch her breath and slow her pulse rate a bit, and then we both went back into the kitchen and peeled potatoes for dinner.

—

Now I stand behind Whitney Ellsworth and begin the dance that will allow me to pickpocket him without becoming an intrusive presence that he instinctively avoids. I am unseen, which is good. But I must also be unfelt, like a true pickpocket who can catch the mark when he is most unaware.

With practiced patience, I gently raise the left flap on the back of Mr. Ellsworth's suit coat. I am a little surprised to find the weapon of choice back here is a large hunting knife in a leather holster. There is no clasp on the holster; I can easily lift the knife out of its resting place, but I decide to pursue the guns instead.

As I gently lay down the back panel of the suit coat, the bodyguard jumps into motion.

I step away as he fumbles with his inside jacket pocket and produces a vibrating cell phone.

"Ellsworth," he says softly into the cell. His eyes light up like a child who has discovered a fascinating insect that he wants to show a friend. "Fox herself? Yes, of course."

There is a moment of silence, and then, "Yes, ma'am. No. No, he doesn't seem to have it, at least not yet. No, ma'am. I—well, I— Yes, ma'am. Well, she's awfully young. Seems like she's pretty much kept out of the— Yes. Yes." He cringes, and I hear a metallic voice speaking indistinguishable words in his earpiece. At the moment he cringes, I see something I haven't noticed before. A weakness, perhaps, that most would keep well hidden—especially someone like Whitney Ellsworth. His eyes flicker for a millisecond and almost roll up into his eyelids. His breathing shortens, and his neck seems to stiffen involuntarily before he regains control of himself. "Yes, ma'am. Thank you, ma'am."

The call ends and now Mr. Ellsworth is a bustle of nervous energy, beginning a short, three-step pacing that takes him side to side in front of the bedroom door. Whatever his orders are, he is anxious to follow them. He stuffs the telephone back into his suit pocket, and I decide that perhaps Baby Doll will want this man's cell in addition to his guns. Before the flap of his coat can fall back onto his chest, I have already stalled the closure and reached in with a two-fingered grab on the cell. I must match his sideways pacing to finish the lift, but it is only seconds since his last call and now I own his phone.

Before I can pocket it myself, I feel it buzz again. A text message appears on the screen, from a sender identified as "vfox." It says only "and give m no cause. we r not savages. yet."

I look back at Whitney Ellsworth. He is walking with his eyes closed, as if deep in thought, still pacing sideways back and forth in front of the bedroom door. Then he takes a deep breath and seems to assert control of himself. He settles back into position, doing his best to look the role of the bodyguard intent on his work.

I now know what he hides; I can read it in his face, in the late flicker of his left eyelid when he blinks, in the nervous twitching that causes him to tip his head slightly backward every few minutes. He covers it well, manages his condition with surprising control for someone his age. It is apparently something he has dealt with since childhood. But I know the weakness and, at this point, patience is all I need.

I can see clearly now the edge of his gun, obviously holstered next to his rib cage, but I feel no need to pickpocket that at present. In time, he will offer it to me without resistance, and if he doesn't, then Baby Doll can easily disarm him when she comes out.

For now, I will simply wait.

My mind retreats and I focus on the ceiling tile at . . . think . . . what is the name? Simon, yes, Simon. The ceiling tile at Simon's place and the box that hides behind it. I feel a pain at not having the box in a place of safety. But there was nothing to be done about it. It was left, and soon it will be recovered, with all its contents, I hope. There are six items inside the box, always six. Never five, never seven. Eternity is visible in six, and six is enough.

Ellsworth has settled into a comfortable rhythm now, slightly rocking on his feet, his mind clearly working through a task at hand, taking him someplace in the future and helping him relax and daydream at his post here in front of Charlie Murphy's bedroom door.

And then the quiet of the moment is interrupted by an unex-

pected thundering, a staccato "bang" that vibrates from behind the door inside the bedroom where Baby Doll and Maurits are meeting. At first I think it might be a gunshot, but then I notice that it sounded a bit dull and dry for that. Regardless, I spring into action. This is the kind of moment I have been waiting for.

Whitney Ellsworth's cataplexy is almost immediate. His neck stiffens, then lolls; his eyes blink rapidly and roll up inside his head. His breathing comes in short bursts, and his muscles fight the limpness that inevitably comes when they finally give in. The man slides, almost gracefully, to the floor. I'm not sure why I do it, but I catch the back of his head and cushion it from cracking hard on the marble below us. Sympathy, I suppose. Narcolepsy is no easy disease to own.

The bodyguard is completely unconscious below me. It is easy work now to steal his guns. First I take the Kahr 9mm pistol out of its strap next to the man's ankle. I will hide this somewhere in the house later; for now it goes into the back waistband of the pants I have borrowed from Stanley. The gun in the shoulder holster is the exact same model, and I find myself a little disappointed by Whitney's lack of imagination. I had expected something different than what was at the ankle. But then again, two Kahr pistols can certainly do a lot of damage. And maybe that's all Mr. Ellsworth needed anyway.

Behind his eyelids, Whitney's eyes roll in what appears to be REM sleep, but I can't be sure of that. He may simply be trying to regain control—and thereby consciousness—over his short-circuiting brainwaves.

It is only a moment before the bedroom door opens and Baby Doll stands, pale and slightly out of breath, beside me. She quickly surveys the situation, and then bites her lip. "Tell me about it—but in my room," she says. She turns and walks down the hall with a purposeful stride in her steps. I can feel the tether warming, loosening, giving me a little more freedom with every moment. I take one last look at Whitney Ellsworth and am surprised to see his eyes open. Inside me there is a ghost of a feeling, an empty threat of nausea and tightness. A single syllable, no more than a grunt really, escapes the bodyguard's lungs. I am frozen.

"Do you see me?" I whisper. In response, Ellsworth closes his eyes, and his retinas are motionless behind his eyelids.

I understand that victims of narcolepsy can experience hypnagogic visions during episodes of cataplexy, and a thought flashes across my mind. I wonder if Whitney Ellsworth has just hallucinated me.

"Come on, Boy."

Baby Doll is waiting. When she sees that she has regained my attention, she continues down the marble hallway toward her room.

I, of course, follow.

When I cross the threshold into Baby Doll's room, I see that she is pointing a small device in my direction. I hear the noisy clicking of an artificial shutter on a camera and see Baby Doll give a satisfied nod toward the image viewer on her cell phone. She doesn't understand. Not yet. In time maybe, if this tether lasts.

"It won't do you any good," I say to her as I close the door behind me.

Baby Doll just frowns.

Nineteen

"It won't do you any good." Boy gave a nod toward the cell phone in Baby Doll's hand. "The picture. It doesn't last."

"What are you talking about, Boy?"

He tossed a Kahr K-series handgun onto Baby Doll's bed. "Why did you take a picture of me on your cell phone?"

"Because, well, it occurred to me that there's no telling when you might disappear. I mean, I know you say that you're not a ghost, but you definitely aren't normal. Someone like you who can simply appear one day is probably going to disappear just as easily on another day, right?"

Boy nodded.

"So, I thought I should have at least one picture of you for that day. So I don't, you know, forget you."

"You won't remember me, even with the picture."

"Of course I'll remember you. How could I not?"

He gave an accommodating shrug. "Well, yes, you might remember that someone like me came into your life. But you won't remember my name, or my face. It will all fade. Even that picture you just took. It's the way things are."

Baby Doll's forehead crinkled. She sighed and sat down hard on the bed. At her feet beside the bed was her old purse, scratched and dirty and worse for wear. She glanced down at it, then kicked it under the bed, apparently done with whatever was inside.

"Who are you?" she said quietly. "What are you? And why have you come to find me, now of all times?"

Boy looked thoughtful, but in the end he said nothing.

"Are you an angel?" She asked the question as though she'd never asked before. The question they all asked.

Boy shook his head. "I'm none of those things." He held out his hand. "I'm flesh and blood, just like you are."

"How old are you?"

Boy shrugged. "I forgot my age a long time ago."

"Work with me for a minute, would you, Boy?" A flash of frustration tinged Baby Doll's voice. "Would you say you are, I don't know, older than me?" A nod. "Older than Maurits?" Another nod. "Fifty years old? A hundred?" More nodding. Baby Doll took a deep breath. "Five hundred years old?" Boy nodded again.

"Baby Doll," he said quietly, "I am older than I can remember. I've lived a hundred lifetimes and died them as well. I've forgotten more than I know many times over, and forgotten that I even knew it once. All I know is that I am a Drifter and you are my Tether. I am bound to you until the bond is broken and another Tether takes your place."

"Can you be killed?"

Another shrug. "I don't think so. No."

"Who controls the tether? You? God?"

A shrug. "Not me. I don't know how it works, just that it is."

"But the mark in your eyes. Surely that's some kind of sign from God, right?"

Boy frowned. "I know that God exists," he said slowly. "I have at times felt his presence, known that he is near. I do not know if Drifters are something that linger on the outside edges of the mind of God. He doesn't answer a Drifter's prayers, at least as far as I can tell. He doesn't imbue me with purpose or give meaning to my life. I am a thing lost in eternity, waiting forever to be found. There is no heaven or hell for a Drifter. Doesn't that also mean that there is no God for me?"

"What do you mean, there is no heaven or hell for you?"

"Heaven and hell are unattainable for me. They are both the same thing. Afterlife is only for someone else. How can there be heaven or hell for someone who never dies?"

There was a moment of silence between them. Baby Doll seemed to be working something out in her head, trying to remember everything she'd learned back in Catholic school, everything she'd pondered from her hidden Bible; Boy stood by the door, waiting.

"I am a lost thing too, Boy," she said. "Clearly. Yet you found me. Does that mean God has found me too? And"—she paused for a moment—"if so, why would God even want to find me?"

Boy shrugged.

"Or maybe I found you," she said quietly. She hadn't thought this deeply about faith and God for a long time. "Maybe you are the one God is looking for, and I'm the one he used to find you. To remind you of his purpose for you. There's a confusing thought."

Boy didn't answer. Baby Doll smiled ruefully.

"Then again, I'm not the most likely tool in God's shed, am I? Particularly after what I've done this past week." She looked at Boy again, uncertain. *Cras credemus, hodie nihil,* she told herself at last. *Tomorrow we may believe, but not today.*

She exhaled, and then slowly breathed a final question. "Can you be trusted?"

Boy looked steadily at her. "Not always," he said.

Baby Doll nodded in contemplation. Almost absentmindedly, she picked the Kahr off the bed beside her, twirling it in her hands as she gave it a cursory examination. Outside the window the skies were still gray and pale, though the snow was apparently done, at least for the afternoon. After a moment she leaned over and stuffed the gun under her pillow. Then she gave an appraising look at Boy, still standing just inside the doorway. She stood and walked over to him, peering deeply into his brown-black eyes.

"I'm not imagining it. I do see a mark there, don't I?" she whispered.

Boy nodded.

"It is clearly a cross shape, almost like a half-tone of yellow lines that intersect in your eyes. Right?"

"It is two intersecting lines, yes. But it could just as easily be an *x* or an addition sign. It has no meaning. It's just a mark."

Baby Doll's lips curled. "You, Boy," she said gently, "are full of crap."

Boy blinked, but said nothing.

Baby Doll turned and walked back to her bed. "Look, I can understand why you're mad at God. It makes sense, given who you are and what you must have lived through. But even if you are mad at him, you can't deny the truth."

"What truth is that, Baby Doll?"

"*Cruce signati,*" she said matter-of-factly. "'Marked with a cross.' That's the symbol of Christ painted in the back of your eyeballs, Boy. I'm certainly no scholar of . . ."—she searched for the words—"mystical things, spiritual things, whatever you'd call it. But I'm sure of this. You are God's property, whether you want to believe it or not." She tapped one finger absently on her lips. "Maybe you are an angel after all. Maybe you just forgot who you are, and that's why you feel lost by God." She turned back to look at him.

"I'm no angel," he said. "Nor demon."

"Shut up for a minute, Boy," she said, then she immediately softened. "Sorry, I didn't mean it to sound so harsh. What I mean is . . . please, give me just a minute to think, okay?"

"I'm no angel, Baby Doll," the Boy said. "It's dangerous to think that way. Others have tried to believe that, and—"

Baby Doll held up a hand, and Boy fell silent and waited. She thought for a few moments.

"Boy," she said slowly. "If God is looking for me, I want to be found."

"I'm no angel, Baby Doll."

For the first time the girl laughed, a sincere, open, happy laugh that even brought a half-smile to Boy's face. "Well, we'll see, Boy," she said, and then she appeared to be ready to change the subject. "Whose phone is that?" she asked, pointing to the device in his hand.

"Whitney Ellsworth's," the Boy said. "I lifted it from him just after he received a phone call."

Baby Doll shook her head to refocus. "I'm so distracted by trying to understand who you are. Yes. Ellsworth. What happened? How come he was unconscious?" She held out a hand for the phone and Boy deposited it there promptly. "Did you get anything else?"

"Long story . . . but I did get his guns. Two of them." He nodded toward Baby Doll's pillow, and also pulled up his shirt to reveal the second in his waistband.

"Both of them K-series Kahrs?" she said curiously. "Hmm. That's standard issue for . . ." She paused and turned on the cell phone, then began scrolling through the call log.

"He got a text a few minutes ago as well," Boy said. "From someone named 'vfox.'"

Baby Doll's eyebrows rose. "Victoria Fox?" she said incredulously. She immediately tapped buttons and pulled up text messages stored on the cell phone. "He's working for Victoria Fox? There's no way. It's not possible. Maurits would never allow . . . unless, of course . . . then he'd have to . . . and . . ."

"You realize you're not finishing your sentences, right, Baby Doll?"

She gave a resigned sigh and nodded slowly. "Of course Victoria Fox is here. She'd be the first to take advantage. That way she keeps both Maurits and Marty Goodman on the defensive." She sat down on the bed again.

"Baby Doll?"

"Listen, Boy, we've got to get that ring back. It's important. It's life or death. Understand?"

Boy shook his head.

"All right, look," Baby Doll said. "I'm going to try and explain this, but it's complicated, and I only know part of the way it works. Here's the thing. Back in the 1920s three main crime syndicates ran the underworld in this city. One dealt in gambling, one in booze, and one in, well, I guess they called it 'property access.' Basically, it was a protection racket. You know, pay the money and no armed goons will break into your business, beat you up, and rob you blind. That kind of protection. When the Great Depression hit in the 1930s, the syndicates started to creep into each other's territories. You can guess what happened next."

"Mob wars?"

"Yep. People getting gunned down at theaters, at restaurants, anywhere. And any innocent caught in the middle was just considered collateral damage. Finally it got so bad that somebody called a meeting with the heads of all three crime families. No one knows exactly who called that meeting, or how he got all three to show up alone. Or how he was able to keep them together for three full days. But when they walked out of that meeting, they declared peace on the streets. A short time later, there was a new crime syndicate in charge, called the Organization, and it demanded absolute obedience in the streets. The new organization was modeled after the U.S. government, with checks and balances, and each family taking on a specific role. Ninety years later, the Organization still runs the way it did back then."

"How's that?"

"There's an Executive. Right now that's Victoria Fox. She runs the day-to-day business, almost like a CEO of a large corporation. There's a Legislator. That's Marty Goodman. He makes the rules about anything that's not under the Executive's authority, like distribution of profits, funding of new initiatives, and so on."

"So the Executive has the power, but the Legislator has the money. Go on."

"And then there's Charlie Murphy. He is, well, he was, the Justice."

"What does that mean?"

"He's the only one that both Victoria Fox and Marty Goodman fear, because unlike the U.S. government, the Executive is not the commander in chief of the army. It's the Justice. Only he has the power to enforce a decision on a large scale, with a full, fighting force behind him. Because of that, he can overturn any decision, any course of action, that the Legislator or the Executive may take—and enforce it with guns and bombs."

"The others don't have arms or soldiers?"

"Sure, Victoria and Marty both have full contingents of bodyguards. But according to the way the Organization is run, they are deliberately limited in the number of armed enforcers they can keep. Only the Justice Department is allowed an army. So you can guess what that means."

"The Executive has power. The Legislator has money. But the Justice has the guns, and that is a constant threat to overrule the other two at any time."

"Right. It's a delicate balance, but it worked, and as a result, Charlie Murphy and his associates have run this city for decades. The police do what they can, but the Organization is too entrenched, too secure. And anytime there was a real threat, Charlie would just make a judgment against them and, poof, they'd disappear, or have a tragic car accident, or suddenly come into an inheritance that takes them off to an island in the British West Indies, or something like that."

"So what does the ring have to do with anything?"

"Each of the three heads in the Organization has a unique, symbolic ring that confers upon them the authority of their office. Possession of the appropriate ring is what gives them the authority to be Executive, Legislator, or the Justice. Think of it like King Arthur's sword, Excalibur, or like the badge of a police officer. If you possess it, you are what it says you are."

"Go on."

"The ring that Linda McDavid stole from me is the one I stole from Charlie Murphy's secret desk compartment. It's the Justice's seal of authority. Whoever holds that ring *is* the Justice. He or she can command the entire army of the Justice Department, and they won't ask questions as long as the orders are sealed by that ring. Do you understand?"

"So you stole the ring so you could be the new Justice instead of Maurits?"

"No, of course not. I stole the ring so there would be no Justice. To create a void in the way the Organization runs. If there is no one giving orders to the army, no one making judgments of whether or not to enforce the decisions of the Executive or the Legislator, then the Organization loses its power. It becomes a shell, in disarray, and ineffective. With no enforcement functioning, it's only a matter of time before the Organization begins to crumble from within. Do you see what I mean? No Justice in place means that somebody like Honoria Lopez can finally start getting through the layers that Charlie Murphy set up against her, accessing the evidence hidden behind people who were previously too scared to talk to the police. You understand?"

"I can see that it would cause some unrest at first, but all it takes is a strong leader—someone like Maurits—to step into the vacuum and set everything back in motion again, right?"

"No, you're not getting it. There is only one Justice. Period. And the only person who can be the Justice is the one who possesses the Justice's ring. It's the basis of the fundamental contract between the three original crime families. It's proof to the others of your right to sit in the Justice seat. If there is no ring, there is no Justice. And that means there is no foundation for the Organization. It becomes like a three-legged stool that has only two legs to prop itself up. Understand? No ring, no Justice."

"But if the ring carries that much significance, then surely that means people would always try to steal the ring. You'd have to be a ruthless, murdering monster to hold on to that ring for any period of . . ." Boy didn't finish the sentence, as the truth of the situation began to sink in.

Baby Doll nodded. "That's why I had to try to kill him, Boy. I switched his pills so he'd go crazy. And it worked, so I'm to blame. Charlie Murphy had been the Justice for sixteen years. I had to do something. There's been so much blood on this house. I had to get my stepfather's ring and then make sure that no one ever could use that ring again. I knew where he kept it hidden, and planned to take it and end this all."

"Couldn't someone just make a new ring—a copy—and step into the power seat that way?"

"Sure, someone could try. In fact, people have tried in the past. Well, one at least. Want to guess what happened when the forgery was uncovered?"

Boy shook his head as Baby Doll continued.

"See, the biggest diamond in the ring has a unique flaw. It's just about impossible to duplicate that flaw. Any jeweler could tell if a ring was a fake. Even if Maurits tried to have one made now the others could tell."

Boy thought about it for a minute. "I see," he said. "As long as the real ring is out there, no one with any sense of self-preservation would try to forge a new one. Not as long as there is an Executive and a Legislator to answer to. Let alone lesser generals in the Justice's army who would be betrayed by such a forgery. Part of the harsh checks and balances of the system."

"Now you're starting to get it."

Boy looked thoughtful. "But even without the Justice's ring, there is still an army out there. Someone will take over that army, with or without the ring."

"They would, if not for Charlie Murphy's last judgment."

Boy cocked his head in curiosity.

"Just before he died—well, just after he died really—Charlie Murphy gave sealed orders to disband the army completely. That was another part of my plan, along with switching his pills. I had it ready for when . . ." Baby Doll trailed off for a moment in thought as she considered what she'd done. "Or when the change of medication went into effect. Paid every soldier a handsome severance package that required them to leave town within twenty-four hours of claiming it. Most took the money and ran. Some stayed behind to see if they might get better terms from the new Justice. But now that Charlie's ring has gone missing, and no Justice has been named, they're all starting to get a little anxious."

"Do you think Maurits suspects you?" Boy asked. "After all, you were there when Charlie died."

"Yes. He's going to figure it out. But I'm not the first person who would come to mind. I'm not sure if he's even aware I knew where it was. Maurits of course knew where the ring was kept when Charlie wasn't wearing it, but he doesn't know who else knew. There were others whom Charlie might have told. And, for all Maurits knows, Charlie might have killed himself because the ring was already missing, and so his power was gone.

"Maurits is certainly thinking over who might have taken it and is hunting those people down. He expected to rule an army when Charlie Murphy died, but without that ring he can't give the order to re-form his platoons. And every hour a few more of his soldiers are opting to take their payouts and leave town. And every day Victoria Fox and Marty Goodman are scheming for ways to put their own people into the Justice position. And every day Honoria Lopez is getting closer and closer to uncovering the evidence she needs to deal a critical blow to Charlie Murphy's Organization. If the ring stays missing, it's only a matter of time before the Organization falls."

"Why not just go to Detective Lopez yourself? Why not try to take down the Organization with your own testimony? You would be a prized witness for the prosecution."

Baby Doll looked at him as though he were a child. "Do you really think that anyone on Police Services staff could protect me if there is a Justice in place at the Organization? There's a reason why Charlie Murphy had four arrests and never even went to trial. And it's not because he did nothing wrong."

"So," Boy said, almost as if he were laying pieces of a puzzle on the table before him, "before you—or anyone else for that matter—can step forward with evidence against the Organization, you have to remove the Organization's ability to enforce its will. To remove the Justice, and by extension, his army. Is that right?"

"Yes."

"And by removing the power of the Justice, you figuratively launch a chain reaction of dominoes that leaves the whole Organization collapsing in its wake."

"Yes. At least I hope that's what will happen."

"And all this occurs because one college coed happened to steal a ring from a dead man."

Baby Doll nodded ruefully. "Except for one big problem."

"Linda McDavid."

"Right. You see, Boy, as long as she wears that ring, she *is* the Justice. She just doesn't know it. But sooner or later, someone is going to recognize that ring and either rally around her to bring the army back together, or do whatever it takes to recover the ring from her and become the Justice himself or herself."

"And if Maurits finds her first?"

Baby Doll sighed. "Then we're back to where we were before Charlie Murphy's untimely suicide. And, more specifically, my life is over."

Boy nodded. Then, as if from nowhere, he said, "You owe me a favor, Baby Doll."

Baby Doll put her head in her hands and pantomimed pulling out her hair in frustration. Finally she said, "I know, Boy, I know." She looked at the afternoon sky outside her window and then flopped back onto her pillow. "Right now, though, I need a break from the world, from the pressure of knowing my life could end at any moment."

"What are you going to do?"

"Maybe I'll just lie here and take a nap." She said it flippantly at first, but as soon as the words left her mouth, she knew that was exactly what she needed. A chance to let her mind slip into unconsciousness, then let her subconscious tackle the problems that overwhelmed her mind when it was alert. "Yes," she said, more to herself than to Boy this time, "I'm going to take a nap."

Baby Doll could feel Boy watching her as she closed her eyes and pretended to sleep.

"You owe me a favor, Baby Doll."

"I know, Boy. Trust me, I know."

He nodded, apparently satisfied, and then he lay down on the floor beside her bed.

Baby Doll listened to his breathing for a while, and then sneaked a peek at him through slitted eyelids. She was surprised to see that he had actually gone to sleep. She looked at the clock on her desk and read the numbers. *Three-nineteen*, she thought. *Where does the time go?*

She closed her eyes again and felt the rush of a million thoughts and worries cascading through her mind. When she opened her eyes again the clock read 4:41. Had she drifted off to sleep without knowing it? She rolled on her side and realized that her body ached with tiredness and sore muscles.

She felt the busyness of problem solving going on below the surface of her thinking and closed her eyes again. She decided another hour's sleep was definitely what she needed. Rest would be important.

She had much to do after dark tonight.

The world is full of mysteries, and all true mysteries are God's. The rest are just charades played by lesser beings and men.

—SOLACE THE LESSER
PHILOSOPHER AND HISTORIAN, 424 B.C.

Twenty

MONDAY, FEBRUARY 21. MIDNIGHT.

It is just after midnight when I awake. At first I'm not sure what day it is. Most times the dreaming sleep takes only minutes or a few hours, but other times it consumes days, weeks, or on rare occasions even months. It feels like I've been sleeping a long time, maybe even a week, but at this point it's hard to tell. I am disoriented, with images still flashing inside my mind as leftovers from the dreaming. They make no sense yet, but I see Baby Doll in them, and a balding man with a hardened face. A gun. A bottle. Snow. Too many fractured visions to understand right now. They will come together more clearly later. Right now, though, I just need to find out what day it is.

I am lying on a floor in a darkened room. I hear someone breathing above me and after a moment I remember that it is Baby Doll's breathing and this is Baby Doll's room. The world is silent around me, save for the lightly textured sound of Baby Doll's breath in the air. I feel a sense of urgency beginning to make itself known in the back of my mind, but it is still too far away to be clear, to be understood.

Wind whips at the window, almost as if a small bird is trying to break through the thick pane of glass and come in from the cold outside. I watch the red numerals on the digital clock blink and change until they read 1:11. The pieces fall into place in my head and I know it is now Monday, in the earliest moments of the day. Instinctively I almost rise to get my box from behind the ceiling tile, ready to dig into its contents again, to remember. It is the memories that are hard for me to keep over time. Just as my Tethers forget me, I find that I remember them less and less until eventually I don't remember them at all—and even forget that I forgot them. But in my box the memories stay safe, stay ready.

Simon never knew about my box. If he had, he would have hidden it away while I slept and laughed about it later. Or he might have held it carefully and made a secret place for me to keep it out of harm's way. You never knew with that boy.

Funny. As much as I disliked Simon, I find myself missing him now. He'd grown almost familiar to me, or at least his apartment had done so. In spite of Simon's weaknesses, he still kept a comfortable home.

I tried to help Simon sometimes, tried to keep him from hurting himself too much, at the very least. But he was young; he thought he was indestructible. And he certainly knew how to throw a party. But even now Simon fades in my mind. I can't picture his face anymore, although I still remember his voice, and his love/hate personality that displayed itself in unexpected kindnesses followed by careless cruelty. He broke a few hearts in that way. I tried to make him a better man. I don't know why, really, other than he was there, and I had time on my hands. But it didn't matter in the end. All that mattered was that he was too drunk to see the turn in the road, and too slow to react to the tree that loomed in the darkness before him.

Rest well, Simon. You deserve that at least.

Even though the memory of Simon is losing its color, I re-

member his apartment with a clarity that grips my mind in its intensity. If I close my eyes, I can almost see the simple layout of its two bedrooms, two bathrooms, kitchen, and entertainment room. The vaulted ceilings in the main living space were what gave me the idea to hide the box in the bathroom. In that kind of home, it was the spacious overhead in the main rooms that got a person's attention, not the fact that each bathroom was enclosed with lower, ten-foot ceilings, and water-resistant, overhead tiles. I put my box above the first tile just inside the door of Simon's guest bathroom. He never went in that room, and so it became my hiding place. My space for memories.

I feel a twinge of longing for that hiding place again, and then a twinge of suffering because I realize I can't remember everything that's in my box right now. And I remember why I feel that vague sense of urgency.

"I need to get my box from Simon's," I say out loud. "Before I forget."

In the darkness of the room I feel the movement before I hear it. I sit up on the floor and turn. My eyes follow the shadows, and I see the door slowly swing open. There is no light in the hallway, but the big man casts an unmistakable shadow without it.

He stands in the doorway, staring inside, but unwilling to take his Italian leather shoes across the threshold into Baby Doll's room. He still wears the suit he had on when he picked us up at the Police Services Center. He's obviously had a long day, yet he stands straight and tall as if he is ready to start another day all over again.

I watch him watching Baby Doll and wonder exactly what he is doing. He stares into the shadows with a patience that I've rarely seen, as if he is waiting for her to wake up and tell him all his suspicions are groundless, that she's just what she's always been, the little girl he protected and corrected as if she were his own.

His eyes stray from Baby Doll and I suddenly notice that Whitney Ellsworth's cell phone has fallen to the floor beside the bed. I look back at Maurits and see him squinting toward the dark spot on the floor. I wait for a blink and then flick my wrist over and snatch the cell off the carpet, tucking it quickly into my shirt, hoping that his subconscious mind didn't see enough of it to help him track it into my hand. If that happened, then he will soon think he sees it again on the floor and simply take it from me and place it where he thinks it is, thus finding it despite my actions.

He squints a little harder, cranes his neck just a bit. But his shoes never leave their place. After a moment, he appears to have forgotten what he saw.

In a quiet, serene movement his right hand reaches into the left inside pocket of his coat. I can't see what he has pulled out, but I remember the small pistol that was in his other coat pocket. I watch him finger the object for a moment and soon my suspicions are confirmed. It is indeed a .22 short minirevolver resting in the palm of his hand. He aims the gun through the doorway at the sleeping girl on the bed. His face is passive, reflective. No anger, no passion. Just thoughtful. After a moment, he relaxes his aim and begins toying with the tiny gun as if he is unaware that it is there. He casually opens the cylinder and dumps the five bullets into his hand. I watch him choose two of those bullets and use them to reload two chambers of his gun. The other three bullets go into an outside pocket on his suit coat. He spins the cylinder and then gently taps the barrel against his right cheek. I am fascinated by the face, still calm. Almost bored, except for the eyes, which are lit with a certain indescribable curiosity.

Suddenly his elbow stiffens and all too quickly the gun is aimed again at Baby Doll's sleeping head. I see Maurits's finger close quickly on the tiny trigger. No hesitation. Instinctively I move to block the bullet with my body, to do what I can to keep Baby Doll from being murdered in her sleep, but I am too slow, too caught off guard by the big man's intentions and the speed with which he carries them out.

Click.

The hammer on the minirevolver fires into place, but no bullet comes out. Maurits has hit an empty chamber. At least this time. Will he keep firing until it hits a live round?

He stands in the hallway a moment longer, staring, arm still outstretched. Then he nods to no one but himself. He retrieves the three bullets from his outside pocket and fully reloads the five shots of the minirevolver. Next he returns the little gun to its place inside the lining of his jacket. I listen in the darkness and am surprised to discover that he is not even breathing hard. He leans inside the doorway now, and whispers.

"Sleep well, Baby Doll. And don't you worry, Maurits is here."

He reaches over and gently closes the door. I hear his footsteps on the marble hallway outside, thinking that they are lighter than one would expect for such a big man. Another moment and the door at the end of the hall—the door to Charlie Murphy's old room—closes with a quiet thud.

The clock on the desk now reads 1:44. Baby Doll sleeps as though she has no worries in the world. But I know better.

"Wake up, Baby Doll," I say with a quiet push on her shoulder. "Wake up."

She opens her eyes, but doesn't speak.

"Come on, Baby," I say. "It's time to go."

Twenty-one

Am I dreaming?

Baby Doll felt slightly confused, but calm, in the darkness of her room. Boy stood over her, his face a mask of seriousness.

"Wake up," he said quietly. "Come on, Baby. It's time to go."

"Am I dreaming?"

She felt an insouciant detachment from herself, as if she were an observer more than a participant in this moment of her life. As if she were part of a dream that was about to reveal a deep dark secret that she really wanted to know.

Boy shook his head. "No." He leaned in close and searched her eyes. "Are you awake?"

With a chill, Baby Doll felt herself settle into reality once more. She nodded and sat up on the bed. A deep breath, and then her feet touched the floor beside her bed.

"I slept in my clothes." She wasn't sure why she said it out loud, but sometimes acknowledging the obvious helped to get her mind moving again. Then her eyes darted to the clock on her desk. "After midnight? Already?" Boy nodded. "Okay," she said. "It's still okay. Still enough time, but we have to be back here before six. The house staff starts their day at six-thirty, and we can't let them know we've been gone."

"It's not safe for you here, Baby Doll."

She rolled her eyes in spite of herself. "You just now figured that out, Boy?" She paused. "Sorry," she said. "Old habits die hard. I meant to say, yes, you're right. But for the time being it's safer in here than it is out there, generally speaking. So we have to be back in here, unnoticed, before Leticia knocks on my door and asks if I want breakfast in my room or at the table. Understand?"

Boy nodded, and Baby Doll stood up from the bed. She took a moment to stretch and realized that sleeping had felt good, restful. Except for the fact that her bladder was remarkably full, she felt energized and ready for action. Almost optimistic even, something that she hadn't felt for quite some time.

"Excuse me," she said quickly.

After returning from the bathroom, she took a minute to ponytail her hair and brush the last bits of sleep from her face. Boy stood impatiently waiting, obviously ready to leave. His appearance never seemed to change. *I wonder why he never smiles,* Baby Doll thought randomly. *Or if he even knows a good joke.* She almost laughed at the thought of such a serious person as Boy telling a joke, but she glimpsed his unease and decided against it. Still, she couldn't deny that she herself felt better than she had in weeks. Was it only because of a few hours of good sleep? Or was there something else? Her mind searched its memory, trying to peek into the subconscious pockets that hid things from her, but it was no use, so she turned her attention to the task at hand.

The night outside her window was glittered with stars, proof that the clouds that had dumped snow on them earlier in the day had moved on past and left cold, clear skies behind. "Must be below freezing out there," she muttered. "We'll have to find you a coat and some gloves."

Boy shook his head. "I don't need them anymore."

Baby Doll cocked her head and tried to process this information. "You sure looked like you needed them when I first saw you at the cemetery."

"I was hostage to a dying tether then. It left me exposed. But the tether now is warm and strong. As long as I'm in a healthy tether, the elements barely have an effect. I don't need a coat, not anymore." He looked meaningfully at her, and she knew he was thinking, *Unless you decide to abandon me again.* And she also knew that his refusing the offer of a coat was an act of faith—faith that she could indeed be trusted with his safety, just as she had decided to have faith that he was an angelic presence in her life right now. She worried briefly that one of them was going to be seriously disappointed before this was over.

Baby Doll nodded. "Okay. Good. Well, I will definitely need to bundle up." She looked at Boy, and then pulled a set of keys from the drawer in her desk. "Can you get to the garage? It's behind the kitchen, a large extension big enough to hold half a dozen cars. Do you remember passing it when we came in?"

He didn't respond at first, then he nodded abruptly. Baby Doll had the impression that he wasn't sure where the garage was, but that he would find it anyway.

"My car is the white Prius."

He nodded.

"Bring it around to the side door. I'll meet you there in ten minutes."

"Why don't you come with me now?"

"I have to time this just right. There are guards that patrol through here day and night. You can walk right past them, but I can't. I'll have to wait until the halls are clear and then go out through the servants' quarters. I'll meet you at the side door."

He hesitated. "I don't know."

"What?" she said, feeling a little frustrated at first. Then she realized the problem. "How tight is the tether now? Is it loose enough to cover this house?"

"I don't know. It's warming and stretching. But I don't know if it will go as far as the garage."

Baby Doll sighed. "Okay," she said. "We'll just have to go together. But at some point we're going to need to know how far the tether can stretch and still hold. We may need to separate a bit, especially when we finally track down Linda McDavid."

Boy looked thoughtful. "The sooner we can know, the better. You go ahead and sneak down to the garage," he said after a moment. "I'll meet you outside the side door in ten minutes. If I start to feel pain, I'll just follow behind you until I catch up. That should give us an idea of how strong the tether is. You're right. We might need to know pretty soon."

She nodded. "What's normal for something like this?"

He shrugged. "Sometimes it stays tight, no more than fifty feet or so. Other times it can stretch as far as a few hundred yards. At least once it expanded to half a mile, or just a little beyond that."

"Okay," she said. "Well, if I can go to the garage while you stay here, that will be at least a hundred yards, so that's a good test." She pointed out the window to the right. "Look for my car at that corner. When you see it, come down."

He nodded. Baby Doll turned toward the door and then stopped. She looked back at him questioningly. "I think I had a dream about you," she said. "Maybe more than one dream."

"Sometimes that happens," he said simply, "though usually not this early in the tether."

"Is it a good thing?"

"What did you dream?"

"I don't remember."

"Then I don't know."

"You're infuriating, you know that, right?" She said it with a smile. He just blinked in response. Baby Doll was tempted to roll her eyes in exasperation. Instead she impulsively asked, "You know any good knock-knock jokes?"

"What?"

"Nothing." She grinned to herself.

She opened the bedroom door and listened. There was no movement outside. She turned to Boy and nodded, then stepped into the hallway. The upstairs landing area was empty, so she moved quickly to the stairs. She caught movement out of the corner of her eye and saw one of Maurits's guards walking lazily across the entryway at the bottom of the steps. She held her breath. If he looked up, he would easily see her near the top of the staircase, but his was an easy, lonely existence. He didn't expect to see anything out of the ordinary, so he didn't see anything out of the ordinary. In a moment, he was gone, strolling his way toward the downstairs meeting rooms at the back of the house.

Baby Doll walked lightly down the rest of the steps into the main entryway. She stopped at the coat closet and pulled out her warmest, knee-length wool coat, along with gloves, a knitted hat, and a thick, soft scarf. She was tempted to add snow boots, but decided against it as her tennis shoes would be quieter. Just as she was about to shut the closet door, she heard a slight sound in the vaulted area above her, on the marble walkway that encircled the second floor. She backed into the closet and looked up. Near the railing up on the second floor, Maurits was pacing, his hand to his ear. She heard his muffled voice speaking into his palm and realized he must be speaking into a cell phone. She wondered where Ellsworth was at this moment, and then decided she didn't want to know after all.

Maurits nodded into the phone, eyes wandering randomly

around the hallway. She hoped she had remembered to close her bedroom door, or that Boy had at least closed it after she left. Maurits turned and looked out over the railing, and Baby Doll heard her name being spoken. ". . . touch Baby Doll. Bring him to me," he said quietly. "I'll deal with him in the morning." Maurits ended the call and turned back toward Charlie Murphy's old bedroom.

I might as well admit that it's Maurits's bedroom now, she thought.

She worried about what she'd just witnessed, and whom Maurits was talking about. She waited a minute longer to make sure Maurits was not going to come back out of his bedroom, and then stepped carefully into the hallway. *It must already be after one,* she fretted. *Time is running short.*

She made it the rest of the way to the garage without incident, and quietly pulled her Prius out of the fifth stall. A moment later, heat blasting on high, she slid the car into place beside the side door and waited. Boy appeared as if from nowhere and climbed into the passenger seat. She questioned him with her eyes.

"A small pull at one point, but no real problems."

"So you've got at least a hundred or so yards of room in the tether, is that right?"

He nodded.

"Okay, Boy," Baby Doll said, "I'm sick of owing you a favor. Tell me how to get to the house you so desperately need to return to."

"Simon's apartment."

"Right, Mr. Simon's apartment. I'm ready to take you there. Where is it?"

Boy looked truly lost for the first time since she'd met him. He opened his mouth as if to speak, and then closed it again. He squinted, turning his eyes up and to the left. Then he looked down at his lap. "I can't remember," he said. He put his face in his hands. "I can't remember." And then all was silent between them.

Baby Doll sat, dumbfounded, in the car. They had been idle long enough for the Prius's gas engine to shut off, though the electric part of the hybrid car was still on and the heater was still blasting lukewarm air toward her feet and face. "Well, we can't just sit here," she said finally. "One of Maurits's guards will see us."

She pressed the gas pedal and felt the Prius engine rumble softly back to life. They rolled quietly away from the house and down the long driveway. Boy was no longer crying—in fact, Baby Doll couldn't be certain that he had ever shed a tear at all. But he didn't speak, didn't give any instructions at all. Baby Doll felt awkward and alone, even with Boy sitting right next to her.

At the end of the driveway, she made a decision and turned left onto the main road.

Twenty-two

Baby Doll is driving through the darkened streets as if she knows where she is going, but I know that we are on a fool's errand.

Curse you, Simon. Is this your last practical joke? To hide your home from my memory, to leave me without a tether to what really matters?

The night is surprisingly bright, and the moon shines clearly above us. An occasional wind buffets the sides of the Prius, suggesting that more clouds may be blowing in before this night is over. The streets are deserted, and the streetlamps illumine acres and acres of empty asphalt and lonely concrete sidewalks. A police cruiser passes by us in the opposite direction, heading lazily toward, and then away from, us. Baby Doll lets off the gas pedal out of reflex, then breathes a sigh of relief when the cruiser continues on its way without noticing us.

She makes a left turn and the map in my head begins to fall into place.

"Where are we going?" I ask.

"Someplace to help you remember," she says.

At her words, I feel an eerie sense of déjà vu. Have I done this before? Have I seen it before? Pictures flicker in my head and I understand that this was part of my dream. I pause to look at Baby Doll, and remember more.

"I have seen you," I say.

"What's that supposed to mean?"

"In my dreams. I've seen you. You were younger."

"Yeah, well, I dreamed about you too, so we're even, I guess." There is a moment of silence and I see that she is trying to remember something as well. She glances over at me. "I feel like"—she hesitates—"I feel like my dream was more than a dream."

"It can happen," I say, "but usually not this soon. Never this soon."

"Alondra," she says suddenly. "Who is Alondra? Is that somebody?"

I feel my breath catch in my throat and the back of my jaw go slack. It seems almost profane for Baby Doll to speak her name, to dream her name. My face feels drained of blood.

"Boy?" she says. "Are you okay? Did I say something wrong?"

"No," I say.

"Who's Alondra? Is that somebody you know?"

"No."

I don't know why I lie. I don't know why I do a lot of things. Like when Simon stole a twenty-dollar bill from his grandmother back when he was fifteen. It would have been easy to let him get away with it. That scatterbrained woman wouldn't have noticed the money missing. And Simon certainly didn't care about the money; he just liked the thrill of the theft. But when I saw that his mother always checked the pockets of his jeans before putting his clothes in the wash, I took that twenty-dollar bill and put it where she would find it. "Where did you get this money?" she had asked her son. At first he tried to lie, but Simon always was such a bad liar. Soon the truth came out. He was punished by having to apologize and then mow his grandmother's lawn for free for an entire summer. He never stole again, though he was guilty of many other things.

I still don't know why I cared that he get caught, why it mattered to me that he become a better person. And I don't know why it matters to me now that Baby Doll not be allowed to know of Alondra.

"It must have been just a dream then," she says doubtfully. I nod, but I can't get my own dreams out of my head. They are beginning to fall into place. The dreams are always important. They tell me who my Tether is and who she might become. Yesterday's dreams finally organize themselves in my mind's eye, and now they start to make sense.

—

I see Baby Doll as a toddler, maybe two years old. A happy smile, a curious face. A woman plays with her in a bedroom full of toys and picture books. "Peekaboo! I see you!" Peals of laughter from the toddler every time the woman's hands snap away from her eyes. In the middle of the game a man enters. Maurits. Younger, fresher, but still a strong presence in any room.

"No," the woman says to Maurits. She sweeps the child into her lap and tries to continue the game, but her eyes are turning red at the edges and her hands are now shaking.

Maurits crosses his arms, but says nothing.

"No, Maurits. No. You can talk to him. You can tell him to change his mind."

"The police are suspicious," Maurits says. "It's either her father or the girl."

"He'll give up looking for her. He will. Her father doesn't know where she is."

The toddler is slapping at the woman's hands, but the game of peekaboo is over. She leans backward in her mother's lap and flashes an irresistible, upside-down grin at Maurits. The big man smiles in spite of himself.

"You know better," he says to the woman. "And besides, Charlie's already made the judgment. The orders with his seal went out last night. The kid's old man is probably dead already. And that means it's time for you to go. Charlie can't afford to be associated with you until the police pin his death on someone else. And they will. Charlie'll make sure of that."

The woman is crying now, but her voice is steady, even. "No, Maurits. You know I can't do it. I can't leave her again. I won't. She's my little Baby Doll."

"Bella Goll!" The child claps her hands at the sound of her own name.

The big man sighs. "Please," he says it without begging. "You got to go. Trust Maurits on this. I'll look after her myself. But you got to go. Before it's too late."

"No, Maurits. I shouldn't have to leave her behind. Not again. Not ever. Where's Charlie? I'll talk to him. I'll make him understand." She sets the toddler on the floor and puts a spinning toy in her hands. "Where is he, Maurits?" The woman is smaller, much smaller, but she looks him in the eye and doesn't flinch. Maurits lowers his head.

"Fine," the woman says. "Wait here, Baby Doll. Uncle Maurits will watch you for a few minutes while Mommy is on an errand." She looks at the big man and he nods reluctantly.

"Come here, Baby," he says. "Want to play horsey on Maurits's shoulders?" The toddler squeals with delight, apparently familiar with this particular game already.

The woman nods and strides out of the room. Maurits plays with the little girl until she is breathless with laughter. Then he sets her on the floor, sits down next to her, and opens a large, colorful picture book for her. She immediately crawls into his lap and slaps a palm against the first page. Maurits starts to read a little rhyme. The toddler points to something on the page and speaks a few words of gibberish. At that moment, a staccato explosion echoes down the hall, startling the little girl to tears. The big man sets the book down and holds her to his chest, rocking and soothing. She cries into his shoulder for a few minutes longer then settles with her ear to his chest and her thumb in her mouth. There are sounds of doors opening and closing, things being moved. Maurits stares out the doorway, an odd juxtaposition. This massive, bodyguard of a man gently cradling a newly orphaned girl.

"Don't you worry, Baby Doll," he whispers into the child's forehead. "Maurits is here."

—

"We're here," Baby Doll says to me now.

I feel the car slow and realize that she is turning the Prius into a near-empty parking lot. A place I recognize at once.

She pulls the car into a parking space on the side closest to the graves. From here I can see Simon's headstone waiting for me.

She turns to me. "Maybe out there"—she motions toward the cemetery—"where he's buried. Maybe something there will jog your memory enough to help us find his apartment."

She smiles, and for an instant I see a two-year-old girl laughing at a simple game of peekaboo.

"You may be right," I say.

"I'll wait for you here," she says.

I don't know why I say it. I don't know why I do a lot of things. "I'm sorry, Baby Doll."

To her credit she doesn't ask what I mean. She just nods. "I'll wait for you here," she says again, this time searching my eyes.

Twenty-three

Sitting in the car at the cemetery, watching Boy stare unflinchingly at the grave, Baby Doll felt the chill of the outdoors begin to seep in through the cracks of the Prius's sleek design lines. The streetlights in the parking lot gave off a pale, almost invisible glow, making Baby Doll feel as if she were sitting in the opening scenes of a cheesy horror movie where the boy and girl go off to an isolated spot and are then brutally murdered by some masked monster. In her mind's eye, she could even see the monster that would attack, and when it took off its mask, she wasn't surprised to see Charlie Murphy's face.

She shook the image from her mind and tried to concentrate on Boy standing out in the cold. Her eyes wandered and finally settled on the spot where she knew that Charles Franklin Murphy's dead body lay six feet underground.

"You're dead, Charlie," she said out loud. "You deserved to die. But I didn't deserve the guilt of being the one who caused your death."

The memories came unbidden, and she knew she would simply have to live them again. That was part of the consequences of what she'd done. She closed her eyes and let Charlie's face fill the space behind them.

—

"You don't stay Justice for more than sixteen years by being stupid," Charlie had said to her. His eyes looked wild and angry, peering at her across the desk in his bedroom. "You know what you get by being stupid, Baby Doll?"

She shook her head.

"You. You're what being stupid gets you."

He sat back heavily in his chair and waited.

"I—I don't know what you're talking about, Charlie."

There was silence between them. Then Charlie Murphy smiled. "I don't blame you, Baby Doll. Not really. I just wonder what you would do if your plan actually succeeded. If you actually did it."

Baby Doll started to stand, casting a glance at the bedroom door she'd closed behind her. "Charlie," she said calmly, "you're not well. Let me go find Maurits. Maybe you need your medicine."

Charlie slapped the Glock 36 pistol onto the desk between them. "Sit down, Baby." He kept his palm on the handle of the gun until she returned to her seat. Then he left the gun on the desk while he reached into a drawer. He rattled the pill bottle in his hand after removing it from the desk. "Got my medicine right here, Baby Doll. You gave it to me last week, remember? Fresh new prescription, straight from the pharmacist."

Baby Doll felt her blood pressure increase. She winced at the throbbing in her temples.

"I see you looking at my gun, Baby. I see what you're thinking, too. Been watching you for right near twenty years now. I know what you're thinking before you do."

"Of course you do, Charlie," she said quietly.

"Got to give you credit, though. Didn't occur to me that you knew enough about chemistry to do this." He shook the bottle of pills again.

"I didn't poison you, Charlie."

"Of course not," he said amiably. "Poison is something they could find in my bloodstream. Poison is something they could trace back to you eventually. That would be stupid."

Baby Doll squirmed uncomfortably in her seat. She wondered how much longer it would be before Maurits came in to save the day like he always did. Her eyes flicked involuntarily back to the gun on the desk.

Charlie grinned lasciviously. He lunged over and picked up the gun, leaning across the desk until the barrel pressed hard against Baby's chest. "Pow," he whispered mockingly. "It's that easy, Baby. You just aim and click."

"Is that how you do it, Charlie?" Her voice quivered in spite of her resolve. She felt moisture above her eyebrows and at the edges of her ears.

Charlie sagged in his chair, dropping the gun on the desk on his way back. "You don't know the half of it, Baby. Your mother didn't either. Shame what happened to her."

Baby Doll didn't say anything.

"You know, she thought you were the world. Thought the sun and moon were made just for you."

Baby Doll remained silent, calculating the distance to the gun, to the door, even to the large, shuttered windows behind Charlie's chair.

"She was stupid, Baby Doll," he spat. "Just like you."

She moved more quickly than she had really expected, even faster than she needed to. Charlie had barely blinked before Baby Doll had snatched the gun from between them and pressed it, hard, against his chest. "Who's stupid now, Charlie Murphy?"

He laughed, a mirthless tone that hung in the air and then dissipated into nothingness. "Still you, Baby Doll. Still you."

She leaned back and away from him, but kept the gun aimed at his heart. She itched to pull the trigger and then to run like mad out of this house, out of this town, to disappear from the face of the earth. But there was something she desperately needed to know before she could do that. Something this slug of a man could tell her. Should tell her.

"What's my name, Charlie?"

"Baby Doll. Same as it's always been."

"No, Charlie. What's my real name? The name my mother gave me."

"Aw, you know I can't tell you that."

"Why not, Charlie?" She spat her fury through gritted teeth. "Without my name, I'm forever lost, never home. Without my name, how do I even know who I am?"

"Home is overrated, Baby Doll." He chortled as if he'd made a private joke.

"What gave you the right to take my name away from me? Wasn't it enough that you took my mother? Why did you have to take my name as well?"

"Because, Baby Doll. I'm Charlie Murphy." There was heat in his voice now. "I'm the only Justice in this town. I say who lives and who dies. I say who goes missing and who gets found. And I say who gets a name and who doesn't. You're just an orphaned nothing. What right have you got to a name?"

"I'm a human being, Charlie. A person. You even call me your own daughter. That gives me the right to my name."

Charlie snorted dismissively. "You're not my blood, little girl. If you were, you'd have pulled that trigger a long time ago. Now go get me a bottle of Scotch and tell Maurits to come see me."

Baby Doll closed her eyes and squeezed hard. The kick on the

Glock popped against the flesh of her palm, pulling her arm backward and to the right. She heard Charlie laughing, a besotted choking sound that made her want to scream with anger.

"Whaddya know, Baby Doll? If you hadn't closed your eyes, you might have actually hit me after all." She opened her eyes and saw him inspecting the top metal hinge on one of the large shutters that covered a window to his right. "Right through the metal," he said admiringly, "and lodged in the wood frame. Gonna have to get that hinge replaced or this whole shutter could come crashing down." He turned back toward the girl, a new steel in his voice. "Now give me that Glock, Baby, and I'll show you how to kill somebody in cold blood."

Baby Doll felt herself frozen, felt helpless to resist when Charlie reached across the desk and pulled the gun from her trembling fingers.

—

A flicker in the shadows outside the Prius brought Baby Doll back to the present. Boy was walking toward the car, new purpose in his steps, new interest in his eyes. He opened the door to the driver's side, letting in an immediate impact of frigid night air from the outside.

"Let me drive," he said breathlessly.

Baby Doll slid over the console into the passenger seat. "Did you figure it out?"

Boy nodded. "Yes," he said. "I remember it. Simon's apartment isn't far from here."

"Okay, good," Baby Doll said. "Now please get in and shut the door. It's freezing out there."

Twenty-four

"Get in and shut the door. It's freezing out there."

I start to obey Baby Doll's request when something catches my eye.

"Come on, Boy," she says. Then she follows my gaze toward the entry of the parking lot. A silver BMW 335 rolls slowly across the entrance and then stops, blocking the exit.

Baby Doll swears softly. "Who is that clown?" She slides back over the console and into the driver's seat. "Get in, Boy. We might need to make a fast getaway. Well, at least as fast as a Prius can go, which isn't that fast. But we do what we can, right?"

I circle around the back of the car and then take the passenger seat. Baby Doll is looking in the rearview mirror, apparently trying to decide if she should risk going off the pavement to get out of the parking lot.

"Maurits?" I ask. She shakes her head.

"No. Maurits wouldn't be caught dead in a BMW." She is tapping her fingers on the steering wheel, thinking. "What's that guy doing now?"

I look through the back windshield and see the BMW back up a bit and then turn into the parking lot. It accelerates slightly and begins gliding in our direction, not fast, not slow, as if the driver of that car knows we won't try to make a run for it.

Baby Doll puts the Prius into reverse and starts to back up. "Maybe it's just some midnight mourner," she mutters to herself. "Maybe it has nothing to do with me. The whole world doesn't revolve around Baby Doll Murphy after all."

As soon as she begins backing, the BMW stops, waiting, now about two hundred feet away. Baby Doll swings the car around so that it faces the exit. The BMW doesn't move. In the colorless lamplight I can see the outline of the driver. He appears to be alone. Baby Doll hesitates, and then the driver's side window of the BMW slides open and a hand reaches out. There is a gun in the hand, and while it doesn't point directly at us, the firearm does wave back and forth in a definite "no, no, no!" gesture of reproof.

Baby Doll curses again, but she also puts the car back into park. "Guess we have an appointment tonight with a stranger after all."

After a moment, the BMW begins rolling again, and soon it pulls up next to us on the left side so that its driver's window is next to our driver's window. The face that grins toward Baby Doll is one we've both seen before. He waves the gun again, this time motioning for Baby Doll to roll down her window.

"Well, well," he says with a nod toward the cemetery behind us. There is an edge in his voice. "Whatcha doin', Baby Doll? Out paying your stepfather a little visit?"

"None of your business, Mr. Ellsworth," she responds, her voice more chilly than the air that now seeps into the interior of the car. "Shouldn't you be back at the house? What good is a bodyguard if he can't stay near the body he is to guard?"

Ellsworth opens the door of his car, leaving it slightly ajar as he leans into the window of the Prius. "Ah, you and I both know that was only a temporary assignment."

"Who are you working for, Ellsworth?"

"Please call me Whitney. I like it better that way."

"It's the Executive, isn't it? Victoria Fox sent you here to spy on Maurits."

"Big, dumb Maurits knows who I work for. But he didn't have a choice in the matter. The Executive, well, she convinced him to invite me in."

"So what do you want with me?" She mocks him with her eyes. "Think I'm pretty? Want to ask me out for a date? Sorry, I don't date morons—or Victoria Fox's flunkies."

Ellsworth reaches inside the Prius window and taps on the button to release the electric locks on the doors. "You should be nicer to me, Baby Doll," he says. "I could be good for you." He opens the back door and takes a seat behind the girl. "Roll up your window," he commands, "it's freezing out there."

"I like the cold," Baby says, refusing to turn around to face him. His left hand flies up and slaps her hard on the ear. She swears and leans out of his range.

"Hurts when your ears are cold like that, don't it, Baby Doll? I know a lot of ways to hurt a woman. Ways to make 'em feel good too."

"You just signed your death warrant, Whitney. Once Maurits finds out—"

"Your big, bad Maurits won't do nothing to me. He won't dare."

"And why is that?"

"Because Maurits knows something you don't know, little girl. I don't just work for Victoria Fox. I'm very special to her."

"Get out of my car, you 'special' creep."

"Make me."

Baby Doll doesn't respond.

"Didn't you wonder why your Maurits would let me in his house untouched, unharmed? Charlie Murphy never would have allowed that, even if it meant war between him and the Executive. No answers? Well, Victoria Fox is family to me. Sister to my mother."

"The Executive sent her baby nephew to spy on Maurits? How sweet."

"She sent me because she knew that Maurits would never lay a hand on me. Not with the current state of things. Not with his army half gone and new Executive Orders ready to declare martial law and consolidate—" He stops.

"Go on, big mouth. Tell me more. I'm just . . . a brainless little girl, remember?"

Whitney Ellsworth frowns, like he knows he let too much information spill from his lips.

"I believe you took something that belongs to me," he says.

"Oh, don't change the subject now, Whitney dear, you were just getting interesting."

He leans forward and presses the barrel of his gun against the corner of her lips. "You talk too much," he says. "That kind of thing can get a woman hurt." She doesn't respond. "That's better," he says. "I found this"—he jiggles his Kahr K-series gun against her cheek—"under your pillow."

"You were in my room?"

"Of course, Baby Doll. Nothing is off-limits to me. Now I had two of these guns before you stole them. Where's the other one?"

"That all you're looking for?"

Another frown. "You took my cell phone too?"

"Maybe. Seems to me that the information in the cell phone would be more valuable than your spare gun. Too bad I already gave it to Maurits."

Ellsworth retreats into the backseat, his eyes working like he's reading a map. I see him lay the gun on the seat beside him and reach toward his waistband.

"Now, Baby Doll," I say quickly. "Get out now."

She looks at me, surprised. She is too slow. Ellsworth has a large knife against her throat before she can move.

"Guns are nice," he says through gritted teeth, "but a knife is so much more personal, don't you think?"

She is frozen by the blade at her neck. One twitch and damage will be done.

"You should learn to show respect for your betters, Ms. Murphy. You never know when one might get tired of your mouth and decide to do something about it."

She says nothing, but I can see her eyes lock onto the rearview mirror. She is gauging distances, looking for any opportunity.

"I ought to slit your throat right here and leave you on top of Charlie Murphy's grave. What would your big, bad Maurits Girard think of that?"

Her eyes flick toward me. "Help me," she says.

"What, are you praying? I heard you went to Catholic school as a kid. Are you still a religious girl after all?"

I am keenly aware that I can't attack Whitney Ellsworth directly. His subconscious will lead him away from any harm by me—and it may cause him to slice the skin on Baby Doll's neck in the process. But I must do something. I feel compelled. I study his face and catch that lazy blink in his left eye. For most narcoleptics, all it takes is a sudden, unexpected emotional shift to trigger a cataplexy. Fear. Relief. Surprise. When something like that happens, the muscles involuntarily relax. Sometimes the victim is overcome by laughter or fear, and often the brain short-circuits and the victim will simply pass out where he or she stands. I've seen that Ellsworth is victim to cataplexy once al-

ready, but then he was unguarded, distracted, and at rest. It was easy for him to be surprised and overwhelmed. Now his adrenaline is flowing. And he is definitely on guard. Still, I must try something.

I reach across the car and press hard on the horn. The instantaneous wailing surprises even me. It sounds almost like an elk bugling of forlorn love. And it shatters the stillness of the night around us. The sudden alarm isn't enough to trigger a full narcoleptic attack, but it does startle Ellsworth enough to trick his mind into starting a cataplexic response.

He blinks hard and his arm involuntarily dips away from Baby Doll's throat. She doesn't hesitate this time. With her left hand she grabs his wrist and pushes the knife out and up. The force makes him release the knife and it falls. Then she rises up in her seat and swings backward, hard, with her right elbow, twisting and smashing the point deep into the side of her enemy's head. For all his faults, Charlie Murphy obviously taught Baby Doll how to defend herself at least. The combination of mild cataplexy and concussive force to Ellsworth's temple does the trick. He sags backward into the seat. Baby Doll rises to her knees and turns fully around in her seat. Once. Twice. Three times she pounds her left fist into his cheekbones until she's satisfied. Blood begins to drip from Ellsworth's lip and from a cut under his right eye.

"Grab that gun," Baby Doll says to me. "And where's the knife?" I reach over the console and pull the Kahr off the backseat but don't see where the knife is. Ellsworth groans and tries to mumble. I think I hear him say, "Where'd he come from?" But I don't feel any weakness in my tether, so I assume he must be dreaming.

Baby Doll swings open her car door and jumps onto the slick pavement outside. "Help me get him out," she says.

I open my door and work my way around the back of the Prius. When I pass the trunk and come around to the driver's side, I see Baby Doll has taken a step away from the car. Her hands are still wrapped into fists.

She looks angry.

Twenty-five

Baby Doll didn't like to admit it, but it almost felt good to smash Whitney Ellsworth in the face a few times. She just wished she were a little bit stronger so she could break something underneath that smirking grin. But she apparently hit hard enough because after only three punches the man's eyes rolled up into his head and he slumped over, unconscious, in the backseat.

"Grab that gun," she said to Boy. "And where's the knife?" Then she opened the driver's side door and spoke quickly over her shoulder. "Help me get him out." Boy responded immediately, opening the passenger door and exiting as well.

Baby Doll jumped onto the pavement and felt her shoes slip on the cold, icy surface. She quickly regained her footing and opened the back door to where Ellsworth had crumpled into the seat, half curled with his legs toward her. He didn't move. She reached in to pull him out by his legs. That was when he kicked her, ramming his heel deep into her left hip. The thickness of her wool coat protected her from any real damage, but he was still strong enough to push her back and away from the door with that kick.

In her peripheral vision, Baby Doll saw Boy swing around the corner by the trunk of the Prius and then stop. But she refused to take her eyes off Whitney Ellsworth at the moment.

"You hit pretty good for a girl," he said from inside the car. "But you need to learn when a guy is really hurt and when he's playing possum."

Ellsworth pulled himself out of the Prius and stood facing Baby Doll, the knife in his hand, poised and ready.

"Shoot him," Baby Doll said quietly. "Shoot him now. Don't kill him. Just hurt him. Shoot him in the leg or something. The knee. That should hurt enough."

"Who you talking to, Baby Doll?" Ellsworth said casually. "Ain't nobody here but you and me."

"Shoot. Him."

There was silence, and into that momentary quiet Boy said, "I can't."

"I don't feel any bullets, Baby Doll," Ellsworth said after a tentative glance around the parking lot and into the graveyard. He made an exaggerated motion as if checking himself for bullet wounds. "Guess that means your backup has backed up and run away."

"He's going to kill me."

"Yes," said Whitney Ellsworth, "I am going to kill you. But don't worry, I'll make it hurt a little bit first."

Baby Doll's face went white with rage. "I trusted you," she said. Boy said nothing, but he took one step, then another, toward the pair.

"Never trust anybody, that's what I always say, Baby Doll," said Ellsworth. He flicked his wrist, faster than expected, and Baby Doll felt the nick of the blade on the outside of her coat. "Look at that," he said happily. "This knife is sharp enough to cut through wool."

She looked down and saw a clear line cut into the sleeve of her overcoat. The knife hadn't gone all the way through the fabric, but it had gone through deeply enough to make it obvious that if Ellsworth put a little force behind it, the knife could definitely pierce the wool of her coat before digging into her flesh.

"Where's my cell phone, Baby Doll? And my other gun?"

"What's the matter? You can't go back home without them? Auntie Victoria might get mad at you?"

He flashed the knife toward her again, obviously comfortable with this weapon of choice. Baby Doll tried to block, but ended up getting sliced across the edge of her palm instead. Thankfully, it was so cold that she barely felt the pain.

"Where's my cell phone?"

"Gave it to Maurits," she lied. "What are you going to do about it?"

Whitney Ellsworth was angry now. "This," he said. He bent his head low and rammed his shoulder into Baby Doll, knocking her back against the BMW that was still parked beside her Prius. Then he turned his palm flat and shoved the blade of the knife toward her appendix. Baby Doll didn't want to, but she screamed anyway. Not long, or loud, but a desperate wail of someone who is very angry that things haven't quite gone her way.

At that moment she felt another shove and realized that Boy had finally stepped into the fray. But instead of attacking Ellsworth, he was pressing Baby Doll down onto her knees and placing himself between her and the knife. He stood with his back to Ellsworth, and Baby Doll could see pain light up his eyes when Ellsworth's knife penetrated his back just below the right side of his rib cage. He let out a grunt and a sigh, blinking as he stared loosely into Baby Doll's face.

Ellsworth twisted the knife, evidently enjoying the feel of flesh on his blade. Boy sagged to one knee and then pressed the Kahr pistol into Baby Doll's hand. A second later he crumpled onto the cold pavement of the cemetery parking lot.

Ellsworth pulled the knife out of Boy's back as he fell to the ground. "Liked that, did you?" he said with a sneer toward the girl. "Well, there's more where that came from." Then his face registered surprise that Baby Doll was unharmed by his first murderous thrust.

"What? How did you—"

"Big mistake you just made," Baby Doll said. "You see, I don't need Maurits to handle a little jimmie like you." From where she knelt, Ellsworth's left thigh was directly at eye level, so that's where she shot him first. He staggered backward and flopped to the ground like a fish caught on a hook. He was yelling, but his words were unintelligible. He grabbed at his leg as if it were on fire.

The bottom of Ellsworth's right foot swung into Baby Doll's vision, so she shot him there next. He screamed and panted and writhed on the ground. Baby Doll finally stood and walked over to where her would-be attacker now groaned and bled.

"You got anything more to say to me?" she said fiercely.

He shook his head and squeezed his eyes tight, gasping and moaning. Baby Doll used the barrel of the Kahr to pry open his teeth and stuff the business end of the gun in his mouth. She watched with a surreal detachment as his eyes opened wide in horror. "Pow," she said. "Just aim and click. That's all it takes."

Ellsworth's frame went rigid and she watched him pass out on the ground before her. She pulled the gun from his mouth and realized with a shake that she had just come millimeters away from literally blowing a man's brains out. If he hadn't passed out first, she realized, she might have actually pulled that trigger one last time and ended Whitney Ellsworth's miserable life. She dropped the gun onto the cold pavement and stared at it.

And then she started crying. She sat down on the ground beside her Prius and let the tears stream and sting down her cheeks, hating the fact that it gave her a headache and clogged up her nose, but knowing that she'd almost killed a man—that she'd wanted to kill him—and wondering what kind of evil lived deep inside of her that she could hurt someone the same way that Charlie Murphy might have hurt someone. What had she become?

Boy groaned, rolled, and pulled himself to his knees. She was only vaguely aware that she saw him ball up the bottom of his shirt and press it painfully into the spot where the knife had penetrated his skin. When he shuffled across the ground to sit next to her, she finally decided it was time to stop crying. She wiped her eyes with her hands and cleaned her nose on the sleeve of her wool coat.

"It was self-defense," Boy said. "He would have killed you. It's not your fault. Not this time."

She nodded. "I know. But . . ." She tried to clear her head, order her thoughts. "I'm afraid of being a person who's able to do what I just did."

"It was self-defense."

She felt him sag next to her and realized there was a more pressing matter at the moment.

"What do we do now, Boy? Can they help you at a hospital?"

He shook his head. "No. I need to sleep. To heal."

She slipped the scarf from her neck, stuffed it into her knit cap, and balled up the bundle, reaching behind him to press it against the wound. He grimaced, but accepted the makeshift bandage. "Sleep heals you, doesn't it? Should we go home? Can you make it back to my room?"

He shook his head again. "Simon's," he said.

Baby Doll leaned her head back against the side of the car. "You can't be serious. In your condition? And we have the problem of this stupid Ellsworth to deal with."

As if on cue, Victoria Fox's nephew stirred, groaned, and rolled into a fetal position.

Boy pulled himself up against the car. He reached into a pocket and produced Ellsworth's cell phone. "Call 911," he said. "They'll get to him before he freezes to death. And let's go to Simon's. Now. Before I forget again." Baby Doll didn't move. Boy looked down at her, locking her eyes onto his. "Please," he said.

Baby Doll sighed. "All right. But you better let me drive."

Twenty-six

The right side of my body feels frozen, yet it burns with an unrelenting fire that seeps through the cold. I feel light-headed from a loss of blood, but with Baby Doll's scarf pressed against the knife wound, I know that soon my blood will start to congeal and oxygen will begin to return to my veins.

I need to sleep, to let the darkness work its healing. But first I must go to Simon's and finally retrieve my box. I can see his place in my mind's eye now. The numbers are erased, and the street signs are blank, but I know where it is, I know how to get there. I also know that if I sleep before I lead Baby Doll to Simon's, the details of that memory will fade. When I awake, even a trip back to Simon's grave may not be enough to bring back the sense of place I have right now.

Baby Doll taps buttons on Ellsworth's cell, then instead of speaking into it she holds it close to the man's mouth, capturing his ragged breathing in the mouthpiece. That apparently isn't enough, so she kicks him carelessly in the ribs and he groans. Satisfied that someone on the other end of the phone heard that, she drops the cell onto his chest, leaving the connection open. She motions for me to be silent, then reaches out to help me stand. The back door on the driver's side of the Prius still stands open from when Whitney Ellsworth made his exit, so she points me in that direction and clumsily lays me into the backseat. I think I should be of more help in this effort, but it seems that the effort it takes to remain conscious has sapped me of strength. Still, in the end, I am inside the car, lying across the backseat. Baby Doll leans in long enough to adjust the scarf and press it into place against the wound. Then she rolls me backward on it so that it will stay in place while we drive.

"Sorry about the blood," I mumble. This car was so clean when we first got inside earlier this night.

She puts a finger to her lips, motioning for quiet. Then she gets behind the wheel. The hybrid engine is still on, waiting in silence for someone to press the accelerator to make it move. In seconds we are once again on the road outside the cemetery, driving away from the wounded man groveling on the pavement there.

"Okay," she says, "we can talk now."

"No one can hear me besides you," I say. "Why the need for silence before?"

She smiles ruefully. "You know, I forgot that. I was so caught up in getting out of there that I forgot that no one could hear you. But it was important for me to be quiet."

"Why?"

"Because I didn't call 911. I called Victoria Fox. I saw her phone number in Ellsworth's address book and I figured it would send a message if she got a distress call from her favorite nephew at four-thirty in the morning. They'll track his cell phone quickly enough. He should get picked up within the next twenty minutes or so—and he'll have some answering to do when he comes to. Maybe even before the surgery to remove the bullets from his legs."

"Why not just call 911 and let emergency crews pick him up?"

Baby Doll shook her head. "People like us don't use hospitals, Boy. We keep our own doctors on retainer. Can't have nosy nurses asking why you happen to have a bullet in your thigh. If the Executive's people pick up Ellsworth, then the police stay out of the picture. And if the police stay out of the picture, then no one will believe that Ellsworth got himself shot up by a little girl who was home in bed all night at Charlie Murphy's mansion. Understand?"

I nod, but she's not looking back at me, so I say, "Yes," and feel darkness tugging at my consciousness.

She looks at the clock on the dashboard. "It's already almost five, Boy. We have to be safely hidden back in my room before six or the household staff will get suspicious. Are you sure we can't wait to go to Simon's? We can head over there right after breakfast. I can skip classes today. It's only a few extra hours. Let me take you home so you can sleep and heal."

"No," I say, and to show I am serious, I lurch into a sitting position in the backseat of the car. I scan the surroundings and immediately know where we are. "It's not far," I say. "But you are heading in the wrong direction."

I see her hesitate for a second, and then make a decision. The street is deserted, so she whips the Prius into a U-turn and begins driving the opposite way down the road.

"Turn right at the corner where there is a bank and a supermarket," I instruct.

"What street is that?" she asks.

"I don't know," I say. "I can't see the names or the numbers. But I know where it is."

She starts to ask a question, then stops herself, and we drive in silence for a while. At the Wells Fargo Bank, she makes a right turn and then looks questioningly at me in the rearview mirror. I close my eyes to help me see.

"It's an apartment complex. A large one. On this road. On the left side of the road. Not far. Turn into the second entrance."

"Okay," she says, and I feel the car shift to the left lane. "Boy," she says. At least I think she says it. My mind is beginning to wander. I think I hear a clock ticking somewhere.

"Boy!"

My eyes snap open. Baby Doll has pulled the car off to the side of the road, and now she is peering at me over the backseat. When did that happen?

"Boy," she says fiercely, "you can't fall asleep. Not yet. If you fall asleep, we're done with this errand and I'm going back home. You understand?"

I nod.

"Tell you what," she says as she eases the car back on to the road. "We'll talk the rest of the way. That will help you stay awake."

"Yes," I say. My speech seems thick; my tongue feels swollen.

"Back at the cemetery," she says, "why didn't you just shoot Ellsworth? Wouldn't that have been easier than taking a knife to the ribs?"

"I couldn't."

"You're not big on explanations, are you, Boy? He couldn't see you. Didn't even know you were there. Why not shoot him?"

"He would have accommodated me."

She looks back over her shoulder at me, a look of confusion on her face.

"Remember the holding cell? Same thing. His conscious mind is unaware of me," I say, "but his unconscious mind senses enough of me to avoid direct contact if possible. He can't see me, but he can accommodate me."

"I still don't get it," she says.

I shake my head and close my eyes, hearing Alondra's voice in the question.

"Boy!"

I open my eyes again. My thoughts feel muddied and brown. "Sorry, Alondra," I say. "You remember. You know, like the landlady in the kitchen. It's like that."

Baby Doll raises her eyebrows toward me in the mirror. Why doesn't she remember the kitchen? I remember it.

"Tell me again about the landlady in the kitchen," she says slowly. "Help me remember. It's kind of, um, fuzzy in my brain."

And so I remind her of when we peeled potatoes with Mrs. Snelling. The memory brings a smile to my face.

"Boy," she says when I am finished, "when did you lose yourself?" She says it softly, like she is speaking in a dream.

"I can't remember," I say. I think we are getting close to Simon's place now.

"I think if you could remember, you wouldn't be lost anymore."

"Remember what?"

"Who you are, Boy," Baby Doll says quietly. "And why you are here."

"I don't know," I say. Why does my head feel like it's floating in a river?

"Maybe I can help you, Boy. Maybe I can find you."

I don't think she expects an answer. Even if she did, I wouldn't have one to give. We drive in silence and I wonder if I am dreaming.

"Here," I say suddenly, feeling the fog lift a bit at the sight of Simon's apartment complex.

"I see it," she says, dutifully turning in at the second entrance on the left. We drive back to the third building. I feel a warmth at being so close again to my box.

"Park in the visitor's space in front of that building," I say. After she's maneuvered the car into place, I point toward a window. "There," I say. "Go up the patio stairs to the landing area. On the left side of the landing is a glass-enclosed fire extinguisher and alarm. The lock on the enclosure is broken. Open the glass panel and lift the fire extinguisher. There's a spare key under there."

I sense the darkness coming in earnest now. A comfortable presence that promises warmth and health, like a quiet room where solitude is a welcome companion.

"Boy," she says. "What are you talking about? I can't just break into somebody's apartment at five in the morning."

"A small box is above the first ceiling tile in the guest bathroom. First floor."

"Come on, I'll help you up the stairs and you can go in. No one will even know you are there."

"You can do it, Alondra," I say. "I'm counting on you this time."

"Boy." There is an edge of panic in Alondra's voice. "Don't go to sleep. Not yet, Boy! Just a few more minutes."

"I trust you," I say.

The darkness begins to swirl around me, wrapping me in its embrace.

"Boy!"

I can no longer tell if my eyes are open or shut. I have a feeling that I have forgotten to tell Alondra something, or that I may have told her too much, but I can't be sure.

"Boy!"

We will sort it out after.

"Boy!"

Right now I need to sleep.

To heal.

Twenty-seven

"You can do it, Alondra," Boy said. "I'm counting on you this time."

Baby Doll felt herself beginning to panic. So there *was* someone named Alondra; she had dreamed that name. But now Boy seemed to be confusing her with this mysterious Alondra person—and he expected her to break into this apartment and get his box?

"Boy," Baby Doll said. "Don't go to sleep. Not yet, Boy! Just a few more minutes."

"I trust you," he said.

"Boy! Boy!" Baby Doll bit her lip in frustration. It occurred to her that he had told her where to find the key, and even where to locate the box, but he had neglected to tell her which apartment she was supposed to break into.

"Boy!"

It was no use. He was so still that Baby Doll worried at first that he might be dead. Then she remembered that for Boy, death was something imaginary. *Dabit deus his quoque finem,* she quoted absently to herself. *God will bring an end to this.* Apparently that little maxim didn't apply to Boy.

She watched his chest rise and fall lightly in rhythm. She rose to her knees and turned around to face him in the backseat. She reached over and gently laid him down so that his head rested—in what she hoped was a comfortable way—on the cushion of the seat. In doing that, she saw that the blood on his back had started to congeal, and that it was now sealing her scarf to his body. She hesitated for a moment, and then decided it would be better to pull the scarf away from the wound now while it was still soft than to wait until it had fully adhered to the wound and thus bearing the risk of reopening it if she removed the scarf later. She reached down and began to pull, feeling the scarf tear parts of skin away from the wound, wincing at the sound and feel of the removal, but grateful that Boy didn't wake up through any part of the procedure. When she was done, she saw a piece of his shirt was also stuffed inside the congealing wound, so she repeated the process again until the wound was fully open to the air. She was surprised that a small slit like that could do so much damage and disgorge so much blood. The area was raw and red and oozing, and she considered pressing the scarf back into it, but in the end decided that while it was oozing, blood wasn't flowing from the wound like it had been earlier. She decided to leave it open and hope that the air would hasten the drying process and help it to congeal better.

She looked back at the clock on the dashboard. It was now 5:17. They were a good half hour away from Charlie Murphy's house—well, from Maurits's house now. If this was going to work, she needed to break into that apartment and get back to the car within the next thirteen minutes. She considered aborting the plan, going home right now, and then bringing Boy back here later in the day. After all, now she knew where it was, so there was no longer a risk that Boy's unreliable memory cells would prevent them from coming back.

But she was here. And whatever was in that box was apparently the most important thing in Boy's existence.

She sighed. "Great," she said to herself. "Now I've only got twelve minutes to get the job done."

She got out of the car, locking all the doors out of habit, and took a moment to look up the half-dozen patio stairs that led to the landing area. The darkness of the night made it hard to believe that the sun would rise before long. She wasn't sure what Simon had done for a living, but this was obviously one of the nicer apartment complexes in the area. From what she could tell, each of the residences appeared to be more like town homes than classic apartments. In fact, it looked as though each of the apartments in this building were two-story homes, though the building was large enough to accommodate eight full apartments. Behind her a similarly styled building seemed to have been split into two levels, creating a set of sixteen apartments that each took only one floor.

Baby Doll walked up the steps to the landing and, just as Boy had said, saw the glass-enclosed fire extinguisher and alarm. She tested it and found it to be unlocked, also as predicted. But the area beneath the fire extinguisher was empty.

Baby Doll glanced back at the Prius. She desperately wanted to leave, but something inside her couldn't face the idea of disappointing Boy right now. She turned back to the enclosure and lifted the fire extinguisher again. Still nothing. And then, unexpectedly, a key fell off the bottom of the extinguisher and clattered inside the enclosure.

"It was frozen to the bottom!" she muttered to herself. She inspected the bottom of the extinguisher and saw crystals of ice where the key had only seconds before been stuck to the metal canister. Then she turned and looked at the eight doors that faced her on the landing. She checked the key for markings, hoping it had a number or letter or something stamped on it to give a clue as to which apartment it belonged, but all it revealed was the name of a locksmith company that apparently made keys for this complex. She sighed again and watched the white mist of her breath fill the air in front of her.

"Here goes nothing," she said.

The key turned on the lock of the fifth door she tried, which also turned out to be the door closest to where she had parked. "Should have tried this one first," she mumbled to herself. When she entered the apartment she was relieved to discover it had been emptied out; there was no furniture in the main room and, she assumed, that meant there was no one sleeping in a bed upstairs either. She reached to turn on a light and then stopped. A light in a supposedly empty apartment would raise suspicion, especially if it was connected with an unfamiliar Prius parked out front. She made her way into the shadowed apartment, willing her eyes to adjust to the darkness until she'd reached the center of the main room. Assuming the bathroom would be near a "water wall" where the plumbing ran behind the drywall, she worked her way toward the kitchen. She found the bathroom in a little hallway close by, situated between the kitchen and the laundry room. In here there were no windows, so she took a chance and flicked on the switch. The bright light in the bathroom almost made her eyes water, but she was glad to be able to see clearly again. Above the door, the ceiling tile looked as though it had never been disturbed. For an instant, she wondered if she had broken into the wrong apartment, or if Boy had been mistaken about where the box was hidden. Then she put her reservations aside and climbed on top of the counter beside the sink.

She had to put one foot in the bowl of the sink and lean at an awkward angle to get the ceiling tile out, but when she had done so, she located what she had come to find.

It was not a large box—it fit in her hand—and was certainly

not big enough to hold much in the way of treasure. The wood was a deep red mahogany. It was covered in filigreed metal and decorative buckles, and it looked very much like an antique. Baby Doll wondered randomly what those guys on *Antiques Roadshow* would say about it. It was not heavy, but Baby Doll could feel items shifting inside the box whenever she turned it in her hands. It also gave off a light scent of perfume or potpourri.

"Strange," she said aloud to herself. "There's no crease anywhere on this box. Nothing to indicate where, or even if, it opens."

She set the box on the counter and hopped down to the floor. "Sorry, Simon," she said out loud. "Gonna have to leave your bathroom a mess if I'm going to get back to the house in time."

She flipped off the light and made her way back to the front door. The box felt cool and mysterious in her hands, and she resisted an urge to flick on a light and give it another look. She made a split-second decision and tossed the apartment key onto a counter in the kitchen. "No time to return that to the fire extinguisher," she said, "and I doubt Simon will be needing a spare key anymore."

A moment later she was outside, closing the door behind her and spying her car waiting patiently in the parking lot where she'd left it.

"Don't believe I recognize you," a voice behind her said. She jumped in spite of herself, turning to find a man dressed warmly in padded mechanic's overalls and wearing a thick knit cap that covered most of his head and ears.

"Oh," Baby Doll said, trying to act natural. "Right. Just visiting a friend."

The man raised an eyebrow. "You're a friend of Simon's?" He obviously didn't believe that was the case.

"Was," Baby Doll said quickly. "Was a friend of Simon's." She tried to look mournful. "Tragedy what happened to him."

The man softened a bit. "Yeah. He was so young." He tilted his head. "How did you know Simon?"

"Girlfriend," she said. "Left my jewelry box last time I was here, and then what with the funeral and all, I never had a chance to come back and get it."

Suspicion raised itself in the man's eyes again. "Thought Simon's girl was blond."

Baby Doll nodded, mind racing. "Yeah," she said. "Turns out Simon liked both blondes and brunettes." She shrugged and dimpled. "I met the 'other woman' at the funeral, but by then Simon was already gone and I figured it was no good to let that ruin my memories of him." She sighed and almost felt sincere. "We had some good times. That's what I decided to remember."

"So Simon gave you a key?"

She nodded.

The man seemed to accept the lie. "Well, you'll probably need to return that to the management office. I understand they've already rented this apartment. Some guy is supposed to move in next week."

"Okay, will do," she said.

He gave her an almost-friendly smile. "Well, I've got to get to work." He turned to leave, and then paused and turned back. "I'm sorry for your loss," he said halfheartedly. "Simon seemed like a good kid."

"Thank you," she said. She waited until the man had disappeared around the corner before practically running to her car. She dove into the driver's seat, tossing the box on the passenger seat at the same time. A moment later she turned out of the apartment complex and swore softly.

"Five forty-one," she said. "Let's hope the household staff sleeps in today."

Twenty-eight

It was 6:09 when Baby Doll pulled her Prius back into its stall in the garage at Charlie's mansion. Boy still slept, unmoving, in the backseat. The wound on his back had dried up some, but still looked like a dangerous mess. She wondered how long he had to sleep before healing would happen. At the jail, it had happened overnight—and he'd been in much worse condition. She was surprised, and worried, that no real signs of healing could be seen yet. She wondered if her distance from him while she was in Simon's apartment had slowed the healing process. She knew that his tether could stretch to about a hundred yards now, but she didn't know if stretching it weakened the tether enough to hinder his sleep-healing.

She looked back at the sleeping Boy and wondered if it was going to be okay to leave him in the car while she sneaked back into her room. She also hoped that none of the household staff would be early this morning. They were expected to start their day at six-thirty, particularly the kitchen staff.

Baby Doll picked up Boy's box from the passenger seat beside her. It still felt cool to the touch, smooth and expensive. "What kind of treasures are hidden inside you?" she said to it. She turned it over and again marveled that it had no opening anywhere, not even a line or crease to indicate where it had been sealed together. It looked as if it were a complete, solid block of wood. But the shifting contents gave away the secret that it was hollow, and that someone had put something inside. That also meant someone could take the contents out of the box. She looked at it for a moment, something tickling at the edges of her reasoning.

"A puzzle box," she said at last. "But not a Chinese or Japanese puzzle box like you'd expect. Some other kind. Italian maybe? Or American?"

She caught herself, realizing that she was wasting valuable minutes with this curious box when she should be sneaking back to her room. But could she leave Boy in this state? Would the tether be tighter since he was injured? She hesitated. As if on cue, the door to the garage opened and Stanley Lieber walked in, heading straight for Maurits's long black Lexus sedan.

Baby Doll felt weak, caught between the impulse to slink down in her seat and hide, or to turn on the car and gun it out of the garage. She pulled the lever on the left side of the driver's seat and reclined the chair to an almost sleeping position, putting her out of view, she hoped, but also making her unable to see what Stanley was doing.

She could hear him open a door, then pop the trunk on Maurits's car. When the trunk didn't shut right away, she figured Stanley was doing a morning polish on the windows and seats. *Figures*, she thought, *Stanley always did the best job possible, which is why Charlie kept him around.*

She worried for a moment that her chair was probably pressing against Boy's legs, but that couldn't be helped right now. She watched the clock on her dashboard tick off one minute, then another, and still Stanley busied himself with his work.

If anyone knows I was out of the house last night, she thought, *then I can easily be tied to the shooting of Whitney Ells-*

worth. My only alibi is that I was home, in bed, when he was shot. That's the only alibi Maurits will believe—and he will demand that Victoria Fox believe it as well.

She heard the trunk close on Maurits's car. It was now 6:27. *Too late,* she thought. *Somebody is surely in the kitchen by now. How am I supposed to get by Stanley in the garage as well as the cook in the kitchen?* To make matters worse, Baby Doll next heard Stanley open the hood of the Lexus, apparently ready to check the car's fluids before taking it out for the day's work. She heard him whistle and rolled her eyes. He was whistling the same little fifteen notes of Disney's "It's a Small World" that played as the ring tone on his cell phone.

Then she had an idea.

Reaching into her inside coat pocket she pulled out the new cell phone that Maurits had given her. She was grateful to see he had indeed had her entire address book transferred over into this new phone. She pressed a few buttons, and then waited. A moment later she heard "It's a Small World" chirping from across the garage.

Stanley took a moment to answer, so Baby Doll figured he was probably drying his hands and then checking the caller ID before responding to the cell. The warmth in his voice proved that to be true.

"Good morning," he said in a loud and friendly voice. "That you, Baby Doll?"

She covered her mouth a bit. She wanted Stanley to just hear her voice in the cell phone, and not from across the garage.

"Hey, Stanley," she said quietly. "How can you be so cheerful this early in the morning?"

"Just happy to be here, Baby Doll. Everything okay?"

"Yeah."

"Where are you?"

Baby Doll froze. Did he know she was not in her room? "Uh, I'm still in bed, Stanley." Then, "Where are you?"

"Down in the garage getting ready for the day. Don't want to be late for your uncle Maurits, you know."

Uncle Maurits. That still didn't sound right to Baby Doll's ears.

"Great," she said. "Hey, listen, I don't have to get up for another hour, but I just started thinking about it, and I can't remember where I put my keys last night."

She heard footsteps. "Want me to check and see if you left them in your car?" Stanley said.

"No," she said, probably too quickly. "No, I remember bringing them inside." The footsteps stopped. "I think I went in through the kitchen, and I may have left them in there. Or else they're in my coat pocket. Lost my purse, and now I can't keep track of anything."

"Want me to pop into the kitchen and look around for them there?"

"Could you, Stanley? That would be great, if you have time."

"Sure thing, Baby. No problem. Let me just finish checking the oil on your uncle Maurits's car and I'll go look. If they're there, do you want me to bring them up to you?"

"No." Again, she said it too quickly. "Just, um, call me and tell me where they are. I'll get them after I take a shower."

"Okay, Baby Doll."

"Thanks, Stanley. Bye."

She shut off her cell and waited. She could hear Stanley whistling again, and then after a moment she heard the hood drop on Maurits's Lexus. She dared a peek out the window of her Prius and saw Stanley's back as he headed out of the garage toward the kitchen. As soon as he disappeared, she opened the door to her car. She gave one last look at Boy and decided he would have to be okay without her, at least for the time being. She hoped that his tether was still loose enough to stretch up to her room and decided she had to take the chance. At the last minute, she reached across the seat and picked up the box again. She wasn't sure why she wanted to take it, why she didn't just leave it with Boy, but something about it made her insatiably curious. She convinced herself she was protecting it for him, and then she quickly sneaked out of the garage.

She sprinted around the corner of the house until she reached the side entrance. She hesitated long enough to make sure no one was nearby, then she entered the house and made her way to the second level, careful to walk softly on the marble flooring. At the end of the hall, she could see the oak door to Charlie's old room was open, but there was no guard standing outside of it. She held her breath and skittered across the floor to her room, never taking her eyes off the entrance to Charlie's. At long last, she reached her own door, slipping silently through it. She'd made it.

The moment she'd softly clicked the door to her bedroom shut, her cell phone rang. She answered on the first ring.

"Hello?"

"Hiya, Baby Doll." Stanley's friendly voice seemed loud in the echo of the earpiece.

"Any luck, Stanley?" she said breathlessly. She quietly set Boy's box on the desk in her room.

"Nope. Sorry, Baby. It looks like your keys are somewhere else."

"Okay, thanks for looking," she said.

"Want me to check the coat closet?"

She looked at the wool coat she was still wearing, with one sleeve cut almost all the way through. "No," she said quickly. "I, uh, I've got my coat in my room anyway. Here, I'll get my lazy self out of bed and check it myself." She went over and sat on the bed to make it sound like she was getting up, then rustled her clothes to imitate digging in her pockets, in case Stanley could hear that far. "Yep, here they are, Stanley," she said after a minute. "Must have stuck them in my coat pocket and forgotten about it. Sorry for the trouble."

"No trouble, Baby," he said. "Glad you found them."

"Okay, thanks, Stanley. I'll talk to you later."

"Baby?" he said.

"Yeah?"

"I'm getting closer on that project you gave me."

Baby Doll was suddenly interested. "McDavid?" she said.

"Yep. Don't have a home address yet, but I did find out where she spends most of her days."

"That's great, Stanley. Where is she?"

"Well, give me another day or so, and I should be able to get you right to her front door."

"What have you got right now? Maybe that's enough."

There was a slight hesitation. "Well, apparently she spends a lot of time at Donenfeld's Pub and Entertainment. Runs a little side business with a few girls there."

"Okay, great. Thanks, Stanley."

"Now, Baby," he said, "don't go running off there by yourself. Donenfeld's is over in the Legislator's side of town. Two weeks ago your name might have been enough to keep you out of trouble. But, well, things are a little tense right now. You might not have the same protection you're used to, if you know what I mean."

"Not to worry, Stanley. I'll be careful."

"Okay, Baby Doll. I think that Johnny Tanaka could probably go with you. You want me to call him for you?"

"No, thanks, Stanley. I'll be fine. I promise."

"Okay. You want me to call you when I get a home address for McDavid? Might be safer to look her up there instead of at a public place like Donenfeld's."

"Um, yeah. That'll be great. Now I'm going to try to grab another half hour of sleep before I have to get up. Thanks for everything, Stanley."

"Anything for you, Baby Doll. Sleep tight."

"Bye."

She hung up the cell phone and felt her heart racing. Donenfeld's. Not the best part of the city, but it had been a long time since Baby Doll was afraid to go anywhere. And besides, her own bedroom was a dangerous place to be right now.

She took off her coat, peeled off her shoes, and then lay down on the bed.

"You'd better wake up soon, Boy," she whispered to the ceiling, "because now you owe me a favor."

Twenty-nine

Baby Doll stared at the ceiling until her breathing settled into a normal, relaxed state. She wondered again how long Boy would have to sleep before his body healed itself. Time was running short, and she knew she couldn't wait too long before going after Linda McDavid and Charlie Murphy's old ring.

She felt restful, but not sleepy, probably because she'd slept away most of the day yesterday before she and Boy had gone on their midnight run to Simon's apartment. She looked across the room toward the box that now sat curiously on her desk. She was tempted to get up and inspect it more, to see if she could get it to reveal any of its secrets. But she decided against it for the moment. She had to figure out what she was going to do about Linda McDavid and that blasted ring.

She heard a loud noise down the hall—a door slamming perhaps? She strained her ears but didn't hear anything else coming from Charlie Murphy's old room. She closed her eyes and saw his face again.

"Leave me alone, Charlie," she whispered. "You're dead and gone now. Why won't you just leave me alone?"

She opened her eyes, but Charlie's voice still rang in her ears until she finally gave in to the remembering.

—

"Whaddya know, Baby Doll? If you hadn't closed your eyes, you might have actually hit me after all," Charlie Murphy said. "Now give me that Glock, Baby, and I'll show you how to kill somebody in cold blood."

Baby Doll felt herself frozen, felt helpless to resist when Charlie pulled the gun from her trembling fingers. She noticed, though, that his hand was also shaking just a bit when it wrapped itself around the handle of the gun.

"Come here, Baby," he said. "I want to show you something."

He walked away from his desk and toward the large bed at the other end of the room. His gait was slurred like speech, not quite stumbling, but not confident and precise either. Baby Doll felt almost insulted that he could so easily turn his back on her, even after she had just tried to put a bullet through his heart. But she followed him nonetheless. One didn't often disobey Charlie Murphy.

A large bookcase stood opposite the bed, filled with titles like Sun Tzu's *The Art of War* and Machiavelli's *The Prince*. Charlie stopped in front of it gazing at the spines of books until Baby Doll stood next to him. Then, without a word, he reached over and pushed hard on the left side of the bookshelf. It swung easily and quietly on a hinge in its middle, revealing a hidden, windowless room situated behind it. The room was not lit, but Baby could see enough of the shadows to know what was in there. Her heart started beating rapidly and she involuntarily took a step backward, away from the secret room.

"What are you doing, Charlie?" she asked.

He laughed, a cold and mirthless sound that reminded Baby more of a metronome clicking than a man feeling joyful.

"I'm showing you how to kill in cold blood, Baby Doll. Just like I promised."

He reached inside the room and tapped a switch, flooding the room with fluorescent lighting. Inside was a hard metal table long enough for a man to be stretched out on. Straps with metal buckles were attached to the sides of the table, and dirty gray handcuffs were set at each corner. There was a sink in the room, and a large metal cabinet. Baby Doll very much did not want to know what kinds of tools were kept in that cabinet.

The floor was concrete. The walls were bare except for one side where a movie poster of Bruce Lee's *Enter the Dragon* had been taped, at an angle, across from the head of the metal table. A mop and bucket stood sentry in the back corner of the room.

"This cell is only big enough for one," Charlie was saying casually, "but it does the job. Sometimes you have to get personal, know what I mean, Baby Doll?"

He stepped inside and motioned her to follow. She hesitated, but then also took a step into the room. He peered with amusement at the movie poster on the wall. "Hmm. Looks like it's time for some new decorations. What's your favorite film, Baby?"

"*The Princess Bride.*" She said it before thinking. It was her standard answer to any question about movie favorites. Charlie seemed to like the choice.

"Yeah, that's a good one," he said happily. "I'll have to make a note of that."

Then Baby Doll noticed why the Bruce Lee poster would be replaced. Upon closer inspection she saw that it had been spattered with blood that had long since dried and cracked on the paper. She felt repulsed, and the smell of stale horror inside the room threatened her sanity.

Charlie Murphy turned to face Baby Doll, seeming to be at ease here in this cell. "A person can live for a while in this room," he said. "But there's no toilet, so I don't usually let them go longer than two, three days."

"You're a monster," Baby Doll whispered in terror, not even realizing she'd said it out loud.

He shrugged. "It comes with the territory," he said simply. "If you're going to be Justice, you're going to need a few prisons."

"I'm leaving, Charlie." She had to get out. "Maurits will be here soon. You don't need me anymore."

"I put myself in here once," he said, almost to himself. "Just to see what it would be like. Spent an entire day shackled to that metal bed over there."

Baby Doll stood transfixed in ugly fascination. She saw a familiar redness appear around the rims of his eyes. His face seemed to age right in front of her. He still held the Glock 36 in his right hand, and its trembling was noticeable now.

"I'm not a well man, Baby Doll."

He was no longer looking at her, but at the table. He seemed to have become immersed in a memory that wouldn't let go. Baby Doll took a step backward and found herself back on the carpet in Charlie Murphy's bedroom. She glanced toward the door that offered an exit into the hallway. She wondered if she could run to that door and be out of it before Charlie could shoot her. She looked back at Charlie and saw him staring at her, gun trembling at his side.

"You just aim and click, Baby," he said dully. "That's all it takes. It shouldn't be so simple to take a man's life, but it is." He stared hungrily at the girl. "It's harder to take someone's soul. But it can be done." He took a step toward her, and she stepped away without thinking. "You start by taking their name. By making them wonder who they really are. Sometimes a little nudge into the darkness is enough to make them get themselves lost in it the rest of the way. You know what I mean, Baby Doll?" He laughed again, but it sounded like crying.

"Sick . . . sick." It was all she could muster in her shock.

"I know, Baby Doll," he said. "That's why I'm on medication after all, isn't it?"

He moved more quickly than she expected, pushing past her into the bedroom. "Close that bookcase, will you, Baby?" he said. "Then come sit down with me again."

Baby Doll felt tightness in her chest, felt trapped by the fact that a crazy man—her own stepfather—stood between her and the exit, holding a Glock 36 and talking about his prescription medicine. She pushed on the bookcase and was surprised by how easily it glided on its swivel. It was obviously kept in working order, which meant it was likely used more than she wanted to imagine. She walked slowly back to Charlie's desk and saw that he had placed the gun next to his computer and that he now held his bottle of pills. He shook the bottle to indicate that she should sit down.

"I know what you did, Baby Doll."

"You're sick, Charlie. You need a doctor." She tried to recover, to turn the conversation.

"Maybe I should just take my Lamictal," he said mockingly. "Maybe I'll just down the whole bottle. That will help me, right?"

Baby Doll said nothing.

"Oh, wait," he continued. "Lamictal only helps with bipolar disorder *when it's in the bottle*. But you already knew that, didn't you, Baby Doll?"

He popped the lid and flung blue tablets toward the girl. "What is this stuff that I've been taking anyway?"

Baby Doll took a deep breath. "Calcium carbonate," she said calmly. She knelt down and began picking up all the little blue pills. "An antacid."

She picked up the bottle and poured the pills back into it, careful not to leave any lying on the floor or the desk. "It helps settle the stomach, and is sometimes used to treat premenstrual syndrome. I came across the powder during a chemistry lab at school, and learned how to compound it into the shield shape of Lamictal as part of a chem lab project."

Charlie Murphy grinned. It was a sloppy, almost-impressed expression that made him look tired and old. "So you switched my pills and hoped I wouldn't notice until it was too late."

Baby Doll nodded, a brief motion that barely registered on her face.

"What were you hoping would happen, Baby? That I might get soft because I no longer had to deal with PMS or an upset stomach?"

"One third of people who suffer from bipolar disorder try to commit suicide, Charlie. One out of five succeed in killing themselves." She said it quietly, her eyes now on the gun situated between them.

"So that's it, then," Charlie said slowly. "You were hoping to kill me by suicide." He nodded in approval. "Maybe you're not as stupid as you seem, Baby Doll." He licked his lips.

"So what now, Charlie?"

"Well, it's not every day that you learn your stepdaughter is trying to murder you," he said. "Of course, the easy thing to do would be to just kill you, now, and then have Maurits get me some real Lamictal. By this time tomorrow I'd feel almost normal again."

He looked thoughtful. Baby Doll waited. For the first time she felt almost serene in Charlie Murphy's room. She was resigned to her fate. Even if Charlie let her live now, she couldn't stay here, not any longer. Not as long as Charlie was alive at least. It would almost be better if he murdered her right now and got it over with. She wondered if she should ask God for forgiveness in the short moments she had left. *Peccavi,* she whispered the Latin in her head. *I have sinned.*

She watched him as he processed the information of her betrayal. He gazed down at the gaudy ring on his right hand and twisted it in absent thought. He pulled it from his third finger and examined it more closely, then he moved it to the pinky finger of his other hand. Finally he removed it and placed it inside his desk. His forehead was moist, but his eyes, for the first time, clear.

"Looks like it's time for a judgment, Baby Doll," he said.

"What's my name, Charlie? I deserve that much at least. To know who I am before I die."

"Exitus acta probat," he said.

Her mind interpreted the Latin phrase involuntarily: *The result validates the deeds.*

"Charlie—" she started, but he silenced her with a frown.

Baby Doll watched as he picked up the Glock and slid the clip out of the gun, verifying that it was loaded. Then he slapped it back into place and stared hard at the girl.

"The ruling is death."

"Charlie!"

"Good-bye, Baby Doll."

He swung the gun into position and with a practiced ease pulled the trigger. The bullet pierced his temple on the right side and spat out next to his cheekbone on the left. His body crumpled instantly, sagging over the desk with a finality that took Baby Doll's breath away. When his hand hit the surface of the desk, it knocked the gun to the floor, but left his arm sprawled toward her as if in supplication.

She felt herself begin to hyperventilate, pushed her chair backward away from the desk but was in too much shock to stand or even turn away from the grotesque sight before her. Blood spilled rapidly onto the desk, thick and red like heavy wine. The smell of death filled the air and made her want to vomit, but still she sat frozen, staring, disbelieving her own eyes.

Charlie Murphy was gone. Dead. Killed by his own hand. She had dreamed of this moment, and now that it was here, she didn't know what to do. Instinctively she reached over and moved Charlie's laptop to keep it from being stained by the ever-expanding pool of blood. When she did so, she saw a kill order still on the screen in front of her. The name on the judgment was Maurits Girard.

"How could you, Charlie?" she asked the dead body. "How could you kill Maurits of all people?" Then she wondered briefly if that was why he had killed himself, if he, the great Justice, found it easier to do away with himself than to murder the one man who had never betrayed him.

Still breathing hard, she closed the file and deleted it. Then she saw the stacks of hundred-dollar bills, the laptop computer in her hands, and Charlie Murphy dead beside it all.

A continuation of her original plan began forming itself in her head. She stepped around his desk and opened the top drawer.

—

A knock at her bedroom door brought Baby Doll back to the present. She stole a look at the clock and saw that it was now exactly 7:30 A.M.

"I'll come down to the kitchen for breakfast this morning, Leticia," she called toward the door. She sat up on the bed and began smoothing the wrinkles in her clothes. She was surprised to discover that she was crying.

"God help me," she whispered to herself. Then she changed

the words of her prayer. "God find me." And for good measure she added, *"Peccavi."*

It didn't help her feel any better. But it didn't make her feel worse either.

The knocking at her door resumed. "I said I'll come down to the kitchen," Baby Doll called out, louder this time and with just a touch of irritation in her voice.

More knocking.

Baby Doll stood and walked over to the door. "Leticia?" she said through the wall.

"Open the door, Baby," a deep voice responded. "It's Maurits."

Thirty

"Wake up, Boy."

In the darkness of my healing womb, a voice is speaking.

"You must wake up."

Alondra?

I am cocooned in warmth, but something feels uncertain, out of place. I hear myself breathing.

Where am I? Alondra?

"Wake up, Boy. Wake . . ."

I feel a cold wind on my face, then an unforgivable stinging beneath my rib cage. I gasp and my eyes open to light and a return to reality. The harm in my back still proclaims itself to me, making it difficult to move. But I am also aware the throbbing doesn't run as deeply inside me as before, my lungs are breathing almost normally, and my heart beats at a steady rate. So, the healing was begun, but I have awakened before it could finish. This is rare, but it has happened before. My eyes flash open. The last time it happened I was in grave danger, and my tether at risk too.

I am surprised to see that I am still in Baby Doll's car, in the backseat. The front doors on both sides are open and two men I don't recognize are peering inside. They are speaking—at least their lips are moving—but I can't hear anything being said.

Am I deaf now too? Or still asleep and dreaming?

The man on the passenger side stands up and slams the door shut. Still, I hear no sound. The one on the driver's side is leaning inside the car, talking, looking in the console and beneath the seat, but finding nothing. I concentrate on his lips as they move.

"—sign of it in here. Mr. Girard said it was just a hunch anyway. We can take apart the door panels, but there's no way to do that without Baby Doll knowing about it." A pause, as if he is listening to his colleague outside the car. Then, "Yeah, sounds good." The man stands up and slams the driver's door shut. I feel the car rock gently at the force of the impact, but still hear nothing.

Alondra whispers in my ear.

"I am awake," I respond, but my lips don't seem to move. Am I only partly awake? In those confused moments between dreaming and waking life?

The stinging in my back flashes in intensity. I find myself blinking, staring, unsure of anything I see. With a rush, as if plugs have suddenly been pulled from my ears, the silence that surrounds me drops away. I hear footsteps walking away in the distance and mumbling voices that soon fade and disappear.

I am alone, I am awake. And I am in pain.

It hurts to rise up to a sitting position, but it no longer feels like I am keeping death at bay. I move slowly, fearful of the wound in my back. But while it feels tender, it does not tear open again. After a moment I feel certain I can move, as long as I am careful and protective of the spot. I come to the conclusion that my internal organs must have healed, but I still bear a serious flesh wound that will need attention sooner or later.

"I need to sleep," I murmur to myself. "To finish the healing."

I feel a tugging inside me and understand that to sleep right now would be deadly. I must find my tether. I must find Baby Doll and let the warmth of a strong tether bring me back to health.

I exit the car and stand in the center of the garage, unsure. Where has Baby Doll gone? And will she come back here to look for me? Or should I leave here to start looking for her? I hear a sound and twist too quickly to follow it with my ears. In the turning, I feel my skin separate at the wound, feel a sharpness almost like the reentry of a knife into my back. The sudden agony is too much for me. I drop to the ground and try to lie still, hoping for relief from the pain.

I need to sleep.

I need to wake.

I need to heal.

But all I can do is whimper, and wait.

Thirty-one

Baby Doll opened the door to discover Maurits's imposing figure filling the opening, and behind him two new bodyguards dressed in dark suits. The one on the left she recognized as John Michael Tanaka, a barrel-chested man with heavy biceps and an easy smile. She'd seen him from time to time working on assignments from Maurits or Charlie, or simply hanging out in the kitchen and looking for between-meal snacks. Right now, though, his smile was gone and his face bore no expression other than a noticeable alertness in the eyes. The bodyguard on the right was new to her, but he definitely looked more the guardian type than Whitney Ellsworth had. This one, she decided, Maurits had hired himself. He was lean but muscled, his bulging biceps and thick thighs pressing tightly against the fabric of his suit. He looked almost like a light heavyweight boxer who had been stuffed into an Italian suit. He also wore no expression, although Baby Doll felt his eyes surveying her with suspicion.

"Good," Maurits said, "you're dressed already."

"Yeah, Maurits," she said, hoping her eyes weren't red from crying. "What's up?"

"I have to go to a meeting today. I won't be in the house until late tonight. I want you to have Stanley drive you to class today, and then come straight back here afterward. Understand?"

"That's nice of you, Maurits, but it's not necessary. I've got my car." Her mind raced feverishly. How was she going to get to Donenfeld's Pub and Entertainment, to Linda McDavid and Charlie Murphy's ring, with Stanley shadowing her every move? "And," she added hastily, "I really need to spend a few hours in the library after lunch. To catch up on some of the work I missed last week."

Maurits frowned a bit, but only with his eyebrows. The rest of his face remained passive and calm. "I need you to go with Stanley today," he said, and now she knew there was going to be no arguing the point. "You can take my Lexus. It'll be safer that way. I'll be using Charlie's old Jaguar sedan for a while."

Baby Doll tried to put on a "scared teenager" face. "What's going on, Maurits? Why can't I drive my own car anymore?"

"Nothing for you to worry about, Baby. Just taking a few precautions, is all. Victoria Fox's nephew fell on a few bullets last night and now there's a little tension between us. Marty Goodman has offered to mediate, so that's where I'll be today."

Baby Doll tried not to shiver. "They know who shot him?"

Maurits shook his head. "The nephew isn't talking. Apparently the bullets came from his own gun, so he either shot himself in the leg or was stupid enough to let his gun get taken from him and then used against him at close range. Either way, it's a career-killer for the boy, and the Executive isn't happy about it. She's shipping him back to his mother in California. Otherwise he'd be a big fat target for anyone with a little ambition."

"So what's that got to do with us, Maurits? Why can't I drive myself to class?"

Maurits let the frown drip down the rest of his face. "Stanley's waiting for you in the garage," he said, and that settled the issue. "You need something, you ask Stanley to get it for you. And leave your cell phone on at all times. You understand?"

Baby Doll nodded. "I understand, Maurits." Inside she was fuming. It was only a matter of time until someone spotted Linda McDavid and that big ring she stole. Baby Doll wondered if she'd been spotted already, if that was really where Maurits was going today. And if he wanted Stanley to stay close by to keep Baby from running again.

Maurits tilted his head slightly to the side, narrowing his eyes to peer at her cheekbone. He reached out and lightly touched the spot beneath the bruise that Linda McDavid had left on her face. "That's looking better already," he said approvingly.

"Thanks."

"And don't worry. We took care of that last night too."

Baby Doll felt her heart race unexpectedly. "What do you mean?"

Maurits gave her a satisfied smile. "It's taken care of," he said. "That's all you need to know."

Baby Doll didn't know what to say. She felt like her eyes were blinking too much, but she couldn't stop them. Was he saying that they'd already picked up Linda McDavid and gotten the ring back? Or something else entirely?

His face softened a bit. He reached into his pocket and pulled out a roll of bills. He peeled off five twenties and held them out for her. "This should tide you over for a couple days. If you need more, ask Stanley for it. He's in the garage right now. Get some breakfast and then he'll take you wherever you need to go. Oh, and I almost forgot." He stuffed the money roll back into his pants pocket, and then reached inside his jacket where Baby Doll knew he kept his spare minirevolver. As he reached in, she also saw his holstered handgun—some kind of Glock that she couldn't identify. Charlie Murphy had always liked Glocks. Apparently Maurits had also picked up that affinity. Baby Doll felt herself stiffen when Maurits's hand dipped into the inside pocket of his suit coat. But then he pulled out something much smaller than a minirevolver and pressed it toward her.

"We finally found this," he said, handing her a smudged library card. "You might need it today while you're catching up at the university library."

Baby Doll was surprised to feel such an emotional connection to that card, but she was glad to have it back in her possession anyway. "Thanks, Maurits."

He turned to walk away. His bodyguards followed closely behind.

Baby Doll wasn't sure what made her do it, but before Maurits had reached the stairs she stepped out into the hallway and called after him. "Maurits," she said. The big man stopped and gave her his full attention. She glanced nervously from one bodyguard to the other, and then looked searchingly into her guardian's eyes. "Maurits." She said it more softly now. He seemed to understand. He nodded for his bodyguards to give them a little privacy while he came back to her door.

"What is it, Baby Doll?" he said, just a trace of impatience in his voice.

"Maurits." She said his name again, feeling foolish, but thinking it was too late to go back now. She almost whispered it. She said it like it was a last chance. "What's my name, Maurits?" she said. "I'm so lost without it, like I don't even know who I am. What is it, Maurits? Please tell me. Charlie's dead now, and you're the only one left who knows."

The edges of the big man's eyes squinted down toward her. There was an uncomfortable silence, and then his face was a mask. "You know, Baby, Charlie used to like that you learned Latin in school. Made him feel proud."

Baby Doll said nothing.

"In fact, he got himself a book, taught himself a little Latin, just to keep up with you. And, of course, that means I had to learn it a little too."

"Yes, Maurits?"

With surprising perfection, he spoke to her in the language of the philosophers. *"Perfer et obdura,"* he said. *"Dolor hic tibi proderit olim."*

Baby Doll felt tiny tears spring unbidden out of the corners of her eyes. Maurits turned and walked away, motioning for his bodyguards to follow. A moment later Baby Doll stood on the marble floor outside her room.

She had never felt more alone.

Thirty-two

The sound of a door opening is a grateful distraction from the throbbing in my back. I turn my head and see Maurits's driver enter the garage, whistling. He walks directly toward my crumpled figure on the floor before swerving, at the last second, to walk around me, completely unaware that he has done so. The driver opens the door of the black Lexus sedan and gets comfortable behind the wheel. He reaches into a compartment and pulls out what looks like a magazine, or a comic book, and starts reading. Apparently he is going to wait here until Maurits or someone else comes down to the garage for a ride.

The stinging in my back has dulled enough that I try to reach behind and touch the knife wound, to gauge how serious it is at this point. But the pain is still enough to prevent me from moving my arm far enough behind me to reach it. My fingers graze across something metal in my waistband and I am surprised to discover that Whitney Ellsworth's second gun is still tucked securely in there. I consider pulling it out and tossing it on the floor of the garage, maybe under that black sedan, but then I decide that if it has stayed in place this long, it might as well stay there a while longer.

I can no longer tolerate lying helpless here on the floor. I brace for the pain and roll over to a sitting position. It hurts—

but not as deeply as I had expected. I risk a deep breath. Again, it hurts—but not as much as it would seem it should. I am not ready to rise and walk yet, but I am ready to prepare myself for that kind of action. Soon, I figure, I will need to move despite the pain. To get to Baby Doll, to a place of safety so I can sleep once more.

The tether is still in place, I can feel this inside me, but I can't be sure how far away Baby Doll is, or whether she will suddenly cross the line of its extremity and plunge me again into a Severance. I close my eyes and concentrate on ignoring the pain in my back. If I can forget it is there, I can forget to be hindered by it. And if I can forget its hindrance, I can follow the tether back to Baby Doll.

Sitting here on this floor, willing my skin to congeal, begging myself to heal, I am struck by the futility of my existence. I remember someone speaking—I can no longer remember his face, or even his voice. Just his words.

"Souls flow through history like a river in time," he had said to me. "And you, well, you are lost in the drifts." It was he who first called me a Drifter, and how I first came to think of myself as such.

Alondra was no philosopher, but she had disagreed strongly with that one's assessment.

—

"If you are simply drifting through time, then there's no reason for you to be here with me," she'd said emphatically. We sat in the kitchen of her boardinghouse, peeling potatoes for Mrs. Snelling as we'd promised.

"Why does there have to be a reason for existence?" I had asked. "What if there is no purpose to life? What if there is only life, and it means nothing more than that?"

"Your problem is not that you have no purpose," she had said, "it's that you've forgotten why God put you here in the first place."

It is easy for me to forget. Even now, I cannot remember.

She had taken my hand then, and led me to the mirror in the bathroom. "Look in your eyes," she said. "You are marked by God. If he has marked you, why would you think that he could lose you? Why would you think he has no purpose for your existence?"

I sighed. In spite of everything, the one thing I do know is that God does exist. I see his fingerprints in the stars overhead, in the dirt beneath my feet. In Alondra's laughter, in the warmth of her loving presence. I know God is everywhere here; I just don't know that he is aware I am here as well.

"God forgot me long ago," I said. And I believed it.

"No," she said. "Repeating a lie to yourself doesn't make it true. It is no accident that you are here with me. That I am here with you. Maybe you are the one who has forgotten God, and in doing so, you have also lost yourself."

"So who am I then, Alondra? Why am I here? I don't even have a name."

She looked deeply into my eyes. "I don't know who you were, or who you will be. But right now you are my Angel," she said, shushing me before I could tell her again that I am neither angel nor demon. "No, not the same kind of angel we see in fancy paintings or read about in stories. A secret Angel, sent from God to give a scared young woman a few moments of peace in what is shaping up to be a difficult life. You are my Angel." She kissed my forehead. "And I am yours."

—

I hear a cell phone ringing and watch in a daze as the driver speaks cheerily into it from his perch in the front seat of the black Lexus.

Alondra called me her Angel. Why had I not remembered that before?

Because I am no angel, nor demon, nor ghost. I am flesh and blood, and spirit can't be flesh and blood, can it?

I try to return to my memories of Alondra and feel a cold fear inside me. Her voice is silent in my mind. Her face is blurred. I am losing her, forgetting, just as I have already forgotten so many countless others. Just as I have forgotten myself.

Is this what I am destined to do for eternity? To forget? To drift through lifetimes and never remember who I am or who I was to someone who once called me Angel?

I sit, wounded, on the floor of this garage. A driver passes the moment talking on a cell phone nearby. Baby Doll hides somewhere behind the walls of this house, and God hides somewhere beyond my soul's vision.

I have never felt more alone.

A lost thing never finds itself. And found things, sometimes, were never lost at all.

—SOLACE THE LESSER
PHILOSOPHER AND HISTORIAN, 421 B.C.

Thirty-three

MONDAY, FEBRUARY 21. MORNING.

It was almost 8:30 A.M. when Baby Doll finally walked out of the kitchen, backpack in hand and wearing her violet-colored ski jacket. She headed toward the garage where Stanley awaited her. She had packed the requisite textbooks into the backpack and tossed in her wallet as well. After a moment's thought, she'd also included Boy's box, just in case. She stuffed her new cell phone in the back pocket of her jeans, and then decided it was time to officially start the day.

Her first class was at 9 A.M., and she figured if they left now she'd arrive about fifteen minutes early. She had tried to delay leaving just a little bit, hoping to give more time for Boy to sleep and heal from last night's injury, but since Maurits had commanded her to let Stanley drive her to school, she knew she couldn't skip classes today. She worried about how she would get Boy from her Prius into the Lexus, and then how she would stay within his tethering distance while she was in the classroom. And she worried about what she would do if he didn't heal in time for her to go get the ring back from Linda McDavid. In the end, she had no answers, so she decided to follow the path before her and see what happened.

When she entered the garage two sights greeted her. First, Stanley smiled and waved from the front seat of Maurits's car. Second, she saw Boy, sitting in a heap, head drooping on his chest, in the middle of the garage floor. The back of his shirt hung over the wound in his back, but was also crumpled behind the handle of a handgun.

He did not look well.

As if sensing her presence, Boy's head snapped upward and turned in her direction. He said nothing, but a look of relief washed over his features. He tried to stand, slipped on a red streak on the floor, and sat back down, hard.

"Hiya, Baby Doll," Stanley said as he exited the Lexus. "Ready to head off to class?"

"Good morning, Stanley," Baby Doll said, forcing herself to tear her eyes away from the struggling Boy. "Um, yeah, I guess so." She let the driver take her backpack and toss it into the car while she tried to sort out how to help Boy. Stanley opened the backseat passenger door for her and waited.

"Um, Stanley," she said suddenly, "I almost forgot. I need to take a lunch with me today." She glanced wistfully back at the door that led to the kitchen. "Any chance you could run back to the kitchen and have them whip me up a sandwich or something before we go?"

"Sure thing, Baby Doll," he said genially. "Be back in a flash."

"Great, thanks," she said with relief. "I'll wait for you here and try to do a little bit of catch-up reading."

"Sounds good," he said. And then he disappeared through the door, leaving Baby Doll and Boy alone in the garage.

"Boy," she said urgently, "can you walk? We have to go, Boy."

He nodded and tried to rise up once more. This time Baby

Doll swept to his side and put her shoulder under his left armpit, bearing some of his weight for him. He wobbled a bit, but then steadied himself.

"I'm glad you came back," he said.

"Hey, you can't get rid of me that easy," she tried to tease, but it felt forced. "We have to ride with Stanley today," she said. "Maurits's orders. I have to go to class because Stanley will be watching, but I'll figure out something. I found out where Linda McDavid hangs out, so we've got to get there this afternoon." She looked at the lurching Boy beside her. "I'm going to need your help to get that ring back, Boy."

He nodded. "I need to sleep. To heal."

"Where have I heard that before," she muttered. She steered him toward the Lexus and set him gently inside. "Sleep now, Boy," she said. "I'll wake you up when we get to the campus. Then you'll have to walk with me to class. After that, you can sleep again. Understand?"

He nodded and closed his eyes. Just then the door to the garage opened and Stanley bounded back in.

"All set, Baby Doll," he said. "Chicken salad sandwich, fruit cup, and cheese stick." He held up a brown paper bag proudly. "You can get a soda on campus, right?"

Baby Doll favored him with a smile. "Sure can, Stanley. Thanks a lot." She took the paper bag and climbed into the backseat next to Boy. The driver slid into his seat, and moments later they were on their way. Almost instinctively, Baby Doll gently pulled Boy toward her, resting his head on her lap. She raised the back of his bloodied shirt and took a closer look at the knife wound in his back. The smell of coagulated blood wasn't pleasant.

"You okay, Baby Doll?" Stanley asked in the rearview mirror. "You look a little pale."

"Fine. Thanks, though," she said. Then she added, "So what's going on really, Stanley? Why do I suddenly have to have an escort just to go to class?"

The driver looked in the mirror and gave a pensive expression. "It's complicated, Baby."

"Come on, Stanley," she said. "Charlie never made you take me to school."

She could see the driver thinking, trying to figure out how much he should and shouldn't say.

"Maurits told me to ask you if I needed anything," she said. "Well, I need to know what's going on." She added a little petulance to her voice. "Tell me something, Stanley. Even if it's just a lie, okay?"

"I wouldn't lie to you, Baby Doll," he said immediately. "I never have, and I never will."

That's what I'm counting on, she thought. Aloud, she said, "So what's going on?"

Stanley glanced back up at Baby Doll's reflection in his mirror. "Well, you see, Baby, something went missing after your father died. Something important. Maurits is doing his best to find it, but now the Executive and the Legislator are involved, and that makes it complicated."

"Why is that?"

"Well, you see, Baby, everybody assumed that Maurits would take over as the Justice when Charlie passed on. You knew that already. But Charlie didn't leave a clear succession plan. And now Victoria Fox is ready to issue an Executive Order abolishing the Justice Department. If she can get Marty Goodman to go along with that, then she'll consolidate the Justice Department into the Executive branch. You see what that means, don't you, Baby Doll?"

She nodded. "War," she said. "Maurits would never sit by and let that happen."

Stanley seemed relieved that she understood. "Right. And when there's war, people who are loyal right now might think it's in their best interests to switch sides, or worse, to open up a few secrets to the police. That Honoria Lopez has already gotten close in the past. Without a Justice to keep her at bay, it's only a matter of time before someone cracks. That's what Maurits is trying to fix right now. You understand?"

Baby Doll nodded. "But what's that got to do with me?" she complained. "I'm just a college kid who lost my stepfather."

Stanley shrugged. "Maurits has got his reasons for keeping you under wraps, Baby Doll. We'll just have to trust him. It's for the best."

Boy let out a deep sigh and Baby Doll decided not to pursue this conversation with Stanley any more. She'd learned enough from him to know that the Organization was starting to crumble from within—exactly what she'd hoped for when she'd stolen Charlie's ring and sent the order to disband the army. But if either Victoria Fox or Maurits—or even Marty Goodman—were able to regain possession of the Justice's ring and legitimize their power, then everything would fall back into the same strangling situation as before and Baby Doll's efforts would mean nothing.

I've got to get that ring back, she thought. *And then I've got to get it out of here and hide it away where no one will ever find it again.*

She looked again at Boy's wound and thought that maybe it looked a little better, less yellow and infected around the edges. A surge of hope threatened to well up inside her. She surprised herself and found herself praying.

There has to be a reason why we are together, God, she thought. *And a Deus ex Machina can't be limited by a knife wound.*

She reached out and touched the area on Boy's back, and felt him flinch beneath her hand. A moment later Stanley pulled the car into the student lot near the humanities building on campus. To her relief, Boy's eyes opened as soon as the car stopped at the curb. He winced, but sat up in the seat next to her and nodded. She kicked her backpack across the floor of the backseat so that it rested beside Boy's feet near his door.

"I can walk from here, Stanley," she said. She jumped out of the car and walked quickly around to the door on the other side. She reached in for her backpack and tried to surreptitiously help Boy out at the same time.

Stanley opened his door and stood up to talk to her. "I'll go park the car and meet you inside," he said.

"Oh, no, Stanley," she said quickly. "My professor hates guests in the room. I'll be fine. Just meet me back here later."

The driver frowned.

"Look," Baby Doll said. "It's going to be a long day for me here. I'll be in the Latin classroom here from 9 A.M. to 9:50 A.M. Then I have my 10 A.M. chemistry class in the science building right next door, and I've got chem lab right after that until 11:50 A.M. Then it's lunch and the library for the afternoon, trying to catch up on all the stuff I missed last week." She gave him a disarming smile. "I'm not going anywhere, Stanley. Just take a break, go wash the car or something, and meet me back here at five and we'll all be home in time for dinner. How's that sound?"

"I don't know, Baby Doll."

Now she tried a pout. "Maurits said you were supposed to drive me, not babysit me."

He looked around at the activity on the campus, students walking to and from class, professors chatting each other up while they smoked cigarettes on the sidewalk. "I guess it is an enclosed environment," he said.

"Right," Baby Doll said. She reached into her coat. "And besides, I've got my cell phone if I need you. Or if you need me."

He hesitated. "All right," he said at last, "but I'll pick you up at four-thirty."

"Fine. That's good. Thanks, Stanley. I'll see you then."

She turned and started walking toward the humanities building, grateful to see that Boy was walking under his own power—a bit unsteadily, but still walking—next to her. She slowed her pace to allow Boy to keep up, and listened intently behind her. She felt relieved when, a moment later, she heard the Lexus pull away from the curb and drive off.

She looked over at Boy. His face was pale and his eyes bleary, but he seemed to be gaining strength. She glanced up at the entrance to the humanities building and back at Boy.

"Okay," she said finally. "I'll go to class. Think you can curl up in a corner and sleep here?" He nodded. "Get better, Boy," she said. "This afternoon I'm going to need your help to get that ring back for me. It could get ugly again, if you know what I mean." He nodded once more, and Baby Doll wasn't sure if he was agreeing to get better or agreeing that it could get ugly.

They followed the stream of students into the humanities building and then into classroom 124 where Baby Doll's advanced Latin class took place. Boy didn't wait for Baby Doll to get her seat. He walked to the back of the classroom, sat down heavily in a corner, and appeared to be asleep before his eyes closed.

Baby Doll turned her focus to the lesson, but for the next fifty minutes, instead of her professor's manicured speech, Maurits's words echoed in her ears: *Perfer et obdura. Dolor hic tibi proderit olim.*

Be patient and tough. Someday this pain will be useful to you.

At the end of Latin, Baby Doll noticed Boy stirring in the back of the room. He stood and looked at her. His eyes were still glazed, but his face was less pale, and he definitely seemed to move a bit more normally. She shot him a look that questioned, "Can you walk?" He nodded and took a few steps toward her. They repeated this routine for Baby Doll's chemistry class and the lab that followed. By the time Boy stirred again, near the end of chem lab, he looked almost normal again. At least Baby hoped he was back to normal.

At 11:47 he rose from his corner in the lab and started toward her station. Then he stopped and fixed his gaze on the doorway. She followed his eyes and saw a woman walk into the room and whisper quietly to the professor. Baby Doll felt like cursing, but instead she gathered up her books and papers and stuffed them into her backpack.

"Ms. Murphy?" the professor said. "You can leave a minute early today so that you can speak with your guest." She nodded toward the woman.

Baby Doll said nothing, but stood up. The woman led the way into the hallway, and Baby Doll dutifully followed, noting that Boy also came a few steps behind her. When they were finally alone in the hall, the woman turned around and flashed an insincere smile.

"Nice to see you again, Baby Doll," she said.

"Wish I could say the same, Detective Lopez."

Honoria Lopez patted her on the shoulder. "This won't take long, sweetie. Just need to ask you a few questions, is all."

Baby Doll said a bad word in her head. It didn't help.

Thirty-four

Honoria Lopez looks worried. And tired. She is playing the part of the confident investigator, unafraid of anything, but the lines above her eyes and the shadows below them give her away.

She is scared of something. No, not scared of something that exists, but of something that might come to pass. I see a clock ticking inside her mind. She is racing to get somewhere before it's too late. And she knows that it might already be too late.

She glances at her watch. "Tell you what, Baby Doll," she says, "let's go get some real coffee this time instead of that swill they call coffee down at the Police Services Center. There's a Starbucks in the student union building, right?"

Baby Doll's lips tighten. "I'm kind of busy today, Detective. Trying to catch up on classes that I missed last week and all."

A slight bow; forced deference. "I would consider it a personal favor if you would allow me to buy you a cup of coffee and ask you a few questions."

"Am I under arrest?"

"No, Baby Doll. And this time I won't make you volunteer either. At least not yet. But time is running short, and I think you may be able to save someone's life. Or at least be able to help me save it."

Baby Doll is thinking. Something in the detective's manner is making her have second thoughts. Lopez is actually asking for help this time. Not demanding it, not playing formalities in an effort to uncover secrets. She looks at me, asking my opinion. I say nothing. It's not my place to decide. She frowns, first at me, then at Honoria Lopez.

"Ten minutes, Detective," she says at last. "We'll go get coffee, and then I'll give you ten minutes. After that, I'm done. And the next time we talk, it will only be through a lawyer."

"Fair enough," Lopez says. She turns and walks toward the exit, confident that Baby Doll will follow.

I feel the strength of the tether warming my extremities and keeping me upright. There is still an uncomfortable stinging in my back, but the knife wound seems less restrictive, less overpowering. I try to reach back to touch the place where the knife entered my skin and am pleased to discover that now I can move my hand far enough back to examine the wound. There is dried blood that cracks when I press on it, and my shirt is soiled with my insides as well. I wonder if it smells as bad as it feels, but I smell nothing, either inured to it or ignorant of it by now.

There is a raised, ragged scar on my back, but the skin is finally sealed again. My fingers trace the scar and marvel that it can be no more than two inches long. It seems such a small cut, yet it did so much damage. The human body truly is a frail thing.

When we enter the student union building, I tap Baby Doll on the shoulder and point. She nods, understanding.

"Just a minute, Detective," she says. Then, without waiting for a response, she slips into the bathroom just inside the entrance to the student union. I follow behind her.

"I'll, uh, just wait out here for you," Lopez calls out as the door closes.

Inside the restroom, Baby Doll turns to me. "Are you okay? Do you need something?"

I turn and raise my shirt. Again, she understands. The tether is growing stronger, knitting us closer together to the point where words are not always necessary. She pulls a few paper towels off the rack and dampens them under warm water in the sink. A rough wash clears away most of the old, dried blood. She then adds soap for the next round, and I feel the sting of cleaning in my back. After one more rinse, she is done.

"It looks awful," she says. "But it's not oozing anymore. And the skin around it looks pink and healthy now that we've cleaned off that dried blood."

"It will be fine for the time being," I say. "But sooner or later I will need to sleep long enough to heal the rest of the way."

She nods. "You could use some new clothes too. There's a bookstore in here with campus gear. How about a new sweatshirt or something?"

I shrug. It makes no difference to me. She motions toward the waistband on my pants. "I see you still have Ellsworth's Kahr back there." I shrug again. She reaches for her backpack and hefts it off the floor, resting it on the edge of the sink. She unzips the opening and spreads it wide enough for me to look inside.

I see my box in there. I can't express the relief, the completeness that fills me at this moment. I think my mouth sags. I am also mildly distressed because I realize that I had actually forgotten, briefly, that this box existed. But now that I see it, I know I must open it soon. And remember.

Baby Doll closes the backpack. "Just wanted you to know it was safe," she says.

"Thank you," I say. And I mean it.

She slips me a small smile. "Hey, I owed you a favor, right?"

It strikes me now that I owe Baby Doll a favor in return. I wonder if I will be able to fulfill that obligation before it's too late.

"How's it coming in there, Baby Doll?" Detective Lopez sticks her head in the bathroom door. "Time really is of the essence on this one," she says.

"On my way out, Detective," Baby Doll says quickly. "Just finishing up washing my hands. Can't be too careful in public places like this, you know."

Lopez holds open the door for Baby Doll, and we all walk into the campus Starbucks. Moments later we are all seated at a corner table in the coffee shop, acoustic pop playing over the speakers, and a press of students sitting all around us drinking coffee, reading books, and having animated discussions about things like Jean-Paul Sartre's play No Exit *and the future of computer radiometrics. Baby Doll seems to have realized that I haven't eaten since yesterday, so even though she ordered a large cinnamon roll with her coffee, she pushes it aside—toward me—when we are all at the table. It is sweet and hot, and I make it disappear quickly.*

"Maurits not feeding you, Baby Doll?" Lopez says with a raised eyebrow when she notices the empty plate. Baby Doll ignores the question.

"Your ten minutes are ticking," she says. "What's this about, Detective?"

Lopez leans back in her chair. "What can you tell me about William Finger?" She eyes Baby Doll carefully for any reaction to the name, but the girl is blank.

"He's got a funny name?" she ventures. "His dad is Tom Thumb?"

"This isn't a joke, Baby Doll."

"Sorry, Detective, I don't know anybody by that name."

Honoria Lopez searches Baby Doll's eyes, but she doesn't

flinch. "Maybe this will help your memory," Lopez says carefully. She reaches into a pocket and pulls out a bent photo of a young man. He has shaggy blond hair and a surfer's grin. Mischievous blue eyes stare out from the picture, and Baby Doll recognizes him instantly.

"Now what can you tell me about Will Finger?" Lopez says. She has spotted the recognition in Baby Doll's eyes.

Baby Doll looks worried. "Why?" she says, anxiety in her voice. "What's happened to him?"

Detective Lopez seems to be weighing her tactics. Good cop? Bad cop? Finally she opts for the good cop role. "William Finger is a student at this very university—but not a very good one. According to records he is flunking most of his classes, mostly because he doesn't bother to show up for them. But he still lives in the dormitory here on campus, and when he didn't come back to his room on Saturday night, his roommate got a little worried. When he was still gone this morning, the roommate called the police. Soon after, the uniformed folks transferred his case to me. Do you know why they did that, Baby Doll?"

The girl nods grimly. "Because he's the same kid that 'stole' your car after Charlie Murphy's funeral."

"Right answer. Now, why is he missing, Baby Doll?"

She brushes her cheek involuntarily; she knows. Maurits hadn't traced her beating to Linda McDavid. He'd wrongly followed everything back to William Finger and was punishing that opportunistic young man for what had happened to Baby Doll's cheek. But she doesn't give in to Lopez.

"I don't know, Detective."

"Do you know where he might be, Baby Doll? I fear for his safety."

She shakes her head, but says nothing.

"He's just a kid, like you, Baby Doll," Lopez says softly. "A

stupid boy who didn't recognize that the pretty girl offering him cash and a car was the daughter of one of the cruelest criminals this city has ever known."

Baby Doll remains silent, avoiding eye contact with the detective.

"His mother is worried sick. She doesn't deserve this. He doesn't deserve this."

Baby Doll still refuses to speak, but her face tells volumes. She stares hard at her coffee cup for a moment. Then she reaches into her backpack.

"Let me ask you a question, Detective," Baby Doll says suddenly, flipping her cell phone out onto the table. She presses a few buttons to retrieve a digital image on the screen. "What do you see in that picture?"

The detective leans in and squints toward the table. "A doorway." She raises up and looks annoyed. "Is that where Finger is?"

"No," she answers. "That's the door to my bedroom." Then to herself, "And to you *it's just a blank space. Empty." She turns and looks very much as if she is staring thoughtfully into space, when she is actually staring thoughtfully into my face.*

"It's no use," I say softly to her.

Baby Doll bites her lips and I see that she's lost something in her eyes.

"That's all you've got to show me, Baby Doll?" Honoria Lopez says, frustration rising in the tonality of her voice. "A picture of an empty doorway? Somehow I had expected a little more than that from you. Will Finger expected more than that."

Baby Doll retrieves the cell and looks into it. She blinks quickly, as if trying to focus, then relaxes when my face in the picture comes into clear view for her. "Not everything is as it seems, Detective," she says softly. "There are some secrets that no one can see. Not even me."

Detective Lopez snorts in disgust and stands. She drops a business card on the table between them. "I'm done wasting my time here," she says. "If you ever get a conscience, you'll know what to do with that." Then she turns brusquely and walks out of the coffee shop without looking back.

After she is gone, Baby Doll buries her face in her hands. "What have I done?" she whispers. "What have I done?" Her hands quiver as she picks up Honoria Lopez's business card and hides it in her pants pocket.

I can't help but wonder, what has she done to William Finger?

Thirty-five

Baby Doll sat at the corner table in the coffee shop and tried not to picture what Maurits had done—or was doing—to William Finger. Boy sat beside her like a statue, waiting. Finally she stood, hefted her backpack, and motioned for Boy to follow her out. She walked into the busy main hallway of the student union building and scanned the walls.

"What is the deal?" she said after a moment. "Are there no pay phones left anywhere in the world?"

"Why not use your cell phone?" Boy asked.

"Because," she said, "any calls to or from my cell can be traced. And I don't want Maurits to know where we're going."

She turned and headed deeper into the student union until they came to the large bookstore that occupied two stories of the building. She marched past the shelves of textbooks and supplies to reach the hats, shirts, scarves, slippers, and such that carried the university logo prominently upon them. She chose a blue, button-down denim shirt with a ferocious animal mascot on the pocket and carried it to the cash register. Just before the cashier rang it up, though, she said, "Can I use your telephone real quick? I want to check the size on that before I buy it."

The cashier gave Baby Doll a short, assessing look, and then said, "Yeah, just make sure it's a local call."

"Thanks." Baby Doll blinked warmly and accepted the receiver of the phone. She recited a number from memory. The cashier tapped the buttons on the wall phone for her, and then his forehead creased in recognition.

"Isn't that the phone number for—"

"Metro Taxi Service?" she said, holding up a finger to silence the cashier. "Yes, I'm calling to find out if Tony would fit in a large shirt, or if he wears a medium?"

The cashier nodded, accepting the idea that she was buying the shirt for someone who worked at the popular cab agency. Then he politely stepped away so as not to eavesdrop on the rest of the conversation. Baby Doll turned her back and spoke more softly.

"Yes, I'm sorry, I think I dialed the wrong number. Still, since I have you on the line, I needed to call you next anyway. Please send a cab to the student union building at the university. I'll meet the driver out front in the loading zone. Um, my name is Bobbi Kane. That's right. Thanks."

She turned and handed the phone back to the cashier. He returned to the register, took the phone, and hung it up. "Right size?" he asked.

"Sure is." She smiled. "I'll take it. No need for a bag."

A few minutes later, Boy crumpled his bloodied shirt and stuffed it into a trash can along with the tags from the new denim button-down. Then he donned the new shirt, and he and Baby Doll walked quickly to the front entrance of the student union building.

"What about William Finger?" Boy asked quietly while they waited for the cab to arrive.

Baby Doll sighed. "The best thing we can do for Will right now is get that ring back, then make sure we hide it someplace where no one will ever find it or use it again."

When the taxi arrived, Baby Doll held the door open long enough for Boy to slide into the backseat before she got in. "Donenfeld's Pub and Entertainment," she said. "You know where that is?"

The driver turned to look at her over the seat. "Yeah," he said. He hesitated. "Not many university kids go down to that part of town. You got friends down there?"

Baby Doll's lips grew thin. "How about you just drive and I'll decide where a 'university kid' is allowed to go?"

The driver threw up his hands in mock surrender. "My mistake, ma'am." He placed special emphasis on the word "ma'am," then started the meter and pulled out of the parking lot, heading south.

Baby Doll followed Boy's eyes and saw his gaze resting intently on her backpack. She reached down and opened the bag, digging inside until she came up with the box. She held it out to him, and he received it with a grateful smile. She watched him as he gently stroked the wood and fingered the metal engravings attached to it. Whatever was inside that box meant more to him than money, than even Charlie Murphy's ring of power meant to her and the Organization. She studied his hands, looking for clues as to how to open the box, wishing that he would just go ahead and open it right then so she could see how it was done. But he seemed content to simply hold the box. He set it in his lap, one palm on each side of the box, and then leaned his head back against the seat and closed his eyes.

"What's in the box, Boy?" Baby Doll asked.

"Treasures," he said.

"What kind of treasures?"

"Irreplaceable treasures," he said.

He didn't say anything more, but he did smile. Baby Doll thought that this was the first time she had ever seen him look so peaceful. A few minutes later she noticed that he had actually gone to sleep again, only this time with a faint smile on his lips. She decided that she liked Boy's smile.

They took the rest of the twenty-minute ride in silence, and Baby Doll almost didn't want the quiet of that moment to end. *I wonder what would happen,* she thought, *if we just kept driving and didn't stop . . .*

"Twelve-fifty," the cab driver finally said when he pulled into the parking lot of Donenfeld's Pub and Entertainment. "Ma'am." He emphasized the last part again.

Baby Doll looked at the seedy establishment and paused to collect her thoughts. The front of Donenfeld's was made up mostly of four large picture windows, tinted brown and encircled with Christmas lights that looked like they might be left over from 1976. Window paints had been used to ink specials such as HAPPY HOUR: 4–6 DAILY to lure customers inside. Concert flyers and announcements papered the window closest to the front door. The rest of the building was a dull brick structure, with weathered-wood framings and a roof that appeared to have been patched in more places than one. Situated behind Donenfeld's was the back of what appeared to be a cheap motel that apparently had its front entrance on a street on the other side.

"Will you wait for me?" Baby Doll said to the cab driver. "I shouldn't be too long."

"Meter will keep running," he said.

She pulled her wallet out of her backpack and took out two twenty-dollar bills. She tossed them over the seat to the driver. "That's fine," she said. "Just wait for me. If I'm not out in thirty minutes, then you can leave, okay?"

The driver picked up the two bills. "Fair enough," he said. "Enjoy yourself. I hear the pool tables at Donenfeld's are some of the best in town. Stay away from the onion rings though, unless you like indigestion." He lowered his cap over his eyes and slouched down in his seat, apparently ready to pass the time with a nap.

Baby Doll spread open her backpack and looked at Boy. Reluctantly he returned his box to the bag, then they both got out of the taxi and walked inside. Their entrance was generally unnoticed by the patrons in Donenfeld's. A man called out from the bar, "Just sit anywhere, honey, and someone will be over to take your order." Baby Doll looked to Boy, and he in turn led the way to a booth on the left that was out of the line of sight from the front door, in a shadowed section of the tavern.

The inside of Donenfeld's was actually much nicer than Baby Doll had expected. There was a row of well-kept pool tables that filled about a third of the space inside, along with all the necessary cues and other accoutrements for the gentleman's game stored against the west wall. A small dance floor and stage took up the back part of the pub, where swinging doors revealed the entrance to the kitchen. The bar filled the center of the space, and the rest was populated by tables and booths that, at this point, were only about one-third full. Lunchtime was apparently not a busy time for Donenfeld's Pub and Entertainment.

Baby Doll sat in the booth and surveyed the room. She saw mostly men drinking alcohol for lunch. A few women in unseasonably skimpy clothing lounged near the pool tables, also drinking.

The red lamps on the tables gave off a depressing glow, but several of the patrons seemed cheery nonetheless. One middle-aged businessman shared corny jokes with some of the women, and all laughed appreciatively.

A waitress came by and put a napkin and a basket of pretzels onto the table in front of Baby Doll. "What can I get you, honey? Do you want a menu, or are you just drinking today?"

"Just a beer," Baby Doll said. She actually hated the taste of beer, but she didn't want to give the impression that she didn't belong in a place like Donenfeld's.

"Sorry, honey, but I need to ask for your ID before I can serve you alcohol."

Baby Doll grimaced. She hadn't thought of that. She wouldn't be twenty-one until next November—and she didn't want her name to get out in this place either. "Okay," she said. "Make it a ginger ale."

The waitress smiled comfortingly. "Don't worry, honey," she said. "You should be glad you're blessed with a fresh young face. Won't be long before you'll be old and wrinkly like me and nobody will card you anywhere!" She laughed at her own joke, and Baby Doll tried to smile along.

A moment later the waitress placed a wide glass of bubbling liquid in front of her. "You need something else, you just wave and I'll come a-running."

"Thanks," she said.

Baby Doll took a sip of her ginger ale and turned to Boy. "What do you think? I don't see Linda McDavid anywhere in here."

Boy pointed toward a woman who had exited the restroom and then joined the women who were flirting with the corny-joke businessman. "Isn't that your sweater over there?"

Baby Doll sat up in her seat, and then slid across the padded bench to the corner of the booth out of clear eyeshot from the pool tables. "Yes, it is," she whispered back. "That's one of McDavid's girls who helped her beat me up in jail."

Boy nodded.

"Okay," she said, taking a quick gulp from her glass. "I'm going to go over and talk to her."

Boy held out a hand, holding her back. "*Nemo dat quod non habet,*" he said.

"Boy, you speak Latin?" She was truly surprised. "You just earned five more 'cool' points in my book," she said approvingly. She ran his words through the translator in her mind. *No one gives what he does not have.* She understood what Boy was saying. Linda McDavid possessed the ring, not that girl over there. It would be unwise to reveal herself to someone who couldn't give her the ring, and then risk someone warning McDavid about her presence. She glanced at her watch. Time was already slipping away. "What do you suggest?"

Boy leaned back in his seat. "Wait. She'll be here. I saw it on the way over here while I slept in the taxi."

Baby Doll fidgeted in her seat.

"Okay," she said at last. "We wait."

Thirty-six

"Wait," I say. "She'll be here. I saw it on the way over here while I slept in the taxi."

I saw more during that dreaming sleep, but I can't make it all out yet. The only thing I know for sure is that Linda McDavid will arrive soon, and she will play a game of pool with her friend who wears Baby Doll's sweater. The other images—a hawk-faced woman, a blank-faced man, and a row of guns—they float in my brain with no real semblance of order or meaning. They will organize themselves in time. I must do what I have instructed Baby Doll to do. Wait.

She fidgets uncomfortably in her seat. She is afraid of being noticed too much in this place, but she is more afraid of not getting Charlie Murphy's ring back, and thus is willing to take a few risks in her impatience. But I can't shake the impression that Baby Doll is exposed to mortal danger in this pub. I can't let her do anything. Not yet.

Back by the pool tables, some money changes hands, then the businessman and a raccoon-eyed girl walk out the door arm in arm. I wonder that she does not put on a longer coat to cover her bare legs, but then realize that she doesn't intend to go far from this place. She returns alone, cigarette in her mouth, barely thirty minutes later. Outside the window I see the taxicab, with the businessman in its backseat, shift into reverse and roll silently out of its parking spot. Baby Doll sees it too.

"At least he waited forty-five minutes," she says sighing. "More than he had to."

Baby Doll has managed to make that one ginger ale last this whole time, but now the waitress seems to be getting a little impatient, so she also orders a burger and fries. Soon after, they sit half-eaten on the table as well. I am grateful for the French fries, but the hamburger I leave for Baby Doll to handle. The waitress has given up on coming to our table anymore, something that suits Baby Doll just fine.

It is 1:41 P.M. when Linda McDavid finally enters Donenfeld's Pub and Entertainment. She doesn't notice Baby Doll huddled down in this booth, and instead calls out to the girls back at the pool tables. She is dressed warmly, and when she removes her gloves and coat she reveals blue jeans and a red, long-sleeved flannel shirt, the collar of which almost reaches her cropped, tan hair. She apparently is not concerned about looking sexy or attractive like the other women who wave to her when she comes in. She stops at the bar and chats up the bartender for a moment before sauntering back to her girls. There is forced laughter and a shuffle of positions. Linda McDavid obviously rules this brood of hookers, but a single look from the bartender reveals that he is in charge of McDavid.

Baby Doll is watching everything, eyes narrowed and appraising. The tavern is only lightly filled now. Two tables host single patrons. Two men are playing a lackadaisical game of pool at the first table nearest the door. Three men and one of McDavid's girls sit at the bar, none of them talking. And Linda McDavid stands with two other girls near the fifth pool table, not far from the kitchen.

McDavid pulls one of the girls off the bench and tosses her a pool cue. "Come on, Cynthia," she says to the dishwater-blonde. "Nothing happening here for a few more hours at least. I'll betcha five bucks I can beat you, best of three matches, at Nine-Ball before Millie over there finishes her drink."

Millie at the bar dutifully raises her glass and sips at some clear liquid.

"No ring," I say to Baby Doll.

"What?"

"She's not wearing the ring. I got a good look at her hands when she took the pool cues off the rack. Her fingers are bare. No ring."

Baby Doll nods. "That's because she's not keeping the ring in plain sight," she says. She taps at her chest, never taking her gaze off Linda McDavid.

In this darkened atmosphere, I am surprised that Baby Doll can see as clearly as she seems to indicate. But she's right. Every time Linda McDavid leans over the pool table, a small bulge outlines itself in the flannel fabric of her shirt, at just about the point where her clavicle rests. A closer look reveals a thick, steel chain around the woman's neck that dips inside the top buttons of her shirt.

"How did you see that so quickly?" I ask.

"I knew where to look," Baby Doll says. "I think maybe Linda McDavid and I are not that much different after all."

Baby Doll looks at me, a desperate plan apparently forming in her brain. "Can you take out that bartender?" she asks.

I shake my head. "He will accommodate me."

"Right." She looks around thoughtfully. One of the men at the bar drops a bill on the counter, wipes his face with a napkin, and heads out of the pub.

"How about a distraction?" she asks. "Can you use that Kahr pistol in your waistband to break a window or something? Just

long enough to distract everyone so I can overpower Linda McDavid and grab that chain with my ring on it?"

I have to admit, Baby Doll sometimes seems to be a fearless person. There are four of McDavid's women in this bar, plus customers and the bartender, yet she is confident she can engage her thief in a fight, grab the ring, and get out without anyone being able to stop her.

I look over at the two women playing pool, and notice again the ring-shaped bulge when the larger woman leans over to take a shot.

"Wait," I say.

"I can take her, Boy. I should have beaten her back in the jail. I just got caught off guard. But she's slower than me, and this time I'm ready. It'll be over fast."

"Wait," I say again. "Vincit qui se vincit."

"'He conquers who conquers himself?' What's that supposed to mean?"

"Be patient."

"Boy"—exasperation is evident in her voice—"pretty soon Stanley Lieber is going to expect to find me at the entrance to the student union building. I've been sitting in this dumpy bar, eating a disgusting hamburger, for much too long. I've finally found Charlie Murphy's ring. And you're spouting Latin and telling me to be patient? No *offense, Boy, but I'm going to get that ring back, and if I have to kick Linda McDavid's wide behind in the process, well, that's just fine with me."*

"Baby Doll," I say. "Conquer yourself. And wait."

The hawk-faced woman appears in my mind again. The row of guns. The blank-faced man. They are starting to make sense. This world melts away and a world-to-come takes its place. I am transfixed by it, not sure that I am understanding everything it means.

"Boy? Are you okay?"

Baby Doll is looking intently at me, rubbing ice-cooled fingers across my forehead. I shake my head, confused. I feel a stinging in my back where the scar from my knife wound is. Baby Doll reads my expression.

"You passed out," she says. "Or something like it. A trance maybe. You were talking, and then suddenly your eyes rolled back in your head, you started twitching. But you didn't fall down or anything. Your eyes were moving around under your eyelids. What happened?"

"How long was I out?" I say.

She looks at her watch. "About three minutes."

I nod.

"What was that? Are you okay?"

I nod. "It was the dreaming."

She tilts her head. "Narcolepsy?"

I shake my head. "No. Different than that. But an important warning."

"Okay," she says. "Let me go get that ring, and we'll get out of here. Grab my backpack." She starts to slide out of the booth, but I am faster. I block her exit and give her a slight shove to push her back into her seat.

"Sit down," I say. "Wait here. I have seen you."

"What?"

"There's no time to explain. And I don't know that I understand it all anyway. But I know you must stay in this booth. As far back and out of sight as you can." I think about it for a second. "In fact, get under the table if you need to."

"Boy, I—"

"You have to trust me, Baby Doll. You have to."

She starts to speak, then stops. Her eyes radiate distrust, but her mouth finally says, "Okay, Boy. I will trust."

Her face says it all to me. She will trust, but not only in me. In this moment, at this place, she is beginning to place her trust in God. I want to tell her that I am no angel, no Deus ex Machina. But I know now that I haven't the time. And for the first time in a while, I wonder if perhaps it might be a good idea to trust in God after all.

"Call a cab," I say.

"I can't use my cell phone, Boy. You know that. It's traceable."

"You have to take the chance," I say. "Call a cab. Wait for me. And no matter what happens, don't get out of this booth until you see me tell you it's okay."

She says nothing.

"Promise me," I say. "You must stay hidden in this booth."

"What are you going to do, Boy?"

"Promise."

A sigh. "Okay, I promise. What are you going to do?"

"I'm going to get Charlie Murphy's ring back."

Thirty-seven

Baby Doll wasn't sure what to make of Boy's sudden change in demeanor or that little blackout of his. One minute he was Mr. Passive, sitting quietly in the booth across from her, scouting the situation and telling her to sit tight and do nothing. The next he'd passed out, or something, sitting straight up at the table, scaring her more than she really wanted to admit. Then he was all chauvinistic action, demanding she hide in the booth while he went off to get Charlie Murphy's ring.

She felt irritated at being relegated to doing nothing, and frightened by Boy's insistence. What did he mean when he said, "I have seen you," and with all that talk about dreaming? Her mind flicked back to her own dreams about Boy, and to the name Alondra that had stuck in her brain afterward. Apparently there was something to that—Boy had inadvertently revealed that to her before. If she could dream about his past, could he dream about her future?

In the end, she heard his call for trust, and decided she would. What she found interesting at this moment was not so much that she trusted Boy, but that Boy inspired in her a flicker of confidence in God.

Is it possible that you are actually involved in my life? She prayed silently. *That despite everything, you haven't lost me after all?*

Something about Boy's presence made her want to think, made her want to believe, that the little girl whose name had been stolen away from her had been placed in this life for a reason, for a purpose. And that maybe, right now, her would-be Deus ex Machina was some kind of sign from God telling her to trust him.

"Call a cab," Boy had said. It seemed a dangerous thing to do, knowing Maurits was already suspicious, and anything on her cell phone could be easily tracked. But she had decided to trust, and that meant calling a taxi. She opened her cell and dialed 555–1111, the number for Metro Taxi Service. She couldn't help singing their little jingle in her head while she dialed it. She hated that ubiquitous jingle, but she had to admit, it did make it easy to remember the phone number. The dispatcher sounded bored and busy at the same time. It would be at least fifteen minutes, he said, before he could get a cab out to Donenfeld's, but he would send someone over as soon as possible. "Bobbi Kane" thanked him and said she'd look for the cab through the window of the pub. Then she worried that fifteen minutes might be too much, or too little, time for whatever it was that Boy was planning to do.

If she understood Boy's earlier explanation, he couldn't just walk up to Linda McDavid and take the ring from her. She would accommodate that kind of action. Something in her subconscious would recognize that he was a threat to her and, without really knowing what she was doing, she would easily avoid his direct approach—and possibly hurt him in the process. That meant he would have to do something indirect to get her to give up the ring.

For some reason the classic Aesop's fable about the wind and the sun popped into her brain. In that little parable, the wind and sun had an argument over which one of them was the stronger of the two. They decided on a contest to determine the answer. On the earth below was a man wearing a long overcoat. The first of them that removed the man's coat would be the winner.

The wind went first, blowing and blasting the man with freezing cold air, trying to rip the coat right off his back. But the harder the wind blew, the more tenaciously the man clung to his coat, wrapping it tightly around him and holding on to it in his clenched fists. Finally the wind gave up, and the sun's turn began. The sun started beaming directly down on the man, gradually warming the air around him, little by little. As the man's world grew gently warmer, he loosened his grasp on the coat. A few more degrees, and he let his coat fall open while he sat down to relax. Warmer still, and the man closed his eyes, letting down his guard completely. Finally he was so comfortable, he slipped off his coat, dropping it onto the bench without so much as a second thought. And so the sun won the contest and was named the stronger.

Baby Doll thought that maybe she was the wind, and Boy was the sun in this situation. Her plan had been to blow over toward McDavid and let the hurricane force of her presence overwhelm the other woman's defenses. Boy, on the other hand, appeared to be more concerned about making sure Linda McDavid was relaxed and comfortable.

She watched him walk over to where Linda and Cynthia were shooting pool, and then was mystified to see him lean in close to Linda's left side. Was he actually blowing in her ear?

McDavid didn't respond at first, and Baby Doll could see Boy's cheeks puff out to blow a little harder. At that point the woman flicked a hand across her ear. "We got flies in here or something?" she said with mild annoyance to Cynthia. Then she leaned over the corner pocket to line up her next shot.

Now Boy placed a hand in the middle of her back. She didn't

respond. Boy moved his hand slightly upward, toward her neck. She didn't respond. He reached the back of her hair and, slowly, nonthreateningly, began to gently tickle it with his fingers. She responded almost immediately, twisting out of her shot stance and scratching the back of her scalp. In the process she grazed the top of Boy's head with her pool cue, but he didn't seem to be affected by it. "Or maybe we got mosquitoes, though it seems too cold for that. Or spiders or something."

She finished her shot, missed, and straightened to watch Cynthia take her turn. Boy stood inches in front of the hefty woman now, staring at the textures on her face. Suddenly, without warning, he swung out to slap her hard on the cheek. McDavid didn't even flinch, but she did casually, absentmindedly, twirl her pool cue in front of herself, easily blocking his effort and smacking his knuckles at the same time.

Boy rubbed the sore spot across the back of his hand and nodded to himself, satisfied.

So that's what he's been talking about, Baby Doll thought to herself. In order for him to be able to interact with untethered people, Boy had to be either unthreatening or stealthy. So when he said that he had spent years practicing his pickpocket skills, he really meant that he had become a skilled pickpocket—not just an invisible man clumsily removing the contents of a mark's pockets.

Baby Doll looked at her watch and willed Boy to hurry up, but he seemed not to notice the minutes trickling away. He followed McDavid around the pool table, mimicking her posture and her rhythms until he could literally do it with his eyes closed. He bent when she did, spread his arms like she did, flipped the back of his hair like she did. Only his expression never changed, his face one of pure concentration and focus.

Outside, a cold wind blew against the large picture windows

of Donenfeld's Pub and Entertainment. Inside, Baby Doll felt herself sweating. Like the man in the fable, she wanted to discard her coat and leave it on the bench beside her, but she knew that she would want it pretty quickly when it was time to leave this place.

She worried again about the taxi. Would it arrive in time? Or would it come early, before Boy had retrieved the ring, and then leave without them like the previous cab driver had done?

The phone behind the bar rang. The bartender picked it up, answering with a standard greeting, and then listened. He turned his back and spoke confidentially into the receiver. He glanced over his shoulder at the front door, then back at the kitchen door. His brow furrowed a bit, and his eyes landed on the clock. Baby Doll could almost see his lips move, as if he were counting minutes on the face of the timepiece. After a moment, he hung up the phone and stood, thinking, staring at a bottle of Absolut vodka. He turned toward Millie, who was still nursing her drink at the bar.

"Something wrong?" the girl said lazily to the bartender. He immediately spread a plastic smile across his face.

"Nope. All good," he said without conviction.

Baby Doll watched him glance toward the kitchen door once more. "I'm going to dig up a few more bottles of vodka," he said while wiping his hands on a towel. He gave a meaningful look to the waitress, and then turned to the girl drinking slowly at the bar. "Watch the counter for me for about five minutes, will you, Millie?"

"Sure thing. Just remember to spill about a glassful of that vodka for me, okay?"

"Anything for you, sweetheart," he said.

Then he disappeared behind the swinging doors to the kitchen. Millie waited for his exit, seemingly unaware the waitress had also set down her utensils and followed the bartender out of the room. Then she leaned over the bar and snatched the partially empty Absolut bottle, filling her glass to the top before returning the vodka to its place.

Baby Doll watched the clock tick another minute away and felt agitation welling up inside her to almost a breaking point.

"Come on, Boy," she whispered aloud.

Boy opened his eyes and looked directly at her, almost as if he had heard her speak. Then he nodded, and she knew what he was saying in the silence.

It was time to begin.

Thirty-eight

I am ready. I think.

I have tested the limits of observance in Linda McDavid's unconscious mind. She is duller than some overall, but more sensitive than others when I am near her head. Still, over the course of the last few minutes, a plan has formed itself in my mind. It will take patience and coordination, so I begin following her around the pool table, learning her rhythms, mimicking her expressive nature, until I feel that I can predict her next movement quickly and accurately.

I chance a look at Baby Doll and see that she grows more impatient with every second. Still, I will only get one opportunity to do this, and I must make it count.

Unexpectedly, the bartender slips from behind his counter and glides into the kitchen. A second or two later, the waitress does the same. Linda McDavid doesn't notice, although Cynthia's eyes follow the waitress through the kitchen doors.

I begin to think that Baby Doll's impatience is justified. The pictures in my head tell me that very soon this room will change, and my opportunity for subtle theft will disappear as quickly as that bartender has.

McDavid has won the first Nine-Ball match, but Cynthia took the second game. Now they are deep into the third match, each trying to work a little magic to hit the lowest-numbered ball and have it ricochet to sink the number 9 ball and win the game. It is slow going this time, though, and the selection of lower-numbered balls is shrinking as more and more are hit into the pockets of the table.

Cynthia is up to the table now. She decides not to even try hitting the number 9 ball this time, opting instead to attempt to pocket the 5 ball in hopes of setting up a better shot afterward. McDavid stands back, watching the table with passive interest. I sidle up behind the larger woman until she seems comfortable with my presence. I place my right hand, ever so gently, on her back in the space between her shoulder blades. She doesn't react, so I place my left hand next to my right. The woman reaches back and scratches the spot, forcing me to pull back and try again. The second time, I am able to set both hands in place without alerting her subconscious. This is what I need.

Cynthia has missed her shot, and it is now McDavid's turn at the table, so I must follow her around, awkwardly, mimicking her movements without letting her subconscious become aware that I am attached, in a manner of speaking, to her back. McDavid sinks the 5 ball, but then table-scratches on the next shot, so Cynthia returns to take another turn.

I have managed to stay with McDavid through all of her last turn, which I decide was good practice for what is to come next. I feel my fingers beginning to tremble from the effort of keeping my hands balanced gently on the woman's back. My scalp is sweating lightly, and I have to blink my left eye rapidly to keep from getting a trickle of wetness in it. Finally I risk wiping my forehead on my shoulder. McDavid doesn't notice. She is engrossed in Cynthia's next shot. I can sense that she is a competitive person, and the thought of losing to her supposed "inferior" is affecting her concentration and her play. But it also means she is less attuned to the unseen world around her, which means she is less noticing of me.

Finally, I raise my fingertips and gently slide my palms up her back until my thumbs and forefingers are level with her neck.

"Ha!" she says triumphantly. "I knew you couldn't make that crazy shot, Cynthia. Let me show you how it's done."

We are moving again, like two dancers in a mirror ballet. She leans over the table, deep in concentration. I squeeze the thick metal chain she wears between my fingers and am disappointed to discover that the clasp has twisted around her neck and sits near the front instead of the back. Slowly, carefully, I begin working the chain to the left, sliding it over until the clasp finally rests between my thumbs and forefingers. When I feel her pull back and jerk forward to smack the cue ball with her stick, I raise up quickly on the chain, hoping to simulate the impression that the force of her shot has popped the weight of the ring up toward her neck. I am successful, and just as the ring should begin falling back down, I flick the chain in my hands so that it falls outside her shirt instead of back inside it.

McDavid has made her shot, placing the 6 ball in the corner pocket and setting herself up nicely for a combination 7 to 9 ball shot that could win her the game. She doesn't notice that Charlie Murphy's gaudy ring now rests between the second and third button on her flannel shirt.

From the corner of my eye, I see Baby Doll sit up and lean forward. She sees the ring too, but no one else in the bar seems to notice.

McDavid is now walking around the table to set up her next shot, talking a little trash to a clearly nonplussed Cynthia. We are now standing on the far side of the table, facing toward the front door. I see Baby Doll's head swing away and lean toward the large, tinted picture window next to our table. I don't have to guess what she is seeing out there in the parking lot. I know time is now short. I have about one minute, maybe less, to complete this theft.

I try to block out any distractions, forgetting Baby Doll, forgetting what I know is about to come through that front door, forgetting the absence of the bartender and the waitress, forgetting everything but me, Linda McDavid, and the chain between my fingers.

The necklace is held together with a medium-sized barrel clasp. I twist in opposite directions and feel the clasp unscrew and then separate. McDavid leans over the side pocket, lining up her next shot and pumping her back arm in preparation. I transfer both ends of the opened clasp into the fingers of my right hand and remove my left hand completely from the woman's back, waiting.

One. Two.

And she stops.

I know that she always hits on the third pump, but why has she hesitated now?

She straightens, walks to the left, then to the right. She kneels down to get a better look at the angles, then stands up confidently and resets her position. She is unaware that her neck now sits inches above the side pocket of the table, and that this means that Charlie Murphy's ring also dangles precariously there. I raise the chain in the back, pulling the ring closer to her neck and making the jewelry less obvious to a casual observer.

One.

I move the clasp into position.

Two.

I hold my breath, even though I know that makes no real difference.

Three.

She swings her pool cue forward, hitting the cue ball dead center and causing a loud crack sound when it careens into the 7 ball. At just that moment, I release the left side of the clasp and pull the right side up and back toward me. The heavy ring does its part, sliding like a firefighter down the falling portion of the chain, slipping right off the end and dropping unceremoniously into the side pocket just below Linda McDavid's neck.

She stands and curses. She missed the angle, scratching the cue ball in the opposite pocket while the 7 ball zips fecklessly across the table and missing the 9 ball completely, setting up a new shot for Cynthia to take.

At that moment the front door opens and a stream of people enters. Six large men in dark suits, three no-nonsense women, also in dark suits. Of the nine people, five have guns drawn, and the other four are fanning out to take positions at the four corners of the pub.

I look hastily at Baby Doll, and am relieved to see that she has already slid down the bench seat where we were sitting and is crouched like a ball underneath the table. It is not a proud posture, but it is exactly what will keep her alive during the moments that are going to follow.

Linda McDavid looks surprised. She stands up next to the pool table and immediately turns to the bar. When she sees that the bartender is nowhere in sight, she exhales a soft curse. Her eyes flick back toward the kitchen doors, but she knows already it's too late. Cynthia backs away from the table, seeking the security of the other girls still sitting on the benches behind the pool tables.

I lean around McDavid and plunge my hand into the side pocket of the pool table. One second later I feel the warm edges of the ring touch my fingers and I spirit it away to safety. I toss the woman's necklace across the floor toward the benches where the prostitutes sit. I then slide quickly away, heading toward Baby Doll and the table she hides under.

One of the gunmen asserts himself as the leader. He nods toward the four others who have guns at the ready, and they begin walking through the pub, corralling anyone they see and bringing them all to a designated location behind the pool tables. Two of the dark-suited ones—a man and a woman—head into the kitchen. They return a moment later.

"Kitchen's empty," the woman says. "All clear."

The man in charge surveys the pub one more time. He turns to Linda McDavid. "Anyone else in here?" He says it as a command more than a question. Her jaw tightens, but she says, "No." He nods and then speaks into something on his wrist.

"All clear."

Eyes turn expectantly toward the door. I slide into the booth where Baby Doll is hiding. I open my palm under the table to show her that I have the ring. I feel her fingers curl mine into a fist over the ring and then squeeze. She wants me to hold the ring, at least for now.

The front door opens and one more bodyguard walks in. Following behind him is a woman, mid-fifties, with a nose like a hawk and dark eyes that flash with disdain for everything around her. She wears a long leather coat and gloves, but she carries no purse. Her thinning hair is pulled back in a bun. And she looks hungry.

"Victoria Fox," I hear Baby Doll whisper. "The Executive herself."

Victoria Fox surveys the room until her eyes land on the blank face of one of the dark-suited men without a gun drawn. He responds immediately, stepping forward and pointing toward Linda McDavid. "That's her, Ms. Fox," he says. Then he steps back to his place.

Linda McDavid curses.

Thirty-nine

Baby Doll heard the rumble of cars in the parking lot, and it was enough to make her tear her eyes away from Boy's awkward dance with Linda McDavid. She pressed her face against the tinted glass next to her booth and saw four black Mercedes GLK-class SUVs pull into the parking lot outside. Three of the cars opened doors immediately, and Baby Doll counted as two, four, six, nine dark-suited bodyguards exited and walked intently toward the front door of Donenfeld's Pub and Entertainment.

She didn't wait for an introduction. She knew Victoria Fox's people on sight. *How did they find me here?* she thought. *And so quickly?*

For Baby Doll, Boy's earlier comment about hiding under the table suddenly seemed to be very good advice after all. Before the bodyguards had reached the door, she had already slid down under the table, pulling her knees up close to her face and trying to make herself as small as possible on the sticky, dirty floor. At the last second she remembered her backpack. She reached an arm up and snatched it off the bench just as the door to the pub opened.

She looked back at Boy, and found that he was now standing next to Linda McDavid, no longer mimicking her or moving his hands along her back. They were both staring at the stream of armed guards coming in through the door. Baby Doll noticed that McDavid no longer wore her necklace, but she also saw that Boy's hands were empty as well. She wondered what she'd missed—and where Charlie Murphy's cursed ring was.

It was difficult for Baby Doll to see everything that was happening, but she gathered the gist of it. Victoria Fox's people had somehow tracked her—or the ring—to this little hole, and now they were taking it over long enough to get what they wanted. She saw the bodyguards sweep the pub and herd everyone into one corner. She felt relieved when they passed by her table without a second look, and then wondered how long she was going to have to stay crunched up under this table before Fox's people were done.

What will I tell Stanley if I'm late? she wondered. Then she decided that was a problem for future Baby Doll. Present Baby Doll had enough to worry about at the moment.

She couldn't see exactly who said it, but she heard a man's voice say, "All clear." Activity in the pub stilled, and the guards assumed an air of expectancy. A moment later Boy sneaked into the seat above Baby Doll and held out his palm toward her. She was relieved to see the Justice's ring resting in his hand. At first she reached to take it from him, then she had second thoughts. *Who better to hide a ring with,* she said to herself, *than someone who is already hidden?*

She closed his fingers around the ring and gave him a squeeze. And then Victoria Fox walked through the door.

Baby Doll had only seen the Executive in person once or twice before, but she knew her by reputation. She had risen to power eight years ago, under clouded circumstances. In this world shady dealings were part of the folklore, and it hadn't taken her long to cement her authority in the Executive position. She and Charlie had not been friends, but at least they weren't enemies either. Still, there was no disguising her lust for power. If she had found a way to eliminate the Justice Department and consolidate it into her branch of the Organization, it would only be a matter of time before she was the only real crime lord in the city, and maybe even the state.

One of Fox's bodyguards stepped forward and fingered Linda McDavid. *So,* Baby Doll thought, *they've tracked the ring to her after all.* She shuddered to think what might have happened if Boy hadn't been able to steal the ring only seconds earlier. Or what might happen if she and Boy were unable to get out of this place while still in possession of the ring.

Victoria Fox motioned and Linda McDavid was brought sputtering before her. Two guards, one man and one woman, twisted her arms painfully behind her and then held her in place before the Executive.

"Who are you people?" the McDavid woman stammered. "You better be careful, you know. This is Harry Donenfeld's place, and he's a good friend of mine."

Victoria Fox smiled like a cat that smelled fear in a mouse. "Oh, I assure you, Ms. McDavid, Mr. Donenfeld is the least of your concerns right now."

That silenced Linda McDavid. She was apparently used to dropping the Donenfeld name—and used to it getting her out of trouble. She stood uncomfortably, bearing the full weight of Fox's silent gaze on her. Then Victoria nodded and the woman holding McDavid brought a crashing blow down on the back of McDavid's head, just above the point where the spine meets the skull. The large woman wobbled in pain and surprise, but the other guard yanked her back, holding her up and keeping her from falling.

A few of the girls at the back of the room started to protest, but they were quickly silenced by similar treatment from the bodyguards assigned to them.

The female bodyguard with McDavid stepped in front of her

and let her companion hold their prisoner on his own. He twisted one of the large woman's arms farther behind her back and also pressed his forearm against her neck.

"Now," Victoria Fox said calmly, "every time you ask a question, Meg here will cause you to feel pain. Your job today is not to ask questions, but to answer them. Understand?"

"What are you talking about?" McDavid choked out. "What do you want?"

The female guard didn't hesitate. First she smashed an open palm into Linda McDavid's face, cutting her lip and causing blood to spurt from her nose. Then the guard closed her hand into a fist and rammed it into McDavid's solar plexus. The large woman yowled and then grunted.

Victoria Fox looked bored. "Every time you ask a question," she repeated, "Meg here will cause you to feel pain. You understand what I'm saying now?"

This time Linda McDavid simply nodded, as best as she could with a beefy man's forearm buried in her throat.

"Your job today is not to ask questions, but to answer them. Understand?"

She nodded again. Sort of.

Victoria Fox seemed satisfied. "My associate"—she nodded toward the man who had pointed out McDavid—"well, he's sometimes careless with his paycheck." She looked at him with a frown, but her eyes showed appreciation toward him nonetheless. "It seems that late last night he visited one of your, ah, friends." She waved dismissively toward the back of the room. "Well, that's his business. And yours, I suppose," she sniffed. "But it became my business when Mr. Wheeler-Nicholson here noticed the jewelry you were wearing."

Linda McDavid's eyes lit with recognition. "The ring?" she said. "You want my ring?"

The female bodyguard responded with a Tae Kwon Do front kick to the gut, followed by a roundhouse kick to the right side of McDavid's face. The force of the kicks was strong enough to knock the woman out of the other guard's hold. She sagged to the floor, groaning. The male bodyguard looked apologetically toward Victoria Fox, then picked up Linda McDavid by her hair and resumed his hold.

"My ribs," she gasped. "I think you broke my ribs."

The Executive looked on with disinterest until the injured woman stopped speaking.

"Every time you ask a question," she said again, "Meg here will cause you to feel pain. And I have to warn you that it only gets worse, right, Meg?" The female bodyguard gave a small smile and nodded. "In fact, I do believe that Meg actually enjoys it when you ask questions. Is that right, Meg?" The bodyguard's smile grew wider, and she nodded again. "So, let's go ahead and get this out of the way. Do you have any more questions?"

Linda McDavid's eyes grew wide. She was rasping with noticeable effort. She shook her head, eyes darting between Fox and Meg.

"Excellent," the Executive said. "Now, you're right. I do want that ring. The large gold ring. Encrusted with diamonds and a center made of onyx engraved with an ax and a scepter. You know the ring I'm talking about." It was a statement, not a question.

Linda McDavid nodded. "What's so important about—" The guard behind her tightened his grip and she immediately stopped. Meg looked toward Victoria Fox as if to ask whether or not the beginning of a question constituted a full question, and therefore its expected, punishing result. Fox gave her head a slight shake from side to side.

"You know the ring I'm talking about."

McDavid nodded. “Yes,” she croaked.

“Give it to me. Now.”

The absurdity of the situation was not lost on Baby Doll. Even if McDavid had still possessed the ring, it would have been impossible for her to move an inch to get the ring from anywhere on her person as long as Fox’s goon had her pinned like he did.

“It’s on the chain,” McDavid said hoarsely. “Around my neck. Take it. I don’t want it anymore.”

Fox nodded toward the female bodyguard. Meg stepped forward and searched the other woman’s neck, making her way carefully around the other guard’s meaty arm that was still entrenched there. She turned back to the Executive and shook her head.

Linda McDavid’s eyes grew wide again. “No, it was there. I just had it. I don’t know where—”

McDavid stopped speaking because Victoria Fox had suddenly produced a Kahr K9094CN handgun and shoved its barrel partway down her throat. The large woman gagged and coughed, but Fox refused to remove the gun.

“I’m not a patient woman, McDavid,” she said quietly. “Now where is my ring?”

Linda McDavid couldn’t talk, but somehow she communicated the concept, “I don’t know.”

Wheeler-Nicholson was standing near the bench with McDavid’s girls. He picked something off the floor and spoke up. “Ms. Fox,” he said deferentially. “This looks like the necklace I told you about.”

She pulled the gun from McDavid’s mouth and handed it to Meg, who promptly wiped the spit and bile from the barrel with the large woman’s flannel shirt. She motioned to Wheeler-Nicholson and he brought the chain over to her. Fox examined it without touching it, then she turned back to Linda McDavid.

"Is that your necklace?" she asked politely.

"Yes, but I don't know what happened to—"

Victoria Fox nodded and Meg hit Linda again, this time in the jaw.

"I know, you didn't ask a question," Fox said casually. "But you also need to know when to stop answering one." She surveyed the room again, and her eyes paused when they reached the clock behind the bar. It said 3:19.

"So," Fox continued, "your bartender buddy warned you I was coming. You hid the ring, but got careless with the chain."

"No, I—" The forearm at her throat constricted and it was obvious that Linda McDavid suddenly had trouble breathing, as well as talking.

The Executive looked again at the clock. "Perhaps we should move this conversation to a more comfortable venue." She turned and walked out of the pub.

The bodyguards all responded as one. The two charged with Linda McDavid immediately began dragging her toward the front door. The others came into formation and carefully backed toward the door, keeping their guns trained on the patrons the whole time.

As soon as the door closed, the people by the pool tables broke ranks and started chattering to each other. One or two jogged through the kitchen doors and disappeared. Everyone seemed rattled by what had just happened.

Baby Doll dared to crawl onto the seat next to Boy. She pressed her face against the glass and saw Linda McDavid being forcibly inserted into one of the black Mercedes. She also saw a taxicab roll into the parking lot, stop at the sight of the obvious abduction, and then inexplicably pull around to a parking spot on the opposite side of the lot. He kept the engine running. The other bodyguards began filling up the rest of the Mercedes vehicles when a silver Jaguar sedan screeched into the lot, followed closely by a tan Cadillac Escalade EXT. The Jaguar and Cadillac didn't bother with parking places.

Baby Doll felt as if her insides had just been pulled out through her nose. The back door of the Jaguar opened and Maurits exited with a snarl on his face. His two bodyguards also exited the car and followed him as he walked toward the center Mercedes vehicle. From the Cadillac a smallish man with wispy hair and a scar on his cheek also exited with two bodyguards. He looked even more angry than Maurits.

"Marty Goodman, the Legislator, is here too," Baby Doll said to Boy. "So, they all three tracked the ring to Linda McDavid. And Marty can't be happy that Victoria Fox entered his traditional territory without notifying him first."

Victoria Fox exited her car and came to meet the two men. Baby Doll saw them exchanging heated words, and was impressed that Maurits could easily hold his own in the face of Victoria Fox. If anything, she seemed a little bit wary of him, while he showed absolutely no fear of either her or Marty Goodman.

Boy pointed, and Baby Doll felt a little more panic set in. The cab was now pulling out of its parking place, apparently ready to get away from this situation. The tan Cadillac was blocking the front exit, however, and the cabbie was obviously trying to work out the way to exit this place.

Baby Doll calculated quickly in her head. Then she grabbed her backpack and pushed Boy toward the edge of the booth.

"Come on," she said. "It's time to get out of here."

Forty

I feel Baby Doll press her weight against me. "Come on," she says. "It's time to get out of here."

"What about Maurits and the others outside?"

"Just come on."

Her feet have barely hit the floor before she is running toward the kitchen. We rush past the others, but no one seems to notice. Except Cynthia. Recognition lights her eyes as Baby Doll brushes past, but then it's immediately followed by doubt, and before she can take a second look at the face she thinks she knows, we are through the doors into the kitchen.

Baby Doll pauses just long enough to get her bearings, and then she flies toward the back door. We burst into the back lot and are greeted by the requisite smell of rotting food in the Dumpsters outside. And, just as Baby Doll had figured, the taxicab driver was looking for a back entrance to this lot.

"Wait! Taxi! Wait!" she calls out, waving to get the driver's attention. He slows and then stops.

"Get in," he says through a cracked window. "I don't think it's very safe here for a young girl like you."

"Tell me about it," she says with appropriate, aristocratic childlikeness. "That's the last time I promise to meet my boyfriend on this side of town." She swings open the back door and

we both climb in. "Jerk stood me up, and next thing I know there's a gang war brewing or something."

"Yeah," the cabbie says. "Good thing I came by when I did. Are you Bobbi Kane?"

"Yeah. Thanks for coming. I think if you pull into that motel parking lot you can exit on that street over there."

"Right, I see it."

A moment later we are streaking away from Donenfeld's Pub and Entertainment, leaving behind Linda McDavid, Victoria Fox, and all the others. The driver exhales, and only now do I notice that he has a gun sitting on the seat beside him. He grins apologetically back at Baby Doll.

"Guess I don't need this anymore," he says brightly. In one swift motion he sweeps it off the bench and deposits it into the glove box. "Never can tell on this side of the world. I grew up not far from here, and most people here are good people. But it only takes one crazy person to ruin your day, if you know what I mean."

"Yeah," Baby Doll says. I can tell she's ready for this conversation to end.

"Where to?" the cabbie says, finally starting the meter.

"The university," she says. "Student union building."

"Have you there in twenty minutes or your money back," the driver says cheerfully. "You just sit back and catch your breath now."

"Okay," she says. "Thanks." She leans back and closes her eyes, pretending to sleep. Through stiff lips she whispers to me. "That was close."

"Yes," I say.

"You still have the ring?" she asks.

"Yes."

She nods slightly. "Keep it for now."

"Okay."

"I almost feel sorry for Linda McDavid," she says after a moment. Then a pause. "Almost."

I can tell she is remembering the beating McDavid gave her in the holding cell. I find myself torn between justice and mercy toward the woman.

"How did you know that I should hide?" she asks.

"The dreaming," I say. "Sometimes it shows me the past. Sometimes it shows me the future."

"Wow. That must be something."

I don't answer. I have come to a place of peace with the dreaming, but I don't think I like it. Sometimes the dreams show me terrible things. I have no control over them; often I don't even understand them until it's too late. But I have learned to pay attention to them. When I can.

An idea begins to work its way into my head.

"Baby Doll," I say. She opens her eyes and chances a look at the driver. He is now preoccupied with a Beach Boys song playing on the radio. She turns to look at me.

"What is it, Boy?"

"Look," I say, "we have the ring. We have my box. We're alone and in a car. Why don't we keep driving? Just leave town, right now, and never look back? I can get us money along the way. If we go now, they can't follow us. They are too busy with other things. If we go far enough, we can bury the ring in the ocean. You can become someone new. Change your name; choose your name. Become who you were meant to be."

She searches my eyes. "I had a similar thought earlier, Boy," she says softly. Then there is silence.

"Let's go, Baby Doll. There's no reason to go back."

She stares hard at the floor. "There is one reason, Boy."

A name floats into my brain. William Finger.

"But if we take this ring back into Maurits's house, it only increases the chance that he will be able to recapture it and assume Charlie's old position of Justice in the Organization. If that happens, everything you've been working for is gone. Evaporated like morning mist."

She nods.

"And your own life will be at constant risk. Maurits is not safe. He already almost killed you once." She looks at me questioningly. "While you slept."

She nods again.

"Who am I, Boy?" she whispers. "Why am I here?"

"Maybe you are here to be a Deus ex Machina for me," I offer. "You have already done more for me in three days than some other Tethers did in years." I nod toward her backpack and the box it holds. She understands and reaches inside it to produce the box.

She hands it to me and I feel the tingle of its touch. I run my fingers across the filigree, counting the spacings on the side without meaning to do so. One. Two. Three. Four. It feels good. I tick my fingernail on the opposite side. One. Two. Three. My thumb twitches involuntarily.

"You are stroking that box like it's a puppy," she says observantly. "What's in it? What makes this box so important to you?"

"Six," I say. I'm not sure how much more to tell.

"That means nothing to me, Boy."

It seems odd to me that Baby Doll is a new Tether. We've only been together a few days, but I already feel knitted to her more closely than . . . than . . . the boy who was my last Tether; the boy whose name is already lost to me and whose face is fading as well.

"I've lived more years than I can remember," I say by way of

explanation. "Sometimes it's difficult to remember. But some things I don't want to forget."

Baby Doll squints, trying to understand. I am going to have to tell her more, or simply stop talking at all. The box feels alive in my hands, like a breathing being begging to be opened. It makes me feel whole to hold it again.

"I won't remember you, Baby Doll," I say at last. "Just as you will eventually forget me. You will fade from my mind after the tether is broken."

"I could never forget you, Boy. How could I?"

"You will. That's the way it happens. And as time goes by, my memory of you will lock itself behind a door in my mind. I will know that I once tethered to a young woman, that we once were together. But I won't know who you are, what you look like, any of that. It's my nature. It's what makes it possible for me to survive."

"Six," she says, coming to the obvious conclusion. "So inside this box you keep mementos. Out of hundreds of years of living, you keep only six mementos. To help you remember people from your past. Is that it?"

She is close enough to the truth, so I nod. And then I change the subject. I pull Charlie Murphy's ring from my pocket and hold it out to her. "You have your treasure and I have mine. Maybe now is the time to go away from here. Maybe that's why we have found each other. To survive."

"Or maybe," she says slowly, "it's not you who is supposed to be the Deus ex Machina. Maybe it's supposed to be me. Maybe I am the broken, dirtied tool that God intends to use to find that boy. To save the boy. Maybe that's why I've been lost in Charlie Murphy's world for so long."

"To save William Finger?" I say, and I already know the answer.

"Yes," she says.

For an instant I can almost feel the whisper of God on my cheek. It is good, and dangerous, to feel that again.

"It could cost you everything to go back there," I say to Baby Doll.

"It would cost me more to walk away."

She reaches over and wraps my fingers back around Charlie Murphy's ring.

"Keep it," she says. "In case something happens to me. Promise me you'll keep it safe."

I can't respond, and she doesn't press me. After a moment, she turns her attention to the window, watching the winter outside pass by on the streets, and becoming lost in her thoughts. She seems to be humming something. I lean over and return my box to the safety of her backpack.

"I promise," I say finally. But I don't think she is listening.

Forty-one

Baby Doll watched the city roll by outside her window and found herself humming. It was an old song, a church song that told a story about a man who found a pearl and then sold everything he had just to buy it. She couldn't remember all the words, but she wondered if she was more like that man in the song, or more like the pearl. Part of her desperately hoped to be both.

Something about Boy, she realized, made her want to be a better version of herself, to be a priceless pearl someone would be overjoyed to discover. And he made her think more about God than she had in some time. It was hard to be so forcibly confronted with the supernatural and not think about God. And that was why she had decided to go back to Maurits's house, to try to find William Finger. Unreasonable as it seemed, at this particular moment, it felt like that single task was what God had created her for, and it filled her with a sense of purpose she had never known before.

We will go back and find William Finger, she thought, *and then disappear.* With Boy's help she could do that, she could disappear and become someone new. *I will do it,* she found herself thinking. And then she felt cold reality in her bones. Something was still nagging at her that didn't sit right. Was this her purpose? *At least I will try,* she resolved, *and I will hope that's enough.*

The last half of the cab ride they took in silence. When they arrived at the student union building, it was ten minutes to four. Baby Doll almost laughed. She had forty minutes to wait before Stanley arrived to pick her up, and for the first time in days, forty minutes seemed like all the time in the world.

They walked inside, and Baby Doll took them to the spacious sitting area outside the fast food shops. There were tables and chairs, and also along one side, a row of couches and recliners. Beyond that were study carrels and a few desks for those who liked to do their homework in public places. Baby Doll wedged herself into a seat at one of the study carrels, turning the large desk slightly so that she was shielded from the view of most of the rest of the sitting area. She tossed her backpack onto the desk area and then pulled a chair over and situated it casually behind her so that it looked like someone had gotten up from it and left it a little askew. Boy took that seat, a look of patient suffering on his face.

It was then that Baby Doll remembered his wound, and his scar. "Let me see how that scar is healing," she said softly.

Boy unbuttoned his denim shirt and dropped it down his back. Baby Doll bit her lip. The scar was swollen and purple, with yellow lines around the edges. It actually looked worse than before, as if it had gotten a little infected while they were at Donenfeld's Pub. She touched it gently with her finger and felt Boy flinch.

"It will be fine," Boy said, shifting his shirt back onto his shoulders.

"Would it help if you took another nap?" she asked. She looked out at the sitting area. It was sparsely populated, with only a few students either reading or eating junk food. Two full couches and five of the recliners were completely empty. "We've got more than a half hour before Stanley will be here," she said. "Do you want to lie down?"

Boy considered the option.

"Of course, if you stretch out on that couch," she wondered, "does that mean someone might come along and sit on you?"

Boy shook his head. "If I'm on the couch, others will accommodate me without knowing it."

"Right," Baby Doll said.

Boy sighed, and she could almost see him sag, as if he were remembering the pain that the knife had brought to his back. Then he nodded. "It's not long enough to heal completely, but it would help."

"Go," she said. "I'll sit right here and pass the time with worrying." She smiled. "I'll wake you up when it's time to meet Stanley."

Boy nodded again, then he walked over and let his body melt into the cushions of the couch. She watched him for a few minutes, wondering at how completely still his frame was. If she didn't know him better, she might have been tempted to check his breathing just to make sure he was still alive. His right hand was still clenched into a fist, holding, she knew, Charlie Murphy's ring. She wondered why he hadn't put it in a pocket, or at least slipped it on his own finger. Then, thinking about Charlie's ring made her think again about Boy's box.

Only six people, she thought. *If I could only remember six people in my short life, I wonder who they'd be? That would be hard to choose.* Then the enormity of Boy's situation finally sank in. *Only six people. Six.* Out of all the many lifetimes he had lived, Boy could only keep six people in his mind, in his heart. She felt a sense of loss that weighed on her like a burden.

How many Tethers, how many people, had he had to choose to deliberately forget in order to remember those special six memorialized in his box? If we are the sum of our experiences, she thought, then losing those memories meant he was constantly losing parts of himself. No wonder he no longer knew who he was or what he was meant to do. For him, life was only something that would soon be forgotten. Except, that is, for the people represented in his box.

Baby Doll reached over to her backpack and retrieved the box from it. Boy slept undisturbed on the couch. A young girl with a fat textbook and a cup of frozen yogurt approached, but at the last minute opted to slump into a nearby recliner instead of sitting on the couch.

Holding the box somehow made Baby Doll feel a deeper connection to Boy than she'd felt toward anyone else in the short twenty years of her life. She fingered the filigree along the sides of the mahogany wood and remembered the way Boy had done the same.

If it's a puzzle box, she thought, *that means it has a combination. Some unique but repeatable step that unlocks the hidden opening to it.* She touched the cool metal that decorated the box, then placed the tip of her forefinger at the corner on the side of the box. *One.* She let her finger dip into the first gap of the filigree design. *Two.* She moved to the second gap. *Three. Four.* At the fourth gap she felt a fine smoothness, as if the box had been frequently touched in this spot. She held her breath and pushed gently with the tip of her finger. The wood beneath her gave way, sliding inward about one eighth of an inch. On the opposite side of the box, below the decorative filigree on that side, a tiny, cubed plank sprang out about half an inch from the wood.

Baby Doll worried that Boy might be awake, that he might be watching and that he might disapprove. But she didn't take her eyes off the box long enough even to look at him. Instead she tapped the tiny notch and was surprised to feel it click like a tumbler under her touch. She tapped it again, and felt the same click. A third time, and she knew she'd reached the end. Boy had tapped this side of the box three times when he held it in the backseat of the cab. She felt certain that three was the correct number for this part of the combination, but nothing happened. She turned it over and examined it, expecting something to pop out or to pop open as before, but the box remained the same.

She closed her eyes and tried to remember Boy's unconscious mannerisms when he held the box in his lap. Four on the right. Three on the left. Then it hit her. *One in the middle.*

She pressed her thumb between the two buckles on the back of the box, as close to the middle of it as she could estimate, and as she did she felt a circular spot there sink inward about one eighth of an inch. And then a seam appeared as if by magic, and the top of the box skated open, like a sliding door on a tiny track. The wood inside the box gave off a flowery smell, almost like lavender potpourri, but soft and aged. She pushed the lid a little farther and the full contents of Boy's box lay open before her.

Baby Doll breathed in deeply.

Forty-two

It feels good to lie down on the couch near Baby Doll. I feel tired, worn down. I think I will drop off to sleep almost immediately, but the minutes pass by and slumber doesn't come. I feel the soreness in my back and know there is still healing to be done, and usually the healing sleep comes quickly when given an opportunity. But this time my body rests while my mind stays alert.

A girl with a cup of frozen yogurt walks toward me as if to sit on this couch, but then she veers to the right and occupies an empty recliner instead. I lie still and unmoving, waiting for the bliss of slumber. I think about how easy it would have been for Baby Doll to stay in that taxi, to drive out of this city and out of danger, at least for the moment. And I see her face resolving itself into a moment of purpose, refusing to leave until she can find a boy she only met once—a stupid teenager who figured a joyride in a stolen car was no big deal. Baby Doll owes him nothing, really. But she stays for him anyway.

Something more to remember about her.

An unexpected tingling runs through me, starting at my fingertips and running up my arms, then into my body's core. Voices whisper in my head, memories that are on the edges of dreaming. The ambient noises of this student union building float by my ears. Random snatches of conversation. Someone laughing. The humming of vending machines. The squeaking of sneakers walking across the floor. Background music from a local radio station piped in through speakers.

And through all these noises, one small sound captures my attention. A slight click, like a tumbler in a lock. I am amazed that a faint sound like this can cut through the density of the background until I discern that I have heard it on the inside of me instead of from the outside. I hear/feel the click a second time, and then a third. My heart begins to race.

I sit up on the couch and turn toward Baby Doll. She is hunched over in the study carrel, intent on something she holds between her hands. At first I am angry, feel betrayed. And then I know better. She cannot unhinge my box unless I have shown her how. I didn't intend to show her; something inside of me revealed the secret when I was unaware. Something inside of me must have wanted *to reveal the secret.*

Four right. Three left. One in the middle.

I see Baby Doll's eyes widen, see an expression of wonder trickle down her face. I wait, knowing that she has opened my box, knowing that my inmost being now lies bare before her. Even Alondra never opened this box. I wonder what Baby Doll will say now, what she will think, when she understands what is hidden inside there. I wait, but Baby Doll doesn't do anything except stare. She doesn't unpack the box, or lay out its contents before her. For the first time, I am unable to read her face, unable to tell what she is thinking or even feeling.

I walk toward her until I am standing behind her, looking over her shoulder at my opened box. She is unaware of my presence. Her hands are trembling. She closes her eyes, briefly, as if sorting out what to do next. I watch her reach over and stroke the hinge, then she starts to swing the lid back to a closed posi-

tion. Something inside her tells her she must ask permission to go further, and so I will give it to her.

I reach down from over her shoulder and stop the lid from clicking back into place, surprising Baby Doll with my presence.

"How long have you been there?" she says to me.

"Not long," I say.

"I, well, I was curious. Too curious, I guess."

"No," I say. "It's okay."

She looks up at me and then back at the box. "Okay?" she asks again, seeking one last confirmation.

"Okay."

She nods and then reaches inside the box gingerly, as if the things inside will turn to dust if she handles them too roughly. She lays them out on the desk before us.

A wooden matchbox, stamped with the words "J. R. Cole's."

A diamond solitaire ring.

An antique paring knife.

A faded photograph of a beautiful woman, standing in an orchard.

An old postcard with a picture of the Uffizi Gallery in Florence, Italy.

A handwritten letter, carefully rolled into a cylinder and tied with a red ribbon.

"Six," she says to herself. "Only six."

"Always six," I say. "Eternity is visible in six, and six is enough."

"But what if you want to add something new? What then?"

"I risk erasing one memory if I replace it with a memento of a new one."

"So if you put, say, a picture of me in here?"

"Then I would have to remove a memento that is in here now. And I would lose its memory over time."

"When was the last time you added to this box?"

I can't remember the exact day, only the moment. I close my eyes and think. "More than thirty years," I say. I nod toward the letter. "That was the last thing I put in there."

"May I?" she says. I nod, and she carefully unties the ribbon and then unrolls the letter. It is written on a flowered stationery, in the shaky letters of an old woman's hand. Baby Doll reads slowly, drinking in each word like it is wine. When she is done, she lays it back down on the desk.

"May 11, 1978," she says thoughtfully. "And when did you find it?"

"A few months later, I think. Or a year. I'm not sure. At her funeral. It was placed in her hands, inside the casket. I took it from her there. I don't think anyone ever knew."

"How did you know? To attend the funeral, I mean?"

"My Tether saw the obituary. He insisted that we go." I shake my head. "I can't even remember his name or how old he was. Only that he was kind enough to accompany me so I could attend her funeral."

Baby Doll looks at the items on the desk in front of her. "Boy," she says slowly. She is beginning to understand what it cost to keep the memories. Who it cost me.

"Alondra was more to me than life," I say. "I would trade all of eternity for her beatae memoriae.*"*

"And so you did," she says. "For her blessed memory."

She picks up the paring knife and holds it toward me with a question on her face.

"From the early days. With Alondra."

She fingers the diamond ring, waiting.

"From a wedding," I say. I feel no need to say more. She understands without hearing the words.

Next the postcard.

"To remember that once she offered to give me the world."

The matchbook imprinted with a name.

"A drugstore. Where we first met."

The photograph.

"Alondra."

"And?"

"Yes, that's me beside her in the picture. I'd actually forgotten I was there."

"She's beautiful," Baby Doll murmurs.

"She reminded me why I wanted to exist," I say. "Sometimes now, I forget even that."

"But how could you give up the others, your own past, for these little things? Wouldn't one memento of Alondra have been enough?"

"I don't know anymore who the people were that I took out of this box, Baby Doll. I may have even taken myself out of there. I only know that, one by one, I knew I never wanted to lose these memories of Alondra. Not ever."

"So you really will forget me, won't you, Boy? After all, I can never replace anything in here, right?"

"Other than this box, I do not control what I remember," I say. "The memories control me. And there are so many, I just can't keep them all." She waits, but I say nothing more, because I can think of nothing to say.

"It doesn't matter," she says at last. She stands and places her hands on my cheeks, looking deeply into my eyes. "Thank you for sharing this with me, Boy. I feel honored."

I still don't know what to say, so I remain silent. She rises up on her toes and kisses me lightly on the forehead. Then she turns and carefully replaces the ribbon around the letter and gently repacks my box. She glances at me once more before sliding the lid to a close. It clicks into place, resetting the com-

bination and becoming once again a seamless, openless, wooden thing.

She hands me the box, and for the first time in decades I wish that I truly were an angel. It seems to me that Baby Doll deserves one.

She checks her watch and sighs. "It's time," she says. She gathers her backpack and motions for me to follow her to the front of the student union building.

She deserves an angel. Today, however, a Drifter will have to do.

Forty-three

Baby Doll's mind was racing with questions and images as she walked toward the curb in front of the student union building. What kind of person would sacrifice everyone he had ever known to keep the memory of a single person in his heart? What kind of person would even have to make a decision like that? It made Baby Doll wonder what she would be willing to lose everything for, or for whom she would sacrifice it all. Then she almost laughed at herself. Wasn't she doing just that right now? Risking all she was, even her very life, to try and save William Finger?

Then she realized she was going back for more than just Will Finger. She was going back to save a hundred Will Fingers, maybe more, from being lost in the abyss of Charlie Murphy's Organization the way she had been.

It was 4:27 P.M. when Baby Doll exited the student union building. She wasn't surprised to see Maurits's Lexus already parked by the curb waiting for her. Stanley hadn't been kept around for so many years by being late. He saw her walking down the sidewalk and got out to open the car door for her. In the sky above the clouds roiled, casting shadows on the late afternoon below.

"Hello, Baby Doll," Stanley said cheerfully. "Right on time. Good for you."

She tossed her backpack onto the floorboard and hesitated long enough for Boy to squeeze in ahead of her, then she took her seat in the back of the car. "A girl would be foolish to stand up a handsome guy like you, Stanley," she flirted harmlessly, causing the older man to blush just a little.

"Yeah, you are a little charmer, aren't you, Baby." He laughed as he shut the door behind her.

Stanley took his place in the driver's seat and soon they were headed down the road toward Charlie Murphy's mansion. Baby Doll tried to maintain a carefree air about her, but inside her stomach knotted up more tightly the closer they got to home.

"How was school today, Baby?" Stanley asked.

"A bit overwhelming," she said. "It's amazing how far you can get behind just by missing a couple of days."

The driver nodded sympathetically. "You'll catch up, Baby Doll. You're destined for greatness after all."

She laughed in spite of herself. "Now who's the charmer?" she said. Then she added, "Anyway, it looks like I'll be spending more time in the library tomorrow. Think Maurits will let me drive myself again?"

Stanley's demeanor suddenly lost its cheeriness. "I don't know, Baby," he said. "Things are getting worse before they're getting better, if you know what I mean."

Of course I know what you mean, she thought. *I saw it all blowing up at Donenfeld's Pub and Entertainment just an hour or so ago.* But she said, "What do you mean, Stanley?"

He forced a smile into the rearview mirror. "Nothing for you to worry about," he said. "But I expect I'll be driving you to school, and anywhere else, for a while."

"Oh," she said. That could cause problems down the road, but, she decided, it was best to deal with one problem at a time. And right now her biggest problem was going to be finding, and then figuring out a way to free, Will Finger. She looked over at Boy and noticed that he still held Charlie Murphy's ring in his right fist, and now also held his box in his left hand. She considered, briefly, taking the ring from him and then thought better of it. Again, she reasoned, it was safer and unseen when he held it, whereas if she carried it there was no telling who might spot it—or steal it away from her.

She motioned toward the ring and spoke softly to Boy. "Why don't you put that in your pocket or something?"

He nodded and obediently slid the gaudy bauble into a pocket on the front of his pants. She was about to offer to take the box for him when he flicked at one of the metal buckles on it. The buckle slid out, and then up, forming a small clip of sorts that jutted out from the top. He hooked that clip over his belt, allowing him to carry the box upside down, hands free, almost fanny-pack style, on his right hip. She wondered what other secrets that box might have, but didn't have the courage to ask.

Stanley drove in silence the rest of the way, and Baby Doll appreciated the solitude. She stared out the window, thinking about Boy, about his mementos of Alondra. And worrying over exactly what she would do when they got back to the mansion.

Traffic was thicker than usual due to an accident on the freeway, but Baby Doll didn't mind. Still, it was almost 5 P.M. when they finally arrived at the house. Stanley dropped her off at the kitchen entrance and then drove the Lexus around to the garage. Baby Doll stood at the door to the kitchen and said a quick prayer before entering. Boy followed after her, and it almost looked like he was praying too. *That would be a first,* she thought, but she said nothing.

She greeted the kitchen staff warmly upon entering, and they informed her that dinner would be served at 7:30 P.M., per Maurits's request. She asked if Maurits would be home between now and then, but no one seemed to know for sure. "He may not even be here for dinner, even though he set the time for it," the cook said with a little irritation in her voice. "He insisted on a 7:30 P.M. dinner last night as well, and then never showed up for it." The round woman looked at her accusingly. "If you're going to skip dinner again tonight, Baby Doll," she said, "at least have the decency to call down and let Leticia know, okay?" Baby Doll promised that she would, and then headed into the main house.

She deposited her ski jacket in the hall closet with the other coats and then made her way up to her bedroom. She tossed her backpack on the floor and, when she did, she noticed the scuffed and scarred Louis Vuitton handbag peeking out from under the bed. She remembered the contents—particularly the small mini-revolver that Maurits had bequeathed to her after the episode at the cemetery. *Five shots,* she thought, *used wisely, would all be deadly.* It was a familiar thought, and one she didn't welcome.

So much had happened in just three days, but she found herself thinking the same things she did on the way to Charlie Murphy's gravesite. *Could I kill Maurits?*

She decided not to answer herself, and instead kicked the Vuitton purse farther under the bed until it was well out of sight. Then she turned to Boy and saw he was staring out the window again. The bulge in the back of his waistband reminded her how hard it was to get away from a gun in this house. She started to speak and then stopped herself. Boy was at peace, at least for the moment. And she had some thinking to do as well. She let the silence rule the room for almost an hour, working up courage she wasn't sure she had.

Outside, the day was done, and a gray presence shadowed the world, pierced periodically by streetlamps and porch lights. Snow began to fall, and Baby Doll felt grateful. The white blanket always seemed to remind her of hope, of second chances. She felt like she needed a little bit of both of those right now.

Boy stood motionless, staring out the window for so long that Baby Doll wondered how his muscles didn't ache or give way beneath him. At last he turned and faced her.

"You know where William Finger is, don't you."

"Yes."

"Why didn't you tell Honoria Lopez?"

"I couldn't. I didn't want to believe it."

"What do you believe now?"

She took in a breath, and then exhaled it. "I believe that I am to keep Will Finger from becoming a lost thing. That I am to be a Deus ex Machina, a representative of God who arrives just in time to save the day."

"And what am I?"

She smiled sorrowfully at him. "You are a Drifter. And I don't know what that means."

He nodded. "You are different, Baby Doll. Not the same girl I tethered to three days ago. I can feel the change inside me. You were blocked to me then. Now I see you more clearly, like a painting that's been cleaned and restored."

"I feel different, Boy. I think it's because of you."

"What do you mean?"

She stood and walked to the window, watching the snow fall gently to the ground. "You remind me . . ." she started. "You remind me that God exists. That loving something matters. That not all lost things have to stay lost. Maybe that's what a Drifter is. Someone to remind us of important things."

"Is that what you believe?"

"Credo ut intelligam," she said. *I believe so that I may understand.*

"Credo quia absurdum est," he replied, and Baby Doll couldn't help laughing.

"Yes," she said, "that's closer to it. 'I believe it because it is absurd.' That sounds about right."

She felt warmed to see a smile slip onto Boy's face. But in his eyes she saw a new sadness begin to cloud up.

"What is it, Boy?" she said.

"I tried to see it, Baby Doll. To find it for you. I couldn't. Not yet at least. I'm sorry."

She felt herself blinking too fast. Why did she know what he was talking about?

"It's okay, Boy."

"You are more than a lost name, Baby Doll."

"Well, I'll never know, will I, Boy? Mine was taken from me before I could speak it. And now the only person left alive who knows it is Maurits, and we both know he'll never tell. He would never betray Charlie Murphy like that, not even a dead Charlie Murphy."

"I'm sorry." He said it again, as if it were his fault.

"It doesn't matter, Boy," she said, speaking to herself as much as to him. "We have a more important problem to deal with right now."

He looked toward the door of the bedroom. She reached out and squeezed his hand.

"If the cook is right, Maurits won't be home for at least another hour," she said. "Guess now is as good a time as any."

In spite of her words, she didn't move for another minute. Then she walked to the bedroom door and opened it wide.

"Amantes sunt amentes," she whispered to herself. And then she walked out onto the marble floor and turned toward the door to Charlie Murphy's old bedroom.

Forty-four

"Lovers are lunatics," I hear Baby Doll whisper just before she screws up the courage to go face the damage that must be William Finger by now. I think she is probably right. There is some element of lucid insanity inherent in any decision to love. It strikes me that perhaps Baby Doll has finally found her calling, and maybe herself in the process. Not to be a Deus ex Machina, or even to be the person who finally breaks the cruel grip of the Organization on this city. Perhaps what it takes to get God's attention is to love enough to act on his behalf. Or perhaps when you have God's attention, you finally can love enough to act. Like so many other things in my existence, it is a mystery to me.

We take only a few steps beyond her bedroom door when Baby Doll stops. "Wait," she says, "I forgot something."

She runs back into her room and emerges a moment later with her new cell phone in hand. "Might need this in there," she says breathlessly. "At least I hope we do."

The upstairs is vacant at present. In fact, this entire side of the house seems empty. This is a good thing. I feel a sense of unease when we walk through the door of Charlie Murphy's old bedroom, but I can't tell if this is more than just a feeling.

Baby Doll hesitates once inside the room, then she turns and closes the heavy door behind us. The room darkens immediately and Baby Doll has no choice but to turn on a lamp to better reveal what is in there. There is a faint smell of furniture polish, and what appears to be a new bed, a large king-sized one with a maplewood headboard and no other frills. The bed is meticulously made up, as if an army sergeant wants to use it for bouncing coins. The dressers and wardrobe cabinets are polished and closed. The shutters on the windows are all closed, with the exception of one that has apparently broken off and is now leaning against the wall behind the desk. The desktop is clean save for a single laptop computer set in the middle of its surface. In all, the room is almost museumlike, as if it were being prepared for a scene in a movie rather than a place where someone actually lives.

"This room was a mess last time I was in here," Baby Doll mutters. "Maurits has definitely made it his own."

She stops at the desk, as if remembering something painful. I watch her, and see flashes of images. It hurts me, but not in a physical way. She stands there, thinking, breathing, remembering. Suddenly she turns back to me, a look of unexpected wonder on her face. She walks to me slowly, and I wait for her to come.

She stands in front of me and I see her looking deeply into the markings in my eyes. She is searching, and whatever she is searching for, she finds.

"You really are marked with a cross, aren't you?" she says.

This time, seeing the belief in her eyes, I can't deny it.

"I think I have finally understood something, Boy. I think it finally makes sense. I don't even know how I know . . . but I do. I know."

"What is that, Baby Doll?"

"You are *a Deus ex Machina," she says, and I see that she believes it. "But not in the way I expected. You're not here to save me from Charlie Murphy or Maurits Girard or any of those people."*

Her words have a familiar ring to them. I almost remember something important about myself.

"You found me, Boy. God marked you and then sent you over centuries to find me. Do you know what that means to me?"

I feel a tingling in my sides, in my heart.

"I'm not lost anymore, Boy. God sent you to find me for him, to seek and to save that which was lost—did I read that somewhere in the Bible?—and because of that finding I have the strength to be the person he sends to find William Finger."

"I don't know, Baby Doll—"

"That's okay," she says, "because I do know. It's clearer to me than anything has ever been in my life." She looks at me and smiles. "I think," she says, "it's clearer to you than you remember as well."

And then a rush of images floods my memory. Of time before time, of stories that have been told and lived, of people—a long, joyful line of people—who sit in the eternal embrace, all of them part of me, part of my past and my future. I see Alondra among them, and she is beaming, as though she's been trying to tell me this for so very long. I am no angel. Not a demon or a ghost. I am something different, maybe something better. I am a secret, something God created and then hid on the fringes of reality. A tool destined to do as he did, to seek and to save that which was lost, to bring lost things back to his hand. I am not an angel. I am a Drifter, and for too long I have forgotten what that means.

"Thank you, Boy," Baby Doll says quietly. "Thank you for coming to me. Thank you for finding me. For showing me that God never lost me. You may not remember me, but I will always, eternally, remember you."

I don't know what to say, so I say nothing. But that's okay, because I know that words are not always necessary between Baby Doll and me. Not anymore.

She reaches out to me and squeezes my hands in hers. Then she nods and turns toward the back of Charlie Murphy's master bedroom. She walks slowly, as though she doesn't want to see what she knows will be there. But she refuses to stop, despite her obvious growing fear.

I feel a freshness inside me, and yet also a sense of dread on the outside. I have not dreamt this moment, nor have I seen it, and it makes me feel blinded, as if unseen things are at work—and they mean to cause Baby Doll harm.

At the back of the bedroom Baby Doll stops in front of a particular bookcase embedded in the wall. She takes a deep breath and then reaches over to the left edge and gives it a hard shove. The bookcase remains solid, and I am unsure why she is surprised.

"No," she says. "Wait a minute. How can . . . ?"

She leans in closer to inspect the bookcase, running her fingers along the edges of both sides. I move to her and now I see that there are creases around the bookcase, disguised by paint and unobtrusive panels. She pushes again on the left side of the case, and again nothing happens. She looks at me with concern in her eyes.

"It opens, Boy," she says to me. "Will Finger is behind this bookcase. I'm sure of it. But now I can't get it open."

I nod. She turns back to the bookcase and begins tearing tomes off the shelves, not bothering to stack them neatly or to do anything but see what is behind them. I move to the right of the bookshelf and begin following the signs. Paint flaking in this spot. Dusty areas that abruptly give way to circles where no dust remains. Chips on the corners of the wood. And then I see it, the wooden plug that covers the almost invisible hole in the right side of the case on the third shelf down. I check the left side and see a similar plug there as well.

"Baby Doll," I say, and she stops flinging books long enough

to look at me. I point to the plug on her side, and she understands almost immediately. Together we remove the plugs.

There is a thick, short iron bar on my side of the bookcase, with a metal ring attached to its end for use in pulling and pushing it into place. It runs through the wood of the bookcase and into the wood frame of the wall, effectively bolting the case in place. It slides out easily, as if it has been used frequently over the years. On Baby Doll's side is a similar metal rod but with one important difference.

The metal ring attached to her rod is clipped inside a padlock that barely fits inside the hole. There is no key, no indication of where a key is kept. Only the bolt and the padlock that holds it in place.

Baby Doll looks at me in desperation, but all I can do is nothing.

"Can we break it?" I ask. "Cut through it? Or through the wood around it?"

"We don't have enough time for that kind of operation," she says. I can see her mind racing through clues, forcing itself to discover where a key might be hidden. "We have to be out of here before Maurits gets back, or we all will end up in this room."

She steps back again, studying the bookcase, following its lines. She kicks aside a stack of books to study the other side, and then she stops.

"I know you, Charlie Murphy," she says to herself. "I know you better than you know yourself."

She bends down and begins looking through the stack of books at her feet. After a moment she pushes them all aside and returns to the books still left on the shelves. I see her whispering titles to herself as she reads them on the spines. The book she is looking for is on the second shelf from the top, about two thirds of the way across.

"The Prince," *she says softly, "by Niccolò Machiavelli."*

She opens the book and finds a small brown envelope glued onto the inside of the back cover. And in the brown envelope, there is a key.

She throws the book onto the floor at her feet and inserts the key in the lock. When it turns, her face registers both relief and fear. She pulls the locking rod from the wall and looks at me. With a deep breath, she pushes again on the left side of the bookcase. This time it swings open effortlessly, turning on a hinge buried somewhere in its middle.

The room on the other side of the bookcase is both a cell and a torture chamber. There is a metal table in its center. And fastened to the table is a young man, with shaggy blond hair and frightened blue eyes.

"William Finger," Baby Doll says. "I've found you at last."

Forty-five

William Finger's head snapped sideways at the sound of Baby Doll's voice; his eyes squinted in the light that flowed into the shadowy cell from the bedroom. His mouth was covered by thick duct tape, and his arms and legs were handcuffed to the four corners of the metal table.

"Boy," Baby Doll said quickly. "Turn on the overhead lights."

Boy stepped inside the room and flipped a switch, flooding the cell with fluorescence that appeared to hurt Will Finger's eyes. The room was filled with the stench of pain and bodily fluids, and when Baby Doll got a clear look at the captive boy, she felt like weeping and like being sick at the same time.

His face was swollen and bruised, with a particularly nasty purple-and-black spot in approximately the same location where Baby Doll still wore a fading bruise from Linda McDavid's fists. A cut above his left eyebrow looked to be the result of a heavy ring forced punishingly into his forehead. He had been stripped down and wore only his underwear, now soaked through with sweat and stained by blood. His chest bore several hostile, raised red welts, as though burned randomly with either cigars or electrical charges. His legs appeared remarkably unscathed until Baby Doll looked at the bottoms of his feet and saw more red welts and fresh scars dotting the fleshy, plantar parts. At least two toes also appeared to be broken.

Whether Will Finger recognized her or not was unclear. His eyes followed her with intense fear, but his body barely responded otherwise to her presence. He didn't strain at his bonds, or even scream for help behind the duct tape on his mouth. But his swollen cheeks and clear blue eyes called for help nonetheless.

"No keys," Boy said after a quick survey of the room. "We'll have to cut the handcuffs off."

Baby Doll stared at William Finger a moment and then walked to his side. She knelt close to his ear and gently stroked the side of his face, trying hard not to cause him more pain. She contemplated ripping the tape off his face, but then worried it would reopen a cut that appeared to run beneath it.

"I've found you, Will," she said. "You are not lost any longer. And I'm going to get you out of here. You understand?"

The young man nodded, but fear still shone in his eyes.

"Keep looking for a key," Baby Doll said to Boy. "Check that cabinet over there. I'm going to get help."

She walked into the bedroom and then heard Boy's voice.

"Baby Doll, wait," he said.

She turned on the carpet and looked back into the cell from the outside. She felt torn between needing to stay near Boy and needing to get help for William Finger. Finally she nodded. She pulled her cell phone out of one pocket and Detective Lopez's business card out of the other. She dialed quickly on the phone pad, never taking her eyes off Will Finger.

"Hello," she said at last. "Detective Honoria Lopez, please." Then she felt a crushing grip on her hand, closing the cell phone and bruising her knuckles as they were squeezed together in submission. Her knees buckled from the pain, and her eyes flew to Boy in alarm. He came quickly to her side, but could do nothing to stop Maurits from threatening to break her hand.

"I tried to tell you he was coming," he whispered.

"Calling a friend, Baby Doll?" Maurits's voice was ice.

"Maurits, please," Baby Doll grunted. "You're hurting me."

The big man let go of her hand, removing the cell phone in the process. She felt herself panting and she cradled her right hand with her left. Maurits made sure the connection had closed on the phone call and then tossed the cell across the room toward the desk.

"Get up, Baby Doll."

"Maurits—"

"Get up."

Baby Doll obeyed, stepping away from the cell until she stood at the end of the bed in the room. Maurits eyed her carefully, then stepped quickly into the cell and turned off the light. Baby Doll could hear Will Finger calling for help now, screaming behind the duct tape that covered his mouth. A sweep of Maurits's hand and the bookshelf closed behind him. Baby was surprised at how effectively that silenced the boy's cries. Maurits seemed to notice her surprise.

"Charlie learned a long time ago how important it is to soundproof a room like that," he said matter-of-factly. "Otherwise he'd never have gotten any sleep."

"Maurits," Baby Doll was pleading now, "you have to let him go. He didn't do anything."

He cocked his head in her direction. "I told you I'd take care of it, Baby. He was the one who drove off with you at Charlie's funeral and the one who got you hurt. No one disrespects Baby Doll like that. I've got it under control. There was no reason for you to come in here."

"Maurits, he didn't do anything. You got the wrong person."

"Can't be helped now, can it?"

"Maurits, let him go."

"Is that an order, Baby? You got the right to make an order like that? Is that something you can do?"

Baby Doll was speechless. Her mouth moved as if she wanted to say something, but no words came out. Maurits eyed her carefully, but let the silence hang in the air, apparently comfortable with the moment. A movement caught the corner of Baby Doll's vision and she saw Boy step in close to her. He reached into the waistband of his pants and produced a Kahr K-series handgun. He held it toward Baby Doll.

"Shoot him," he said quietly. "He's going to kill you if you don't."

Baby Doll placed a trembling hand on the gun. *Could I kill Maurits?* she wondered again. *Could I place a bullet behind his ear, and then run like madness out of this room, out of this city, out of this world?*

"I'll distract him," Boy said. "Just give me one minute to tear down one of those shutters." He pressed the handle of the Kahr into her palm, but something in her made her refuse to clasp it with her fingers. She pulled her hand away.

"No," she said. "No. I can't."

"I'm glad to hear that, Baby Doll," Maurits said. "Because only the Justice can make an order like that. But there is no Justice right now, you know that already, don't you, Baby?"

Boy looked somber, but he didn't force the gun any further on her, dropping it on the bed beside her instead. Baby Doll didn't respond to Maurits's question. Again, he seemed satisfied with the silence. After a moment he leaned back against the desk. His face relaxed a bit, his eyes glazed, remembering. He seemed to age a bit before Baby Doll's eyes.

"You know, Baby," he said, "when you were little, you talked all the time. Couldn't get you to shut up, really, not until after your mom died. Gibberish mostly. Imitating sounds more than words, if you know what I mean. But you were a smart little thing. Knew how to get what you wanted from whomever you wanted. Even from me."

Baby Doll watched the big man speaking. His body language was tense, firm, ready for a fight. But his voice, that was different. His voice felt warm, almost nostalgic. Tinged with affection.

"You used to make your mama laugh. A lot. She thought you were the world, so much so that I almost believed it too."

"Maurits," Baby Doll said, "don't do this."

He reached inside his coat and unholstered a Glock 37 big-bore handgun.

"You couldn't say your name right, Baby Doll," Maurits continued. "Kept getting it garbled whenever you'd try. Made us laugh so much. You thought it was funny too. I think you enjoyed the attention."

"Maurits," Baby Doll said. She was crying now. Not sobbing, just allowing the tears to stream down her cheeks without holding them back. She reached a hand in his direction. Baby Doll saw Boy walk over and peer closely into the big man's face.

"Your mama, she thought it sounded like 'Baby Doll' when you garbled your name. She started calling it back to you, and the name stuck."

Maurits opened the clip on his Glock 37 and checked the number of rounds. He seemed satisfied with it and replaced it in the gun with a sharp snap.

"Charlie Murphy, he always hated that name. Thought 'Baby Doll' was silly, not something that people would respect. Then someone made the mistake of making a negative comment about it, and he knew he couldn't have that kind of disrespect, not in his Organization. He came down hard. 'The girl's name is Baby Doll,' he said after your mama died. 'Anybody disrespects that name has to deal with me.' We all understood, even Charlie's enemies. And so your name was Baby Doll. That was it."

Boy stepped away from Maurits and nearly stepped on Baby Doll's cell phone. He picked it up and came back and stood close to Baby Doll. She took his hand in hers, and waited.

"You know, Baby, you told me this morning you felt lost without your real name." He nodded, as if talking to himself. "You aren't lost, Baby. You never were lost. Just hidden. Charlie Murphy hid you away for a while, that's all."

"Maurits," Baby Doll said. "Let me go. Let that boy behind the bookcase go. It's not too late."

"Oh, but you're wrong there, Baby Doll," the big man said, standing to his full height again. "Past the point of no return for us now, as they say. *Facta non verba* and all that." He pointed the gun toward her head. "Where's the ring, Baby Doll? I need that ring. I have to have it, and soon. So much that I might even be willing to kill you for it, Baby. Even you."

Boy released Baby Doll's hand and stepped solidly in front of her. "Get down," he hissed, passing her the cell phone. "When he shoots, run. Run to your car. Lock yourself in and call 911. I'll follow you. I promise. If you have to leave before I get there, I will know that you'll come back for me as soon as you can. Understand?"

"I can't tell you where the ring is, Maurits," Baby Doll said over Boy's shoulder. "Only that it's someplace where it will never be found. Not ever."

Maurits shook his head. "Anything can be found if you look long enough for it, Baby Doll. I just don't have enough time to keep looking. Tell me what you did with the ring, Baby."

"And then what, Maurits? What happens after you get the ring?"

"Then I will be the Justice, just as Charlie Murphy always said I would be. And after I get the ring, I can hide you away, far from here. I always took care of you, didn't I, Baby?"

The smell of Maurits came into Baby Doll's memory, of the gentle man who comforted her when she was alone, who chased away the demons of the nighttime when she was just a little girl.

"You used to read books to me, didn't you, Maurits?" The memory was faded and rain-soaked, but for some reason it came to her anyway.

"You always did like books, Baby Doll."

"And I think it was you who taught me to ride a bike. It was you, wasn't it, Maurits?"

"That was fifteen years ago, Baby Doll. You got a good memory."

"Can you really shoot me, Maurits? You're the closest thing to family I've ever had."

"You're the closest thing I got to a daughter, Baby Doll. But the Organization demands complete loyalty. Not family. And if I don't get that ring, I'm a dead man anyway. I'm not a coward, so I won't run. But they'll kill me unless I have that ring. What are my options? So tell me, Baby. For old times' sake. Tell ol' Maurits where you hid Charlie Murphy's ring."

She shook her head, pausing only long enough to wipe her nose on the sleeve of her shirt. "I love you, Maurits. It's not too late for you."

Maurits sighed and his whole body sagged. The Glock fell to his side. He leaned heavily against the desk.

"Belinda," he said softly. "Your name is Belinda Gayle Marston. That's who you are, Baby Doll. That's who you are."

Then, in one swift motion he raised the Glock, aimed, and fired.

Baby Doll screamed as his arm moved. She knew from the instant he began to say her name. She pushed Boy out of the path of the bullet. The metal slug pierced her larynx first, twisting her scream into a gurgling silence, and then it imbedded in the third vertebra of the cervical portion of her neck. She crumpled immediately to the floor, eyes wide, mouth still open, spilling blood both inside and outside of her body.

Maurits slumped even further against the desk. "I love you too, Belinda," he said. Then the big man put his face in his palms and wept.

Forty-six

I feel the bullet in my soul as though it has struck me instead of Baby Doll. I am completely caught off guard by Baby's actions. Why would she push me out of the way? Why would she sacrifice her own life to save me from a temporary pain?

She wilts to the floor, landing in a distorted mess, with the right side of her cheek pressed to the carpet and the back of her head barely touching the footpad on the bed.

There is so much blood.

Even I am taken aback by the amount of blood that spills. I drop beside her, mixing my own tears with liquid life that pools up beneath her wound. Baby Doll is motionless, except for eyelids that flutter. The bullet has clearly severed her spine, cutting off all nerve connections to the rest of her body. I hope that, at least, spares her the pain associated with dying.

Maurits is alone by the desk, head in his hands as he cries. But he is irrelevant to me right now. All that matters is Baby Doll.

I reach for her limp hand, grasping, squeezing, willing my own life into it, but it does no good. She can't feel me; she can barely see me.

Her eyelids flutter again.

I am struck by how slowly death comes, even when it only

takes minutes. And I feel a great sorrow. Baby Doll goes where I cannot follow. Not ever.

I lie beside her on the floor, her blood smearing on my face, and I bring my eyes level with hers. She cannot speak, but it's okay. We no longer need words between us. There is still a flicker of life in the back of her eyes. She sees me, I know it. I believe it.

Another flutter.

"Baby Doll," I whisper. "I will remember you. I promise, Baby Doll. I will remember."

A flutter. More slowly this time.

A candle shines unsteadily in her retinas, as if a soft wind is blowing by.

She hears me. I know it. I believe it.

"You found me too, Baby Doll."

And she is gone. The light of life turned to dullness in her eyes, leaving behind it only flesh and blood.

I cannot bear to leave her, to have her leave me. Not yet, not now when we have only just begun to find ourselves again. I long for the pain of Severance, if only to turn my attention away from the pain of losing her. But death only weakens the tether; it doesn't break it. Nothing breaks an existing tether except a new tether.

"I won't forget you, Baby Doll." She can't hear me, but I make the promise again anyway. And I know what I must do.

Maurits moves from his perch on the desk. He is done crying now. A man like him can never cry for long. He doesn't wipe the tears from his face. He stares with a relentless sorrow in his eyes at the girl he has raised, at the woman he has killed. He moves closer to her, touches her cheek as if expecting to find she will wake again after all. Finally he reaches inside his pocket. "This will end it," he softly says. "It is done."

I rise from beside her and lean heavily against the bed. I know what I must do.

From my belt I unhook the filigree that holds my box by my side. Four right. Three left. One in the middle. The lid swings open, releasing the faint aroma of lavender. There are six things inside, and I must choose carefully. After a moment, I steal the diamond solitaire ring from the box, then rest the box on the bed behind me. Baby Doll's hand lies limp and distorted beside her stomach. The ring is too big. Again. I place it securely on the middle finger of her right hand, and it fits there.

"I will remember you, Baby Doll," I whisper.

Maurits is now fingering his own cell phone. In the silence of the room, I hear the numbers as he presses them. At first it strikes me as odd that he has them memorized, and then I remember the idea of keeping friends close, and enemies closer.

"Detective Honoria Lopez," he says flatly.

"I will remember you, Baby Doll."

"Detective Lopez," Maurits says after a moment. "There's been a murder. At Charlie Murphy's old mansion. Yes. The killer is still in the room. Come and get me, Detective. It's over. It's all over."

He drops the cell phone to the floor, not bothering to hang up the call. Then he walks to the bookcase in back of the room and gives it a shove on the left side. The case swings silently open. He stares inside there for a moment, and then returns to the bed where he sits down gently beside Baby Doll. His eyes are glazed and dry. Empty. He stares at the bedroom door, waiting.

I take the Justice's ring from my pocket and look at it once more. I wonder what would have happened if I had simply dropped it in front of Maurits before he had pulled the gun. If I had simply given him what he wanted—power, authority, purpose. And saved Baby Doll's life in the process.

But I know she wouldn't have let me do that. Not today.

Maurits sighs, the deep sighing of a man who suddenly real-

izes how old he really is. Of a man who no longer cares about life, or death, or power, or love.

The Organization is finished. With Maurits's testimony, and the evidence he provides, Honoria Lopez will be able to flush through the criminal underworld like a fire hose drowning rats. But even that won't bring Baby Doll back to me.

I feel the tether beginning to stiffen, like gum that hardens in the dry air. I don't know how much longer it will be before I must stay right beside Baby's side. But I don't care; there's no place else I want to be right now anyway.

My box sits open on the bed behind me. I know what I must do. I must hide this ring, keep this memory, for eternity. Baby Doll is lost no more; God found her before the bullet pierced her neck, and right now he calls her by a new name, one that he has held for her since before time began. God found her, and I cannot allow myself to lose her either.

I drop the Justice ring into my box and seal it shut again.

In the distance, sirens begin to wail.

In the losing, sometimes we are found. After all, God did not come so that he might forget his children, but to seek and to save that which was lost. May this be the truth that I always remember.

It is so easy, sometimes, to forget . . .

—SOLACE THE LESSER
PHILOSOPHER, HISTORIAN, AND
DRIFTER, A.D. 39

Forty-seven

FRIDAY, FEBRUARY 25

I am cold.

What was once a dry February has grown moist over the past week. There are drifts of snow in neat, snowplowed piles around the edges of this place. The sleet of the morning covers my frame, stinging my face and neck. There is numbness in my fingers and toes, and a biting that seems to come from inside my earlobes robbing me of comfort.

The dirt beside me is tumbled and stirred, but already I can see the hardness forming within the mass that extends six feet below me. Baby Doll lies beneath that mound of earth, her body colder than the frigid air that now surrounds me. The cemetery is empty, though I see cars pulling up in the parking area to the north. There is another casket that has been set up for a ceremony about a hundred feet away, but right now that means nothing to me.

I tethered to Baby Doll a week ago. Only one week, yet it already seems like forever.

She was too young to die, too young to leave me locked to her in an unforgiving world. In the cold.

I am not angel, nor am I demon. I am not a ghost as some would like to believe. I am a Drifter, marked by Christ and sent out to seek and to save that which was lost. I feel the cold in my pure physicality. In my skin, in my pores, down into my bones. I want to moan and cry, not for myself, but for the child who lies buried beside me. But I cried my tears out days ago. She would not want me to cry forever.

A few mourners enter this graveyard. They pass me by without notice. No surprise.

More mourners move toward the other casket. Not many. A few faithful friends, I suppose. And one companion, a woman in her mid-fifties with dark eyes and graying skin. She is apparently the widow of the man in the casket over there.

I am unseen by any of them, and I wish desperately to share one of those wool coats draped over the backs of any of the people who pass me by. But they are too far away for me now. Baby Doll's death has weakened the tether, but not broken it.

My eyes hurt from the cold. I close them and finally give in to the ground below me. It is cold like me, but it holds me without complaint. I sit next to the freshly filled grave and curl into as much of a ball as I possibly can, rocking back and forth like a baby wishing to sleep in his mother's warm arms.

Baby Doll was only twenty years old when I found her. Funny to think that was just a week ago, right here in this very place. And now, when we should be smiling together and watching the snow fall from inside a warm home, she is gone already, and I am left here to remember. I will remember.

—

Honoria Lopez came to Charlie Murphy's old house and barged through the door waving a warrant she must have had waiting for probable cause. She came into the master bedroom with four uniformed police officers behind her and found Maurits Girard sitting next to the dead girl in silence.

To her credit, Detective Lopez didn't say anything except for reciting the Miranda rights to the big man. He stood and nodded, telling her that he understood. He handed her the Glock 37 by the barrel. She received it in a cloth and passed it to a uniform who produced a plastic bag meant for holding evidence and dropped it in there. He nodded toward the open bookshelf, then reached in his pocket and passed over a set of handcuff keys. One of the uniforms radioed for an ambulance while two of the others rushed to release poor William Finger.

Honoria Lopez held out handcuffs of her own, and Maurits let himself be shackled without a fuss. She started to lead him through the door, back to the squad car waiting in the driveway, but he stopped.

"You're going to want that," he said with a nod toward the laptop on the desk. "If you leave it now, it will be gone before you get back."

She nodded, and the last uniform unplugged it from the wall and wrapped it in plastic as well. And then they all walked through the door, into the marble corridor of the second floor, and out of my sight.

—

I have not seen Maurits Girard since last Monday night, but I have heard bits of news about him and seen his name on TV news and in the daily paper. They are saying he's given up everything and everyone. That Honoria Lopez has so much evidence stacked in the Police Services building that not even Charlie Murphy could have made it all disappear.

Victoria Fox is gone. She disappeared with a few close allies within an hour after Maurits's arrest. Rumors are that she has gone to California. Or to Barbados. Or to the moon. No one really knows for sure.

Marty Goodman was not so lucky. When word got out that Lopez was on the way, two of his own bodyguards gunned him down in cold blood. They got away with murder and a sizable chunk of the Legislator's cash that he'd collected from lobbyists in the past week. Maybe they are with Victoria Fox now. Or maybe they also have gone to the moon.

The remnants of the Organization are left in disarray. Maurits's hoped-for army has melted away into nothing. Mid-level bosses are falling over themselves in holding cells and interrogation rooms, trying to cut their own deals with Honoria Lopez. Trying to save their own skins. The rest are either long gone or holed up in jail. All because of a college coed who was smart enough to steal a ring from a dead man.

Rest well, Baby Doll. You deserve that at least.

The thought of her name warms me inside just a little.

"Rest well, Belinda Gayle," I whisper to the dirt beside me. "Rest well."

—

I feel my rocking stop, feel my body stiffen. I raise my head a bit, listening to a sound I don't quite recognize. Or maybe one that I do recognize. One that requires my attention.

My breathing relaxes involuntarily and I let a spurt of warm breath fire from my mouth. I feel mild dizziness accompanied by a churning, a knotting in my stomach. My head turns slowly, and then my eyes lock onto hers.

The widow at the other grave site. She appears to be looking right at me.

Do you see me?

I mouth the words, and somehow she understands them.

She nods slowly.

Epilogue

To Whoever Finds This Letter:

If you are reading this, my dear family, my dear friends, it means that I have passed away without finding him.

Rest assured that as I write this, I am of sound mind and body, in full control of my faculties, and not in any way impaired. You will even notice that I have written this on the same date that I have formalized my will in front of witnesses and my lawyer, who have all testified to the above. In fact, I am writing this letter within an hour after the signing of that will, and in my own handwriting so that it may not be confused with another's.

I need to tell you of a boy, well, a man, I once knew. I know you will disbelieve these words that you read here, but, for the love of an old woman, please hear them. They are irreversibly true, whether you believe them or not.

I found him on July 19, 1920. He was bleeding in a gutter outside Jack R. Cole's Drugstore, which was then at the corner of Fifteenth Street and Binder Avenue in Lehigh, West Virginia. I was twenty years old, and had recently gained a position teaching English to grammar school children. I was walking home from the school that day, when I noticed people stepping over and around something at the edge of the sidewalk—yet they didn't seem to be aware that anything was there at all. As I got closer, I saw the damaged figure of a boy in the gutter. There was blood all around him, but no one seemed to notice. I dropped my bags and raced to his side. His face was dirty and scarred, and the blood appeared to be coming from a wound in his side. But his eyes were open, aware.

"Do you see me?" he asked when I knelt down.

"Of course I do," I said. "What happened to you? What can I do to help you?"

He didn't respond at first, just looked directly into my eyes. The worry and fear I felt at first subsided and, to my astonishment, I noticed the faint sign of a cross illuminated behind his pupils. The cross grew slightly brighter in intensity, and then faded again to the point where it was almost unseen.

The boy sat up, breathing heavily.

"Do you see me?" he asked again, but his voice had fewer rasps and more tone in it now.

"Yes," I said, "I see you."

He nodded. "I need to sleep," he said. "To heal."

"Of course," I said, not really knowing what he meant. "I'll get you to a hospital."

He shook his head, and instinctively I knew that a hospital could do nothing for him. I would have to take him home with me.

And that was how I met a Drifter.

If my research is correct, the first recorded evidences

of Drifters appeared as far back as the days of King David and King Solomon. Traces of them show up in Egyptian artifacts, in Roman ruins, and even in engravings from the crews of Columbus when they reached the new world. I'm not sure if they are human or otherwise. Some have been mistaken for demons, others for ghosts. But they will tell you, they are none of those things. It's almost as if they are a completely different, yet similar creation of God. A hybrid of angel and man, of spirit and flesh. A secret, so to speak, of eternity that has not been revealed in any traditional way.

A Drifter appears to be caught in the shallows while the currents of time flow past.

The boy I met when I was a young woman stayed tethered to me for more than thirty-five years, unseen by anyone but me. In many ways, he was closer to me than any soul I've ever known—closer than a husband, a mother, a brother, sister, or dearest friend. No, he was not a lover. But he was a soul mate, if there is such a thing.

Robert, you remember when we almost perished on that rafting trip in the Colorado River? He was there with us. It was he who salvaged the raft that saved us.

Marianna, you recall on your wedding day when the drunk stumbled in through the back door thinking he had found himself some new kind of tavern? I lured him outside of the chapel with a bottle of wine, but it was my Drifter who made sure he stayed safely locked in one of the anterooms of the church until he could sleep off the influence of alcohol.

And C.C., you recall when, as a boy, you accidentally

fired off that handgun you found in your uncle Steven's gun cabinet? It was my Drifter who stepped between the bullet and your friend Billy Parker, saving both your lives at once. Didn't you ever wonder why that bullet was never found?

My Drifter was taken from me on October 31, 1956, at a Halloween party.

He once told me that when our time was up, my memories of him would fade until I one day thought of him as only a dream. But that hasn't been the case with me. True, I can no longer picture his hair or see the exact shape of his face, or even remember the color of his skin. But his eyes and his memory stay bound to my soul, even now in these grayer, paler days.

I have spent the last twenty-two years of my life searching for him, trying to find him. Sometimes I think I see his reflection in a mirror, or catch a faint fragrance of his smell. But whenever I turn to embrace him, he is not there.

I am now an old woman; I feel within me that my days are not long for this earth. And so, I leave this note to you, my family, to you, my friends, and to anyone who may stumble across it in the months and years to come.

If you see my Drifter, please remind him of me. Tell him of my gratefulness that one day he found me. Yes, yes, I know it was I who first came upon him in the street. But it was he who kept me from being lost in a difficult world. And it was in his finding that I learned to be found by our Creator as well.

Tell him that I love him still. Tell him that even if he doesn't believe it, he was, and forever will be, an angel of God sent through centuries and into my life.

Please tell him for me. I think he may have forgotten it, and it's very important that he know.

Please tell him.

Please.

Alondra Noelle Kane, Ph.D.
May 11, 1978

READER'S GUIDE FOR PERSONAL REFLECTION OR GROUP DISCUSSION

A NOTE FROM THE AUTHOR:

After I finished my second novel, *Unpretty,* I started something I called *Two Graces.* I wrote the first twenty-five pages or so, liked it quite a bit, and felt pretty confident that would be my next book.

Then, one night when I couldn't sleep, I entertained myself by imagining an opening scene to a brand-new movie. (This is a familiar theme for those of you who have read my previous books—it's often how a good idea comes to me, though it plays havoc with my sleep cycle!) In my mind's eye I pictured a cemetery in winter. "Okay, who's in the cemetery?" I asked myself, and then I saw a boy—the Boy—sitting beside a freshly dug grave, freezing and alone.

"Hello, Boy," I said to myself. "Who are you, and why are you here all alone?"

As I looked him over closely, his story began to reveal itself to me. I became captivated by the idea of Drifters. What could they be? Why might they exist? How would their being there but not being there work? Yes, I know these beings are just a figment of my imagination without any basis in Scripture, but . . . what if?

The next day, when I was supposed to be writing more of *Two Graces,* I instead wrote the first chapter of *Drift,* surprising even myself with the memory of Alondra that popped up in there. I was intrigued. But seriously, I had to get to work on *Two Graces,* right?

But Boy was haunting my thoughts. Another sleepless night came, and I turned my attention to the girl marching unwillingly to the funeral of her stepfather in that very same graveyard where Boy sat freezing. "Baby Doll," I wondered to myself, "why don't you have a real name?"

So I found myself writing chapter two of *Drift.* I read the two chapters aloud to my family. "It's good," they said. "But we really want to know what happens with the rest of *Two Graces.* Finish that one."

But now something had happened. *Drift* seemed to be moving on ahead in my mind without my permission. So what could I do? I wrote *Drift.*

As for *Two Graces,* I published it as a short story on Amazon.com. (Yes, you can download it from there for only 49 cents—such a steal!) Someday I may pick it up again and see if I can remember why I wanted it to be a full-length novel. If I do, I'll be sure to let you know.

In the meantime, I hope you've enjoyed reading *Drift.* I'd love to hear from you, if you want to share. You can contact me at: www.SharonCarterRogers.com.

May God bless and keep you!

SCR

QUESTIONS FOR GROUP DISCUSSION OR PERSONAL REFLECTION

1. Which character in *Drift* is most like you? Why?

2. If you were casting a movie of this book, whom would you pick to play the main characters? Why?

3. If a friend asked you what *Drift* is *about*—not what happens in the story—what would you say?

4. Why do you suppose it was so important for Baby Doll to know her real name?

5. Because he never dies, Boy says that heaven and hell are unattainable for him. How do you think that affected his attitudes and actions?

6. How would your life be different if heaven and hell were not attainable?

7. Do you think Baby Doll is guilty of "murder by suicide" in regard to the death of Charlie Murphy? Explain.

8. At one point, Baby Doll says, "If God is looking for me, I want to be found." What do you think it means to be "found" by God?

9. When have you felt "lost"? What made you feel that way?

10. Maurits Girard loves Baby Doll, yet is also willing to kill her in cold blood. How do you explain that contradiction?

11. What meaning do you find in the names of Boy and Baby Doll?

12. Is Solace the Lesser actually Boy, millennia before he meets Baby Doll, or is he another Drifter? Explain your opinion.

13. If you kept a box of only six memories, what would be in it?

14. Bonus question (just for fun!): Can you spot any homage to the "Golden Age" of comic books sprinkled throughout this book?

FOR FURTHER REFLECTION

To dig more deeply into the spiritual themes explored in *Drift,* get a Bible and check out the following Scripture passages:

- Psalm 139:13–16
- Matthew 13:45–46
- Luke 15:1–6
- Luke 19:10
- Romans 8:38–39

ACKNOWLEDGMENTS

Although I work in solitude, I most definitely do not work alone. Writing this book was an effort that included more people than I can mention here. But I still need to say thanks to some very special people.

Thanks to Gail Simone, Todd Michael Green, Eric Wilson, Chris Well, Kevin Lucia, Caleb Newell, M. E. McFadden, Nancy Moser, Deena Peterson, and my pals at MySpace.com. I thought of you often while writing *Drift*—after your previous kindness toward me I was petrified of disappointing you this time around! (Hopefully you weren't disappointed!) Your frequent encouragement regarding my earlier books, *Sinner* and *Unpretty,* really helped me keep going when I felt like giving up.

Thanks to Stephen King, just for giving me something to shoot for. Someday, maybe, you'll actually read one of my books, and then I can tell everyone, "Yeah, Stephen King read one of my books," and then die happy.

To Jeffrey Osborne, Elliott Yamin, Earth Wind and Fire, Nicole C. Mullen, tobyMac, Frank Sinatra, Club des Belugas, Johnny Hallyday, Chaka Khan, Whitney Houston, Cindy

Morgan, and Chris Botti: thanks for keeping me company during the long, dark winter when I was writing this book.

To the team at Howard Books / Simon & Schuster: my heartfelt gratitude for bringing me into your family. Thanks especially to Dave Lambert and Lissa Halls Johnson for all your hard work. Also to my agent, Mike Nappa at Nappaland Literary Agency. Thanks for believing in me when no one else seemed to notice.

And, last but certainly not least, eternal thanks to the One who found me, and keeps finding me anew each day. You make it all worthwhile.

PS. If anybody out there wants to contact me, you can find me at: www.SharonCarterRogers.com

ABOUT THE AUTHOR

Who is Sharon Carter Rogers?

On one level, she is, of course, the popular thriller author of the National Best Books 2007 Award Finalist *Sinner*, as well as the suspense novels *Drift* and *Unpretty*. There are some who suggest, however, that Sharon is not the author's real name, and that she has chosen to hide her true identity from the public view. Others dismiss this as pure speculation and a publicity stunt—that is, a "mysterious author who writes mysteries." Ms. Rogers refuses to confirm or deny any of these speculative assumptions, but Internet rumors about her background have included the following:

- She is a former English teacher and is now a homemaker.

- She is a group of Christian romance writers who got together to experiment with a more gritty, thriller style of novel.

- She is actually Dean Koontz or some other well-known author who wanted to write something with a spiritual emphasis but did not want to interfere with a publisher's current "author brand."

- She is a former covert military agent and skilled combatant.
- She is married to one Steven Rogers.
- She has never married for fear that her work would put her loved ones in danger.
- She is married to James Barnes.
- She is an elderly woman living in Connecticut.
- She is an aspiring actress living in southern California.
- She is blond.
- She is brunette.
- She is a redhead.
- She is bald, and wears wigs that are blond, brunette, and redhead.
- She is a former mob moll who now lives in the witness protection program.
- She is a high school drama teacher in Alabama.
- She doesn't exist at all.

Regardless of the rumors, there is one thing we can be sure of about Ms. Rogers: She's an astonishingly good writer of fast-paced, suspense-laden, mystery novels.

So who is Sharon Carter Rogers? Perhaps it doesn't matter, as long as she keeps delivering high-octane entertainment like *Unpretty, Sinner,* and *Drift.*

To contact Sharon directly, you can send her an email through the MySpace.com social network. Her profile page is at: www.MySpace.com/SharonCarterRogers.

ONE

A man had three daughters.

The oldest was a treat for the eyes, with long, silky hair, a carefully constructed face, and a workout-toned feminine physique. The middle daughter was the happy rebel, with body piercings here and there, hair that changed color with her moods, and a smile that made her face light up like a sunbeam. The youngest was the plainest—and smartest—of the bunch, with ordinary skin, a studious manner, and a glint of secrets in her eyes.

A man had three daughters.

But only one of them was unpretty.

Do you know which one?

EXCERPT FROM THE MICHELANGELUS RECORDINGS,
TAPE 4,
TRANSCRIBED BY H. J. COLLINS

— — —

THURSDAY, SEPTEMBER 18, EARLY EVENING

Jonathan Shelby heard the concussive crack behind his left knee before he felt the actual blow. Flooding pain made him gasp for breath and briefly wonder if his leg had been broken.

He collapsed onto the gritty pavement of the bookstore alley, the aged slime of a well-used dumpster disgustingly close to his face. A moment later an elbow hammered against the back of his skull and disrupted the functions in the occipital lobe of his brain. Temporary blindness prevented him from seeing the concrete that now rose up to meet him.

Missed that third guy, Jonathan thought. He must have been standing in the shadows near the entrance to the alley. My mistake.

Jonathan felt a sticky warmth ooze out of the place where his forehead had scraped along the concrete. He tried to roll over onto his back, tried to blink away the roiling blackness that shadowed his vision, but his captor dug a knee into his back and twisted his arm.

"Check his pockets," a voice said.

Jonathan heard a switchblade flick open, felt it cut the back right pocket of his jeans. Another hand began patting down his jacket and quickly discovered the standard-issue gun strapped next to his ribs.

Not good, he thought. Not good.

"How long has he been following us?" A different voice this time.

"Since Sixteenth Street. Maybe longer."

Red and yellow lights began flashing at the edge of Jonathan's vision. He blinked, and darkened shapes appeared again. He had a terrible headache. And it was getting worse by the second.

"Jonathan Shelby," the man holding him read. "Correction. Detective Jonathan Shelby."

He couldn't see it, but he heard the soft slap of someone catching the leather wallet that held his badge. Heard someone muttering halfhearted expletives. He blinked again and was relieved when his vision cleared a bit, revealing a dirty streak of oil and sludge inches away from his face on the pavement. He was losing feeling in his arm and fought for breath. He hoped for a split-second opening when the guy on top of him would relax. A quick roll and a kick should be enough to—

"Stand him up."

This voice spoke with authority. Obviously the boss.

Jonathan felt the pressure release on his back. The man, surprisingly strong, gripped the back of his head and dragged him to his feet. He cranked Jonathan's arm harder behind him. Then, before he could do anything significant, the second guy stepped close and placed a blade under his chin. Jonathan blinked again, letting his eyes adjust to the stark evening gray of the alley.

Okay, he thought. One guy trying to break my arm and yank the hair out of my head. A second one dangerously close to cutting a second mouth in my neck. Not good at all.

The boss stepped closer and appraised him. After a moment he reached out and placed a finger under the detective's chin, gently adjusting the position of his profile.

Jonathan started to speak, but the boss frowned and shook his head. Jonathan took the hint.

The boss reached inside his coat and pulled out a cloth—a handkerchief perhaps? Or a bandanna? Jonathan couldn't tell. The throbbing in his leg threatened to make him stumble, but the knife at his throat provided motivation for him to support the bulk of his weight on the right leg. The boss dabbed the cloth at the blood on Jonathan's face, wiping it away from his eyes, brushing it back into his ear and hair.

Jonathan glanced desperately toward the alley entrance and the row of shops across the street. He knew this part of town well. The bookstore. Coffee shop. The sandwich place. A shoe store. The little art gallery on the corner. It was just past quitting time for most folks. Maybe one of those little doors in the back of one of those little shops would open, and a laughing group of employees would discover what was going on in this hidden alleyway. Maybe help would come.

Then again, maybe not.

The boss folded up his cloth now and stuffed it back into a pocket inside his jacket. He spat, carefully avoiding Jonathan's shoes. Finally he spoke.

"He'll do."

Jonathan felt panic finally break to the surface. He screamed for help and shifted hard to his right. The knife nicked the surface of his neck, but he didn't care. He just knew he had to get out of this alley, right now. He could not be taken. Could not.

The third man twisted Jonathan's arm until it loosened in its socket, pushing down until Jonathan's legs gave out, dropping him to his knees. Then the man pressed a meaty forearm against the detective's larynx to silence him.

"Sedate him," said the boss calmly. "And put him in the trunk. We've got some errands to run before going home tonight."

Jonathan felt his tongue go thick when the big man released the pressure on his throat. He tried to take in a fresh gulp of air, ready again to yell for help. Then the sting of a needle in his neck sealed his despair. *But I promised Aurora I'd be home by six*, he thought absurdly.

He fought it for a moment, but too soon his body involuntarily relaxed, and the night came crashing down in pieces. Jonathan blinked again, felt the goon finally let go of his mangled arm, saw the streak of oil and sludge near his face again. He struggled to maintain consciousness, feverishly twitching on the dirty concrete, but he knew it was a losing battle. A soft, electric whine filled his ears, and for some reason, he thought he smelled onions.

"Let's go," a voice echoed hollowly. But Jonathan knew he was already gone.

—

At 6:15 p.m., Aurora Shelby was just a little annoyed. True, Jonathan was always late. And true, she'd known this about him when she married him. But still, he had promised her—solemnly vowed almost—that tonight, for once in his life, he wouldn't be late. Yet here it was 6:15, and once again, her husband was absent from the dinner table.

Aurora let the candles burn and turned the oven down to a setting that would simply keep her chicken cacciatore warm without drying it out. She turned off the stereo midway through the fourth Norah Jones song, took a sip of wine, and sat down to wait a little longer.

At 6:45 p.m., she was downright angry. She called Jonathan's work number, but there was no answer. She tried his cell phone, but all she got was voice mail. She put the wine away and turned off the oven.

At 7:30 p.m., Aurora moved from anger to depression. She picked a bit at her dinner, then wrapped it all in Tupperware and foil and changed her clothes into something more comfortable. She tried to read a magazine.

At 7:45 p.m., she went to the movies. If Jonathan didn't have the decency to call or come home, then she would just go out and have a good time without him. There was a new Kate Hudson movie they both wanted to see, so Aurora opted to view that one, just to spite him.

At 10:30 p.m., Aurora couldn't remember anything about the movie she'd just watched. She entered her apartment and was surprised to see it had apparently remained untouched the whole time she was gone. For the first time that night, a glimmer of worry crept into her conscious mind.

She called Barry, one of Jonathan's coworkers. He told her that Jonathan had left the station around 5:15 p.m., and he hadn't seen him since. Aurora bit her lip then and called her mother-in-law, who immediately freaked out when she heard her son hadn't come home. Jonathan's mother hung up quickly, intent—as usual—on calling hospitals and mortuaries to look for him.

At 11:15 p.m., Aurora finally called 911 to report that her husband was missing.

Of course, by then it was much too late.

—

Kinseth Roberts breathed heavily for at least twenty minutes, then finally reached down under the covers to remove their shoes. They'd been in such a rush to get into bed by eleven o'clock—just as they'd promised Elaina they would—that they hadn't had time to change into pajamas, let alone take off their shoes. So when their heart had finally slowed down, when the excitement of barely making curfew had finally worn off, Kinseth had reached down and unlaced their left shoe, then their right one, and flicked them both out onto the floor. They would just have to sleep in the rest of their clothes tonight.

Kinseth also removed the glass eye from their left socket and dropped it into the bowl by the bed. It was too uncomfortable to sleep very long with it in. Out of habit their fingers paused to gently trace the long red scar that dipped below their left eyebrow and stretched out across their cheek. Only when they felt confident that they were ready for sleep did Kinseth allow them finally to reflect on what they'd seen tonight.

Those three men had dragged that other man up to the porch of the house across the cul-de-sac and then waited. Kinseth had moved the telescope out of their closet and back to the window of their second-story bedroom and watched the men through it, wondering if this new man was a guest or a prisoner. Kinseth guessed it was the second, because at one point the new man had appeared to try to jump off the porch, but the others had quickly pulled him back. Then one had stabbed a needle into the prisoner's neck. At least it looked like a needle. Sometimes Kinseth had trouble sorting out details.

The men had waited for several minutes before the door opened and all four slipped quietly inside. That was when Kinseth suddenly realized it was 10:59 p.m. and that they'd promised Elaina they'd be in bed, covers drawn and lights out, by eleven o'clock sharp. Kinseth already had the lights out, so they leaped into bed, clothes and all, and slid under the covers just in time to watch the red numbers on the clock flicker and change.

That was close.

Kinseth let their eyelids close and thought some more about the men at the house across the cul-de-sac.

It sure was interesting to live on this street.